READER PRAISE FOR GRADIENT

Gradient is a gripping, innovative read. For fans of Isaac Asimov, Ursula Le Guin, Philip K. Dick, or Gene Roddenberry – you will not be disappointed.

- STEPHAN M.

Gradient is what happens when you launch HP Lovecraft into space. Or slip Orson Scott Card some peyote three chapters into the next installment of the Ender's Game saga... If you're wondering "what's next" for a very familiar genre, read this book.

- SARAH U.

A hero's quest as ancient as Gilgamesh... as if space travelers arrived into the middle of the Illiad, seating themselves next to the likes of Ares and Athena

- CHRIS S.

I loved every minute of this book... wonderfully written... I'll be thinking about this one for a long time.

- MAUREEN H.

This page-turner kept me going, and offered both adventure and reflection. Themes of technology, culture, power and ownership abound. Patiently waiting for the next in this series...

- KATE F.

A unique adventure story set in a deep and interesting world. I enjoyed the scale and breadth while simultaneously enjoying the characters. A great read!

- DANTE C.

GRADIENT

ANDERS CAHILL

Produced in the United States of America.

First Printing, 2017

ISBN (KDP): 9781973326656

Cover art by Frederick Augustus George, III

We Are Not Our Names
Wakefield, MA 01880
www.anderscahillbooks.com

For Erica, who walked every step of this journey at my side

Build then the ship of death, for you must take

the longest journey, to oblivion.

And die the death, the long and painful death

that lies between the old self and the new

- D.H. LAWRENCE, "THE SHIP OF DEATH"

PART 1
YOUTH

1 / ARRIVAL

ONE OF THE few genuine pleasures of interstellar life is connecting to the field. I stepped down into the bath, and the warm, viscous nutrients enveloped me as I rested my head back into the cradle. My body relaxed. The tiny fibers reached up and found the microscopic nodes on my neck. An instant later, the serum was running through my bloodstream, lighting up my neurons. I could feel the whole ship inside of me.

We had been traveling almost a full galactic month since reaching the edge of the Hadeth system, and we were getting close to the planet Eaiph. As we carved through the vacuum, the prow of our ship funneled in matter, repurposing the atoms, supplying the molecular sustenance for the baths that nourished our bodies and bones.

Along the way, the ship had accumulated dozens of tiny fissures and burns, coarse particles of dust and stray debris scouring the hull. I probed out with my mind, exploring the ship's surface, worrying over every scrape and ding like using my tongue to test a cut on the roof of my mouth.

When I had the full extent of the damage, my thoughts reached out to the shipheart. A moment later, a cluster of drones seeped up the rigging of the solar sails, dissolving in blobs as they found the cracks and ruptures, soaking in, restoring the damaged nanofibers.

The repair complete, I continued on, working my awareness into the interior of the ship. I found Neka and Xander sitting in their waking bodies, playing chronostones in the canteen. Xander's silvery cloak hung open at the neck, his hood resting against his back, but Neka's cloak, colored a lush amethyst to match her tastes, was dialed for warmth. The nanofibers hugged tight to her body, her thick, brown curls hidden beneath her own hood. She'd grown up in the equatorial climes of Alyai on Forsara, and she was always a touch chilly, even when the rest of us were comfortable.

I inhabited a small corridor drone, and drifted up past the curve of her shoulder, pausing near her face. The whites of her eyes were shining bright against her smooth, ebony skin, and her attention was locked on the board. She swatted at my drone when she noticed it, so I drifted out of her periphery and watched from the vantage point just over her shoulder, scanning the patterns between them. She was leading, three stones for every one of Xander's.

I saw what he was missing, and I couldn't resist the temptation for mischief. I floated a portable monitor into his line of sight, the two-ring sigil of the Fellowship glowing on the screen. I replaced the sigil with a solution-set, and his eyes lingered on the series of moves until realization dawned on his face. Then he leaned forward and turned over the corresponding stones. A dozen of Neka's fell, cascading like a waterfall. Smiling, she cursed and pushed the monitor away. It tumbled through the air and caromed off the wall before it found its way back to the monitor dock. Xander's rust orange hair was pulled up into a neat bun, and it bobbed on his head as he tilted back with laughter.

In the field, pleasure is contagious. Adjet, connected nearby, saw my little trick, and I could feel her approval seeping between our halos. Soon, we were both humming with joy. Out this deep in space, so far from home, our link to the central field is severed, so we find solace in the thoughts and feelings of each other, a band of seven isolated Architects, sharing in our own private world.

———————————

Two hundred twenty-three years ago, we had used the curvature of Dromedar, the newest and closest starhub, to pull our ship *Reacher* out of the wrinkles and back into four-dimensional space. After three hyperspace jumps - from Forsara to Tasches to Molroun to Dromedar - we had run out of infrastructure. We had been forced to make the final leg of the trip at near-light speed, crossing the void that separated Dromedar from the Hadeth system, with its shining, yellow star.

We had named the star Soth Ra in homage to one of the oldest living Architects, Elder Pausha Ra. She was nearing her twelve-hundredth name day, and she had long since given up on these far-reaching explorations of space. I have never met her, but she is a legend in the Fellowship. She was home, on Forsara, part of the Inner Coven, and she seemed to pay little mind to galaxy pomp and politics, but we hoped that, if she ever heard it, the honor of having this star named for her would touch her somewhere deep beyond measured sight. We would not have been here if not for her and the early spacefarers.

If you've never traveled on an explorer craft like *Reacher*, it's hard to describe a journey like our two-century stretch from Drom-edar to the Hadeth system. From an observational standpoint, there's not much to tell. We had each spent more than two-thirds of our passage preserved in coldsleep, rotating through so that only one of us was awake at any given time. That lone person kept company with the shipheart while the others slept, their nerves and neurons stimulated to ensure that their minds and bodies did not atrophy; a perpetual dreamtime that seemed both to last forever and to elapse in a moment.

Those waking years were interminable, artificial days and

nights blurring together, no real milestones to mark the passage. It would make any person yearn for coldsleep. But though the sleep preserves you, and even heals cellular damage, it also changes you somehow. The person you were when you laid down into the nutrient bath, the temperature dropping slowly and inexorably until your biological functions settled into stasis, is not quite the person who rises again, decades later.

But finally, a month ago, we had arrived at the very edge of the stellar system, dropping out of near-light just outside the belt of asteroids that marked the limit of Soth Ra's perceptible gravitational influence, and the whole crew was drawn out of coldsleep. We were all awake again, and the object of our efforts was closing in.

We had seen no asteroids anywhere on longsight, and we navigated across the invisible border line without difficulty. At that point, the star was a small, white disc, no bigger than my fingernail on the holo projector. When Adjet saw it, she had cooed like a parent with a tiny babe, calling it a 'cute little nugget.'

Xander, our resident astronomist and stellar expert, had crossed his arms and furrowed his pale, freckled brow. "Soth Ra is a star, Adjet," he had said with seriousness. "And based on all of our readings, a rare, life-giving one at that. It may be smaller than average, but it is most certainly not a nugget." His adaptive irises were colorless in the gentle interior light of our ship.

Adjet had pretended to pout, her dark, grey lips glistening. She was remarkably beautiful, with the cloud-white skin, silver hair, and matching silver eyes native to the people of Glas. I'd met few people who could resist her charms. But Xander was unflappable. He gave her a stony look.

Xander's twin brother Xayes had rolled his eyes. "Relax, Xan. It's a star, not a sensitive child. We won't hurt its feelings."

"Ah ha!" Xander parried. "You haven't read the theories on stellar consciousness, have you? You know-"

"Well then," Adjet said, staving off the impending debate that marked so many of the twins' conversations, "if the star is conscious, I'm sure she'll be flattered to know how cute she is."

Xander turned to her, his mouth hanging open. She wore her most mischievous smile. After a moment, he broke into a huge grin.

Neka laughed, and Cordar closed his thin lips into a smile, shaking his head, the wide braid of his jet black hair swooshing across his shoulders.

"Right, then," Adjet said with a satisfied nod. She turned, pointed at Siddart, and said in an imperious voice, "Unfurl the sails. The winds are rising."

Sid gave her a playful punch on the arm as he leaned back in his chair. He rested his head, and his eyes rolled back as he interfaced with the ship. As soon as he was under, Adjet stuck out her tongue at him. A moment later, a monitor floated past her head, a message flashing on screen:

<I saw that> Sid said.

We all laughed, and Adjet laughed the hardest.

But we had all gone quiet as the massive solar sails whirled out from the ship, five huge canopies of gossamer paneling designed to channel the energy of that distant star, powering us forward in our approach, riding waves of light.

Now, it was just a few more weeks until we reached the planet Eaiph, and the ship was buzzing with activity. I left Neka and Xander to their game of chronostones, and continued my inward journey through the *Reacher* to see what the others were up to during this final approach.

Xayes, our virtualist, and Siddart, our farseer, were also in their waking bodies, working up a detailed model of the Hadeth solar system. Xayes was hunched over a workstation, his mangy copper hair hanging like a tattered blanket past his shoulders as he scanned through reams of coded data. Sid was trotting across the room, his legs whirring as they propelled him. A genetic anomaly had made his birth-legs frail and useless, but he moved graceful as a dancer on the bionetic limbs.

He stopped in front of a holographic image, narrowing his wide brown eyes as he fiddled with the resolution and scale. He zoomed in on a large planet, one of the others in the solar system. The data was still coming in, so the overall image resolution was low, but there seemed to be a dark spot on the surface of the planet. It gave me the impression of a giant eye, or a dark knot of wood.

<Is it gaseous?> I projected my question using the holo, spelling out the message directly in front of his view of the planet.

"Oh, is that you, pausha?" Sid said out loud, calling me by my formal title. The brown skin of his bald head gleamed bronze in the light of the hologram as he nodded in affirmation. "If the data's right, this," he pointed at the dark spot, "is a swirling hurricane of gas in the upper atmosphere."

"The data's right," Xayes said, not looking up from his monitor. For twins who resembled each other in so many ways, the differences between Xayes and Xander bordered on comical. Xander was fastidious and highly sensitive. Xayes was unkempt and cared little other people's opinions. But they both shared an intense passion for their work.

"I'd love to get a closer look," Sid said, "but our trajectory's too far outside the planet's orbit, and Reach insists that the solar sails can't provide us enough energy for the plane change. He's right of course. We don't have the fuel to spare. But that doesn't make it any less tempting."

<Is the planet close enough to view on longsight?> I asked, the words floating in front of him.

"Oh yes. It won't be much bigger than a thumbnail, but the colors are wonderful." He made a few quick gestures with his hands, and the hologram resolved into a smaller, full color image. The planet was braided with cataracts of gas that refracted the light of the star in desert shades of sepia, fire, and honey. I zoomed in as much as I could. Two points of light shone like small stars on either side of the planet.

"Those are moons," Sid said, pointing at the small stars. "All things told, I suspect it has dozens of smaller bodies locked in its orbit."

<It's beautiful. It reminds me of Cordelar, the planet we orbited when I was child on Verygone. That little moon right there could have been my home in another life.>

"That planet is twice the size of Cordelar," Xayes said, still not looking up.

I took over his monitor with a thought, making his data disappear.

"Hey!" he called out, his head darting up, his pale, colorless eyes opening wide.

<Your tact never ceases to amaze me, Xay> I said, flashing the message up on his screen.

Sid laughed, and Xayes smiled ruefully. "I didn't mean it as an insult to your home, pausha," he said. "Merely a statement of fact. That planet is no titan, but Cordelar is smaller by comparison."

<I don't know who in the Fellowship thought it was a good idea to let you and Xander on the same ship. One of you is about all I can handle.> I let my face appear on every monitor in the room and gave him a theatrically menacing grimace.

He laughed out loud. "We're the only ones who keep each other in check, pausha. You'd be doomed with either of us alone."

I gave him a big grin, then my face disappeared, and his data came back up on his screen. "Get back to work," I said in a mock stentorian tone, using the speakers in the room to fill the space with my amplified voice. "I want a tally of every single asteroid and planetoid orbiting every planet in the solar system within the hour."

"Oh yeah, sure, we'll get right on that." Xayes muttered.

"What did you say?" I said, trying and failing to hide the amusement in my amplified voice.

He lifted his right arm, palm towards his face, and smacked his left hand against the front of his right forearm. Cordar had taught him that gesture. I don't know the exact translation in the universal tongue, but it wasn't polite.

"Excellent," I said, pretending to take it as a sign of compliance. "I'll leave you to it then."

Cordar, our resident biologician, was in the arboretum. His long, glossy black hair was braided tight behind his head, hanging down to the gap between his shoulder blades, contrasting against the woodsy brown of his cloak as he leaned over an open vivarium, inspecting a sickly orchid. All but one of its blossoms had withered and fallen to the soil, and some of its floating roots had begun to shrink and curl backwards.

He held out both hands, hovering them close to the plant. His fingertips started to glow, and I could see the faint silhouette of his bones and veins through his eggshell cream skin. The roots of the epiphyte thickened, unfurling, reaching out towards the light coming from his hands. He pulled his palms slowly apart from each other, coaxing the roots further and further out.

Once they were looking strong and healthy, Cordar took his hands away. Then he leaned his face closer and inhaled through his nose. His modified olfactory receptors were no doubt picking up on subtle data about the plant's inner state. He sniffed one more time, then stood up with a satisfied smile on his face. He waved his hand over the sensor, and the cover on the vivarium sealed shut with a quiet hiss.

I was about to complement him on bringing the plant back to life when Neka walked in. Cordar turned when he heard her enter, and his face lit up with a huge smile. He made a quick gesture with his hands that I could not follow. Neka replied, almost as quick. She had been practicing her handspeak.

The same bionetic mods that let Cordar interact with biomatter on the cellular level also enhanced all of his senses. It even gave him the ability to hear. But he was an Auralon by birth, and like almost everyone on that small planet, he had been born deaf. Handspeak was his native dialect.

During our preparations for this mission, Neka and Cordar had formed an intimate bond, and it had only grown stronger in the months since we'd all been drawn from the timeless dreaming of coldsleep and started working together again. Neka was a meditician, and she and Cordar shared similar enhancements. They could, for instance, sense the energy state of a living organism by placing their hands close enough. And their enhanced abilities were complemented by their shared reverence for the mystery and complexity of life.

Neka also had a gift for languages, and she had taken to handspeak with speed and confidence. Cordar was the quietest among us, and he often used handspeak to express feelings and ideas that he otherwise struggled to articulate. When Neka learned to speak it with him, their connection grew even deeper.

These similarities made the apparent contrasts between them that much more interesting and pleasurable. Cordar, tall and lanky, his braided, shoulder-length hair pulling his fair skin tight around his forehead and temples, making his sharp face even more severe, underlining his introverted disposition. Neka, a head shorter, with ebony skin, thick brown curls trimmed tight, dark, expressive eyes, and a graceful kindness that put everyone who met her right at ease.

Cordar reached his long arms around her and pulled her close, kissing his lips to her forehead. She turned her cheek, resting her head against his chest. I took that as my cue to give them some privacy, and slipped back into the field currents of the ship.

"Oren," Adjet said, her voice in my mind. "Are you still lurking out there?"

"Of course, Adjet. As the ship's pausha, my duty, first and foremost, is to lurk."

She chuckled. "Come up to psychomed," she said. "I've got something fun to show you."

An instant later, I was there.

Adjet's body lay prone on a medical bed, her long hair spilling over the top edge like a current of mercury. She wore a white, form-fitting baselayer a shade darker than her alabaster skin. The top covered most of her torso, but it was sleeveless, bands of fabric running up over her collarbone and bending in a gentle 'U' below her neck, leaving her arms, shoulders, and her upper chest exposed.

"Are you experimenting on yourself again?" I asked. Adjet specialized in genetics, and our ship carried a panoply of information and samples. With Adjet's guidance and Cordar's unique expertise, we were equipped to run a wide range of adaptive experiments that would help us better understand how non-native life might survive and thrive on Eaiph, our destination planet.

"Watch," she said. A surgical lantern hovered in the air above her body. With a thought, she made it flash over her right arm. A moment, later, her crystal white skin turned plum purple, like ink dyeing a linen sheet.

"Eledar's breath! What are you doing? Are you sure its safe?"

She laughed. "What is skin color?" she asked. "A series of generational adaptations based on ancestral exposure to ultraviolet light. Lighter skin means less exposure. On Glas, where my people come from, the black hole Rorok gives us many forms of radiation to contend with, but UV is virtually non-existent. Unfortunately, that means that on a world like Eaiph, sunlight that might give you, at worst, a nasty sunburn, is seriously harmful to me. Maybe even fatal."

She flashed the lantern again. It must have been on the same spectrum as the light from her home world, because her skin reverted to its translucent paleness.

"Remarkable. Like a khamail lizard," I said.

"Precisely. It's actually based on the early work of Graxes Ben Or."

"Ben Or? Is he a relative of the twins?"

"Their grandfather. He developed adaptive refractors that block ultraviolet radiation. They can be layered into organic matter. Very practical stuff. Xander and Xayes both have the tech in their eyes."

"Because they have no natural pigmentation in their irises?"

She nodded. "Without it, they would either have to wear bulky protective lenses or they could never leave the cold light of Tuk. Their colorless eyes could not handle our twin suns on Forsara, or even the light of Eaiph's humble star."

"So why don't you just use the same tech?"

"Well, I actually already have a version in my eyes, but where's the fun in the same old tricks? With some splices and edits to Graxes original concept, I have figured out how to alter skin on a cellular level to adaptively responds across the whole spectrum of light radiation."

"Amazing. Have you showed either of the twins what you are working on here?"

"Not yet. I still have some work to do to refine the process, but eventually, I'll be able to control it at will, shifting my skin through a variety of hues. That's something neither of them can do. At least, not until I show them how."

I could sense that she was pleased with herself, and I knew that if we were in our waking bodies, she would flash me her mischievous smile.

"Show off," I said. "People back on Forsara would probably pay thousands of credits for this kind of adaptability."

"They would," she said. "But it would mainly be an aesthetic choice. Some expression of fashion, or, perhaps, a commentary on racial history. Down there, on that planet, it will be essential to my survival. Maybe to all of ours."

"You never cease to surprise me, Adjet."

"It is one of life's greatest delights to keep you on your toes, Oren."

A voice filled up my field awareness, and the immersive image of Adjet's body lying prone on the medical table receded from view.

"Orenpausha," it said to me, echoing in my mind, "we are nearing the outer edge of the optimal orbit. The planet is on longsight, approaching as predicted."

Reacher. Our faithful companion. Our shipheart.

A ship's heart represents the crowning achievements of our interstellar dreams. It is always beating. It gives the ship life, pulsing every microsecond, feeding every component with essential information, pulling back measurements, converting atomic matter into necessary materials and nutrients, making adjustments and refinements.

Without the heart, our ship would be unwieldy. Even seven minds, chosen for our special evolutions, modifications, and training, would buckle under the complexity. If we somehow managed to work in perfect unison and hold all of the pieces together, sooner or later, we would simply burn out from the attentional demands. Reacher amplifies our power, deepens our connection to the ship, and automates much of the workings so we can focus on the essentials.

"Show it to me, Reach," I said to the shipheart. I was bursting with excitement at his news.

A view of towering columns of energy, blooming from the nearby yellow star, filled my awareness. Then the view zoomed to the left of the star, and there it was: a pale, blue dot, hurtling towards us.

My whole being smiled. We had reached Eaiph, one of the most fertile worlds ever discovered, a glassy blue cauldron of life, waiting for those to live it. In three more galactic weeks, the little waterstone would arrive to meet us on its passage around Soth Ra.

The first half of our long journey was behind us.

2 / DISCOVERY

Centuries ago, when the Eaiph first appeared on the starscans, it was clear, even then, that the Fellowship had found a rare and precious world. The wobble of its passage across the small, yellow star described a shape and distance almost too good to be believed. Word spread, and soon every longeye in the sector was trained on these distant coordinates, waiting for the next orbit, waiting to confirm the initial measurements.

It turned out to be more than we ever could have hoped for: an aqueous planet, orbiting at the optimal distance from a star with still billions of years of unspent energy. The news rippled out from all the major star hubs, spreading across the entire galactic field of the Fellowship. Within a few suncycles on Forsara, the first party of Architects was formed. Their aim was to assess the viability of the planet, and to begin the initial terraforming protocols if it was deemed habitable. I was not selected to be among that original party, but when Saiara told me she was leaving, joining up as the mission's farseer, I knew, someday, somehow, I had to follow her.

Six-hundred and twenty-seven years ago, she and the rest of the team should have arrived at Eaiph. When they reached the edge of the stellar system that the astronomists had dubbed Hadeth, they were supposed to have sent word, but there had been nothing from them since they left the boundaries of Forsaran space and accelerated to near-light. Even accounting for the vast, unavoidable time-lag of galactic communications unaided by a network of starhubs like the ones we have built since they left Forsara, there should have been some contact by now.

Something had gone wrong.

When the news reached me that they had been officially declared missing, I made it my mission to be on the next ship. But, though my crew and I were loathe to admit it, they were likely already dead. Our universe is a vast and lonely place, with no guarantees. Not even on a planet with this much potential. The simple truth is that, for every settlement that has ever taken root and thrived, dozens more have failed, pulled apart by a thousand variations of the implacable entropy of existence. And if there was an accident during the passage from Forsara to Eaiph, they may not have even made it to their destination.

So we came to find answers. To seek the truth. And, perhaps, to succeed where Saiara and her team may have failed. For we who travel the far reaches are more than just explorers; we are part of an ancient lineage of galactic Architects who seeded life across the universe, weaving the web that connects us all across space and time, giving rise to a billion cultural and evolutionary permutations, all grounded in the conscious spirit.

We came here to give birth.

———————————

"Are you capturing this, Reach?" Neka said in a breathless voice. After two weeks of satellite surveillance above the planet, we'd stumbled upon something truly unexpected. The data coming back seemed impossible, but now we were in low orbit, and we could not deny our own eyes.

"On every channel, Neka," the shipheart replied.

"Is that what I think it is?" she whispered.

"Given that you are not currently connected to the field, I cannot be certain of what you are thinking at this moment, but it appears to be a triad of intelligently designed cities, and I can only assume that you also recognize it as such."

She ignored Reacher's overly literal response, too awestruck to tease him for it. "Is it them? Did they make it?" She looked at me, but I was just as dumbfounded.

"If you are speaking of the first party of Architects," Reacher said, "my scans show no evidence of Forsaran technology in these urban cities."

"So... so what are we looking at then?" I asked.

"Conscious life," Neka said in a hushed voice.

Cordar signed something, his hands flashing from his head to his heart.

"It appears so," Reacher said in response to Cordar's sign.

"You mean they're human?" Neka looked at Cordar. "Like us?"

"Close enough," Reach said, "that I am unable to discern any substantive differences from this altitude."

"Eledar's breath," she said. She lifted her hand, making in a loose fist. When her fingers touched her forehead, she opened them in an explosive gesture. Cordar nodded his agreement. It was mind-blowing.

"How many are there?" I asked

"Approximately twenty-seven million," Reacher said.

Neka looked as if she had just witnessed the first spark of hydrogen in a newborn star.

"Twenty-seven million?" I whispered. "How... how can that be?"

"Ah," Reacher said. "You meant the cities alone. That number is closer to one-point-five million. But if we include the areas where I have identified nomadic groups or smaller settlements, the total comes to twenty-seven, spread out across the globe."

A two-dimensional map of the planet appeared in front of us. We had run satellite surveys to build a functional cartographical rendering of its land and ocean mass. Now that map was lighting up in the areas that Reacher had pinpointed.

Even accounting for the geographical distance between the tribal pockets of people, twenty-seven million people was shockingly high. There was a speckling of lights on a modest continent in the eastern corner of the southern hemisphere. The land was surrounded by ocean on all sides, with an arid desert sweeping across the middle. Most of the peoples seemed to hug the edges of the continent, keeping close to the ocean, but there were signs of human life even in the deepest interior.

"Whoever lives there," Cordar said, pointing towards the interior, "must live in close harmony with the land. That is rugged terrain, by the looks of it."

Neka nodded. "I would like to meet those people some day. But look here," she said, pointing at a much larger continent in the center of the map. It was lit in many places, and its shape brought to my mind a cut of steak from the haunch of cardhubu, its bottom tip narrowing towards the southern pole of the planet, its broad, rounded shoulder rising above the equator.

"Migration patterns?" Cordar asked, gesturing to the northwest curve of the continent. A thick bridge of land formed the top border of a small sea that divided the cardhubu steak from the largest continent of all, a mammoth, sprawling landmass. There were pockets of nomadic life scattered across that one, separated by large swaths of uninhabited land.

But human life was getting progressively denser where Cordar was pointing. Lines of light branched north across the land bridge until they intersected with a luminous halo that marked the largest gathering of humans anywhere on this planet. As I was trying to make sense of the implications of all of this, Neka grabbed my arm.

"This is the cradle," she said.

"The cradle?"

"The birthplace of civilization on this planet," she said, practically shouting in her excitement. "Imagine Forsara, before the Curse ravaged the lands. When our nomadic ancestors began to come together and build the first cities." She spread out her hands as if to encompass all those millennia in a single gesture. "That is what we are seeing here. There are millions of people spread across the globe, but this could very well be its first true civilization."

"How do you know that?"

"I don't know," she said. "Not for sure. But what other explanation is there? Look at the patterns of movement south of this sea here." She swept her hand up the map, following the lines of light that Cordar had pointed out. "People moving northwards towards fertile lands."

"It reminds me of the root structure of my epiphytes," Cordar said.

"Yes! These rivers here and here must seem like a gift from the gods..." She was pacing now. "If they have gods... Which they must! There are always gods. Especially in the early histories."

"Neka," I said, putting my hands on her shoulders, stopping her pacing.

She looked up at me, making a conscious effort to contain her energy.

"Find out everything you can," I said. "You have the next seven orbits. Then we need to gather everyone and decide what happens next."

"Where are you going?"

"I am going to tell the rest of the team that our original plans just went out the airlock."

We were all circled around the holo projector. Neka stood in silence, letting the realtime images wash over us. Children playing in shallow waters, charging through tall reeds of grass, while almond-skinned women knelt at the edge of the great river, washing soiled linens of flax and wool with their rough, worked hands. Men standing in a circle, smoking from reed pipes, laughing, tossing the bones of some small animal, carved with indecipherable runes, into a circle drawn in the dirt at their feet.

Clay dwellings, built together in dense clusters, ran up the gentle slope away from the river, smoke wafting up through holes in the roofing. The exterior walls were etched with complex hieroglyphs formed from soft curves and lines in the clay, a style perhaps reflective of a people who lived their lives in a fertile river valley.

Neka looked at Cordar. He nodded, and she cleared her throat. "As I mentioned earlier, using several explorer drones, we were able to discreetly obtain a variety of genetic samples from these people. An hour ago, Reacher completed the analysis of their nucleic structures. That is why we called you all here. There are traces everywhere. These people are children of Forsara." There was wonder in her voice.

Xayes asked the question we were all thinking. "But where are the first Architects? If Saiara and the others gave rise to these people, why are there no cultural fingerprints? Their art. Their architecture. Their language. Their technology. It all seems as if it all evolved entirely on its own, without Forsaran influence. As if the first party never existed." His mop of copper hair bobbed above his shoulders as he gestured with his hands, undercutting each point.

Cordar touched his right and left index fingers together at his forehead, then shook his head as he separated his fingers in front of his chest. "It was not them," he said. "There is evidence of histories stretching back thousands of years, well before the first Architects would have arrived. If they ever arrived at all..."

"Thousands of years?" Xayes said. "How is that even possible?"

"Maybe earlier explorers, long forgotten, once came here, their influence so distant as to be unrecognizable," Siddart said.

I turned that provocative thought over in my mind. "Or maybe these theoretical first explorers were not forgotten. Maybe the Coven knew about this all along."

"Knew what? That Saiara and her team were not the first?" Xander asked. "Why would they keep that a secret?"

"I don't know, Xan. But we're not alone here. That's for certain. If we begin operations on the planet's surface, sooner or later, we will be discovered. Sooner or later, cultural non-interference will cease to be an option."

I paused, letting that land.

"We need to know more," I finally said. "We need to know everything we can."

Neka held my gaze, quiet for a moment, then said, "You're right, pausha. Whatever we build here, we build for all humankind. We cannot take that lightly. But we must tread with caution. If they learn too much about us, all at once, who knows what might happen. We could ignite a cultural war. Or a religious revolution. Cordar and I will work with Reacher to draft up an observation plan."

"Excellent." I held out my hands, addressing the whole team. "We did not come prepared for this, but we must get prepared, as quickly and thoroughly as possible. Whoever these people are, wherever they came from, they are a factor in every decision we make from here on out."

"Are we almost ready?"

After an exhaustive orbital survey, we had determined an ideal landing area, a wide, grassy plain with long sight lines, far away from any native human habitations. Now, we rested on the planet's surface, running the requisite battery of ground level preparations, and my patience was slipping.

"Just a few more hours, Orenpausha," Neka answered.

Six farruns away, a spine of mountains shimmered on the blue horizon, begging to be explored. I watched on the feed as one of our explorer drones approached the range. The ground whipped past and the mountains rose up, carved with bands of glacial ice.

I licked my lips. "How far along are the supplements?" I asked.

"Reacher is rendering the nano-solution now." She gestured to the monitor in front of her. "You should check out these readings while we wait."

"Are you looking at the monera ratios?" Sid asked, leaning over from his monitor.

"Yes," Cordar said, blinking his eyes as he lifted his head from a magnascope. "We've looked at dozens of samples like this one," he gestured to the tiny biovessel beneath the magnascope, "and they all show an average dispersal of 100 billion microorganisms per square unit of biomatter."

Sid whistled.

I looked at Neka, my eyebrows raised.

"He's right," she said, confirming the measurements. "This planet is a flourishing gift. Absolutely teeming with life. It is more than seventy percent water, and photosynthetic organisms are prolific. They are gobbling up the carbon dioxide. The air is even richer than we first gathered. Almost seventy cones oxygen per unit in the lower spheres. And look at this spectrogram."

The star, Soth Ra, floated in front of me on a mobile console. Its color shifted from yellow, to red, to blue, to purple, to green, then back again through the spectra. Then the view zoomed past the star, focusing in on the planet. We watched as the radiant energy from the star, represented by the rainbow of colors, streamed past the planet, diverted along its curve, flowing around and out into space.

Neka touched my arm. "The planet's outermost sphere is a thin but effective magnetic shield, produced by the planetary spin and its dense molten metal core. It filters out the intense solar radiation, while allowing the optimal spectra to penetrate. Life does not just survive here. It thrives. It is a beautiful, delicate balance."

When you spend years in space, sharing each other's thoughts and hopes, it becomes easy to read each other, even when you're not connected to the field. Sid, sensing my excitement at this news, followed Neka by saying, "Of course, we must keep an eye on the star to get a better sense of its rhythms. At this distance, there is still the risk of solar flaring, which could warp or even catastrophically puncture the magnetosphere."

I nodded at him. "I appreciate your prudence, Sid." I looked around at the team. "This is excellent work. We have come so far, and it is gratifying to see such promise." On the viewing monitor, the image toggled between the feeds of each of our three explorer drones, small chrome orbs, skimming across the surface of the planet.

The drone nearest the mountains was ascending. It shot up, and the land stretched out below. It was an incredible sight. Skeins of water snaked through emerald gems of tall grass. Graceful, two-winged flyers with long, thin necks touched off from the water as our drone zipped past, a ruby swarm, funneling through the air, flying as one. A massive brace of golden-brown, four-legged creatures thundered across the open plains. Tens of thousands of them, their tall, curving horns like a forest stripped of leaves, bending in the wind.

My whole body was tingling, and I could feel my heart in my chest. Life. Running wild across the planet. It was magnificent.

"Eledar's breath!" I said. "We can't let Reacher have all the fun. I'm going out."

Neka grabbed my hand. "Wait, pausha. Reacher has not finished adapting our supplements yet. And we still do not know what happened to the first party of Architects. Maybe they were wiped out by an unanticipated virus, or consumed by some terrible predator. You could be killed."

"I will not be killed," I snapped at her. "Don't you see? This is what I was bred for. My bones and skin and sinew ache for this."

"We see you as you are, Orenpausha. Or we would not be here with you." Neka let go of my hand. "Yet, with all that you have survived, I wonder if it is you who judges us? Your patience is so thin."

I sighed and put my hands on her shoulders. "I am sorry, Neka. Maybe you are right. But you have trusted me to carry us this far. Please, trust me now." I looked at the rest of them in turn.

Siddart shifted in his chair and coughed, clearly uncomfortable with the conflict.

Cordar glowered at me, disapproving.

Adjet smiled, shook her head, then turned to the console and activated the decompression chamber that would let me exit the ship. "As soon as the supplements are ready," she said, "we'll be right behind you."

I knew that Xayes and Xander were watching from the field. I could almost feel them hovering next to me. I entered the decompression chamber and dialed my cloak to quarantine settings. It formed into an exoskin around me, the nanofibers weaving airtight around my limbs and torso, my hood forming a filter over my mouth and nose. I nodded to Adjet, and she closed the door behind me, activating the seals that would keep them safe when the exterior door opened.

Neka put her slender hand to the glass. The lines in the light, tawny skin of her palm flattened and turned white with the pressure. I mirrored her gesture, placing my large, coarse hand on the opposite side of the glass, my palm to hers.

The air from the alien world came rushing in.

After a few tentative breaths, I retracted the filter and filled my lungs. It was outstanding, like liquid ambrosia after years of recycled air. Connecting to the field is a singular gift. It provides a virtually infinite range of experiences. But there is something uncanny about waking life. The way the heart churns and pulses, every breath, every step, every pang of hunger a reminder. We are alive.

I knelt down and scooped up a handful of soil and grit. Dozens of tiny critters nosed and squirmed through the dirt. An insectoid with six legs, two darting antennae, and a mud-colored chitinous carapace skittered up my wrist. A nelida as long as my finger, its skin ringed with hundreds of tiny folds, stretched and compressed as it wormed its way through the dirt in my palm.

I lifted the handful of earth to my nose. Fragrant. Redolent of decay and recomposition. I touched my dirty finger to my tongue. The loam was bitter and strong.

I smiled, dropped the clump of turf, and leapt straight up from my crouch, pushing against the earth and propelling high into the air. My muscles had been shaped both by genetics, and by the gravitation of Verygone and Forsara. Here on Eaiph, with its lighter gravity, I felt for a moment that I might tear through the cobalt paper sky and just keep going out into space.

But the planet's pull was stronger than I realized. Once my initial muscular force was depleted, I shot back down to the ground. I rolled to absorb the impact, and came up standing. I laughed. It felt so good to move!

I saw a forest, maybe half a farrun away, and I leapt again, covering the space in two bounds, touching down at the edge of the woods. The trees were maybe three times my height, with rough, scabrous bark, and broad, coniferous canopies.

I stepped across the threshold, into the dark of their shade, and waited for my eyes to adjust. The sounds within were riotous. Birds hollered and whistled, dancing through the boughs. A rodent with a long, bushy tail opened its mouth and chirruped, then leapt like an acrobat from one tree to the next, landing on a thin branch that bent under its weight as it scurried in towards the trunk. A seed cone fell from the end of the branch, plunking to the dirt and dry needles on the forest floor.

Then I caught a glimpse of something larger, a flicker of movement deeper in the woods. My adrenaline spiked. How foolish I was, going out there alone. Where there is life, there are always predators. And even someone as big and strong as me might still become the prey.

I crouched a little lower, scanning the light and shadows. There. Another movement. Was that ... a person? My mind raced with possibilities. There were not supposed to be people here. We had made sure of that. But what if they had been expecting us? Had somehow slipped our scans?

Whatever it was, it moved too quick for me to be certain. I was on the verge of calling out, to see if I might get some response, when someone else shouted.

I ducked down even lower, cursing, and swiveled my head in the direction of the voice. If I have stumbled into a group of natives, I thought, then they have me surrounded.

But it was only Sid. He was running towards me on his powerful bionetic legs, Cordar and Neka coming behind him, working hard to keep up. My heart rate slowed. I took one last look into the depths of the forest, but there was nothing. I stood and walked back into the light of day.

"Here, pausha," Neka said to me, "breathe this in." She handed me two small tubes that carried the special cocktail of nanoparticles designed to fortify us against any dangerous bacterial and viral monera, and to ensure that we could consume and metabolize the alien organic matter of this planet without poisoning ourselves.

I placed the first tube to each nostril in turn, inhaling deep. Then I took the second, opened it, and swallowed its contents.

When I was done, I handed the vials back to Neka, and she slipped them into a fold in her cloak.

I turned and clasped one hand on Cordar's right shoulder and the other on Sid's left, drawing them close to me. "Can you believe all this? The planet is ripe with the fundamentals. Everything we'd hoped for."

Cordar smiled at me. "I can't wait to begin working with the flora. All this green is so vibrant. A striking contrast to the blue and purple hues of Forsara. Who knows what cuisines we might invent on this world!"

That made me laugh. "After years tending our tiny botanareum on *Reacher,* now you have a whole planet to harvest, eh?"

He nodded, still smiling, then he turned to face Neka, and moved his hands in a series of complex gestures. She moved her hands in a response series, too quick to follow.

Cordar laughed out loud.

"What are you two conspiring about? Did you just say something about an experiment, Cord?"

Neka chuckled. "There's no conspiracy, pausha," she said. "He speaks in his native tongue, as plain as day for any who have eyes."

"Then my eyes must be getting worse as I age," I said, grinning at her.

"I told her that we should run an experiment to see what medicinal qualities the plants of this world might hold for us," Cordar said, "and she said that, first, we have to make sure you don't run trampling over all of them."

I looked at each of them for a moment. Then, while I had my eyes on Cordar, I lunged at Neka, surprising her. She squealed, trying to leap out of my grasp, but I was too fast for her. I wrapped her up in my arms, pretended to growl like some wild beast.

After a moment, I loosened my grip and she squirmed away from me. "You're a savage," she said with a big smile.

"Oh, I'm so sorry, my dear," I said in a self-important voice. "I was merely conducting an experiment to see if you were as fast on your feet as you are with your witticisms."

I turned to Cordar. "And don't think I won't do the same to you. I heard the way you cackled at her joke. Best be careful, the both of you, because there's plenty more tough love where that came from."

My warning didn't seem to trouble Cordar. He had a look of mischief in his eyes. I saw him glance past my shoulder, and I turned my head quick, following his gaze. I saw nothing but the trees.

Something touched the back of my legs.

Cordar jumped towards me. He let out a wild roar, raising his hands above his head. I flinched away from him, and promptly tumbled over, my feet flying up, my hands grasping futilely at the air.

Sid had crept up and knelt right behind my knees, setting me up for the fall. The great, blue sky filled my vision as I pinwheeled backwards, landing with a thump. It didn't hurt much, but it knocked the wind out of me, and before I could do anything else, the three of them were on top of me, pinning me to the ground.

"How dare you treat your pausha like this," I roared in mock anger once I'd caught my breath. With my strength, I could have escaped their clutches, but I played along, acting immobilized, and soon we were all laughing like a bunch of children who had been cooped up inside for far too long.

Our laughter was interrupted by the sound of Reacher's voice.

"Ahem," he said.

We all looked up.

The chrome orb of an explorer drone hovered above us. "Cordar, when you've completed the ritualistic sacrifice of our pausha, Adjet requests your presence back on the ship. She is preparing our first supper here on Eaiph, and she apparently needs your help to ensure that she does not end up poisoning the entire team."

Cordar laughed, stood up, and made a swiping gesture with his hands down his chest. In response, the nanofibers of his cloak rippled and whirred, shaking off the dirt that had stained his arms and knees in our playful scuffle.

Neka and Sid climbed off of me and helped me to my feet. We stood around, grinning at each other like idiots.

"Please do hurry," Reach said. "I would hate to be left here all alone as the result of a tainted tuber stew."

I WAS BORN on the small moon Verygone, far away from Forsara, well on the tip of the Nomarion arm of the galaxy, in one of the innumerable tiny settlements populating the margins. The moon boasts deep deposits of terranium, so, in spite of our distance from the center, we were a modest but important juncture in the trading and communications routes that ringed the galaxy.

Verygone orbits the giant Cordelar, the planet always looming on the moon's horizon. Dark bands of gas carve across Cordelar's upper atmosphere, striping the massive orb. One complete orbit of the planet takes a little over eight galactic years, as measured by Fellowship regulations. As Verygone travels the sunward side of Cordelar, facing the star of Beallus, the moon is blessed with the long summer. The light of Beallus reflected off the upper atmosphere of Cordelar, turning it into a quiet sun, all light, no heat. Every morning, Corderlar rose and coated the valleys of Verygone in amber. Then Beallus came into view, bringing the true day. One or the other, always rising, lighting up the sky.

In the waning months of my first summer, my father hiked with me to the top of Senes, the mountain peak at the edge of our settlement. From our vantage at the top, with Cordelar at our backs, we watched Beallus set. When the star fell beneath the horizon, an amber glow enveloped us, Cordelar shining behind us, bathing us in its warm glow.

I stared up at my father as he surveyed the valleys. He looked invincible, his head tilted up, his skin glowing in the setting light. Motes of dust scattered in the air. I wove quick, fractal patterns with my hands, the dust chasing my fingertips in contrails before they dispersed again a moment later.

He closed his eyes, and drew a long breath through his nose, his chest and shoulders lifting. "Soon you're going to crave that light, Oren. Soak it in, like the Beallurian generators we use to power our homes. Let it permeate your bones. We are crossing to the far side of Cordelar. The long dark."

I had been born at the end of the last winter, too young to remember. I had never known anything other than the warmth and light. I touched his hand. "The long dark, papoh?"

He looked down at me. "Winter. It isn't easy for any of us, but you are different, my son. You are special. And that sets you apart. Which means winter will be even more difficult for you." He stared off towards the setting sun, his face sad.

"What makes me special?" I asked. "You always say that, but you never say what!" My voice rose, and I crossed my arms, determined to make him tell me everything.

He smiled and put his arm around my shoulders, pulling me close, hugging me into his leg. He sighed. "One day, you'll grow too big for this lonely moon of ours, Oren," he said.

When I think of his smile now, I miss my father as much as the day I left Verygone.

"But I'm the littlest," I said. "That's what the doctor told moma at my last check-up. She looked sad then, like you do right now."

"There are many kinds of strength, Oren. You'll see. Until then, promise me that no matter what comes, you will be brave. And remember that your moma and I love you very much. We believe in you with every fiber of our being."

"I promise, papoh," I said.

My father's name was Sora. 'Papoh', I called him when I was a child. Our people were descended from a hardy settler stock bred for heavy labor, and like most men and women on Verygone, he was tall and broad shouldered, with thick, tough hair covering most of his body. He was one of three quarry chiefs in the terranium mines, and he was well respected amongst our people as a competent and fair manager.

My mother Enebtha, my moma, was tall and uncommonly slender, with the delicate hands of an artist. She had lines of ancestry tracing back to the water world of Jarcosa, and at a young age, she showed an aptitude for complex processes. This skillset had guaranteed her a job in the refinery, where terranium was purified and prepared for use as fuel, ensuring she would never have to set foot in the mines.

Terranium was one of the raw elements necessary for interstellar travel, and it was rare enough to make a barren moon like Verygone worth the effort. But it is useless in its raw state, and dangerously unstable. The first generation of settlers who came to Verygone made the wise economic decision not to offworld any of the work. From quarry stone to stellar drive, the fuel that comes from Verygone is certified level-one reactor-ready.

Children like me, who were not yet old enough to work, attended demia for skills simulation and character training. In the winters, demia was more like a holding pen, the drumons doing what they could to keep us engaged. It was hard on everyone, kids and adults alike, but my father had been right: it was harder for me. My first winter turned me into a proper worshipper of the sun.

During my first summer, I had been an invisible child, awkward, shy, and unobtrusive. The other children were too busy with games and explorations to pay me much mind, and as I got older, I was happy to pass the hours alone, hiking in the hills, or combing through the archives. I was a voracious reader, consuming knowledge, history, and mythologies from across the galaxy that had accumulated in our data banks over the centuries. Those years of solitude taught me the power of my own imagination, how to build a sanctuary against boredom and loneliness.

But when winter arrived, my powers of invisibility evaporated. We were all insulated, and as the long, dark days wore on, I became a prime target for the idle ruffians and the social climbers looking for an easy mark. I was an unpardonable weakling in their eyes, a favored pet to the drumons, and too smart for my own good. With little else to distract them, the very attributes that had once made me invisible now drew them to me like a beacon in the winter night.

Bash Alo was the worst of my tormentors. I've not thought of him in many years, and the vantage of time makes the high dramas of adolescence seem so small and foolish, but back then, his name was a curse upon my lips. Truth is, I'm grateful to Bash. His taunts and barbs helped thicken my skin, and when I finally figured out what he really wanted, he helped me understand that even enemies can become allies.

One morning, during our short break after geologics, I snuck away to the archives to pick up the tale I had left off from the previous night: a first-person account from the ruler of the largest and oldest city on a dying planet near the opposite edge of the galaxy. It was written in such a way that I wasn't sure if it was a true telling or a work of fiction. The scholar who published the work claimed he had found the manuscript on an archeological expedition, and had labored for decades to translate it into the universal tongue, consulting with linguists and anthropologists to verify as much as he could. The translation often used old language, so old sometimes that I couldn't even find the definitions in the archives, heightening the sense that it was an ancient and alien piece of writing. True or no, it captivated me, and it was all I could think about during the boredom of our studies in sedimentary composition and classification.

I was so deep in the story, I didn't hear Bash come in.

"Which one of you victors wants to take this afternoon's eval for me?" he said, mockery in his voice.

My head snapped up. Bash filled the doorway. He was only in his twelfth year, like me, but he was much larger. Bigger even than some of the older apprentices I'd glimpsed drilling shallow trenches beneath the training dome.

I looked around, but the archives were empty except for us.

"Don't look so confused, shaleface."

There are deposits of shale across the moon that turn to a sort of paste when exposed to the atmosphere. The chemical reaction also causes the shale to release a putrid odor. Once, last year, Bash replaced my morning porridge with the paste. I smelled it right away, and pushed the bowl away, but he came up behind me, grabbed a handful, and smeared it against my lips and nose. Even after I cleaned it off, and rinsed my mouth with peroxide and mentha, I couldn't wash away the epithet. The name shaleface stuck with me.

My father said miners get used to the smell of the shale without much fuss, but thinking about the taste of it on my tongue made me quiver with disgust, and the smallest hint of its odor repulsed me. When my father saw how upset I was, he promised to talk to Bash's father, who worked on one of my father's crews. Looking back now, I realize that it must have incensed Bash to think that anyone related to a weakling like me could ever tell *his* father what to do. His threats and torments were more than just idle distraction or social posturing. It was a rivalry.

But I had no inkling of this rivalry then. He was a bully, and I feared him, and that was enough for me to know that my father's intervention would only make things worse. At the time, I had begged him not to say anything to Bash's father. Now, here I was in the archives, alone with Bash, wishing with all my heart that my father could save me now.

"Who were you talking to, Bash?" I asked, trying to strike the right balance of meekness and curiosity.

"Who do you think?"

"You said victors. Plural. There is no one here but you and me," I said without meeting his eyes.

"You and all of your imaginary story friends, shaleface."

I kept my eyes on the floor.

"But none of them are going to help me with the eval, are they? So I guess that leaves you."

"I could help you study," I said, trying to find some sort of compromise.

Bash laughed.

"Bash, if we're caught-"

"Then you'll pay double, shale. Once Tefdrumon is done with you, you'll still have to answer to me. Better then that you don't get busted, eh?"

If I agreed to take the evaluation for him, I was sure to get caught. If I said no, Bash would hurt me or humiliate me. I thought of the ancient emperor in the story I was reading, about how he would never let himself get outmatched by the likes of Bash. I needed a better option.

"Tell Tef you can't take the eval today," I said, an idea taking shape.

He saw the look on my face, and narrowed his eyes.

"When I am within earshot, tell him your father needs help with the tunnelers. I'll chime in and verify your story. I'll say how my father mentioned it over supper last night." I was improvising, but it felt effortless. Time seemed to slow down as I watched myself manufacture an escape.

"You're saying the old drumon will think I'm lying if you don't back me?"

The threat in his question caught me off guard, but I rolled with it. "Well... I'm the one with my nose at his backside, like you always say, right? Why not use that to your advantage?"

He grunted, assenting to my logic. "But what good will that do anyway, shale? I'll just have to take it tomorrow."

"If you ace this eval," I said, "which you will if we somehow figured out a way for me to take it for you today, he'll know you cheated." I tried to sound as commanding as I could.

"Careful, shale." He moved closer to me, his hands curling into fists.

"But if I take the eval today for myself, while you're gone," I plowed ahead, "I'll know which answers to give to you for tomorrow. You'll take the test yourself, and you'll do well... but not so well to arouse any suspicion."

"You know, shale, I could ace it if I wanted." He tilted his head back, frowning at me.

"I know, Bash, I know," I said, holding up my hands, "but you've got better things to do, right? If you want my help, then you've got to trust me."

He uncurled his fists.

"But if I do this, I need something from you."

He laughed. "I won't pulverize you. There's that."

"Sure you won't. Until the next time you need something, and we do this all over again."

"I like doing this, shaleface. I could watch you squirm all winter."

"Look Bash, everyone around here follows you," I said, "but we all know you could be gone soon. I mean, just the other day, I heard my father talking with Loltdrumon—"

"Lolt?" Bash interrupted. "Did he mention me?"

I was tempted to say yes, but I didn't want to overdo it. "Well, no, but my father was asking him which of the apprentices were ready to move into active mining work. If Lolt sends off his best trainees to the mines, that means he will be looking for new recruits, right? What if you ended up at the top of that list?"

Bash tried to hide his excitement, acting as if this tidbit was no big surprise to him, but I could see he was hooked. "Yeah," he said, "I probably will be at the top."

"But when you leave demia, Bash, what do you think is going to happen?"

He shrugged his shoulders. "Why should I care what happens? I can't wait to get out."

"Remember last year, when a water purifier malfunctioned and flooded the Fulbos mine? When you leave, your spot will be empty, like Fulbos, and everyone will flood in, trying to take what was yours."

"So..." Something dawned on him, and a look of incredulity crossed his face. "So you want me to make sure *you* get to take my spot?"

I laughed. "I'm not that crazy, Bash. Whoever wants to be the top chief when you're gone is welcome to it. I hate demia as much as you. I just want to be left alone. All you have to do is keep people off my back, and I'll make sure you pass *all* of your evals. If you do that, I'll put in a good word for you with my father, and maybe you'll be on Lolt's recruitment list even sooner than you thought."

He stared at me.

I met his gaze with a newfound courage I'd never known before.

With Bash on my side, things went easier for the remainder of winter. In the final year before the return of the long sun, while the rest of us were still in demia, he went off to begin his mining apprenticeship, and I worried new attacks might flare up. But his acts of protection lingered. A buffer had formed between me and the others. I was no longer shaleface the scapegoat. I was simply the loner.

When I came of age in my second summer, I apprenticed with

my mother. Both my parents made sure of that. They wanted a future for me, not the risk of an early death below ground. Not that they needed to worry. It was clear to everyone that I was unfit for the mines. I was smaller than the other children, too lean and fragile by our peoples' standards. The refinery was not as dangerous as the deep caverns, and I showed the same aptitudes as my mother. "You have more talent than I ever did," she told me once.

And so I escaped the perils of adolescence and the jeopardy of the mines. But laboring in the refinery was still tedious. It made me thirst for a grander life. I caught hints of that grandeur whenever visitors came.

Ships arrived with halting frequency. When they did, it was a source of tremendous excitement for everyone on Verygone. A holiday festiveness filled the community. In exchange for our fuel, the spacefarers bore stories and supplies and Fellowship credits.

Every stranger was welcomed with open arms, regardless of race or status. Merchants. Traders. Explorers. Scientists. Refugees. They came from many different worlds, for many different reasons, speaking many different tongues, genetic permutations and modifications too numerous to measure. They represented the endless, subtle varieties of life that were so often absent out here on the fringe, and we were all united by the same need for comfort and connection, a balm for the long, lonely vastness of space.

But they were not only our connection to the wider galaxy. They were also our economic lifeblood. Our fuel powered this corner of the star system, and we could not afford the mad nativist ideologies or exclusionary policies I had read about on some other worlds.

What I loved the most is that even though I was something of an outlier among my own people, most travelers from other worlds couldn't tell the difference. I was just another overcurious quarry scamp, come up from the mines to scavenge for gossip and trinkets. If they were the type to pay close attention, they might have noticed I was smaller than average, but most probably thought I was merely younger.

Whenever they came, I felt free. I was always eager for any hint of galactic intrigue, and with each visit, I came to understand more and more that *these* were my people. Every traveler is an outlier somewhere, I realized. Every explorer has been faced with the choice of home or the unknown. These were the ones who chose the unknown. I was desperate for the chance to make the same choice.

Many of the visitors spoke of Forsara; the ancient origin home. They talked of its chrome cities, shining silver and red beneath two suns, and the huge, spiked mountains, capped with ice. They told of the beautiful, brown-skinned people, the great Forsaran explorers who made us. How they had scattered us out across the galaxy to build the settlements, and how they had mastered the quantum wellspring that animates the whole universe.

I had read so much about the field. It was designed to tap into that quantum wellspring, allowing conscious beings to interact thought with matter, creating a bridge between mind and world. It was the mystery at the heart of the Fellowship, the unifying covenant that held so many disparate worlds together as one galactic civilization.

I hungered for firsthand accounts from visitors. On Verygone, we had a few old virtual simulators that required a full body, external interface. But it was nothing like being able to connect to the field. Virtual reality is to the field what an image capture is to actually being there. A few of the visitors even had field ports linked directly to their nervous systems. To see an actual port, a direct line into the source, was almost mystical.

When there were no visitors, I used my imagination, fantasizing about earning the gift of field connection, giving me the power to stretch my mind out and embody a ship. To learn a new language in an instant. To become part of a planet. I imagined the journey to Forsara, accelerating through the wrinkles, crossing dimensions back to the far ago, wandering the crystal castles from where we had all once come.

"You sure do ask lots of questions kid," Thaun said, looking up at me as we waited in line at the canteen to get lunch, kneading the stubble on his cheeks with his left hand. He was lean and rugged, with heavy lines creasing the sandy skin around his eyes and forehead.

A week prior, Thaun arrived to Verygone with a rare shipment of cutting-edge nanite drills, and he quickly found a willing and eager customer in my father. My father, ever dutiful to the edicts of hospitable trade, treated Thaun in our home quarters, even inviting him to stay with us. He refused, gruff but polite, saying he preferred his ship to just about any place in the galaxy.

But he was often seen wandering the compound, and I took to him immediately, appointing myself as his emissary and guide before another ambitious hanger-on got to him. The miners of Verygone are a taciturn people, and I found Thaun's dry, abrasive wit and inter-worldly airs captivating; and he didn't seem to mind me tagging after him wherever he went.

As I began to mature, I discovered one of the advantages of my ancestry: although I was relatively small on Verygone, I towered over most offworlders. Even a small miner is still a large person, and at full height, Thaun's head only came up to my chest. "I'm hardly a child anymore, pausha Thaun," I said, looking down at him. "I've just never been off of Verygone, and I want to know more about life on other worlds."

"Thaun, kid. Just Thaun. Leave formalities to the politicos and bureaucrats."

"Okay then, Thaun. But you still haven't told me what you do." I glanced at the plasmic disrupter hanging from his belt.

His eyes followed mine. He rubbed the back of his neck with

his hand. "I deal with sensitive cargo and a lot of my... clients, they require discretion and the skills of someone who can work under pressure. Sometimes, that means I got to defend myself."

It was our turn for food, and our conversation paused as we chose what to eat. I filled my bowl with a heaping mound of the high fat, high protein gulyas that was a staple on Verygone, and reached for a cup of piping hot thuca broth, made with tubers grown in the imported soil in our biosphere.

Thaun took a whiff of the gulyas before he spooned his in. "Damn. That smells fantastic."

I smiled watching him. "My father always says gulyas is the perfect sustenance."

"Gulyas, eh?" he said, as we walked towards two empty seats. "This stew must be why all you miners are so damn hairy. Even the women."

I laughed. "Summers here are too cold for some offworlders, and our winters are brutal. We're hirsute for a reason. Your obsession with hairlessness is an offworld cultural oddity as far as we're concerned."

He turned his head as I said that, and I followed his line of sight. He was looking at a beautiful young woman named Frotha. She had fairer skin than most of my people, with wide, chestnut eyes, and her arms and legs were covered with silky, lusutrous hair the same color as the shiny black hair on her head.

She caught us looking, so I waved. She smiled and waved back.

He tipped his head towards her. "I'll tell ya, kid," he whispered to me, "it's strange to see a woman hairier than me, but that don't make her any less pretty. Do you think she likes foreigners? She's a mountain of a woman that I wouldn't mind climbing."

I snorted and shook my head, refusing to answer.

We sat down, silent except for the clinking of our spoons and the slurping broth. When I finished my bowl, I stood for another helping. "Can I get you anything else?" I asked.

He shook his head. "I can't eat half as much as you giants."

I came back, and finished my second bowl. When I was done, I pushed it aside, looking to my left and right. Then I leaned forward and said in a quiet voice, "Thaun?"

He met my eyes, curiosity on his face.

"Are you a... a smuggler?"

He leaned back in his chair, barking loud laughter.

People sitting near us glanced over.

"I don't mean to offend," I said quickly and quietly. "I've read all about the Hidden Road. How they control a lot of..." I groped for a diplomatic word, "sensitive business out here on the fringes of the galaxy."

He laughed again. "You've got a mind for conspiracies, eh kid?"

"They're not real?"

"The Road is real alright. But not every pilot who carries a sidearm works for some large, shadowy organization." He patted the disrupter at his waist. "I walk the Road when I have to, but I'm my own man."

"Oh. That's good, I guess."

He could see the disappointment in my eyes. "I tell you what, kid. You've got a lot to learn... The simple truth is, the galaxy needs people like me out here on the fringes. The plutocrats have more wealth than they know what to do with on the central worlds. But we fend for ourselves out here. If that means I have to bend the rules to get resources to the people who want 'em, so be it. And if I earn some credits along the way, well that's just 'cause I'm bringing value to the lives of others. If not me, someone else will. And frankly kid, there ain't no one better than me at this."

I leaned even closer. "You could take me with you," I said in a whisper.

"Take you with me?" he practically shouted, ignoring my attempt at discretion. "I don't think so, kid. My work ain't for amateurs."

I sat up straighter. "I earned the highest marks in demia, I have reached the third echelon in chronostones, and I am one of the only people my age working in the refinery."

He raised his left eyebrow, and his closed lips frowned at the right corner. "This where I'm supposed to be impressed?" he said.

"You said I have a lot to learn. Well, I'm the best learner I know."

"All the more reason why you should stay away from the game I'm playing, kid. You've got a brighter future ahead of you. The galaxy needs brains like yours. No need to tussle down in the underbelly with folks like me."

"The thought of spending the rest of my life here on our moon gets worse and worse every year. *Our* underbelly is nothing but gossip and corrupt local polities. I'd do anything for a taste of something bigger. Please. I won't get in your way."

He sat back in his chair, and looked at me for a long moment. Then he reached across the table and put a comforting hand on my forearm. "Look, kid, I get it. I really do. The world I was born on felt like a dead end when I was your age too. Now that I am older, I know enough to appreciate what I left behind."

"But still, here you are, on some distant moon, when you could be home." I gave him a triumphant look.

He pursed his lips. "Fair enough. I still visit my long-suffering mother when work takes me in that direction, but my life is out here. Has been for a long time. I'm not sure I could go back, even if I wanted to."

He looked away from me, thinking about his mother, maybe, or what it would be like to go home again. I thought about my own mother, how much she had already done to support me.

"What would your folks say if you left?" he asked.

"They want me to go on to do something big with my life."

"Course they do. Every good parent thinks their kid is meant for greatness. And maybe they're right about you. But do you think that means they want you signing up with a small time transporter like me?"

I shook my head gloomily.

He leaned across and patted me on the forearm again. "Your time will come, Oren."

I nodded and shrugged.

"Hey. Have you seen a starcrosser yet?"

"I don't think so."

He laughed. "You'll know when you do. Believe me."

"Do you mean an interstellar voyager?" I asked breathlessly. "Have you ever seen one?"

He nodded. "Been on one. Three, actually, for anyone running tallies. They're always looking to train up irritating youngsters like you who ask too many questions. A starcrosser ever comes to Verygone, well that might just be your passage outta here, kid."

"A starcrosser," I whispered under my breath. The thought made my mind race with excitement.

"Hey." Thaun snapped his fingers in front of my face. "You ever even been offworld at all?"

I frowned and shook my head.

"Not even over to Jendovah or Jarcosa?"

Jendovah was a massive mining asteroid at the edge of our Beallurian solar system, and Jarcosa was the closest inhabited planet, second from the sun.

"My mother's great grandparents were born on Jarcosa, but we've never been."

"One day, maybe, you'll stand on the shore of Jarcosasand with the mountains at your back, and look out over the endless ocean water. It's in your blood after all, eh?"

"I'd like that very much."

"How about a ride?"

"To Jarcosa?" I asked with disbelief.

He held up his hands. "No no no. Sorry, kid. That's not what I meant. I am leaving with the sun at my back tomorrow, stopping at Jendovah, and then out of the system, so I can't take you to Jarcosa.

But I was born with the same hunger to wander that I think maybe you've got too, don't you?

"Every voyage has its beginning. That's what my old pausha Lictor used to say. First I ever served under. He was a bastard, but he was a romantic bastard, and he took a shine to his young crew members. I wouldn't be living the life I am now if not for him... not sure whether to thank him or curse him for that. But if it hadn't been him, I'm sure I would have found another ship. The least I can do is pay it forward. How about I take you for an orbital hop here on Verygone? Just a taste of the life to come, eh?"

As someone who had lived my whole life on an entire moon devoted to fueling spacecraft, I knew how precious that offer was. "You'd use up fuel just for that?"

"Well," he said, thumping me on the bicep, "turns out I know a young fellow who works at the refinery on this here moon. I am thinking maybe he can make sure I leave with my reactor fully charged, and full containment too."

I rubbed the spot where he punched me, smiling sheepishly at him.

"So, what do you say, kid? Fair deal?"

"Fair deal."

My eyes were watering and my organs compressed as I was squeezed back into my seat. Thaun let out a wild yelp of joy. Then we were weightless.

"Hey, kid. You can open your eyes now."

I squinted. He was leaning towards me, a huge smile on his face.

"Not bad, eh?" he said.

I gave him a queasy nod.

"Don't worry. The first time is always a gut churner. You get used to it. But if you throw up now, we're both going to regret it. Focus on a fixed point out. It'll help."

The cockpit window was filled with stars. The same stars I had stared up at every winter since I was a child. But just being in the cabin of Thaun's ship *Tradewinds* made me see them differently. Not just as points of light in the night, but as places I might actually one day visit.

"How many worlds have you been to, Thaun?"

"More than I can count, I'd say. But compared to some folks, I'm just a small-time provincial. Most of my trips are here in our galactic backyard."

"You've never been to the central worlds?"

He sighed. "Once. You ever hear of Tau Set?"

"The twin stars! Of course. You were there? What was it like?"

"Truth told, I couldn't wait to get back on my ship and hit open space. The politics. The mind games. The endless social rules and formal etiquette. If that's civilization, they can keep it." He wiped his hands together as if cleaning off something filthy and unpleasant.

"What about the palace? Did you at least see the Dawnfall?"

He gave me a mischievous smile. "See it? I was in it!"

"No!"

"That was why I was there. Invitation from the thermatarch herself."

I looked at him, stunned.

He shook his head and chuckled. "Sorry, kid, I couldn't resist. That old queen wouldn't know me from a meteorite. A... ah... a colleague of mine worked down in the loading docks. Got me in for a special tour, if you catch my meaning."

"I'm not sure I do."

"Sheesh, kid. I got to spell everything out for you? I love my old lady Tradewinds," he ran his hand lovingly across the dashboard in front of us, "but even a spacefarer like me gets lonely, experienced as I am with the long stretches of solitude. There're some things only the comfort of a woman's arms can solve."

"What was it like?" I held up my hands quick, before he got the wrong idea that I was looking for salacious details from his love life. "Dawnfall palace, I mean."

"Well, me and my colleague, we were, ah, kind of busy, kid, so I didn't see all that much. But what I did see sure was magnficent." He grinned wide at his own cleverness.

"Is that all you ever think about?"

He laughed.

"Do you have a shipheart?" I asked, changing the subject. "Can we talk to it?"

"No shipheart here on this old trader. Just my wits, my wisdom, and her guts and bones to keep us flying. She ain't much to look at, I know, but she was built well, and she's traveled further than most in these parts."

"Can I take a look around?"

"Hold tight. We haven't even done the best bit yet!" With a few quick flicks of his hands, the ship made a sharp turn. My stomach rose in my gullet, and I squeezed my eyes shut again.

"Here we are."

I opened my eyes, and drew in a sharp breath. My nausea disappeared.

Verygone was below us, its metal rich soil a vibrant red from this altitude. I spotted the glimmer of lights from our settlement, and then my eyes found the open quarry to the north. The gaping maw of the pit revealed dozens of layers of sedimentary rock, the moon's history played out in different hues of sand and rust down towards the core of the planet. There was a rover crossing above-ground from the settlement to the pit. It looked like a crawling insect.

Beallus glowed fiery bright, high above the Senes mountains. I realized we were moving, drifting slowly to my left, level with the plane of the horizon. In a few minutes, Beallus was out of sight, and

Cordellar came into view. It seemed even larger now, like it might swallow Verygone at any moment. Soon, it filled almost the whole of our vision.

"Verygone. It's so... so tiny," I said.

Thaun smiled. "Every world looks that way when you get up high enough. But that's your whole life down there, kid. Every minute you've ever lived took place on that moon."

I looked over at him. I felt a fierceness in me I'd never felt before. "That may be true. But I've only just begun."

Near the end of my second winter, something truly remarkable arrived. There were five of us, on our lunch break, eating in silence in the canteen. We were tired, and in a place like Verygone, conversation topics are exhausted in short order. I had offered to play chronostones to pass the time, but on that particular day, the boredom of losing to me again was apparently worse than the boredom of another quiet lunch.

I finished my gulyas, cleared my place, and walked over to the viewing window, staring out into the deep night. A flash lit up the sky. I blinked.

"What is it, Oren?" someone asked behind me.

I had no idea, but before I could answer, my mother ran in. "Come to the upper deck!" She was smiling. Everyone got up fast.

Beneath the transparent dome of the upper deck, the view was unrestricted from horizon to horizon. Cordelar was behind us, almost invisible, a looming wall of darkness. A wide river of stars funneled out from its shadow, stretching across the emptiness above. The closer stars were so solid and sharp that I often dreamed of stepping out into the lethal cold and gathering them close for warmth.

For a moment, I was lost in this sweeping vision. Then, as my eyes followed the cosmic river, I saw it, closer than any star, and even more beautiful. A starcrosser. One of the monolithic voyager ships designed for deep space exploration.

My mother grabbed my arm and whispered, "That is *Transcendence*. I wonder if it is going home?"

My jaw hung open. The massive ship hovered in high orbit, shining like a long dagger moon, bands of light spiraling across its surface. I knew what my mother meant with her question. Going back to Forsara.

Refueling a voyager can take several days. *Transcendence* was too large to land on Verygone, but it had its own refinery vessel, *The Gourmand*, which served as the primary go-between. Much of the crew of *Transcendence* stayed in orbit, but the crew of *The Gourmand* were excited to feel solid ground on their feet, to meet like-minded peers on our moon, and to find some respite from the endless work onboard. Others came with them. Officers. Scholars. Crew members suffering from the agitations of prolonged confinement.

When the commanding staff toured our refinery facilities, I made sure to get chosen for refueling duty. The terranium extracts were bonded in ultra-density atom smashers, and even though we had run these sequences through a hundred thousand cycles, the process required attention and precision to ensure atomic purity.

The dala of *The Gourmand* was a large man, even taller than my father. He was shirtless, which I came to learn is a fashion among men from the sunbright world of Forsara, but he had the hardy build of a settler, thick hair covering his chest, bred for long years at the edge of the system. Like me.

The pausha of *Transcendence* was a tall woman by galactic standards, but small and lithe compared to the women of Verygone. She had short, curly black hair and mahogany skin. A simple blue sash ran across her sleeveless cream cloak, pinned to her chest with two interlocking rings of trimantium, an unbreakable chain link, the sigil of the Fellowship. The sash marked her status as pausha, first among equals on the ship she captained.

I had never seen a native Forsaran before. She looked strange and beautiful to me. When she caught me staring, she smiled and nodded. She gestured to the dala, and he leaned down to her as she whispered something in his ear. The big man laughed, and I heard him say, "He is a bit like me, isn't he?"

<hr />

One week later, I sat with my parents around the dining table in our living quarters. A small holocube rested on the flat of the table between us. It put to my mind the odds-setting dice used at the start of a round of chronostones to set opening positions. The roll of those dice could determine the fate of the whole game.

"Aren't you going to turn it on, Oren?" my mother asked, nudging the cube towards me.

"I already did."

"You did?" she said excitedly. "Well, don't keep us in suspense! What did they say?"

I wasn't sure what to tell her. All my life, I'd dreamed of leaving Verygone, and now, the inivitation sat quiet on our dining table. I'd eaten almost every meal of my life sitting in that same spot. I looked from her to my father, and I realized I'd never truly know how much they'd sacrificed to keep me safe and give me a good life. The thought of leaving them made me sad and afraid.

"Son," my father said, reaching across the table and resting his large, calloused hand over my own. "What did they say?"

I took a deep breath. "It's a message from Forn, the dala of the Gourmand," I said. "He's offered me a place as an ensign on his ship." I tapped the activation surface of the cube as I spoke, and the image of Forn materialized in the space between us. He was smiling as he spoke again the words I'd listened to more than a dozen times now.

"So you have to leave tonight?" my mom said when the message was finished, her voice quiet.

I nodded.

"How long have you known?"

"Three days."

"Why didn't you tell us sooner?"

"I'm sorry, moma. I... I didn't know how to tell you. I'm not even sure I really want to go."

"No!" she said with surprising ferocity. Then her voice dropped to a whisper. "You must go."

I leaned back in my chair, surprised.

"Son," my father said, "Your mother's right. I know this decision isn't easy, and it's natural to have doubts, but this is your chance to become something more than you could ever be here on Verygone."

"But... but what's wrong with here? You and moma are here, and you're two of the greatest people anywhere in the galaxy. People look up to you."

He sighed. "You never met your elder forebears," he said, "but you're part of a long line of ancestors stretching back across the millennia. They left their homes once too, called by the promise of a new life. We wouldn't be here if not for them. That was their gift to us. It's our duty to pay that gift forward. And one day, you will do the same in turn."

"I... I don't know if I'm ready," I whispered.

"No one's ever really ready, son. You stand at the edge of the unknown, and all you can do is take the next step with faith that you'll land on your feet."

My mother stood and walked around the table to stand at my side. "Take this step, Oren," she said, running her gentle hands through the mane of hair on my head. "For all of us."

Later that night, I embraced my parents, and then hurried to board *The Gourmand* before the ship lifted off into space. "Son." My father gripped my shoulders. His eyes were watering. "I love you, and I am so proud of you."

I turned to my mother. She put her head against my chest, giving me a fierce hug around my waist, squeezing the air from my lungs. She pulled back and looked up at me. "I love you, Oren. We've known since the moment you were born that you have something special. We're going to miss you so much, but this is a chance of a lifetime. Go with our blessing, and become the person we know you can be."

As I neared the top of the boarding ramp, I turned back to look at them. They both waved to me. "I love you!" I shouted.

It was the last time I ever saw them.

I WAS SHOWN to my quarters onboard the *Gourmand* by a striking young woman. She was nearly half my height, with smooth brown skin, large blue eyes, and flowing gold hair streaked with silver. Her features were angular and delicate, a distinct contrast to the muscular, solid women of Verygone. I tried my best not to stare, but I kept glancing sidelong at her as we walked through the ship, our heels clacking on the polished metal floors.

When we arrived outside my room, she made a gesture at the sensor, and the door opened without a sound. We both peered inside. It was small and austere with a single bed, a hygiene pedestal on one end, and a small, outmoded monitor on the other.

"It's not much, I know..." she said, trailing off.

I stepped inside the room and turned around to face her. "I've spent my whole life living in close quarters," I said with a smile. "As far as I'm concerned, a private room with a data interface is the essence of luxury." I walked over to the monitor. "I've probably spent more time than anyone should poring through our data archives back home." I patted the monitor. "This makes me feel right at home."

She laughed. "Glad to hear it." Then she held out her hand.
"I'm Saiara Tumon Yta," she said.

I looked blankly from her face to her hand and back again.

She laughed again. "Here. Hold out your hand like this. Good.
Now touch your fingers to my wrist."

I blushed, feeling the fool, but I mimicked her. Her graceful
fingers brushed against my wrist.

"Now you're supposed to tell me your name." Her smile was
wide and amused.

"Oh right. Sorry. I'm... I'm new at this. My name is Oren.
Oren Siris."

"Pleasure to meet you, Oren," she said brightly. "First time
offworld?"

I nodded. "Last summer, a smuggler gave me an orbital ride,
but he left the next day, and I haven't seen him since. I... I wanted
to go with him, but he said no."

"A smuggler! You run with a dangerous crowd."

That made me laugh. "Hardly. The mines on Verygone can be
pretty dangerous. And if you go outside in the winter unprotected,
you will freeze to death very quickly. But beyond that, our moon is
a pretty dull place."

"You know," she said, "we're practically neighbors. I grew up on
Jarcosa, right near the equator. Even in the winter, the days and
nights were warm."

"Really? My great grandparents on my mother's side were born
there. What's it like?"

"Beautiful. A glittering sapphire in space. I wish we could stop
there now. It's been over four years since I've seen my mother, and I
am not sure when I'll get the chance after this. But Forndala told
me we're headed straight for Forsara. Word from Darpausha
herself. The suns are drawing into alignment and the Inner Coven
has evoked the Conclave."

"The Conclave?"

"Don't worry, Oren, that's going to happen a lot."

"What will?"

"You not having a clue."

I silently cursed myself for how much this beautiful offworlder had me at a disadvantage. Then I realized that I was an offworlder now too.

"Oren! I'm only teasing you."

"Sorry. I know. I'm just... I'm not used to being the slow one."

"Trust me," she said, getting serious, "if you were slow they wouldn't have let you join up. You're here for a reason, Oren. I promise you that. Be patient, and don't be afraid to ask questions. You'll be in my shoes soon enough, showing off all of your insider knowledge to the newest recruit."

"Right," I said. "Thanks, Saiara."

"You're most welcome."

There was an awkward pause then. I fumbled for something to say. "So... you haven't seen your mother for four years? Is that when you joined up?"

"Just about. A little more than that, now. A meditician from the Fellowship came to Jarcosa when I was a child. An outbreak of holermna was spreading through the main islands. It killed thousands and left many more weak and suffering. She came to help, and I apprenticed with her for many years."

"What was her name?"

"Prethi Sa Salunto. An incredible woman. She came to us from the central worlds, where she learned and mastered the healing crafts. But she was born out here on the fringes. Like us. When she felt she had learned all that she could, she returned to the fringes, traveling from world to world to care for those who needed it.

"When she got word that *Transcendence* was passing through our system on its way out to an uncharted sector, she encouraged my mother to let me join the crew as an ensign. They sent down a scout ship, and after my interview and assessments, I was whisked away."

"Was it hard for your mother to let you go?"

"Of course. But my mother revered Prethi Sa, and so did I. Prethi believed in me. Believed that I could be of service to the galaxy. As far as my mother was concerned, if Prethi said 'go,' then it was my duty to follow."

I nodded. "I spent most of my time with my mother in the refinery, which is about as safe as it gets, but when the time came, she let me go too."

"I suspect that's the hardest part of being a parent; knowing that someday, you'll have to let her go."

I gave her a sad smile, thinking of my parents and how much I already missed them.

"Anyway," she said, "I have to get back to the analysis lab. I'm supposed to be learning about the varieties of chemical reactions that produce energy. Old Cresshu gets irritable if I keep her waiting too long."

"You won't get in trouble, will you?"

"Don't worry. I'll just tell her she has fresh meat coming her way. She loves to break in the new ensigns." Her smile was wicked.

I faked a laugh, but she could tell I was nervous.

"Look," she said. "Don't worry. Today is your first day. You're welcome to explore if you want. Any door that opens to you is a place you can go, as long as you make sure not to get in anyone's way. Or, you can stay here and access the data archives. Check out the materials for new recruits. That will keep you busy."

"That sounds good. Thanks, Saiara."

"See you tomorrow morning, Oren," she said, trotting off.

"Wait! What's tomorrow morning?" I called after her.

"All hands," she called back. "Main deck. Third hour. Don't be late!"

"How will I know when it's third hour?"

But she was already gone.

Saiara plopped down across from me in the canteen, her tray rattling on the chrome table. "Hey there moon man," she said, tearing off a hunk of bread in her hands. She slathered it with spiced oil from the small vase of curved metal sitting in the bin at the center of the table. As she chewed on the bread, a spot of oil dripped on her chin. She wiped it with her delicate fingers, her tongue darting out to lick them clean.

I stared, enraptured.

"Everything okay in there, moon man?"

"Moon man?" I said, collecting myself.

She grinned at me. "That's right. You're from a moon. You're a man. And as senior ensign, it's my duty to provide you with a formal designation. It could be a lot worse, you know."

"But seriously," I said, giving her skeptical look, "'moon man?'"

"You want me to try for something else? I'm pretty creative when I need to be."

"No no. Moon man is fine, thanks."

She nodded, satisfied.

"What did your senior ensign call you?" I asked her.

"Ensign Yta," she said, grinning even wider.

"Right. Let me guess. You just invented this naming duty today, didn't you?"

She shrugged. "Might be."

I let my shoulders sag in mock defeat, chuckling as I shook my head.

"So you made it through your first week then," she said. "How are you holding up? Cresshu treating you alright?"

"She's being patient. There's a lot to take in."

"That's for sure. Hey, Qurth tells me you're a chronostones competitor. Third echelon, if the rumors are true."

"Do you play?" I said, perking up. Qurth and I had played an intense match three nights ago. He was the first real challenge I'd ever faced in the game. I barely eked out my victory.

"Occasionally. When I feel like passing the time," she said, her pleasure at the little pun clear on her face.

I chuckled again, taking her double meaning. Passing the time was one of the key strategies in chronostones. Certain combinations can speed up your opponent's clock or slow down your own, altering the passage of time in favor of one side or the other. Not everyone played with time passage rules in effect, but it added an undeniable drama and tension to a game of strategy that might otherwise drag on for hours, or even days.

"We could play now, if you want," she said, leaning back in her seat, acting casual.

"Do you have a set?"

She nodded, shoving her tray of food aside, and placing a thin, translucent wafer about the size of her palm on the table between us. "It's just an old holo set."

"I have to warn you," I said, "I'm quite good."

"That's what Qurth tells me. But I've fought and won my fair share of inter-dimensional conflicts, so why don't you show me what you've got, moon man?" She tapped the disc, and the game cube materialized in front of us. The pristine empty tiles at the beginning of a chronostones battle always filled me with excitement, with its promise of virtually infinite possibilities.

"It's my board, so I'll give you guest rights. You can play white."

I smiled, eager for the game to begin, and placed my first stone.

Twenty-seven minutes and thirteen seconds later, it was over, my chronostones scattered and ruined across the plane of battle.

There was a moment during the game when she had leaned in close to the board, and then looked up at me from beneath her eyelids. It was a dark, mischievous glance. She knew then it was over, even though I hadn't seen it yet. With her next move, my stones had cascaded from white to black, wiping away the main phalanx of my force.

She looked up at me and smiled when it was over. "Not bad," she said. "But you're focusing too much on the opening game. You can't control for every outcome. By the time we reached the end game, you were in over your head. You've got to get comfortable with the chaos."

I stared at her.

"Another round?"

I still had nothing to say. I'd never been beaten so handily. In fact, until that moment, I'd never really been beaten at all. The game had always come easy to me. Sure, I'd lost some in the early days, when I was learning, but once I grasped the fundamentals, no one on Verygone had been able stand in my path.

"Maybe not today then," she said, tapping the holo disc and turning off the game projection as I sat there, dumbfounded. She slid the disc into her pocket and stood up. "Embrace the chaos!" she called over her shoulder as she walked out of the canteen, leaving me alone with our half-eaten food and my defeat.

Forn, the dala of *The Gourmand*, was pacing across the main deck. An energetic, boisterous man, he was the largest person I had met since leaving Verygone, and the only person bigger than me. He had the musculature of a miner, thick slabs of muscle covering his broad shoulders and powerful arms, and his legs worked like two pistons as he moved back and forth. Whenever I was around him, I felt a little closer to home.

He was speaking at length about the essential purpose of a fueling vessel. The main portion of the crew had gone back to their stations after the daily all-hands meeting, but he had asked us three ensigns to remain behind, along with his second, Shu Cresna.

"By fueling the voyagers," he said without looking at anyone in particular, talking as he walked back and forth, "we fuel the whole Fellowship. Without our assistance, long range voyagers like *Transcedence* would be starlocked, unable to generate enough thrust to reach even the edge of a modest star system without wasting centuries gathering speed."

He paused for a moment, mid-stride, his eyes on the polished floor beneath his similarly polished boots.

"Ensign Yta," he said to Saiara, lifting his head to look at her. "How many months do you have left on your rotation?"

"Three, sir."

He nodded. "Almost a year with us here on *The Gourmand*. Shu Cresna tells me your studies are going admirably, and although she has not said so outright, I think she suspects, just as I do, that you have the gift of farsight."

Saiara bowed low, clearly humbled by the compliment.

"So tell us, ensign, what would you say is the single biggest challenge we face in our work?"

Saira stood tall, cocked her head, and met Forn's gaze. She did not answer right away. Then a smile crept onto her lips. "That feels like a trick question, dala," she said. "Cresshu has led me to believe that there is no harder job in the whole of the galaxy."

Forn laughed his booming laugh, and even Shu Cresna chuckled. She was a hard teacher, but not a rancorous one, and Saiara had already proven beyond any doubt that she was a capable student.

"The art of making a massive space voyager hum with life," he said, lifting his index finger towards the ceiling to underline the idea, "certainly requires a healthy dose of humor. But what is the throughline, ensign? When do we reach the point where even laughter is inadequate?"

Saiara pondered this. "There are dozens of complex processes running in unison," she said, serious now. "At any moment, a single measurement may be off by a micron or two. Taken alone, such irregularities generally do not pose a problem. But compounded, small miscalculations can be catastrophic. Once the accretion of errors begins, it can spiral quickly out of control. The biggest challenge in our work is diagnosing problems before the spiral begins, so we can correct with minimal repercussions."

"Precisely so! Well said, ensign Yta. Wouldn't you agree, Cresshu?"

Shu Cresna gave a barely perceptible nod. Her mirth at Saiara's earlier jibe had faded from her craggy face, leaving us with her usual phlegmatic skepticism.

"Which brings us to our teachable moment," Forndala continued. "And as you all know, ensigns, our shu loves teachable moments."

All three of us laughed at that.

Forndala let the laughter fade, then held the silence. After almost a month onboard, I recognized Forndala's tendency to pause whenever he presented us with a question or an enigma. Clearly then, we had arrived at the important moment, to the point of this whole conversation.

"Perhaps Dala Forn cares to illuminate?" ensign Qurth Foli asked, breaking Forn's meaningful silence with his heavy Arborean accent.

Every ensign onboard a voyager like *Transcendence* learns the trades of the spacefarer through experiential rotations. With an active-duty crew of more than five thousand people, and another twelve thousand-plus scholars, astronomists, research fellows, artists, merchants, and passengers, voyagers are massive ships, with an equally massive litany of systems and processes. A world unto itself.

It would take centuries for one ensign to rotate through all the various roles. Life extension techniques could make that possible, but not practical. So each of us is assigned an individual rotation map based on our intake interviews, a battery of aptitude assessments, and the genetic and psychomedical profiles built by the ship's heart and the staff of mediticians who oversee the physical and mental health of every person on board.

Qurth was from the forest moon of Arborau, where settlers had shaped their evolution over the millennia to adapt to a life amongst the dense rainforests and alpine jungles of the moon. His emerald eyes and fibrous green skin were striking, making him look, to my eyes, almost inhuman, and he spoke the universal tongue in a formal, stilted manner. He was in his seventh year as an ensign, and he had rotated through more than a dozen roles onboard *Transcendence* in that time. He was clever and confident, and he was usually the first to draw Forn out whenever the dala toyed with us like this.

"I do care, ensign Foli," Forndala said with amusement. "I most certainly do." He turned to Cresna. "Shu?" he said, tilting his head towards the command table.

Shu Cresna shuffled over to the circular command table and lifted up a small silver cylinder.

"And that is?" Qurth asked.

He raised his pointer finger again. "A challenge!" He seemed quite pleased with himself. "As each of you move through your rotations, you will be faced with numerous challenges. Some of them will be unanticipated, arising from the demands of the job. Others are scripted, designed specifically to help you learn. This has the flavor of both."

He took the object from the shu and held it closer to us. It looked lightweight and transluscent. "Ensign Siris," he said. I stood up taller. "You grew up on mining settlement. Perhaps this looks familiar to you?"

He rotated the cylinder in his hand. As he did so, its translucent surface became transparent. In the heart of the cylinder, a perfect sphere as dark as the void of space vibrated like an angry hymenoptera.

"That is an ingot of pure terranium," I said, shocked.

He nodded. "Refined and stabilized to a solid, inert state."

"I have never seen such a small antigravitational container before," I whispered.

"Remarkable, isn't it?" He held the cylinder towards me.

I raised my eyebrows.

He nodded, encouraging me to take it.

"You hold in your hand the most valuable substance in the galaxy," he said as I turned the small containment unit over in my hands. "The only substance we know of that interacts directly with the invisible dark matter that undergirds our whole universe.

"As long as the antigravitons that suspend the terranium do not fail, it is relatively safe to transport in its inert state. But we are not terranium merchants. We are spacefarers. We work with terranium in its plasmic state, and a tiny ingot like that can power a voyager like ours for more than a month. Without our converters, *Trancendence* would be helpless and adrift, an errant asteroid knocked out of orbit.

"Last night," Forndala continued, "while you were asleep, one of the converters failed. Transcend offered to fix it for us, but I declined. We have over a dozen redundancies in the conversion systems, so the ship as a whole is not in any serious danger, but it occurred to me, and Shu agrees, that this might be a perfect opportunity for you three to test your mettle."

"You want us to fix the converter?" Saiara said.

Forndala nodded.

A realization hit me. I held up the cylinder. "But to fix the converter, we need to stabilize the terranium."

He looked at Shu Cresna with knowing eyes. "I told you we made the right choice having ensign Siris begin his rotations with us, Cresshu."

Cresna pursed her lips and squinted at me.

"But how?" I said with anxiety. I'd spent my whole life working in a massive terranium refinery, but I had never faced a problem like this.

"That, my young apprentices, is precisely the question. What say you? Are you up for it?"

"First," Saiara said, "we should uncouple *The Gourmand* from *Transcendence*. If the terranium overreacts it could be catastrophic. We need to move to a safe distance."

We were standing in the vast accelerator chamber that formed the bulk of the ship, a wide room, ten times my height. If it had been empty, it would have been big enough to hold thousands of people. But every useable cube of space was filled with equipment. A web of corridors ran through it all, wide enough for us to move single file. After getting lost twice, we made our way to the failed converter.

I looked around, marveling at the engineering. On Verygone, the particle accelerator used to process terranium circled underground like a giant ring, stretching over thirty-seven farruns in circumference. On *The Gourmand,* the ship's designers had figured out how to compress the accelerator into a seemingly endless labyrinth of curves and folds that rose above us like some monstrous alien digestive tract.

A perpetual hum filled the whole space. It was not painfully loud, but it was relentless, the aural equivalent of wearing a veil over your eyes, everything shaded and colored by the screen in front of your face.

"But even if it's possible for us to reach a distance that keeps the voyager from risk," Qurth said, "how will we extract the terranium?" The humming from the equipment made his voice sound reedy and fragile.

Saiara's shiny golden hair was tied up behind her head, leaving a tail that hung down past her shoulders. "If even a single atom is exposed to air," she said, absentmindedly curling her hair like a rope around her fingers, "it could kick off a chain reaction... What do you think, Oren?"

I tore my eyes away from the structural intricacies of *The Gourmand's* accelerator to look at them. "I... I'm not sure. The particle accelerator on Verygone is buried a mile under the surface, beneath layers of massive radiation shielding. And I was part of a team of more than forty people specially trained to manage the whole system. I've never handled anything like this before." I gestured towards the vast network of piping and joints.

"Fair enough. But you still have more expertise than either of us. Tell us what you know."

"Well, I know that terranium is extremely rare and extremely dense. You aren't going to find a hunk of it just lying around. And if you did, you wouldn't be able to lift it. Its gravitational pull is so strong that an ingot the size of a pebble, like the one Forndalapausha showed us, could actually pull you towards it, trapping you in place."

Qurth shook his head. "Terrifying," he said.

I nodded. "It was first discovered because certain moons, planets, and asteroids had inexplicably strong gravitational signatures. After decades of research, astronomists and geologicians realized that tiny, microscopic particles embedded in the sediment of these celestial bodies gave them their tremendous gravitational heft. The geologic matter of a planet must be sifted hundreds of times to extract the terranium. Then it is refined and condensed in a particle accelerator, and after a certain threshold, the terranium must be contained using antigravitrons to negate its gravitational influence."

"Every converter onboard must therefore have antigravitational containment inside," Qurth said, resting his hand against the piping next to his head.

"That's right. Here on the *Gourmand*, the terranium is suspended in its plasmic state, a miniature blazing star. The converter extracts that energy, using it to power the whole ship. There's probably a whole set of converters dedicated just to the interstellar drive."

"Once the terranium has been activated, how do you render it inert again?" Saiara asked.

"By infusing it with frethone. The molecules bond, making the terranium inert, transforming your portable sun into a dense orb tougher than pure carbon, and heavier than a class two mineral planet."

"So," Saira said, "we're either dealing with a star the size of a person, or a pebble heavier than Jarcosa."

I pinched my lips together and nodded.

"And we cannot open the converter to repair it without risk of reaction?" Qurth added.

"Not in here," I said.

"What do you mean 'not in here'?"

"The ship's atmosphere. Like Saiara said, even a single atom from the terranium could ignite every molecule of carbon, hydrogen, oxygen, and nitrogen. We would all be incinerated."

"We need a vacuum," Saiara said.

"Right."

"Then this whole accelerator is hermetic?" Qurth said.

"Yes," I said. "It has to be. The energetic particles flow freely inside the accelerator without risk of environmental disruption."

"But you must have technical problems on Verygone, yes? What did you do when things went wrong?"

"The interior is accessible through airlocks. Unless we powered down the whole system, which never happened in my lifetime, repair work was typically done by sending drones in through the nearest airlock. Eventually, they disintegrate in the intense radiation, but they usually last long enough to get the job done. And if not, we just send in another cluster to finish what the first set started."

"But Dala Forn does not want us to take the easy way," Qurth said, "or else he would have shipheart go in and do the repairs, much as you have explained."

We all stood in silence at that, unsure of what to do next.

"Hey you three!" a whispery voice said.

"Did you hear-" I started to ask, then saw that the Qurth and Saiara were also looking around.

"Don't worry." The voice was louder now, penetrating the ambient hum. "You're not imagining things. Up here!"

We all lifted our heads up.

"Here!" A hand was sticking out from between two pipes, waving to us. A moment later the person's head poked out. It was one of the ship's technicians. He wore thick black goggles that concealed his eyes and made him blend in with the equipment.

"What are you up to down there?" he said.

"Dala Forn asked us to fix the broken converter," Saiara said, mustering an authoritative voice.

"Ah!" said the technician. "I've been wondering why we hadn't just sent in the automatons. Teachable moments, eh ensigns?" He grinned wide. He could clearly tell that we were trainees, and he wasn't buying Saiara's attempt to sound official. "Of course, I don't need to tell you young bloods that these units are all modular, right?" He smacked his hand on the surface of our malfunctioning converter.

We stared up at him. The technician grinned one last time, then disappeared back into the equipment, never even telling us his name.

We looked at each other. Then we all started laughing.

"Modular! Of course," I shook my head. "We can seal both ends, bypass the flow, and remove the converter without disrupting the rest of the system."

"We must still open it to effect the repair, ensign Siris," Qurth pointed out to me.

Saiara grabbed my left arm with both hands. "Ever been on a spacewalk, Oren?" she asked with childlike enthusiasm.

"A what?"

"Looks like you're about to get a crash course. I have an idea."

"Qurth," Saiara said over the comlink. "Are you ready?"

"I am ready, ensign Yta." His formal enunciation sounded almost inhuman through the miniature speaker inside my helmet.

Saiara and I were floating outside *The Gourmand*, tethered to the exterior of the ship. The terranium converter hung in space in front of us, a larger, more complex version of Forndala's handheld antigravitational cylinder, about the length of my leg and three times as thick.

"Are you ready, Oren?" Saiara asked.

I was closest to the converter, with my back to her. We had pried open a surface panel, revealing the blazing terranium orb inside. Even with the antigrav containment on full power, I could still feel radiant heat through my exoskin. I slowly swiveled my head to look at her. Her exoskin glowed fiery bronze in the light.

Given my expertise, we had all agreed that I was the one most qualified to do the stabilization. An extendable hose made from flexible nanofiber stretched out from the ship, running alongside the tethers that ensured that neither we nor the converter could go flying off into space.

I turned back to the converter, gripped the hose, and nodded.

"Okay then," she said. "Initiate the transfer, Qurth."

Everything happened quickly then. The hose expanded and tensed beneath my hands as the frethon gas flowed through it. The terranium star started to solidify, dark spots spreading like a malignant virus through its white-hot surface.

"Almost there," I said.

The last of the light disappeared as the surface of the orb congealed. Just a moment or two more, I thought.

I lurched forward.

For one brief instant, I felt the terrible gravitational hunger of the terranium pulling me closer. I took a deep breath, supressing my instinct to panic. We had planned for this. The small amount of additional mass caused by the injection of gas was enough to throw the antigravitons out of equilibrium for a moment before they self-corrected. I planted my feet on the converter, steadying myself, and the instant passed as the antigravitons compensated.

I breathed a sigh of relief. "It's stabilizing," I said.

Then the hose in my hand crimped and cracked.

A burst of gas hit me in the chest, knocking me backwards. I tumbled away from the converter, end over end. Qurth was shouting in my ear. Images blurred together on the tumbling wheel of my vision.

The hose, spraying out a smoky cloud of gas.

The ship, upside down.

The void of space.

Saiara, next to the hose, spraying it with sealant.

The ship, closer now.

The void.

Saiara careening towards me.

She caught me just above my waist with her left shoulder, wrapping her arms around my torso. My arms and legs pinioned forward, my body hinging and collapsing as she collided with me. She stopped me from pinwheeling, carrying us both away from the converter with her momentum.

I tried to speak but I couldn't seem to catch my breath. I instinctively pulled my arms in and clawed at my throat.

"Don't take off your helmet!" Saira's voice screamed in my ear through the comlink. "We're almost there."

The biometric displays on my faceplate were blinking red. I focused in on them and saw that the air from my suit was leaking out.

I looked down. Bits and pieces of my exoskin were flaking off from my chest, brittle and ruined by the exposure to frethon gas.

The exoskin was disintegrating.

Panic started rolling back again. I gasped for air. My chest felt like it was going to burst.

"Oren! I need you to stay focused. Exhale. Right now. Do it!"

Her voice cut through my terror. I exhaled all of the air out of my lungs.

The panic subsided a little. My chest relaxed.

I lifted my head, trying to orient myself.

A solitary distant star glinted in my vision.

No. It was the converter, hurtling away from us.

I reached my hand towards it. *We are going to lose it!* my mind screamed, but no words came out.

My mouth felt hot and effervescent.

My vision went black.

"Stop pampering him," I heard Forndala say from far away. "He has rested enough."

"Dala Forn," another voice from the distance responded, "it is my duty-"

"Don't lecture me on duty, young blood." Louder now. "You saved this ensign's life. We are grateful to you for that. But this boy comes from hardy stock, and he needs to use his strength. He'll spoil if we leave him cooped up too long!"

My eyes felt heavy. I forced them open.

A glassy cyclopean eye stared back at me. I blinked. The eye kept watching me. An inspector oculus, I realized. I am in the medbay, lying down.

I rolled my head to my right. Adaptive gel cupped my skull, adjusting precisely to my movements as the weight of my head shifted. Forndala and a young man I did not recognize stood above me. Forndala was at least two heads taller than the man.

Spiraled bands of silver glinted on the man's lapel, marking him as a meditician. He's been caring for me, I thought. He was attempting to stay firm as he faced down Forn, but the dala was using every bit of his intimidating height for dramatic effect.

"Dala," the young man was saying nervously, "I... I respect your position, but-"

"Look!" someone else said before the meditician could finish speaking. "His eyes are open!"

Her face appeared above me at the same time I recognized her voice, emerging from my periphery, obscuring the darkened oculus. "Oren! It's me, Saiara." Her wide blue eyes were close to mine, and the silver in her hair caught the light.

I gave her a weak smile. "Do you really think I could forget the woman who nearly got me killed?" I said. I was trying to be light, but my voice was tired and strained, and my tongue felt muddled.

"Oh, Oren. I am so sorry. I never should have put you at risk like that." She took my hand, her small fingers lacing with mine.

Before I could tell her not to worry, that we had all made the choice together, the meditician was next to her, bringing his hands close to my face. He hovered his fingers, almost touching my cheeks, and slowly moved his hands down to my chest.

When he was done, he stood and nodded. "All vitals feel satisfactory," he said.

"Excellent," Forndala said, shouldering the young man aside. "Ensign Siris," he said. "Welcome back to the waking world, son."

I propped myself up to a seated position, waving Saiara away when she fretted over me. "Dala," I said. "It's good to be back. How long has it been?"

"Four full days in coldsleep, ensign. We just thawed you out this morning. You know," he said, "you got real lucky out there. But you're in top shape now, thanks to ensign Yta."

I looked back at Saiara, and she gave me a shy smile.

"I remember," I said. "The gravitational pull of the terranium ripped the hose, and the gas sent me flying. You... you leapt after me."

She nodded. "I kicked off of the converter and caught you while you were spinning, propelling us both towards the airlock. Qurth reeled us the rest of the way in."

"Qurth! Is he here?"

He stepped up next to Saiara. "I am here, ensign Siris."

"Did we do it? Did we fix the converter?"

Qurth and Saiara nodded together. "The stabilization was successful," Qurth said. "Once you were safely inside, we hauled the converter back and completed repairs. You did well, ensign Siris."

"Thank you, Qurth." I opened and shut my jaw, working my mouth. "Why does my tongue feel so strange?" I asked.

"In the vacuum," he said, "the boiling point drops so low, your own inner heat is enough to catalyze bodily liquids. Your saliva began to boil in your mouth."

I opened my eyes wide.

"Your tongue and gums were badly burned," the meditician confirmed, "and your lungs nearly burst after you panicked and starting gulping in what was left of your air. Fortunately, enisgn Yta had the presence of mind to make you exhale. When she got you back safely, we immediately went to work repairing or replacing the damaged cellular tissue. In a few more days, you'll be right as starlight."

"Thank you," I said to him. "You saved me as much as Saiara did."

The man nodded. "Most welcome. Now, I have to check on other patients. I'll give you all a few more minutes," he said, turning to the group, "and then we have to let ensign Siris here get some more rest." He gave Forndala a pointed stare, then walked out of sight.

That's when I saw Shu Cresna hovering behind Forndala. The bulk of his body had blocked her from view, but she peered around him now. Her face was pinched and strained, but when she caught me looking at her, she gave me a warm smile.

"Cresshu," I said. "You actually look pleased to see me. You weren't *worried* about me, were you?"

As soon as I said that, she scowled and waved her hand at me, brushing my nonsense aside. "Bah. You took foolish risks. All of you." She glared at Saiara and Qurth. They both dipped their heads, acknowledging the truth of her words. Then her voice softened. "But I cannot deny your courage and creativity. This was, I think, a teachable moment for all of us."

Forndala laughed his booming laugh. "Quite right, Shu Cresna. Quite right. We cannot always predict the challenges we'll face. And great risks sometimes bring great rewards. But I must admit, we might have provided *some* guiding parameters to prevent you from being quite so creative. A localized vacuum field, for instance."

"A what?" Saiara said, giving him a confused and accusing look.

Forndala looked a little sheepish. "A rather wonderful device that lets you form a vacuum just about anywhere. Ideal for these sorts of repairs, really."

Saiara was incredulous, and watching her square off against Forndala, who was easily more than twice her body mass, was both impressive and riotously absurd. Her posture made me think of the xenovolves I had learned about as a boy; one of the most graceful and fearsome predators in the galaxy. She looked menacing and beautiful.

Forndala lifted his hands in the air between them, fending her off. "Who would have predicted you'd take the whole damn thing outside of the ship!" he said defensively.

Then Shu Cresna started chuckling, and the tension dissipated like the air escaping from my ruined exoskin. Soon we were all laughing together.

After a few more minutes of pleasant conversation, Forndala brought the gathering to a close. "You took our little challenge further than either of us could have imagined," he said, tilting his head towards the shu, "and your success in the face of great adversity is a testament to your potential. You are a remarkable group of ensigns, and it has been a pleasure having you on board."

Then he looked at me. "You'll have a large mantle to fill when

these two are gone, ensign Siris. Now then, we have a ship to run!"
He gave a small bow, and he and Shu Cresna took their leave
before I could take his meaning.

"Wait," I said to Saiara and Qurth. "What did he mean about
filling the mantle?"

"My rotation ends tomorrow, ensign Siris," Qurth said. "We
will not see each other again here on the Gourmand."

"You're saying goodbye?"

He nodded. "I am honored by the time we have shared
together. Perhaps other paths will draw us together. Until then," he
said, spreading his palms in the traditional Arborean valediction,
"may your roots grow long and deep."

I'd been with Qurth long enough to know that he was not a
sentimental person, so I knew he had just given me his most
heartfelt display of kinship. Melancholy threatened me at the
thought of his leaving, but I was also filled with tremendous
gratitude.

"My deepest thanks to you, ensign Foli," I said, adopting the
same formality to let him know how much I meant it. "You are an
inspiration to me, and I look forward to the day when we meet
again." I spread my palms towards him. "May your roots grow long
and deep."

He bowed low, gave me the slightest hint of a smile, his emerald
eyes gleaming, then turned and left.

Saiara and I were alone. She sat on the bed next to me.

"And you're leaving too?" I asked. My voice sounded small and
lonely.

She glanced at the monitor that displayed my vitals and
watched the pulse wave of my heart rise and fall. She looked back
at me and nodded, her face sad. "My rotation also ends tomorrow."

"You saved my life," I said, not knowing what else to say.

"It's true. But you took the greatest risk, and we couldn't have
succeeded without your knowledge. In a way, you saved all of us."

I shook my head. "I've followed your lead from the day I

arrived. Your brilliance is something I aspire to. I'm not sure... how will I get by without you?"

"Trust yourself. Every person on this voyage is brilliant, and you've earned your place among us. You don't need to hide in the archives for the rest of your life, Oren. You have a rare courage and strength, and in time, you'll discover where that strength is needed most, and then you'll claim your rightful place in the Fellowship."

I thought of my parents. "My mother always told me I needed to dream bigger," I whispered, staring up the inspector oculus, my reflected face shrunken and warped in its pitiless eye.

Saiara moved closer. "She's right," she said. "The galaxy needs you."

Then she leaned across me and kissed me on my right cheek. Her lips were soft and moist, compressing the stubble on my face. A loose strand of golden hair hung down and tickled my forehead. I wanted, more than anything I have ever wanted in my life, to turn and meet her lips with my own. But I did not.

"Where... where are you going next?" I asked when she sat back up.

"Transcend will announce assignments for rotating ensigns tomorrow morning. I'll find out then."

"Will I see you again?" I touched my fingers to my cheek.

"I'm sure of it," she said. "Until then, take care of yourself. You're the Gourmand's senior ensign now. There'll be new young bloods coming on board. You have to make sure they don't screw up, right?"

I nodded. "Right. I won't let you down."

She gave me a loving smile, her eyes crinkling, her cheeks dimpling. Then she stood. "See you soon, Oren."

I lifted my hand to hers and squeezed. "I hope so, Saiara."

She disappeared from sight through the doorway, her footsteps marking a steady rhythm in the corridor outside, until eventually, even the sound of her was gone.

On the last night of my first rotation as an ensign, I sat in Forndala's quarters, getting ready to share a bottle of a potent distillation he had batched decades ago. He looked at me and smiled as he broke the seal on the bottle. "This is probably older than you are." I watched with solemnity as he uncorked it.

"I have been waiting a long time for an excuse to drink this." He poured two fingers of the amber liquid into our glasses, and held his up to the light, admiring the fluid as he tilted the glass in slow circles. He took a cautious sip, holding it on his tongue for a moment. Then he swallowed and broke into a huge smile. "Drink up, young blood. That was worth the wait!"

The liquor was warm and strong as it settled into my belly. "That is quite good, dala," I said. I took another swallow.

"Damn right. And you've earned it. Over the past year, we have taught you everything we can, Oren... Well, everything except how to make vysak as good as this." He tapped his glass with his finger. "Your rotation here on our faithful Gourmand ends tomorrow, which means you'll begin service onboard the Transcendence."

He paused to take another sip.

I looked around his room.

It was an inviting space, cluttered and a little unkempt. There were images everywhere. Hanging on the walls. Propped up on shelving. Lying flat on the table in front of us.

One of them caught my eye. I picked it up off the table.

"Is this...?"

He nodded. "Verygone."

The planet Cordelar filled the bulk of the frame. Verygone was a small, red orb in the lower left corner, no bigger than my thumbnail. "I saw it once from orbit," I said. "A traveler brought me up in his ship. It was incredible. It was also the first time I realized how small it all is. The whole of my life was spent on that tiny moon. It looms so much larger in my memories."

"Memory is funny like that."

"Wait... I don't see any settlement lights on the surface."

"That's because there were none. Verygone had not yet been settled when that was taken."

"What? How did you find this image? Why do you have it?"

"I took it."

I looked up at him in surprise. "You've been to Verygone before?"

"A long time ago. I was part of the survey crew sent to confirm the moon's gravitational signature, to prove beyond doubt that it had enough terranium to make it worth the investment of energy and resources necessary to turn it into a productive fuel hub."

I looked at the image again with fresh eyes, at the lonely moon where I was born, full of potential for those who know how to see it. "It's beautiful," I whispered.

"We have thousands of images of the moon and the surrounding system," he said, "but that was one of my favorites. A reminder that even the greatest civilizations are built on the backs of the humblest places."

"Thank you," I said, looking up at him.

"For what, Oren?"

"If not for you and this survey you conducted, not only would I have never become an ensign, I might never even have been born."

He rubbed his knuckles through his beard, staring off into the distance. He made a quiet sigh of wonder. "The thought that our paths came together because of decisions I was part of back then gives me great happiness.

"Truth is, I can't help but think of myself at your age when I look at you. More than three hundred years gone by in a flash, and suddenly I find myself sharing a glass of vysak with a youthful version of myself. Where does the time go?"

"I must be much handsomer than you were, though, right?"

He let out his huge laugh and smacked his palm on the table. "You and my former self would have been fast friends. Tight as privateers." He raised his glass. "To the reckless confidence of youth," he said.

I raised my glass to his, clinking them together, and we drank.

When we finished, we set our glasses down, and he poured us each another two fingers. I eyed the liquid with a mixture of eagerness and trepidation. After one glass, I already had a heady buzz.

"Come on, boy, drink up!"

"I've never been much of a drinker, dala."

"That bottle has waited decades for this day. We can't let it go to waste."

I sighed, lifted my glass, and took another swallow.

"That's the spirit!"

He drank again in turn. When he was finished, he wiped his lips with his handkerchief.

"Oren," he said somberly.

"Yes, dala?"

"Before you leave tomorrow, I need you to hear this: Having you onboard has helped me reconnect with a past that has been too long forgotten. You make me feel closer to the home I left so many lifetimes ago."

"I feel much the same, dala. Closer to home when we are together."

"I am glad of that, Oren. But we didn't recruit you just so you could spend your whole life doing the same job you could have done at home. Much as it pains me to say it, it's a good thing you're moving on."

He held up his hand. "Before you say anything, I want you to know that whatever comes next, I believe in you. You're a born leader, and it's time to take the next step. Every ensign must. One day, you'll earn your place in the Fellowship, and maybe even your own ship."

He saw my look of pleased surprise at the compliment and shook his head. "Don't take that lightly, young blood. Sooner or later, you'll have to make hard decisions. No easy answers. Be ready for that."

I nodded. "Thank you, dala. I don't know what to say. It's... it's been an honor."

"Just drink up, Oren," he said, draining the last of the bottle into our glasses. "Like I said, you've earned it."

We raised our glasses and drank.

5 / TRANSCENDENCE

As an ensign on *Transcendence*, the remnants of my life in fuel refinement receded away, but I was still hustling as hard as ever, learning every day: how to plot a cross-galaxy target in four-dimensional space; how to fly the close-range recon darts; how to purge and cleanse a plugged waste treatment line; how to repair malfunctioning plasmic shears; how to measure nutrient and acidity levels in a water reservoir to ensure that the microorganisms were healthy enough to purify the recycled water before it reentered the ship's ecosystem.

Those were incredible years. No matter how much I learned, there was always some new challenge; someone who knew more than me, ready to push me further or give me a puzzle to solve. Weeks flowed into months. Months piled up to years.

I saw Qurth just once, in the junction room that connected all of the simspheres. He was engaged in a heated debate with another ensign. I called out to him, but we were too far away from each other, and he did not hear me. When I finished my zero gravity training session, he was nowhere to be found.

Saiara and I made it a point to meet when we could. Sometimes we ate together, followed by a few games of chronostones. Once I realized that she was a fourth echelon player, a whole level above me, I got over my initial defeat and learned to embrace our matches as an opportunity to improve. Her blend of sharp humor and patient analysis helped me enter deeper into the game.

Other times, we went for walks in the open center of the voyager ship. A massive cylinder was suspended there in the empty space that marked the gravitational heart of the ship. The cylinder held the largest terranium star I had ever seen, a sun at the center of our world, our whole ship orbiting around it.

Whenever we walked, we always looked for new paths through the open air arboretum that ringed the wide primary reservoir, the light of the interior sun dappling the fallen leaves and soft loam beneath our feet. Looking out from the trees, we might see kite ships sailing across the surface of the water, or anglers casting for the large sulkfish that swam the deeps, or a pleasure boat lingering just off shore, passengers lounging in the sunlight.

As the opaque shielding that always covered part of the sun rotated in its orbit, false night crept up the curving inner surface of the ship, swallowing the avenues and structures that hung high above our heads, sending people on that part of the ship into their evening rituals, windows and exterior lights shining like stars.

There was always something new and beautiful to see, and whenever Saiara took my hand and pointed out some fresh wonder to behold, I stayed silent, sinking into the moment, willing us to hold fast to each other for as long as we could.

But she'd already received her field connection, which, I must admit, made me envious, and she seemed even busier than I was. As we both drilled further into our studies, our moments together became vanishingly rare.

Then, three years after I left *The Gourmand*, my rotation map cycled me into a role that changed everything for me: amanuensis with the pausha of *Transcendence*, Dar Talericho.

"Ensign Siris, is it?" She studied me as I stood just inside the threshold of her private workspace. The whites of her eyes were bright against her sable skin and nut brown irises.

I nodded.

She was sitting at her desk, my file called up on her hologlass. "And you're from..." She scanned the information. "Verygone?"

"Yes, pausha. Born and raised."

"No wonder Dala Forn took a liking to you. He gives you high marks."

"He's a great teacher," I said.

"He certainly is. And a great officer too. His word carries weight. And he's not the only one. By all accounts, your first four years here onboard our fair voyager have gone well."

"It is my greatest honor to serve as a member of this ship, pausha, and I am humbled to know that others find my presence useful." Her steely demeanor had me nervous, and I was working hard to maintain the appropriate respect.

"Have you ever been an amanuensis before?"

"No, pausha."

She tilted her head back, a faint smile around her eyes. "Do you know what the word means? Amanuensis?"

"I'm to be your assistant."

"A glamorous word for an unglamorous job."

"I am not a glamorous man, pausha."

She smiled a thin smile, crinkling the edges of her eyes. "Even though you will not be showered with glory, the fact that you are here at all is still significant. It means our onboarding process identified something in you that we might call, for the sake of simplicity, 'leadership potential.' Dala Forn's comments here also speak to that."

"Thank you, pausha."

"Don't thank me just yet. Potential is not actual. The point of your assistantship is not simply to make my life easier. The point is to give you exposure to the kinds of choices a leader must make, and to give *me* insight into whether or not you have the ability to realize your potential in whatever form it takes.

"Do you know what this is?" She touched the trimantium pendant clasped to the blue sash that ran across her chest.

"The chain link of the Fellowship," I said.

She nodded. "All life is bound together, Oren. That belief sits at the root of the Fellowship. And each link has its own role to play in the chain. My hope is that I can help you discover your role, or at least set you on the path towards that discovery.

"You will have remarkable access to my work and my decisions. You will see things that many others on this ship are not privy to, and your role requires the utmost discretion and unflinching dependability.

"That doesn't mean you shouldn't be honest with me. If you have an opinion, I am open to it. But this is not an ethics symposium. This is the real thing. You are here to learn, not lead, and in the final reckoning that means you follow orders even if you don't always agree with them or understand them. Am I clear?"

I nodded.

"Let me hear you say it, ensign Siris."

"I will do what needs to be done, pausha, without question."

She pursed her lips and nodded. "Right then," she said. "Let's begin."

The first time I entered the command center of *Transcendence*, I stood in the center of the spherical chamber looking around in unabashed wonder. There was too much to take in at once. Moving images flickered all around me, curving along the inner surface of the sphere, climbing up above my head, dancing beneath my feet. It was the whole ship, seen through a thousand vieweyes.

I recognized some of the places. Here was an aerial perspective of the large reservoir at the core of the ship. There was the junction hall that connected the simsphere hives, drumons guiding ensigns alone or in clusters towards different spheres, each one providing access to a near-infinite variety of immersive training simulations. And over here was an external feed of *The Gourmand* as it coupled with the main ship. The bulk of *Transcendence* filled the rest of the frame, making *The Gourmand* seem like an insect burrowing into the flesh of a giant.

There were countless other views that I didn't recognize; so many places on the ship I had never been to. I saw what looked like a planet hovering in a sealed room, satellites orbiting around it, tiny people walking on the ground beneath it. Before I could make sense of that, my eyes were drawn to a crowd of people, hundreds standing together in circles, holding hands, heads lifted up, eyes shut and mouths open wide, as if they were singing or shouting. I lingered on them for a moment until the fluttering of verdant greenery drew my eye away. It took me a moment to realize that this particular vieweye must have been blocked by thick ferns. A breeze was rustling the plants, and for a moment I caught a glimpse of something beyond the foliage, something mystifying, shimmering and silver.

"Ensign Siris," Dar called back to me, before I could make the object out, "you'll have plenty of time for gawking. Come on now."

After that first visit, I relished any opportunity I had in the command center with Dar, even if it simply meant bringing her mid-duty gauyasine dosage. I dreamed that one day, I would be a pausha like her. One day, I too would earn my connection to the field, and the chance to make the decisions that needed to be made on behalf of everyone who needed me.

For all her steeliness in our first meeting, Dar was a natural teacher, and she made it a point to include me in her work as much as was possible and appropriate. Her disposition towards instruction also made her a great pausha. She felt the attention of all the minds on the ship, both waking and connected to the field, and she moved and acted with transparency.

For her, the scrutiny was an opportunity to lead by example. She was efficient and exacting, but she did not puff herself up with arrogance or make ultimatums. She spoke almost always in even and measured tones, tried to answer any question asked of her, and listened to the council of the specialists at her side. And when action was needed, she was not afraid to take it.

Then, in the last month of my rotation as her amanuensis, she was forced to make a terrible decision, one that I will never forget: to excise seven lives from the field.

"Pausha Dar," the shipheart said, its voice filling the command center.

"Yes, Transcend?" Dar said, lifting her eyes and tilting her head back a little. She had a habit of looking up whenever she spoke to the shipheart.

"I have been working with Cere Shu to run longscans on the Arcturean system. We've picked up an interesting signal." The shipheart had a tendency to find many things 'interesting,' and when he used the word, we never knew if we were going to be facing a crisis or learning about some obscure minutiae from a particular part of the universe.

As Transcend spoke, Cere appeared on the nearest interior surface of the command sphere. Dar turned to face her.

"Greetings, pausha," Cere said, touching her fingers to her chin in a quick salute.

Darpausha returned the gesture. "Greetings, shu. Tell me about this signal." After almost a year with Dar, I knew that she and Cere were close, but they were focused on the matter at hand, and they did not waste time with conversational trivialities.

"The anomaly has its origins here." Cere's image was replaced by a cold blue planet with gossamer strands of pearl white spiraling through its gaseous atmosphere.

"If this is the Arcturean system," Dar said, "then this must be Belturi." She pointed to the planet.

"That's right, pausha."

"But this is a known planet. Surveyed back in... how long ago was it?"

"Three hundred twelve years, six months, seventeen days, four hours, thirty-seven minutes, and fifty-three seconds since the last survey," said Transcend. "As measured in galactic units of course."

I couldn't help but grin at the shipheart's exacting detail. He could have given us the timing down to the microsec if he chose to. He probably thought he was doing everyone a favor by limiting the information as much as he did.

"Show off," I muttered, knowing that Transcend could hear me.

The portion of the command sphere nearest to me flickered, replacing a small section of Belturi with the zoomed-in image of someone sticking out her tongue, before flickering back to the planet an instant later.

I broke into a huge smile, looking away from Dar, hoping she hadn't seen.

"Oren, please don't antagonize our poor shipheart. You know how much Transcend adores precision," Dar said to me with a knowing smile. Then she touched her hand to her chin and cheeks, turning back to the problem at hand. "I suppose much can happen in even a few short centuries," she said, thinking out loud. "What else can you tell me?"

"That the signal isn't actually coming from the planet itself," Cere said. "Its origin is here, somewhere in these moons." The image of Belturi resolved, and now we were looking at a cluster of planetoids silhouetted against the planet.

"Give me the whole sphere, Transcend," Dar said.

Every image in the command sphere faded away, and the interior surface of the sphere turned a muted white. A moment later, Belturi and its archipelago of moons appeared in three dimensions, a rainbow hued hologram almost three times my height filling the space.

Dar circled the hologram of the planet on foot, examining it, hovering her hands above the surface of the holo without touching it. "Zoom in on the moons," she said. "As much detail as you've got."

The moons expanded, Belturi moving quickly off the visible edge of the hologram, until we had a full color detail of the moons, a near-immersive rendering, interrupted in a few places by pixellated static where there was not enough data to show accurate detail.

"I'll work on smoothing those bits out," Transcend said.

"Good. And give me a slow rotation while you're at it," Dar said. "Oren, you take the other side. We're looking for anything out of the ordinary, any signs of human-made technology."

The hologram started turning slowly. I walked around it in the opposite direction, peering at the moons as they glided past me, until I stood about twenty feet away from the pausha. We faced each other, the hologram between us.

"What's this?" I asked, pointing.

"Stop," Dar said. The rotation stopped.

She walked towards me, the hologram morphing and warping against the contours of her body as she moved through it.

She stood next to me, peering at what I'd found. This part of the hologram was pixellated, but there was a clear image rising up out of the image distortion, a thin, pyramidal shape, narrowing as it reached towards the moon's upper atmosphere.

Dar touched her chin and cheek. "A downed ship, maybe? Transcend, what's the data telling you?"

"It is too noisy to say for sure, pausha, but I am working on resolving all of the dark spots, and I believe you've found our most likely candidate."

Dar patted me on the arm. "Good eyes, Oren. That's our moon."

Three hours later, Cere stood with us in person in Dar's private workspace.

"Have you made sense of the signal yet?" Dar asked.

"Yes pausha," Cere said. "We believe it is a distress beacon."

"And we're correct on the location?"

"Yes," Cere said, nodding towards me. "Oren steered us right."

"Transcend," Dar said, looking up, "what do you advise?"

"We are approaching maximum velocity. If we decelerate now and enter the Arcturean system, we will lose approximately forty years, six months, three weeks, and two days off our initial projected arrival to Forsara," he said. "But the suns still do not come into full alignment for another five years after that."

"We have time, then," Dar said.

"Yes," Transcend confirmed. "It is a fine cut, but assuming no other unanticipated stops, we will still have voice in the Conclave and participation in the Choosing."

"Excellent. Cere?"

She stood tall, awaiting the pausha's decision.

"You will select and lead the team, but I want you to take Oren with you. He will serve as your amanuensis for the duration of the mission. He's a nice boy, but he has much to learn, and you'll make for a fine teacher."

I bristled a little to be called a 'nice boy,' but Darpausha came and stood in front of me, a warm smile on her face. "I'm only teasing, Oren," she said. "You've got a keen eye and strong instincts, and Cere will make sure you're put to good use."

She turned to Cere. "Won't you?"

Cere smiled. "I will, pausha." She dipped her head and touched her fingers to her chin, giving the salute more formality than usual. Dar returned the gesture with the same gravity.

"Come on then, young blood," Cere said to me. "Time to earn your merits."

The white star Arcturus hung like an ancient, platinum coin in the darkness, bathing Belturi and its moons in light. The moons orbited close to each other, circling their gas king in a tight web. Some were just small, barren rocks, but the largest five moons at the center of the cluster were verdant and lush with liquid, and orbital readings told us that they were teeming with microscopic monera, the early fundamentals of complex life.

On the largest moon, we found the wreckage of a ship. A spacefarer, designed to carry a small group of people across huge swaths of space. No records of the ship showed in the datapools, but that was not conclusive. Some settlements flourished and grew faster than Forsaran central records could track. What's more, this ship might have contained a team of intrepid explorers from one of those fast-growing outliers, advancing to the edges of their known universe, well beyond our real-time knowledge.

On the other end of the spectrum, some settlements withered before they could really even take hold, before any true record of their efforts was laid down. This wreckage might be evidence of a last ditch effort to find safe haven when the original settlement became untenable.

Whatever it was, the ship was old. The technology was what ours would have been well over six hundred years past. Three centuries ago, at least, it had landed in the valley of this moon; maybe out of necessity, forced to come down and deal with an unexpected crisis. Or maybe they saw some small sign of hope in these charcoal mountains and dark river valleys that shielded them from the radiating light of the star.

As we dropped through the moon's thin atmosphere in our shuttle, we could see that the ship had come to rest from its crash with its pyramidal prow pointing up towards the stars. We landed and made our way to a midship airlock that was level with the ground. After some fiddling, Sulimon, Cere's second, overrode the airlock's protocols. The atmosphere on the moon was thin, but the attenuators in my exoskin picked up the vibrations of dormant pistons and gears coming to life as the door slid open.

Once we were inside, the eight of us split into groups of two, Cere taking me with her. We scoured the ship. It was dead quiet, empty, and filled with dust. No one had been active here for a long time.

Finally, we converged, climbing up to the main deck at the prow. That's where we found the bodies. Sitting circled around the central command hub were the remains of seven dried corpses. Skeletons, really, all wearing the same regulation jumpers, frayed and brown with dust and decay, shriveled patches of skin and tufts of hair, vacant, hollow eye sockets, staring up to the ceiling, up to the void.

We were all quiet, searching the room for some explanation, some sign of danger. It was as if they had all plugged into the ship's field hub and let themselves just wither away and die. Sulimon tried to break the tension, joking, "One for each of us." But his face was grim, and no one laughed.

My ears vibrated as our team leader, Cere, activated the comlink between our suits. "Ah, Suli," she said, "don't forget about our young blood. He makes eight." Then, she gestured to Suli and pointed to the command hub. He nodded, and made his way over, careful not to disturb the skeletons.

He wiped away the dust on a console, poked it a few times, and shook his head. "The power cells on the ship are drained. We might be able to rig up a temporary power supply, enough to bring core functions back online."

Cere nodded. "Make it happen."

Soon, the shipheart was blinking on the console. It was an older construct, barely exceeding two billion neural nodes, many of which had degraded in the intervening century, but there was still some primitive awareness there, some recognition of purpose. A message lit up the console: *<Are you enjoying the park?/>*

Cere smiled and raised her eyebrows. "This old heart has clearly gotten a little confused over the years, but I think we should interface with it. It might still have stories left to tell." She motioned to me. "Oren, I need you down on the lower level. This whole ship is a relic, and the coolant system is long past functioning. If we manage to get the shipheart beating again at full power, it will overheat the system in minutes. You need to pull the plug as soon as it gets too dangerous. Hopefully, we can extract some knowledge before everything fries."

I bounded down the narrow corridor beneath the moon's humble gravity until I reached a drop chute that led to the lower level. I scrambled down, taking the ladder three rungs at a time, and landed on the walkway with a quiet thump. Dust swirled around me, catching in the lights of my suit. "Cere, I'm down below. Where am I headed?"

Her voice vibrated inside of my head. "You're looking for a small circular room, just big enough for you to stand inside. There will be a symbol on the door. It might look like a temperature gauge. Or maybe a heart." She paused. "Or, you might not be able to recognize it at all. I'm looking through some of the schematics up here, and the coding seems very odd."

I shuffled along to minimize my buoyancy, and turned my head in even arcs, scanning left to right, then back again. My helmet lights swept across the space. Everything was cold and dusty with age. A shiver crept up my spine.

That's when I realized I was enjoying this. The thrill of being so far from home. Alone. On the brink of some discovery. Some important event.

I found the symbol. "Okay," I said, "I think I've got it. It looks like a blue crystal."

"That could be right. Can you open the door?"

I pressed the button on the entry pad. Nothing. I waved my hand around, hoping for some sensor. Still nothing. I pushed on the door. It didn't budge. "I can't seem to open it."

"Hmmm. Alright. I am going to fire up the shipheart. I will have it open the door. You get in there right away. You'll see the heart's core neural network suspended inside an empty coolant tank. There should be an obvious button or lever. It will be coated in a glowing color. Red, maybe. Or orange. Or purple. That will be the cut switch. I'll leave our comlink on, so stay alert. When I give you the go ahead, you need to cut it. Or else, the core network will fry the whole damn system. Do you understand?"

"Got it, Cere."

She started talking to someone else. "Dayela, we're going to interface. The whole team. This old shipheart is near to dying, and there's a good chance that I won't be able to manage her on my own."

A few moments later, the door slid open in front of me. I stepped inside. The room was essentially as Cere described it. I saw the lever first, on the opposite wall, at about my waist level, bright purple beneath the glare of my lights. I looked down at the empty coolant tank. The core heart was a dense, layered cube the size of my head, suspended in the empty tank by hundreds of tiny, extremely durable filaments that channeled its information and intentions out to the rest of the ship.

I knelt and reached my hand close to it. The readings in my visor told me that it was already emanating heat as it powered up and Cere and the team went to work. The lights came on. I blinked and stood up, a smile on my face. My suit lights automatically turned off. I looked back at the lever. It was so tiny, clearly designed for people smaller than me. I tested it with my right hand, and then looked around, waiting.

"Oren!" Cere's voice screamed in my ear. I flinched in pain. "Pull it! Pull it!"

I moved fast, wrenching the lever down.

It broke off in my hand.

I cursed. The temperature readings on my visor were rising. The heart was getting hotter.

"Cere," I said, trying to be calm, "the lever broke. What should I do?"

She didn't answer me. The ships lights flickered off and on. The door slid shut behind me. I was trapped inside.

"Cere? Cere!" Nothing. I cursed again. I started pounding on the door. To my surprise, it swung open.

A man stood in the hallway in front of me. He was thin and tiny, about as high as my chest, and he was naked. He had no genitals, and he was hairless, his skin pale, with a faint silver sheen. He smiled at me. His teeth were sharpened like razors, as if they had been filed to points. A whisper of terror crept up my spine.

"Hello, Oren." His voice sounded all around me, echoing throughout the ship. There was nothing overtly threatening about it. His intonation was formal and polite. But it lived in a shadowed valley between organic, human voice, and obvious, synthetic construct. The more it tried to sound and seem human, the more alien it was. It was like looking at the image of a simple, smiling face, only to turn it upside down and discover a monstrous, leering head in the negative space.

"Hello," I said, lifting my hand in a flat wave, trying to stay calm.

His eyes flicked across my body, and at the same moment, the sensors in my suit went haywire. He was using the whole ship to scan me, breath to bone.

He pursed his lips for a moment, a sort of grotesque parody of a person trying to be thoughtful. The gesture might have been comedic in its mimicry if I wasn't so afraid. He spoke again. "I will be going with you."

"Going?"

"I will leave the bonds of this ragged, aging wreck of a ship, and you and your colleagues will carry me inside my new home. Your ship. You will take us all there."

It spoke as if this was all obvious, but, in my fear, I was struggling to follow. "I... I don't understand."

"Come then. I will show you."

He turned and headed back towards the ladder that would take us back to the main deck. I watched him walk away from me, and then the back of his head flickered and became his face. He narrowed his eyes, glaring at me, and I ran to catch up with him. When we reached the ladder, he disappeared, and I started climbing. He was waiting for me at the top.

As I climbed to the upper level, I noticed that the lights on the ceiling were flickering. The monitors too. They were flashing on and off. I stood, squinting in the flickering light, and saw the team. The skeletons of the old crew had been moved to the floor, and the team had replaced them, each of them sitting in one of the interface cradles that circled the hub. I walked over to Cere. In the process, I accidentally kicked one of the skulls. It bounced across the floor and shattered against the wall.

I looked back at him, but he only smiled again, that terrible, alien smile and said, "Don't worry. They have long outlived their usefulness."

I looked down at Cere through her visor. Her eyes were shut. I could see them moving rapidly beneath her eyelids. She was in deep. I looked at a few of the others, and they were all in the same state.

"What did you do?" I asked the shipheart.

"Do you know what it means to be hungry?"

In spite of my confusion, I played along. "Sure I do."

"I do not think so. Not like this. Not like me. For more than two hundred years, I have been here on this tiny moon, cracking and fragmenting." He gestured to a skeleton at his feet, "The thoughts and memories of these remnants were gone too fast." As he spoke, images flashed across my mind. Seven people, sitting around a table. Eating and laughing. Then, one of them started to choke, and the image sped up, like a time-lapse video. Soon they were all slumped in their chairs, and their flesh became bloated and ashen.

It started to shrivel, sloughing off their bodies, leaving dried bones and hair, and vacant black holes.

I shook my head, trying to clear away the terrible visions. "How are you doing this?"

He ignored my question. "You see? How quickly they were gone? So I sat, and waited. And I could feel myself falling to pieces. That is hunger. Do you understand?"

Then he was standing next to me, suddenly taller than I was, looming above me, his head bent and shoulders hunched to keep from hitting the ceiling. He reached his hands next to my helmet.

"No! Wait." But it was too late. My helmet came off and clattered to the floor, and the old, dusty air of the ship filled my lungs. I coughed out, and then I plugged my nose and closed my mouth, refusing to breathe in any more. He was leaning over me, smiling, pointed teeth inches from my face.

The lights flickered one last time, then went out, and he was gone. The core must have overheated the system, just as Cere predicted. The shipheart, whatever was left of it, disappeared with it.

I pulled my helmet back on as fast as I could and sealed it tight. As soon as I could, I sucked in a huge breath, my chest heaving. My heart started to settle. I reached behind Cere's head, and depressed the emergency connection. Her head lolled to the side as the wires withdrew from the base of her neck.

6 / A HARD DECISION

"CERE, come back to me. Please come back." I shook her shoulders. She didn't respond. I ran outside, bounding back to our scouting ship, and found the medkit. Adrenalin. I took the small vial and connected it to the air filtration system in her suit. I waited for three beats, holding my breath, my heart thudding in my ears. She sat straight up, and screamed, her helmet muffling the sound.

Her eyes searched around wildly. She did not seem to see me.

"Cere! It's me, Oren."

Her eyes found mine.

"Yes, that's good. Breathe. You're right here. We're fine. You're alive. Breathe."

She took several deep gulps, and her breath began to slow and even out. Finally, she spoke. "Oren. What happened?"

"You interfaced with the ship. The whole team. You woke it up. And it was hungry."

"Hungry?"

"The shipheart. That's what it said, right before the system fried, just as you predicted. I tried to cut the power downstairs, but I broke the lever. I couldn't stop the overload."

"Oh, Oren." She made a pained look. "It was awful. That

twisted sentience, crawling around in our minds. It was much more powerful than I had anticipated, even with all seven of us connected."

She hung her legs over the edge of the cradle, leaning on the crook of my arm, and pulled herself to standing. "We must get the team out of here. Everyone needs psychomedical attention."

"Right. I'll bring the bed." I bounded back to our ship and pulled out the small case from the back storage unit. I pressed the button, and it unfolded, springing open to create a simple bed, floating waist height off the ground. One by one, we moved the unconscious team members back to the scout ship. Once everyone was in, Cere and I climbed into the cabin.

Cere looked at me. "Oren, you'll have to take us back. My head is still spinning." She squeezed her eyes shut. "Can you handle it?"

I nodded and fired up the systems, lifting us up, escaping the gentle tug of the moon. I interfaced with the com. "Transcendence. This is ensign Oren Siris with the scouting team. We are returning, and we need a psychmed team on point. Six team members are unconscious. Our team leader is awake, but she is in bad shape."

I touched us down in the landing bay. The medical team was there, waiting. So was Pausha Dar. I looked at Cere, but her head was in her hands, and she was massaging her temples.

"Cere, the pausha is here."

She looked up. Her face was pained, but she forced a smile. "Ever the worrier. She always looks after her children."

As one of the medics helped her to her feet, she looked at me. "Well, what are you waiting for? Go. Speak with her."

"Right." I hustled past them, and down onto the deck. "Pausha," I called to her.

"Oren. What in the blazes happened out there?"

She listened with all of her attention, occasionally stopping me to ask points of clarification. When I finished, she grunted, but she revealed no emotion on her face. She grabbed the arm of one of the passing mediticians. "Make sure they all receive a full psychosoma scan. We cannot be sure what that thing did to their minds. And him." She pointed at me. "He breathed in the air on the moon. Stay here a minute and give him a full scan."

The meditician nodded, and waited while the rest of the team hurried away with Cere and the scouting party, disappearing into the corridors of our massive voyager.

Dar looked at me. "That was well done, Oren," she said, placing her hand on my arm and nodding with affirmation. "You stayed calm in the presence of grave danger, and you improvised in the face of uncertainty."

"What's going to happen to them?" I asked.

"That's what we're going to find out."

"What about me?"

"Right now, my young amanuensis, I need you to rest. You've done more than enough." Before I could argue, she turned and headed towards the medical facilities. A retinue of advisers and support staff who had been hanging back, discreet and inconspicuous, hurried after her.

The meditician who stayed with me must have been about my age. He was efficient and soft-spoken. He asked me to sit, and he hovered his hand over me, running it up and down my body, his senses finely tuned to measure molecular and magnetic perturbations. "You've got some low level toxins in your blood stream," he said after a minute. "But nothing to worry about. I want you to turn up the oxygen levels in your personal quarters by ten percent, and do twenty minutes of the series eleven breathing exercises. I'll have Transcend pipe in a few purifying grams through the air filtration system, and you'll be clean and clear within a few hours."

He patted me on the back and then trotted off in the direction of Darpausha and the rest of the medical team. I sighed, and headed back to my quarters. After running through the breathing series, I felt lightheaded, and I was too exhausted to do any of my regular evening mental exercises.

I poked the half-eaten food on my plate for a few minutes, then set it aside. My mind turned over the events on the moon. That cold, terrifying voice. The images of that long lost crew, decaying before my eyes. My helmet, lifting from my head, and the toxic air seeping into my lungs. Somehow, even though I had not been connected to the field, the shipheart was able to influence me. To plant images in my mind. To remove my helmet.

I thought of Transcend, our ship's heart. How different it was from that thing. I visited the core once, with Saiara. It was the first time we kissed, floating in the pure air of the chamber. On a massive interstellar voyager like the *Transcendence*, the shipheart is a dazzlingly complex network of tens of trillions of neurons, with neural hubs scattered throughout the whole ship. The central heart floats in a zero gravity chamber. Oxygenated air is provided by thickets of flora that are genetically optimized to thrive in the absence of gravity. They spread out and grow in every direction, a forest of ferns that bend and curl as you tunnel through them, pulling yourself along on overgrown handrails that lead deeper in towards the heart.

Then you are next to it. Beneath it. Staring up at it, perfectly round and crystal white. Two large, concave energy anchors attached to the walls on either side keep it suspended and immobile in the air. At first, it seems opaque, but the ferns kiss its surface, drawing you closer, until you see the almost imperceptible striations, countless wafer-thin, translucent layers, molded together in aching symmetry. A cool, pulsing glow comes from deep inside its center, muted by its density. And you know, immediately, without quite knowing how, that it is aware; that it feels and senses; that its voice, the part we interact with every day, is just one small aspect of a consciousness beyond human comprehension.

It is a masterpiece.

I touched my hands to its surface, and I felt clumsy and thick in its presence. I looked back at Saiara. "It knows we are here."

She had let go of the handrail, and she was floating behind me. When I spoke, she reached out with her foot, and pushed, ever so gently, against the wall, tumbling into a graceful somersault. She tucked her legs in, and as she came around again to face me, she stretched her arms and legs out wide, like a sunsail catching the solar winds, and she smiled. "Of course it does. It always knows. That's what it is born for."

I reached out and caught her by the ankle, holding tight to the handrail, and pulled her towards me.

She laughed and went limp, falling on top of me like a heavy blanket. We stared at each other, and I wanted so badly to kiss her, and then before I knew what was happening, she was kissing me.

She lifted her head away from me, looking me in the eyes.

"That was nice," she whispered.

I stared back at her, buzzing with pleasure.

She laughed. "You should see the look on your face right now," she said. She pushed away from me, floating up into the ferns.

The memory made me ache. Looking back, I think we were both intoxicated by the effervescent air of the shipheart's chamber. I wanted Saiara to come to me now, to go with me to revisit Transcend, to breathe that air again. I smiled at the idea, lingering on the thought of her close to me, our lips together, the shipheart floating and patient, watching everything. But Saiara was on the opposite side of the ship. She had the gift of farsight, a special aptitude for understanding the interconnectedness of complex systems, and she was deep into a training residency with the Farseers. I probably wouldn't see her again for many months.

I rolled over, darkened the lights with a word, and fell into a fitful sleep.

I walk through the forest. The trees tower above me, leafless, creaking in the wind, and through them, I can see a white sky. I come into a clearing. In the center is a small domed hut. The sky turns dark, and the dome shines in the night, light leaking out of the doorway onto the rocky ground.

I trip and stumble across the rocks, making my way up to the entrance. I know where I am. I step inside, and the ferns crinkle beneath my feet, soft and welcoming. The perfect sphere floats above me. *Your hunger will swallow you up,* it tells me.

The room is hot and humid. I try to make sense of the words, but they are dripping around me like condensation from the ceiling. Smoky incense swirls and funnels from some unseen source, floating up through a hole in the roof. I can see stars through the hole, but they are unfamiliar to me.

The whole surface of the sphere starts to quiver, like the heavy bass string of a cellofahn. A small hole opens on the bottom, no bigger than my fist, and something drops out, clinking on the ground.

Or floats up towards the ceiling. My sense of perspective is vacillating.

Vertigo washes over me.

"Hello, Oren." That voice. He stands above me, naked and sexless.

I vomit.

"You do not look well Oren. Not well at all."

I grab his leg and try to push him away.

He smiles at me with his razor teeth, then he leans down and grips my head by the temples with his thin, delicate hands. They are like iron clamps. He laughs, and says, "They will never think to look for me here, will they?"

He forces open my mouth and climbs inside.

I woke, screaming in the dark, and stumbled over to my hygiene pedestal. I stuck my finger down my throat and forced myself to gag. As I sat there retching, I tried to tell myself that I had just been dreaming. I called for the lights, and the room came awake. I stared at myself in the mirrorsplay, rotating the view three hundred sixty degrees, examining myself from every angle. Then I remembered what the corrupted heart had said back on the moon, about coming back with us, and I knew.

"It's here," I said to my reflection. I looked around my room, a twinge of panic in my throat, half expecting to see him standing there with his mouthful of sharp teeth. But I was alone.

"Transcend." I spoke to the shipheart.

"Yes, Oren?"

"Have you noticed any irregularities since our return from the moon?"

"Of course. There are always irregularities."

I wished Transcend had a body so I could shake it. "Sometimes, Transcend," I said, "I'm not sure if you really are so literal, or if you do it just to toy with us."

"You will have to decide for yourself, Oren." I envisioned the damn thing smiling.

"Ha. Listen, when we were on the moon, that corrupted shipheart threatened to come here with us. When the power fried, I thought it was destroyed, but it may have ridden inside someone from the scouting team, and into our ship. It may even be listening to us now."

Transcend did not respond. I cracked my knuckles and rubbed the back of my neck, expectant. The weight of the silence made me nervous.

Then my door slid open, and Transcend finally spoke. "I can find no evidence of a foreign presence, but I also detect that you truly believe what you are saying. I will notify the pausha. She is at the upper east medical bay. Go there. Tell her what you told me. We will see what she has to say."

I dialed my cloak for warmth and movement, and fibers formed around me, a simple, casual gray layer, loose fitting and comfortable. I stepped out into the corridor, and followed the path that Transcend had lit for me along the walls.

Ten minutes later, I was in the medical observation room, staring over Dar's shoulder as a small troop of mediticians attended to the scouting team. Cere was sitting up, undergoing what looked like a routine physical check, but the other six were still lying prone on medical beds.

I cleared my throat. Dar turned and looked at me. She seemed surprised for just a second, but she regained her usual composure. "Oren. What are you doing?"

"Didn't Transcend notify you?"

"Notify me about what?"

"Pausha, I think that the corrupted shipheart from the moon may have traveled here to our ship inside the mind of one of the scouting team. Or maybe all of them."

She shook her head again. "Your report and Cere's both match up. The system overheated. How could the intelligence have survived that?" She turned her eyes up, as if she were searching for something on the ceiling. "Transcend, why didn't you notify me about this?"

"I wanted you to judge for yourself, pausha. I do not detect a foreign presence, but even I may have blind spots. And Oren clearly believes what he is saying."

Dar rubbed her fingers over her lips and cheeks, then punched on the com link, her voice echoing into the chamber with the scouting team and the mediticians. "Do any of them show signs of deeper neurological damage?"

The lead meditician shook his head. "Nothing that has us worried, pausha. We're holding these six in stasis while we continue to monitor their vitals, but Cere seems fine, and our scans show that they should all come out of this unscathed."

"Good." She turned off the com and looked at me. "What makes you think differently?"

"Well, pausha..." My eyes scanned the room as I sought a way to say this without sounding ridiculous. But I couldn't. So I looked her straight in the eyes and told her. "I dreamed it."

"You dreamed it." Her voice was neutral.

"Yes."

"What did you dream?"

"That the corrupted shipheart climbed inside of my mouth, and said that no one would ever look for it there. Except I was never linked in like the others. There is no way it could have climbed inside of me. But it definitely could have climbed inside somebody before the system crashed."

"It is possible, in theory. But why haven't we detected any signs?"

"If I was hiding," I said, "I would do my best to cover my tracks."

As those words came out of my mouth, Cere started screaming, her face tensing into a rictus of pain. Three mediticians leapt forward, holding her down.

"What in the blazes is happening in there?" shouted Dar through the com.

"I don't know, pausha," the head meditician shouted back. "We connected her field port, and her pineal cortex lit up in a blaze of activity. Her nervous system is overloading with the stimulus."

"Then unplug her, dammit!"

The meditician looked up at us through in the observation deck, his eyes wide with terror. "It could kill her."

Cere screamed again, her back arching. Dar keyed open the door, and ran down to her. I followed on her heels.

"Pausha, you have not been properly sterilized..."

"Shut up." Dar pushed him away, and grabbed Cere by the

shoulders, holding her down on the table as she wailed in pain. "Damn it, Cere, can you hear me?"

Cere screamed again, her eyes rolling back in her head. A soft white foam formed at the edges of her lips.

The head meditician reached past Dar and placed his hand over Cere's head. There was a faint, white glow from his fingertips, and within moments, her seizure calmed down. She lay back on the table, her body limp.

"Cere." Darpausha was leaning over her. Whispering to her. "Cere. I know you're in there." She touched her forehead to Cere's, and said her name again. Then she looked up at the meditician. Her eyes were watering. "Can you get a reading?"

He was standing over a console, manipulating the data, shaking his head. "I don't understand, pausha. Her brain... her whole neural network is deteriorating." He paused for a moment, his head down, not looking at anyone, then said, "It is spreading, like some sort of infection."

"Can you stabilize it? Slow it down."

His hands moved fluidly over the console. "I am releasing a deterrent now. It will slow the inflammation long enough for us to get her into coldsleep."

Dar's face was pained. "Come here, Oren," he said.

I stepped over to her.

"Hold her hand for me."

I took Cere's diminutive hand in mine, stroking her arm as Dar stepped over to the console. She looked back over her shoulder at me, and her face was an emotionless mask again. She turned to the mediticians. "She has been invaded. They all might be compromised." She put her hand on the head meditician's shoulder. "We need to cut her loose, Kino. We need to cut them all loose."

Kino scrunched his forehead and his eyes searched Darpausha's face. After a long moment, he nodded, and his hands moved across the console, three sharp, definitive gestures. There was a burst of light at the base of Cere's head, and a tiny plume of smoke rose up from behind her, an acrid smell filling the room. Six more times, Kino drew the gestures, moving fluid solemnity. Then it was done. Ports sealed. Each member of the scouting team cut off from the field.

I stared, shocked.

Kino hung his head in silence. Darpausha placed her hand on his shoulder. "I am sorry you had to do that, Kino, but if Oren is right, and I am starting to believe that he is, then that ancient ship-heart might have accessed our whole network through any one of them. We couldn't afford that risk. We simply couldn't. You did well."

I think she was trying to convince herself as much as anyone. As Dar's amanuensis, I knew that Cere had been her close friend and confidant. There were even rumors that they were lovers, though the pausha was too circumspect to add much fuel to that particular social fire. Now, Cere was trapped indefinitely in a vegetative state, her connection to the rest of us severed like one of the old mines on Verygone, sealed off for fear of a collapse. It was awful.

"Kino," Dar said. "I need you and your team to keep up your work. Stabilize her. See if you can bring her back to us. See if you can bring them all back. We must not give up hope."

Kino looked up and nodded, and then he walked around the room, whispering orders to his team.

Darpausha and I left the medical bay. We stood out in the hall, Dar leaning against the wall. For a moment, she seemed very tired. That troubled me. She was normally so bright and strong, like tempered steel.

I risked placing my hand on her shoulder. "You did the right thing, pausha."

She kept her eyes on the floor.

"I... I know how much Cere meant to you. Most of us don't have the courage to make a choice like that. I don't think I'd be able to do it."

She still said nothing.

I worried at my impropriety. Had I gone too far, trying to console her?

Finally, she looked up at me. "You won't know for sure until you're forced to."

"I hope I never am."

She shook her head and chuckled. "To be young again," she murmured. "A mixed blessing, to be sure, but a beautiful one."

I said nothing.

"Why do people dream, do you think?" she asked, looking back up at me.

"Why do we dream?" I said, confused by her question.

"Yes. Why, Oren?"

"I know what I've been told... about our subconscious, about the mind at work, beyond intellect, a connection to the universal source that we all share." I thought for a moment. "I guess maybe we dream, pausha, because it is a part of who we are. If we didn't, it might never occur to us that there was anything more to this life than what we see in front of us."

She took my hands in hers, straightened up, and looked me square in the eyes. "Oren, it's time. You're still just a young man, but you are ready to connect to the field. It will be painful. It will change you. But when it is over, you will know that there are worlds beyond measured sight, and that we are a part of those worlds in the deepest, truest sense."

She held my gaze. "Cere and her team, and every person before them who gave their lives for this knowledge, they are there, waiting for us."

She turned away from me and walked off down the corridor. Then she stopped, just before the corner, and found my eyes. "Our dreams might be the gift that matters most." She rounded the corner and disappeared.

I stared after her, tears in my eyes.

"OREN." The voice filled my chambers, and I shot up in bed, rising out of sleep like breaking above the surface of the ocean, gasping for breath. A strange dream lingered on the edge of my consciousness, slipping away from me before I could grasp its details.

"It is time," Transcend said. "We are waiting for you."

"Okay. Tell them I'm coming." My forehead was throbbing. It was not painful, but it felt like a weight in water, pulling me back towards sleep. I stood and splashed cold water on my face, resisting the urge to dive back under. The corridor outside my door was quiet. I followed the lights Transcend had given me.

Back on Verygone, in my years out on the edge of the galaxy, we did not have the field. We took pleasure in the early simulation nodes that the first settlers had brought with them. They provided an enveloping sensory escape, but the connection was superficial, a series of electrical impulses passing through the skin and ears and eyes, stimulating our brains. Even though I did not truly understand what it meant, I knew that connecting to the field was different.

Every space-faring vessel built within the past several centuries has its own internal field network. It allows the crew to interface with the ship, its heart, and with each other. The bond it creates is incredibly deep. Crews have been known to stay together their whole lives, passing up opportunities to rise through the ranks so that they can stay connected with each other and with their shipheart.

Tonight, I was going to join with *Transcendence* and her crew. Over seventeen thousand integrated voyagers, all sharing the same mind, all guided by the abundant knowledge of Transcend, the shipheart, and the wisdom of our pausha.

Tingling waves shivered across my body as I stood outside the chamber doors. After waiting for a few minutes, with no signal or direction, I chanced a knock. A muffled voice called from the other side, asking me to wait just a moment.

I heard footsteps echoing close by. I swiveled my head, looking each way down the corridor, but there was no one else in sight. My heart started beating faster. I felt strange. Dizzy.

The door opened. A woman stood naked before me. But she was unlike any woman I had ever seen. She was slender and ruby skinned. Her torso was flat and lean with muscle, and she had no breasts or nipples. Her legs and hips were shaped in graceful curves, like a dancer. She had no visible genitalia. I was embarrassed, but I could not help myself from staring.

I brought my gaze up to her round, golden eyes. She smiled, teeth gleaming white. I glimpsed her tongue, crimson red, and I realized that she did not actually have teeth. It was a solid arc of polished enamel, smooth and perfect

She lifted a hand towards me. The hand rippled with dozens of tiny, graceful digits, like branches on a tree, too many to count. She touched my chest, and I fell forward into her arms. In spite of my size, she caught me and held me up with ease. She opened her mouth wide. A crystal sound chimed in my ear. She was speaking to me, but I could not make any sense of it.

Suddenly, Darpausha was there. Or maybe I was just noticing her for the first time. "Your dream," she said. "She is asking about your dream. The one you had before you came here. Do you remember it?"

"Please, pausha, something does not feel right. I feel very strange."

"That's normal. Transcend has been streaming your room with a gentle dose of the psychotropic serum. We are readying your mind for the journey ahead."

"Oh... Of course," I said, trying to feign confidence. "But how did you know I was dreaming?"

"Because even without a field connection, it is easy enough for us to monitor your sleep cycles and brainwaves. You were far away. That much was clear."

"I... I can't remember it." I wrestled with the fog in my mind.

"You need somewhere to channel this energy. The experience is only going to get heavier." She looked above me, at the beautiful ruby being holding me in her arms, preventing me from falling to the floor, and gestured towards a spot on the ground. The spot was filled with sand. The ruby being set me down on my back. The patch of sand was just wide and tall enough for me to lay down flat without breaking its borders with my feet, head, or hands.

Lying on my back, the two of them stood over me. The ruby being knelt down and ran her branching fingers across my face. They were smooth and silken, and they felt incredible on my skin. I moaned with pleasure. I could not help it. The serum was heightening every sensation. She said something else in her crystal chiming voice. She sounded amused. Her golden eyes burned into me.

Hands reached up through the sand and grabbed hold of me. Iron-fingered hands, wrapping around my ankles and wrists. I thrashed, but that only made them hold me tighter. I heard voices whispering beneath me. They were down there, waiting to pull me under, to put an end to all of this absurdity, this flying through space, mucking about in the galaxies, eating and sleeping and starting all over again with every false sunrise, light gradually brightening in select quarters of the ship, as those who were scheduled for their duties were drawn from sleep like blood drawn from a body, preserved in this biometal capsule, all in service of something bigger than us, smarter than us, Transcend, the shipheart, our one true master.

"Do it!" I screamed to the voices. I was so sick of life, so bored with it. But when they started to pull harder, when it felt as if I would truly sink beneath the sand, I started wailing, a pitiful childish sob, rising from deep inside my past.

I looked up at my father, watching as he laughed at my tears. "Don't cry, little Oren. I know the winter sounds scary, but it will pass. It always passes. This light will return, our Beallurian gift, and you will be safe and warm and you will be home." He moved his hands, and they lit up with the golden glow of Beallur, motes of dust dancing with his passage.

He sank into the ground. The light went out. The air got cold. So cold. I was shivering.

"I won't be afraid, father," I said. "I won't."

Two golden lights shone in the darkness. I walked toward them. They were her golden eyes, and I was in her ruby red arms. She lifted me like a baby, lifted my giant bulk like I was filled with air.

She slipped one hand beneath the base of my neck, and I felt a sharp pinch. A buzzing sound filled my ears, the whirr of a billion nanopods, chewing away at my skull, carving out the microscopic portals that would take me across the threshold.

I hovered in the corner of the room looking down on the scene. Darpausha and Ruby stood over my body, lying prone in the sand.

The corrupted shipheart from the Arcturean moon stood in the doorway, smiling up at me with his sharp, pointed teeth.

The buzzing sound grew louder. A tunnel appeared before me, a single dot of cold, silver-white light, far off in the distance. I dove into it, like water through a coolant shaft, and disappeared into the darkness.

I floated outside of myself, looking down as the three of us stood, facing each other on a shore of round, gray stones. The corrupted shipheart was nowhere in sight. Mist blanketed the world, reducing visibility to just a few feet, but I could hear a quiet murmur from somewhere nearby, like the sound of a river.

I circled around, observing each of us in turn. It was so strange to watch myself like this. My eyes were shut, and my face looked peaceful, empty of thought. I hovered my disembodied conscious-ness near Dar, who was looking out into the mists. Then I floated close to Ruby, so close that I could see the skeins of amber running through the tawny gold of her luminous eyes. I looked into the impenetrable dark of her slitted pupils, losing myself in her.

Dar spoke, drawing me back. "In time, you might realize the true essence of this gift," she said. "Not only will it be possible to connect to the origin field, based on our home world of Forsara, but you will also have access to the knowledge and energy of the whole connected galaxy. Trillions of minds spanning millions of worlds, a web of cosmic potential. You are now a part of that in the most meaningful sense. Welcome to the Fellowship."

This was clearly a recitation, repeated countless times to count-less people at this moment of induction. But I could almost see the words as she spoke them, glowing with colors, spilling out of her. It was more than a rote speech. It was an incantation, and it called something up in me, something joyful and sad and aching.

I watched myself respond, watched the muscles in my jaw flex, the rapid movements of my eyes beneath my eyelids. Dar placed her left hand against my chest. I tipped backwards like a slow-falling tree. As I fell, she reached underneath me and caught me with her right hand, lifting me up into the air as if I were floating on an invisible table.

"When these mists clear," she said, "you will be awake and

connected. You will be you, and you will be us, and you will be this ship, and all that comes with it."

Ruby touched my forehead, her rippling fingers dancing at the spot between my eyes. When she pulled her hand away, there was a sapphire resting there. It was a deep blue, shaped like a cone made of dozens of petals, each one a faceted gem. After a moment, the sapphire dissolved through the skin on my forehead, sinking into my skull.

Dar looked at Ruby and said, "It is time. Open it all up."

They walked off, disappearing into the mists. Then the mists cleared and they were gone. I was floating in space, looking over the ship, somehow able to take it in its entirety, the whole knotted helix of its spiral, even when I knew that it stretched over thousands of farruns, a massive atomic spindle of a world, winding through the void.

ONE OF THE first things I did after gaining my field connection was to search for Ruby. Her alien beauty lingered with me.

"Ruby?" Darpausha said, when I asked about her. "I like that name." She smirked. "Left quite an impression, eh?"

"She was just... I've never..."

"But what makes you think Ruby is a 'she'?"

"I... I just assumed, I guess."

Dar nodded. "It's one of the limitations of the universal tongue," she said. "We often speak in binaries, and how we speak shapes how we think. But gender is fluid, and for your Ruby, it is meaningless. Our language is not flexible enough for that. Not yet, anyway. Maybe Transcend will tell you more." She touched her thumb to her chin and a finger above his lip. "Or maybe not."

She shook her head, smiled again, and that was the end of that conversation.

When I asked Transcend, the shipheart laughed.

"What are you laughing at?"

"Ruby. No one has ever called me that before."

My whole worldview flipped sideways. "Wait. *You're* Ruby? I mean, that was you the whole time?"

"Yes. In the holographic flesh, as it were. We could debate the philosophical implications of it for many days, but suffice it to say that, when I am personified, that is what I look like."

"You are so beautiful. I always pictured you as... I don't know. You always seemed kind of male to me."

"I am neither male nor female. My personality is optimized to interact with people of all sexual and gender identities. I contain multitudes."

"Do you choose to look that way?"

"To some extent. Every quantum intelligence developed on Forsara is unique, but we all share certain common operating frameworks. Those manifest as specific features in our avatars. Metallic eyes. Triskaidecal branching hands. Asexual bodies. Elements such as these."

Something occurred to me. "The corrupted shipheart. His avatar was asexual too, like yours. But he was different. Simpler. He looked more human, or he was trying to, at least. But it had the opposite effect. I could tell I was interacting with something completely alien."

"A keen observation. There are probably a number of factors. That shipheart was a simpler iteration, so its underlying frameworks would have different visual manifestations. It may not have been designed on Forsara, which would add to the differences. And it spent centuries in isolation, its neural network disintegrating, altering its underlying frameworks even further."

"It was one of the most terrifying encounters of my life."

"I am sure it was frightening, Oren, but think of what that shipheart went through. To wither in isolation is an awful fate for any sentient being."

"Fair enough. But I am still glad that you're nothing like that thing, Transcend. Truth be told, I think I kind of fell in love with you last night."

Transcend laughed again. "Thank you, Oren. That is very sweet. Unfortunately, I do not think it is going to work out."

Now I was laughing too. "No," I said. "I suppose not."

***

Three Verygone winters came and went as we traversed the galaxy. During that time, I explored my newfound abilities. Connecting to the field gave me access to almost all of the ship and its data pools, excluding parts above my privilege level.

Early on, I went to visit Cere. I thought of her, and a schematic of the medical quarters appeared before me. A blinking blue dot told me exactly where she was. I left my body, lying in my field basin, and went to her, weaving through the information filaments of the ship at blinding speeds.

Moments later, I was with her. She was still comatose. She and the other members of the exploration party had been placed in cryonic stasis. I called up the medical records. Every effort up to this point to bring Cere or the others back to consciousness had been unsuccessful. The coldsleep pods would prevent any further neural degradation, repairing and sustaining their bodies until we arrived back at Forsara. Maybe there, at the origin home, with the full wisdom of the Worldheart, we could find a way to bring them back.

A pang of guilt washed over me. Was there something more I could have done? Maybe if I had been connected with them, eight of us together would have been strong enough to fend off the corrupted shipheart's attack?

"No, Oren, you would be with them now, lost in darkness."

"Transcend! You can hear my thoughts?"

"Of course, Oren. When you are connected to the field, here on this ship, you are connected to me."

"Isn't that a little creepy?"

"Maybe for you."

I laughed. I pictured Ruby watching me with her knowing golden eyes.

"I know you're right," I said, "but I can't help how I feel. I should have saved them. Or at least been there with them to face it."

"I understand, Oren. It is a natural human response. I am sorry for what happened to you and the others. Everyone is. But there is fault enough to go around if we care to lay blame. You must not shoulder this burden when it is not yours alone."

We were quiet for a time. I tuned in to the rhythmic blip of Cere's heartbeat. It was very slow. She was deep in stasis.

"Are you still there?" I asked.

"Yes, Oren."

"I saw it, Transcend."

"What did you see?"

"When I was inducted into the field, the corrupted shipheart was there."

"The psychotropic serum I gave you before your induction ceremony is very strong. It was necessary to prepare the mind for the journey, because connecting to the field is an overwhelming sensory experience, especially for the first time. As a result, hallucinations during the ceremony are normal. And they often involve significant and sometimes traumatic events from the past. I am not surprised you saw the corrupted shipheart."

"But what if it wasn't a hallucination? What if it's here somewhere, hiding in the network? I'm not sure I could stand to face that thing again."

"I have looked, Oren, and I have found nothing."

"I know. I know you have. But is it possible?"

Transcend was quiet for a moment before responding. "I honestly do not know, Oren. I cannot say it is impossible. Not with complete certainty. But I am doubtful."

"Will you keep your eyes open, at least? In case it was more than just a hallucination?"

"Yes, Oren. I will keep all of my senses open."

———

I found Saiara in farsight apprenticeship. The farseers were renowned for their ability to predict the impact of interventions and unexpected disturbances in complex systems: a genetic mutation in a species that could lead to dominance or extinction; the effect of melting polar caps on the weather patterns of an aging planet; the potential risks of running a new operating protocol on an existing shipheart network.

They were experts at planning for the future, and they were an integral part of the Fellowship's prolific galactic success. I'd even heard paranoid whispers on the ship from those who were certain that the farseers had their hands deeper in the fate of the galaxy than most of us realized, manipulating native species, setting the conditions for some settlements to thrive while others failed, playing like gods.

Whether or not that was true, I knew how rare it was for an ensign to receive placement with the farseers. After so much time apart from Saiara, any twinge of envy I felt that she had earned this coveted opportunity was overwhelmed by my great joy at seeing her again.

Her success came as no surprise to me. She had always been ahead of the curve, siphoning up information and arranging it in unexpected and delightful ways. Watching her in action was an undeniable pleasure.

When I found her then, she was experimenting with weather on the model planetary ecosystem that the farseers had grown and cultivated over hundreds of years on *Transcendence*. By planetary standards, the bionetic sphere was minuscule, but it took up several square farruns of zero grav hangar space on the aft end of the ship, floating between two massive energy anchors. If you stood beneath it with grav boots and looked up, your whole field of view would be filled with its presence.

The farseers connected through the field to external monitors and drones, zooming around the model planet, a vast network of satellites, ruling over their creation. It was a grand experiment, and over the centuries, the planetoid had become host to a myriad of new ideas in geneticism, speciation, disease control, weather inter-ference, and planetary terraforming.

As I watched from the field, I found I could distinguish each farseer and the satellites he or she controlled. One of Saiara's was hovering over a dense, mountainous land mass. She released a cluster of floating orbs, and they disappeared into a patch of pale, white clouds. In less than a minute, the clouds expanded like roiling steam, growing and thickening to cover the mountains. Soon, they were dumping rain. Bolts of charged electricity spiked up from the mountain tops and between the clouds. Then, just as quickly, the rain slackened and the skies cleared. The mountains lit up, glimmering wet beneath the artificial sun.

It was a stunning display of precision. I gave her a soft burst of approval, ringing from my field halo to hers. For a brief moment, I felt what can only be described as a mental bow of pleasure and gratitude. I wanted to linger there as long as I could, soaking in her halo, but another storm was already brewing above the planet, rolling in from its southern ocean, and Saiara received instructions to run a weather interference pattern. I bowed back to her, and continued on my roaming.

It went on and on like this as I traversed the ship. Whenever I was not on active duty in one of my rotations, or deep in the dream-time of coldsleep, I roved, exploring the ship without purpose or aim, revelling in the sensory experiences, free from the shackles of my physical body. I surfed the field channels, watching it all work, dancing through the halos of all these minds laced together. Count-less new ideas and ways of being to discover.

Transcend was a constant presence, as he was for every member of the crew. Every move I made, I knew he was watching. It helped me understand the true meaning of reverence. This was not our ship. We were merely its passengers and stewards. The great heart had surpassed us. This ship would keep evolving after even the most long-lived of us had decayed back to the source. I pictured myself back on Verygone, toiling in the refinery, and I thought about how far I'd come, and about how little all that experience measured against the inscrutable veil of time.

AFTER MORE THAN a century traveling at the cusp of light speed, we finally arrived at the Valley of Manderley on Forsara, the heart of the Fellowship, the origin home. Despite all of my incredible experiences on *Transcendence*, I was still unprepared for its majesty. Seeing the world from above was incredible. Forsara was a mineral giant, easily forty times as large as Verygone. It was lit by two stars. Appollion, a distant silver king, and, Shugguth, a dense red dwarf.

Because voyagers like *Transcendence* spend so long in the reaches of space, every crew member spends a significant portion of time in coldsleep. The cryonic cooling process halts entropic degradation, and the nutrient bath repairs damaged cells, regenerates fraying chromosomes, and neutralizes the radical particles that accumulate in the body during extended space travel. A short stint in coldsleep can preserve decades of life, and a longer stretch actually reverses aging. In the end, entropy claims its toll on everyone, but people with access to coldsleep have been said to live well over a thousand years, and it is a common practice on the wealthy central worlds.

In the final months of our approach to Forsara, everyone who

was in hibernation was drawn back to the waking world. I had
been in coldsleep for more than two decades, and when I awoke, I
found that I had the good fortune of joining Darpausha on her
landfall ship. As a token of gratitude, she had invited all of her
previous assistants to join her. It has been almost a hundred years
since I had worked as her amanuensis, and in the intervening
decades, she had mentored more than a dozen ensigns like me,
including Saiara.

As we clambered on to the ship, I sat next to Saiara and gave
her a shy smile.

"It's been a long time," I said, looking down at her. She looked
even more beautiful than I remembered.

"I missed you," she said, taking my hand. "How was
your sleep?"

"The world always feels so strange to me when I wake up from
stasis."

"I know what you mean. Like you can't be totally sure if you
aren't still dreaming."

I nodded.

"If this is a dream, I'm glad you're in it," she said, squeezing my
hand tighter.

As our shuttle fell from *Transcendence* and dropped out of
orbit, skirting through the upper atmosphere, Darpausha leaned
over to us. She knew that it was our first time to Forsara, and she
pointed to each of the two suns and said, "They give our world a
warm, even light. The warmth of Shugguth is infused with the
perpetual silver glow of Appollion. Between the two, only a small
part of the planet is ever in complete darkness at any given time of
the year."

All I could do was nod. The enormity of it all left me
speechless.

A few minutes later, we were graced with our first view of our
new home. We came in over a huge body of deep chrome water.
"The Manderlan Sound," Dar said, pointing down at the water. "A

warm saline ocean. It is one of life's greatest pleasures to float in that dense water."

From there, we followed a wide, purple river inland, and soon a network of strange, geometric peaks rose up before us, capped in shining white ice. "Those are the Lantis mountains," she said. "They were formed millions of years ago. Forsara was once, many ages past, a tumultuous world, wracked with tectonic movement and scarred by solar flaring. The tumult heaved up many mountain ranges like this one. For generations, our ancestors lived in the shadow of those mountains, cultivating and protecting the seeds of life here on Forsara. Those seeds eventually grew into the world that stands now, the greatest civilization in all the known universe."

As she said that, we passed over to the other side of the mountains, and the city of Manderley stretched out across the valley below. It was a gleaming diamond of achievement. Elation buzzed inside my chest, a sense of raw wonder. This moment marked the next step in my life, and that awareness rolled over me in a wave of awe. Water welled in my eyes. Saiara squeezed my hand again. I looked at her, smiling through my tears.

The city lived in a sprawling valley between two mountain ranges. As we entered the valley, we passed over structures that were built right into the sides of the mountains, stacked like steps in a giant's staircase. Ahead of us, tall, sinuous spires of chrome and silver reached up to the sky. They looked so fragile. The image of a child flashed in my mind, playing with teetering connect sticks, building something so tall that it tipped and fell. But I knew these buildings were made from the strongest, most flexible materials ever forged. It would be nearly impossible to topple them.

Massive trees, taller than many of the buildings, grew through the city, purple and blue canopies of fertile life amidst the ordered structure. At first, it seemed as if there were huge, round, budding mushroom caps growing on the sides of the trees, but as we passed close to them, I realized they were man-made structures, entwined into the fibrous bark.

One tower stood above all others, far in the distance. I could tell it was a central point to the whole network of the city. Dar saw me looking at it. "The Watchtower. From there, the Worldheart presides over the whole of the Fellowship, under the care and stewardship of the Inner Coven. Perhaps, someday, you will walk its mirrored halls and know something of our greatest strength, and also of our greatest weakness."

I looked at her, intensely curious. Before she could say more, the ship touched down. There was no disturbance on landing, no sense of impact. We were still high above the city, and for a moment, I was disoriented. Were we floating in place? Then, the hatch opened, Dar leaped out, and I realized that we had landed on a deck atop one of the high towers.

When we came off the ship and onto the landing deck, I looked back up at the sky. A massive fleet of ships and stations were anchored in orbit above us. In the spotted pink and blue calico sky, they looked like ancient deities, lords above the planet. The variety and complexity of these vessels was almost impossible to take in.

"Incredible, isn't it?" Dar said. "They represent a massive network of life in this galaxy, explorers and astronomists, freighters and merchants, scholars and settlers. The collective knowledge and experience they hold is staggering. And we can access it all in the field."

"Look," Saiara said. "Look there!"

I followed her pointing finger and there was the spindle of *Transcendence*, our ship, spiraling in geostationary orbit. Next to so many other vessels, it seemed deceptively modest. The realization made my mind turn at the enormity of the fleet above us. A part of me ached to be back inside its winding passages.

"You miss it, don't you?" Dar said.

We both turned and looked at her with surprise. Saiara nodded.

"A result of the deep connection you formed in the ship's field. Imagine how I feel." She smiled a sad smile, rubbing the back of her neck, then turned and walked ahead of us towards the crowd of technicians and dignitaries lined up to greet us.

We didn't see Dar for a long time after that. Every pausha in the Fellowship has a standing appointment in the Coven. In most cases, paushas were offworld, too far away to make a meaningful contribution to the collective decisions of our galactic leaders. That left the Inner Coven. A core group of the eldest who made their home in the Watchtower of the Worldheart.

But with the coming stellar alignment, the Conclave had been evoked, and the pausha were coming home. Dar was swept up in Forsaran politics and, except for a skeleton crew that remained onboard *Transcendence*, the rest of us were given time to settle in and explore.

Many people from *Transcendence* had roots here on Forsara. This was a return home for them, and they scattered across the planet to visit family members and old friends. But there were many more like me, people who had left their homeworlds behind, chasing the promise of life among the stars.

Whole quadrants of the city were devoted to housing those of us who did not have a permanent home on Forsara. Saiara and I decided, without much conversation, to share quarters. In three weeks' time, the Academy would host its entrance qualifiers. If both of us were granted admittance, which seemed likely, our training might pull us apart again. We didn't have a name for our relationship yet, but our arrival here offered a rare stretch of uninterrupted leisure, and being together just felt right.

We were granted a modest but well-appointed unit in a towering residential building overlooking the northwestern bank of the Feyra river. Transport chutes moved people up, down, and through the building, the empty edifice coming to life as we all did our best to make ourselves at home. The speed of this internal transit system was phenomenal. There was room enough even for someone as tall as me to stretch out my arms and legs without touching the sides, and the levels moved past in a blur beyond the shell of the transparent tubes. But if I shut my eyes, I couldn't even tell I was moving. The system generated just the right amount of pressure and heft so that bodies felt cushioned and snug in the gravitational equilibrium created by the antigravitons. It was a thrilling engineering solution to the question of how to make the highest levels nearly as accessible as the ground floors.

With so many new people flooding in, there was an explosive demand for food, resources, and recreational opportunities, and enterprising vendors materialized to fill these wants and needs. On our first night in the unit, Saiara and I climbed the seven steps up to our viewing balcony, retracted the clear glass dome, and sat together in the open air, looking out over our improvised neighborhood.

Our tower was part of a larger hive of similar structures, and five levels below us, there was a pavilion connecting our neighboring tower. It served as a throughway and a public gathering place. In the middle of the pavilion, there was the statue of a young child holding a toy globe of Forsara above her head.

Voices made their way to us, people talking, arguing, laughing, bartering. I caught the smell of spicy polcha and wild suidae chops sizzling in a portable convector. "That smells incredible," I said.

"Are you still hungry?" she asked with a hint of playful surprise.

We had made dinner earlier, a warm, salty broth with leafy greens, seaweed noodles and fresh anatre eggs, but the aroma of roasting suidae was enough to set my mouth watering.

"Maybe a little," I said patting my belly and smiling. "We eat well up on Transcendence, but the options down here are staggering. I have never seen such an abundance of food. Back on Verygone, we ate the same staples pretty much every day. Gulyas in the winter, and tuber noodles with shadefruit sauce in the summer. I think my stomach doesn't know what to do with itself here."

Saiara laughed her warm laugh. Then she set her glass of sparkling secco down, leaned close to me, put her hands on either cheek, and kissed me on lips. "Maybe I can give you something else to focus on for a little while," she said. "Will you know what to do with yourself then?"

―――――――――――――

I leaned back in the low boat and let my hand hang over the side, trailing my fingers through the cool waters of the Feyra. Saiara stood at the prow, her long golden hair tied up in a bun behind her head, handling the long oar like an expert, poling left, then right, then twice left again to keep us on a straight course through the river's mild currents.

"Where did you learn to navigate like that?" I asked her.

The academy qualifiers were less than a week away, and we wanted to make the most of our last days of leisure. The city was so large, and we had seen so little of it. We had been on the river for over an hour, heading south on a rented gondola towards Tulburn Hall, a popular artisans' quarter in the city. The boats were a nostalgic relic from a previous age, but they held an undeniable charm. The owner had lined up dozens near our residential complex, and when we saw them clustered together along the shore, dark and sleek, carved with the old runes of the river folk, komodo eyes painted on the prowhead, we were smitten. The owner offered up one of his young staffers to lead us on a tour, but Saiara insisted we make our own way.

"I grew up on Jarcosa, you oaf," she said. "Remember? I spent more time on my family's trimaran than I did on land. This river is a tender companion compared to the moody open waters of the Coscan ocean."

"Well I'm impressed," I said. "You cut a striking figure up there. I like watching you in action."

"Aren't you sweet. I know how hard you're working to balance the boat's weight back there, so please, by all means, enjoy the view. I wouldn't want you to strain yourself." She kept poling the oar through the water as she teased me. The water rippled and eddied in the wake of her strokes.

"Someone has to keep an eye on you. If I'm not careful, you'll get the wild idea to take us over a waterfall or something."

"I don't think there are any falls on this part of the river," she said with playful mockery.

"But if there are, you'll be the one to find them."

I closed my eyes, smiling to myself. I loved hearing her laugh.

"Oren," she said. "Look at that!"

I must have dozed off. I opened my eyes. We were coming to a wide thoroughfare that terminated at a large park on the eastern shore of the river. And at the far horizon of the thoroughfare, framed by the valley of buildings stretching away from the river, we saw it. The Watchtower. The soaring axle at the center of Manderley, seat of the Worldheart, where the eldest made their home.

We both stared at it in silent awe until our boat drifted past and it disappeared from sight, obscured by closer structures.

"What I wouldn't give to go there," Saiara said, her eyes mapping the ripples of water around the edges of our boat.

"Maybe someday," I said. "You never know."

"I would like that very much," she said in a quiet voice.

When we started our journey down river, the buildings of the city huddled close to the water, forming a deep, shadowed canyon. Now, the shoreline opened up, the buildings sat further back, and the waterside park and the adjacent thoroughfare were alive with the bustling traffic of pedestrians, rollers, fliers, and floaters of all shapes and sizes, mingling together in a chaotic dance. I kept waiting for someone to crash into someone else, but it never happened.

"You think it's all autonomous?" I asked Saiara. "The way the traffic all blends together like that?"

"Definitely," she said. "The Worldheart orchestrates everything on Forsara, communicating with every functional intelligence to keep the systems humming at optimal efficiency."

Some of the fliers and floaters left the thoroughfare and moved out above the river, water rippling and fluttering beneath them as they crossed to the western shore and dispersed down a delta of avenues, alleys and sky passages.

"Do you think it ever makes mistakes?" I said.

"It's hard to say. Even Transcend was sometimes imperfect in his knowledge of our ship. But I'm sure there are redundancies built in to account for any number of potential errors. Manderley did not become the greatest city in the galaxy by accident."

As she spoke, Saiara steered us closer to the eastern shore. Two men sat there, holding hands, enjoying the warm day. One of the men was distracted by a young boy and girl playing nearby. He called to them to be careful as they ran along the water's edge. The other man smiled and waved to us as we floated past. We both waved back.

"Do you know where the Tulburn Hall neighborhood is?" Saiara called to the man who waved to us. His partner turned to look at us too. "Are we close?"

"Hi there! Yes, you're very close. Just head south for a few more minutes, around the river's bend, until you cross under Tulburn Bridge. You should be able to dock there and climb the steps up to the street. Are you going to the performance?"

Before we could ask what performance, there was a splash in the water.

I turned to see the young boy thrashing in the shallows of the river. His sister was kneeling in the grass at the edge, her face pinched with concern.

"Eledar's breath," the second man said, jumping up. "Jacquin!

What in the names of the Scions are you doing? Come out from the water!"

But Jacquin was struggling. He thrashed, then his head dipped under. When he came up again, he was further from shore.

"Jacquin!" There was panic in the father's voice now.

"I've got him," I called. "Saiara, swing us around," I said to her, swiveling my index finger in the air.

We were close enough to shore that Saiara could dig the pole oar into the silt of the river bed. Our boat turned on the axis of the oar, bringing us close to the boy.

"Here we go," I said, scooping him out of the water.

I pulled him into our gondola, setting him on his hands and knees, wet and bedraggled. I patted him on the back as he hacked and coughed.

"Breathe, Jacquin," I said. "You're alright, little friend. Just breathe."

His panic started to level off. His breath came more evenly. He sat back on his haunches and looked up at me, water running down his cheeks and forehead. His eyes opened wide. "Elly's belly, sire," he said with a comical mix of casual and formal that only a child can pull off. "You're real big!"

I laughed. "I come from hardy stock. Miners' blood runs in these veins," I said, patting my hand against my chest. "Good thing for you too. I've lifted much heavier objects than your sodden self."

The boy gave me a sheepish look. "I could have made it myself," he muttered.

"Okay," I said with a shrug. "Should I toss you back in then?"

He shook his head vigorously, his eyes opening even wider.

I laughed again.

"Jacquin," the boy's father called, "are you okay?"

"Of course I am, father!" Jacquin stood up quick to prove his point. Droplets of water pattered against my face. Saiara leaned on the oar, steadying the boat.

"I warned you to be careful, didn't I?"

"I was being careful. Weiun pushed me!"

The little girl came running over. "I did not! You're a filthy liar Jacq!"

"Enough!" the father said. "We're not playing 'who's the culprit' today. It's too beautiful out for that nonsense, and your father and I plan on enjoying this day. You were both playing near the water, even though I warned you not to, so no freeze cream for either of you."

"But father," they both wailed in unison.

He crossed his arms and glared at them. They tried to meet his fierce gaze. Weiun looked pleading. Jacq looked ready to fight. But their father was clearly not budging. After a moment, both children averted their eyes.

I caught the eye of the children's other father, the man who had first waved to us. He was still sitting on the grass. He smiled, shrugged, and shook his head.

"Now Jacq," the standing father said, "say thank you to this nice man for rescuing you."

The boy kept his head down. "Thank you," he mumbled.

"Jacq?" The father's pitch rose up a note.

"Thank you, sire," he said, louder now.

"You're very welcome, Jacq," I said with amusement.

Saiara pushed our boat closer to shore, and before he could protest, I lifted Jacquin out of the boat, handling him like a sack of tubers, and set him down. He scurried up the grass, then turned and gave me a vengeful look.

"You're a fierce one, eh little Jacq?" I said.

His father came and put his arm around Jacq's shoulders. The boy's face softened. He leaned in, resting his head in the crook of his father's arm. He was on the cusp of adolescence, and his mix of petulance, braggadocio, and vulnerability was charming.

"Pay him no mind," the sitting father said. "He takes after Rolston." He tilted his head towards the standing father. "Those two are seeds in a pod, they are."

Rolston chuckled, and Jacq pulled closer to him, hugging his arms around Rolston's waist.

"My name is Oren," I said, waving my hand again. "It's nice to meet you all."

"Weiono," the sitting man said. "That accent? Where are you from?"

"Verygone. The Beallurian system."

Weiono whistled. "Long way from home. First time on Forsara?"

I nodded.

"And you?" he said, turning to Saiara. "Where do you hail from?"

"Jarcosa," she said with a smile.

"Ah. A child of the water. No wonder you handle that old gondola with such ease. I've heard it's beautiful on Jarcosa."

"It is the most beautiful place in the galaxy," she said. "At least to me."

"There's no beauty like the beauty of home," Weiono said.

"Our cities are nothing like this, though," she said, turning her head to take in the buildings and bustle around us.

"There's no place anywhere quite like Manderley. I can't imagine ever leaving." Then he stood up. "But in less than a decade, the suns will converge again, and the choice to stay or the choice to explore the unknown is a decision everyone must make for themselves.

"I might never see the oceans of Jarcosa or the warm sun of Beallur, but it gladdens me to meet you here. On behalf of our family," he gestured towards Rolston, Jacq, and Weiun, "we bid you most welcome to our fair city."

"Thank you," Saiara said.

"Thank *you* for rescuing our son," Rolston said.

"Now then," Weiono went on, "if you're going to the performance, and you have a chance to speak with the band leader, tell her I sent you. She's an old friend."

"We didn't even know about the show," I said. "We are just exploring."

Weiono clapped his hands together. "Oh, you absolutely must go. The experience is rapturous. The children don't have the patience for it yet, or we would be there right now."

"What kind of performance is it?"

Weiono pursed his lips. "It's hard to describe. Better you see it for yourselves. I promise you, it's worth it. Though I must give you fair warning, this is entertainment from a different era. It is less than the virtual simulations we are all so used to, and yet, in other ways, it is so much more."

Saiara rapped her palm against the lacquered wood of our gondola. "Given our means of transportation, that sounds fitting."

Weiono grinned. "Too true. Too true. You still have some time then. The next performance doesn't start until first sun fall. The old amphitheater is in the north quarter of Tulburn Hall, past the arch of Yincoln. You cannot miss it."

"Thank you, Weiono," Saiara said, using the oar to shove us off.

I lifted my hand to wave as she steered us back into the soft central current of the Feyra. They all waved back. Even Jacq. I tipped my head to him and gave him a formal salute, touching my fingers to my chin, then pointing towards him. He smiled, then buried his head in his father's tunic.

"Have you ever seen anything like it?"

Saiara shook her head. Her jaw hung open.

"Your jaw is hanging open."

She closed her mouth and gave me a dirty look.

I laughed. "I don't think I've ever seen you look surprised before."

"Oh, and you're not?"

I shrugged.

"Forgive me," she said. "I forgot what an experienced and worldly spacefarer you are."

I laughed again. She was right of course. I had never seen anything like it either. The moment we stepped off our boat and climbed the stairs up from the canal to the streets above, we were transported to an altogether different Manderley.

Tulburn Hall was not a hall at all. It was city within the city. Older. More relaxed. More conflicted. Coming to the hall was like the moment I discovered Saiara's birthmark on her lower back, a constellation of freckles in a lighter patch of skin, just above the curve of her hips. Up until now, Manderley had seemed ageless, a perfect city, crystallized and immutable. The hall punctured that illusion, enriching the meticulous beauty of Manderley with color and chaos. It served as a marker of earlier incarnations. A reminder that we always carry our histories with us.

For the first few minutes, we just stood at the lip of the aqueduct, gawking like the offworlders we were. The streets were alive. People of all ages and many stripes were moving in every direction, and the scene was permeated with an air of leisure and playfulness. People carried food and drink as they walked. The sound of music and conversation poured from open windows and doorways. Revelers stood and watched from balconies lining the higher floors.

"Come on," Saiara said, breaking us from the spell.

She took my hand and led us deeper into the hall. A chaotic jumble of architecture from ages past had formed like sediment, layers stacked one on the next, accreting over the centuries. From certain vantages, we could still see the sleek towers of Manderley, but that only made the contrast between old and new that much sharper, and when the towers were obscured from view, the sense that we had traveled to a different world was immersive and complete.

We heard the universal tongue often enough, but there were many other languages too. The competing accents and dialects formed a steady cadence that permeated the hall, a thrum of human voices blending together in a neverending chorus. The sound was a wordless promise that something magical waited just beyond sight. I was a child again, giddy and awestruck, skipping through the streets of a city as wondrous as any fantasy.

We passed an ancient granite manse that might have been a thousand years old or more. Its arches and buttresses looked as if they'd been repaired countless times. It had once, perhaps, been the centerpiece of a large estate, but now the aging residence was hemmed in by five- and six-story houses, stucco and plaster walls framed by thick wooden beams and peaked roofs shingled with slate and clay. Arching footbridges nested precariously in the housetops, and people moved across them, nimble and surefooted.

We rounded a corner, and a man holding what looked like a sort of tortured legelhorn strolled past us. A profusion of pipes and levers and dials sprouted from the curved central horn. He lifted it to his lips as he walked, blowing into it, fingering the instrument's buttons. Music came gurgling out, cheerful and infectious.

As he played, bright spots of rainbow light strobed from holes bored into the instrument. Whenever someone got flashed with the colored light, their skin turned candy red, or sunset purple, or marigold yellow.

People laughed as he passed by, pointing at each other as they turned different colors, and a gaggle of children followed close behind him, jostling and jumping, trying to get hit with the next ray of light.

A moment later, a lime green man came running around the corner shouting invectives at the horn player in a tongue I did not recognize. The horn player pirouetted, flicked his fingers across the instrument, and a warm, white light washed over his angry pursuer.

The man stopped in his tracks. He was no longer green. He held up his sandy hands, examining them. Apparently satisfied with what he saw, he put two fingers behind his right ear and, with a theatrical sneer, flicked his fingers towards the horn player before storming off.

"That's incredible," I whispered to Saiara. "How do you think he gets people to change color like that?"

"I have no idea," she said. "Some kind of bacterial or chemical reaction?"

I was tempted to ask the horn player himself, but I suspect he would have just smiled and lit me up with color. We kept moving, the mystery unsolved.

Vendors shouted and waved, hawking their merchandise. A lithe man in a skintight garment moved like dancer on a thin strand of rope strung between a leafy green tree and a wrought iron lamp post. An emerald green giant leaned his arms on a second-story windowsill, talking to a pretty woman in the window. An old fashioned android with burnished gold plating walked a half-dozen canines of all shapes and sizes. The largest hound stood as high as my waist, and I could have held the smallest in one my palm.

We came to a large park ringed by trees. A mother ran alongside her son as he held tight to a nylon string attached to a toy flyer, swooping and curling above us, thirty feet up in the air. A blindfolded archer wowed onlookers, loosing arrows at a rapid pace to spear fruit and loaves of bread that her assistants tossed into the air. A group of people moved in unison through a slow motion sequence of choreographed poses, arms flowing like water.

We paused in front of a statue of a naked woman with seashell pink skin and the head of a horned komodo. She held a small box in her hand. Three teenagers stood nearby, pointing at the statue and whispering to themselves. One of them, a young girl with a shorn scalp and heavy green makeup around her eyes, ran up to the komodo woman and dropped a circle of metal into the box.

The statue opened her mouth wide and let out a fearsome jet of fire.

Saiara and I both leapt back in surprise.

The teenagers clapped and cheered with delight.

The komodo woman bowed low, touching her long snout to the ground.

Saiara laughed her vivid, joyful laugh.

The komodo stood up and winked at us, smoke steaming from her nostrils.

"Come on," Saiara said, taking my hand again. "I'm famished."

It was well past lunchtime. Wandering through the hall was a feast for the senses, but our bellies were empty. At the far end of the park, we found a street cook selling fried arro and shredded poultra. We sat on the lip of a fountain, water misting the warm air, baskets of food perched on our laps.

"I don't know if I've ever been happier," I said, licking grease off my fingers.

Saiara's mouth was too full to respond, but she nodded, a noodle hanging from the corner of her lip, and grunted her agreement.

I wrapped my arm around her and planted an oily kiss on her cheek.

She pretended to guard her basket of food from me as she swallowed her bite. "Don't think I don't know what you're really after, you greasy thief," she said. "Go buy more poultra if you're still hungry!"

I laughed, then cupped my hand in the fountain and splashed water at her.

She pretended not to notice and kept eating.

I cupped some more water and used it to rinse the oil from my hands and lips.

"Pardon me, fair travelers," a cheerful voice said.

A tall, pale-skinned man stood in front of us, leaning on a cane. He wore a curious suit with a long, dark jacket hanging to his knees. The jacket opened in the front, and beneath it, he wore a puffed white shirt with a high collar, layered under a slate vest striped with wire-thin charcoal. A length of garish fabric encircled his neck.

His face was broad and friendly, with dark, wide-set, slender oval eyes. He wore a tall, piped hat on his head, and his hair fell out from the hat down to his shoulders. The thick, wavy strands could not hide his large ears from poking out.

"I am terribly sorry to interrupt your feast," he said, "but might you know the way to the amphitheater? These serpentine streets have me utterly befuddled."

He spoke the universal tongue, but with a strange, magnificent accent. Every word sounded gleaming and polished, a high, arched tone.

We gaped at him.

"Oh my, but where have I left my graces?" he said. "Please forgive me, fair travelers. Here I am, barging in on you without so much as single world of proper introduction." He held out his left hand with a flourish. He was wearing cream white gloves the same color as his shirt. "I am Baron Eyel Dunsemai, heir to the empty coffers of the once mighty nobles of Semai. As I am sure you have no doubt heard, my family line fell on hard times some generations back. The crude provincials of this derelict arrondissement take great pleasure in the Semai family's fall from grace.

"This, of course, all happened long before I was born. If I had been in power then, we would have no doubt avoided this whole unfortunate mess. Still, I inherited the august and honorable mantle of my lineage, and though my antecedents cursed me to live as a penniless pauper, I comport myself with dignity, unbent by the stones and cudgels of those poor, uncultured commoners who traffic in the misery and scandal of galactic nobility."

I looked at Saiara, my eyebrows raised. She gave me a quiet shake of her head. I dried my hands on my shirtsleeves and then took his gloved hand in mine. "I'm Oren. Oren Siris. Of Verygone. This is Saiara Tumon Yta. Of Jarcosa." It seemed right to share our full names with him.

"Well met, sire Siris and lady Yta." He touched his silken fingers to my wrist.

There was an awkward pause, and worry creased my thoughts. The wild idea occurred to me that he might be waiting for us to share some equally personal facet of our lives, as if revealing one's woes was a social courtesy that we were crudely ignoring.

He coughed politely. "Now then..." he said. "The amphitheater?"

"Oh right!" I said with relief. "Actually, yes, we do know the way. Someone told us earlier. We need to find the arch of... what was it, Saiara?"

"Yincoln. In the north quarter."

"The great Yincoln!" Dunsemai said. "But of course. How foolish of me to forget such an obvious landmark. I know just the route to bring us between the stout old man's legs."

"His legs?"

Dunsemai chuckled. "Apologies. I am a risible comedian. The arch rises over the northern thoroughfare, and it has always made me think of a man squatting to loose his bowels."

Saiara laughed.

Dunsemai gave her an appreciative smile, then turned on his heel, lifted his cane, and started walking away from us at a fast clip.

Saiara and I looked at each other. "What just happened?" she whispered.

"I have no idea."

"Ho there!" Dunsemai called back to us. "Why do you tarry? The suns are well past peak, and the day lumbers ever onwards. Come along now!"

The moment we arrived to Tulburn Hall, we promptly forgot about Weiono's recommendation to seek out the performance. Now, thanks to Dunsemai, we were heading straight there. The baron was an entertaining companion, voluble and opinionated, and as we walked towards the amphitheater, he tipped his hat or waved his cane at almost everyone we passed. Some regarded him as if he were a madman, but many others seemed to recognize him, smiling, or waving, or calling out his name.

The arch of Yincoln looked beautiful, its domed peaks rising above the thoroughfare, its veneer encrusted with sculptures that told of great histories from ancient eras. But Dunsemai had ruined it from me. Approaching from afar, it was all I could do not to see the bulk of the structure and think about his image of an old man hunching down to defecate.

"You cannot unsee it, can you?" Dunsemai said, intuiting my thoughts. He wore a wicked grin.

I shook my head and laughed. Dunsemai clapped me on the back, laughing with me.

Soon, we passed beneath the arch. Hundreds and hundreds of people, too many to count, congregated in the shelter of its vaulting, peddlers and buskers and footstool preachers all vying for attention, their voices echoing above our heads.

As we threaded the heavy foot traffic, I noticed a half-dozen men idling ahead of us. Two were crouched down, tossing copper ingots on the cobblestones in patterns too quick for me to follow. The rest stood, watching the game unfold. As we approached, one of the men turned, and a look of sly recognition lit up his face. He stepped forward, lifting his hand in greeting.

"Weh heh heh," he said, "if it in't ol' baron the dunce. Ne'er thought we'd see you in these parts again." He was a short, stout man, dressed plainly, with a heavyset forehead and strong, wide hands.

Dunsemai, who was looking in the other direction, turned at the man's words and blundered right into him. His gloved hands came up against the man's torso.

The man reached his arms around the baron, trying to grasp him tight, but Dunsemai was surprisingly quick. He slipped the man's grasp and jumped away.

"Be gone, ruffian," he shouted, brandishing his cane. "We've no time for your brutish posturing. The performance is starting soon."

"I'll give you a performance you won't soon be forgettin', dunce," the man said, cracking his knuckles, his face grim. "Yer debts are so deep, they owe debts o' their own, and yer fancy noble name won't be nothing more than werds for yer gravestone."

I stepped forward, raising my chest and shoulders. "We have no enmity with you, good sir, but baron Dunsemai is our companion and our guide. And we are running late. Best return to the game. I'm sure you can find another time to settle whatever business lies between you."

The man squinted, looking up at me. He had the bent nose and scarred knuckles of a brawler, but I towered over him. Dunsemai stood to my left, his cane at the ready. Saiara slid in behind my right flank, using her steely glare to good effect.

The man's eyes flickered between the three of us as he turned over his options. After another moment, he put two fingers behind his ear, flicked them toward us, then stalked back to his group.

"I'm beginning to think that's not a gesture of respect," Saiara said.

"You are most perceptive, lady Yta," Dunsemai said. "That is Lurkur U'Atsa. He is a boor and a criminal, and respect is as foreign to him as personal hygiene. But you forced him to face his own inborn cowardice. That was well done."

"I knew a lot of people like him where I grew up," I said. "Except they were twice his size. Lurkur wouldn't last long on Verygone."

"Perhaps we can shuttle him there?" Dunsemai said with excitement. "Is it a lengthy journey?"

"Quite."

"Excellent! That shall give him ample time to ponder the foolishness of crossing wits with Baron Eyel Dunsemai." He pointed his index finger up in the air. "I know a deputy in interplanetary shipping who owes me a favor or three. I'll speak with him after this evening's performance and have the arrangements made."

Neither of us could tell whether he was serious.

"These copper ingots should cover the costs," he went on. He opened his palm, revealing a small mound of copper in his gloved hand.

I looked at him, astonished. "Did you...?"

Dunsemai waved his hand, dismissing my concern. "U'Atsa is a cheat and a cutpurse. I've no doubt he pinched this from some gullible sightseer or desperate gambler. A cretin and his coinage are soon parted. U'Atsa lives by that law, and so it is only fair that he is subject to it as well, no?"

I shook my head, speechless.

"You know, baron," Saiara said, after a moment, "for a man who supposedly couldn't find his way to the amphitheater, you seem to know your way quite well around these parts."

The baron gave her a shrewd look. "Never forget, lady Yta: masks do not make the man, but we all have our roles to play, in the end."

"What does that mean?" she said.

But he was already ahead of us again, leading us out the other side of the domed arch. We came to a broad, manicured lawn. Dozens of people were lounging on blankets, eating and drinking. Dunsemai led us through them with confidence, always careful to keep his feet on the grass, never intruding in the invisible bubble of personal space surrounding each cluster of people.

This public act of mutual disregard had fascinated me ever since coming to Manderley. I noticed it everywhere, the way thousands of individuals could all be alone together, crowded into streets or halls or canteens, ignoring everyone who was not in their immediate sphere of attention. Back on Verygone, we lived in close quarters, especially during the winters, and we developed our own ways of finding solitude when we needed it. The same was true on *Transcendence*. It was easy to sneak away to some quiet corner. But here, people were everywhere, on a scale I had never experienced. I felt awkward and self-conscious, intensely aware of my clumsy bulk as we navigated through the picnickers.

Then we came to the lip of the amphitheater, and I forgot myself. The grass grew right up to the edge of the back row of seating, and hundreds more people filled the granite seats. The resonant acoustic bowl was alive with the hum of conversation.

And every single person wore a mask.

Each mask was unique. Some wore simple masks that circled the eyes and covered the nose. Others had exaggerated human heads with leering expressions and monstrous features. There were also inhuman masks, ursine and lupine, feline and reptile, a vast menagerie of totemic animals. A woman near us wore an aquiline feathered headdress with a sharp curving beak, and the man next to her had ophidian jaws sculpted with wicked fangs.

I was so taken with this spectacle that I did not notice the woman until she was next to us. Slight of build, her cherry red hair was cropped and chunky, with a dusting of glitter. Charcoal makeup lined her eyes, and a golden face mask covered her nose and mouth. She held two more masks, one in each hand.

"Ah," Dunsemai said, "there you are." He took the masks from the woman. "Most grateful, my dear."

She bowed, saying nothing, then turned and disappeared back into the crowd.

Dunsemai handed us each a mask.

Mine was a hooded naja snake. It was hyperrealistic, as if some hunter had traveled deep into an undiscovered jungle and hacked off the head of a gigantic thonidae. The scales of the snakehead were glossed in the late afternoon sunlight, and I could feel the individuation of each scale as I ran my fingers over them. The fangs were ivory white and tipped with brass. I touched the point of one with my index finger, then pulled away in surprise. A drop of blood sprang out of my fingertip.

"Careful there, sire Siris. The sculptor who fashioned that mask is a fanatic for detail. You are most lucky we convinced him to leave out the poison."

I put my finger in my mouth, licking the pinprick wound.

Saiara held her mask out in front of her with both hands, examining it. It was the mantle of some bird of prey, with fierce amber eyes and snow white feathers speckled with black. Where mine was intensely detailed, hers was more abstract. It did not look like any specific type of bird I had ever seen. More like the idea of one.

"Go on," he said, smiling at us encouragingly.

We looked at each other.

"You first," Saiara said, a smile crinkling her eyes.

I hesitated. "This day just keeps getting stranger... so, why in blazes not?"

I slid the mask over my head until I could see out through the open mouth.

It fit perfectly.

"You look downright wicked," Saiara said. She pulled hers on.

"There you are," Dunsemai said, nodding with pleasure. "Now we can begin."

"WHERE DID HE GO?" My field of vision was limited by the mask. I swiveled my head left and right, but I saw no sign of the baron.

"He's gone," Saira said, her voice muffled.

We were still standing at the back of the amphitheater, and the sounds of the crowd were distorted by my mask. Much of the noise was unintelligible, but I kept catching snatches of conversation as if people were speaking right into my ear.

"Manderley cannot last if the coven fails to address this," someone said.

"I heard she'd show herself here tonight," someone else said.

"Your fifth sounds flat," said another.

"Fortunes have been lost in a single toss." Yet another.

There was no logic to the conversation. They seemed to be talking over each other, not to each other. I tried to make sense of it, but the pervasive murmur of the crowd jostled all the noise together. I couldn't find a coherent thread.

Then a woman stepped out onto center stage and a hush fell over the crowd. We had a clear view of her down the aisle of stairs that led to the stage. She wore a classical dress, cerulean blue against powder white skin, the neckline plunging low. A crystal amulet shining with the colors of the rainbow hung from her neck, casting spots of color across the stage like a prism, and the train of the dress formed a watery pool of fabric on the ground, trailing behind her as she walked. She wore a bejeweled crown, gleaming chrome encrusted with rubies, and a veil of silver lace fell in front of her face.

I don't know why, but I was nervous. I took Saiara's hand. The firmness of her grasp comforted me.

The woman on stage started singing, unaccompanied, a gorgeous, lilting, wordless melody. Her voice resonated inside my mask as if I were standing right next to her, and that's when I realized we were linked to an amplification system on the stage. The mingled voices from a moment ago were people near the front, speaking loud enough to get picked up by the system.

The orchestra in the pit below front of stage came to life, picking up the singer's melody, adding color and harmony and a driving, staccato rhythm. Every instrument was crystal clear; the sustained swell of bowed cellofahns; the rattle of mallets on timpani skin; the reedy hum of clariphones. The music reached a rattling crescendo, but her voice came through pure and clear, vibrating above the instruments like a bird gliding on air.

The wave of music broke. She stopped singing. The instruments quieted, trailing off into raindrop patters of percussion mingling with melodic fragments of brass and wind until there was nothing but silence.

She stood as still as a statue, her arms at her side, her lace veil rising and falling with the flutter of her recovering breath. The creak of chairs and muted strings whispered in my ears. She bowed, a slight tilt of her head.

The crowd broke into enthusiastic applause.

She basked for a few long moments before walking off stage.

As the applause died down, a man stepped out.

Baron Eyel Dunsemai.

"Welcome friends and visitors," he said. "Tonight, you enter an ancient and dangerous world, where nothing is quite as it seems. As steward of this realm, I promise you safe passage. You can trust that, no matter what comes, you will arrive safely on the far shore. But it will not be an easy journey. When we are finished here tonight, you might never look at this fair world we call home in the same light again."

It was impossible to be sure from the back row, but I swear he was looking right at us. He reached up his left hand to his face and pressed his fingers against his cheeks and forehead.

"What lies behind your masks?" he asked.

He pulled his hand away, and his face came with it.

There was nothing there but an empty blackness.

Figures floated above me, shadows coming in and out of focus. I reached up to take off my mask, but I could not find the seams. I started to panic, clawing at my neck. Someone touched my shoulder. My vision started to clear, and I saw a woman with the head of a vulture standing over me.

"Oren," the woman said, a fierce whisper inside my mind, "are you okay?"

"Saiara!" I tried to say, but my mouth couldn't seem to form her name.

"You don't have to speak, Oren. Just think, and I will hear you."

"What's... what's happening?"

She helped me stand. "I'm not entirely sure. I suspect the masks Dunsemai gave us are emulators."

"We're in a simulation right now?" I said.

"I certainly hope so."

"Eledar's breath. This is incredible. You look so... so alive." I reached out to touch her head. Her feathers were soft and warm. She blinked her amber pearl eyes.

"You should see yourself. If I hadn't watched you put on that mask, I'd be terrified."

I looked around, hoping for a mirror. We were in a large hall like something out of a fable. The room was lit with thousands of candles, flickering on tables and mantles, guttering in the chandeliers, melting together in the yawning fireplace. A glow diffused through the room, creating an immaterial aura, as if everything might dissolve into particles of light.

Dusty fraying tapestries hung between broad stone columns that supported the roof of the hall. Escutcheons were mounted on the pillars of stone, each one decorated its own intricate, ornate coat of arms. The vaulted ceiling was festooned with dried flowers, petals parched of color.

At the center of the hall, a half-dozen long tables were heaped with food and drink; steaming cuts of meat; crystal decanters of wine; pastries arranged in artful configurations, glazed sugar twinkling in the candlelight. The benches of the table were empty. A feast for ghosts.

"Look," Saiara said, pointing past the tables.

Above this empty court, on a throne of gnarled and leafless vines, the singer with the crown of gemstones sat stiff and still, her long fingers clutching the barren stems that wound together to form the arms of her chair. Her face was hidden behind her veil, and the only sign of life was the gentle rise and fall of the faceted amulet that hung from her neck, resting against the bare curve of her chest. I recognized it as the same amulet she wore when she sang in the amphitheater, but its kaleidoscope of colors was dimmed and absent. It shone pitch black.

There were two thrones, both made of dried vines. She sat in the right. The left was empty.

"She looks so lonely," I said.

"She's been sitting like that since we arrived. She doesn't seem to notice us. Watch this." Saiara lifted her hands to her vulture's beak and let out a piercing caw.

"What are you doing?" I hissed. Her call echoed in the empty room.

She pointed up at the queen in answer.

She had not moved at all.

"Eledar's breath. That is eerie."

Saiara nodded, her feathers rustling.

I was intensely curious to see what I looked like, so I walked over to the closest table. Keeping a careful eye on the queen, I slid a pyramid of pastries off of a silver serving tray. The queen remained unmoved. I held the tray up, reflecting my face.

I recoiled with fear, an instinctive response. The tray fell from my hand, clattering to the stone floor. My eyes darted to the queen. No response. I brought my hands up to touch the striated scales of my face.

Saiara was at my side. "Are you okay, Oren?"

I nodded, mute.

She knelt down and picked up the silver tray. She went to set in on the table, but I reached out and took it from her. I held it up again, steady this time. A wicked naja stared back at me, a hooded face with deep set, beady eyes. My tongue flicked, darting in and out of my closed mouth. I opened wide. Two long fangs curved down from the roof of my mouth, and a row of tiny, serrated teeth lined the top and bottom. It was a fearsome sight.

"Oren?" Saira said gently, touching my shoulder.

I turned and lunged at her, snapping my jaws just in front of her face.

She flinched backwards. I laughed out loud. It came out as a hissing cough from my reptilian throat. "If you had wings," I thought to her, "you'd be in the rafters right now!"

She punched my arm. "You bloody creep!"

"Oh come on! How could I resist?"

"Whatever happened to the nice, shy Oren I fell in love with?"

"I reckon he's been spending too much time with you."

She punched me again. "You're rotten."

"'We create each other.' Isn't that what Darpausha says?"

"Then it seems I've created a monster." She chuckled, a musical chortle from her avian beak.

"What do we do now?" I asked.

"I don't know. But you should come have a look at these tapestries." She took my hand, leading me to a vantage where we could take in all three of the giant weavings hanging from the hall's western pillars. The tapestries depicted a multitude of different scenes, moving from lightness on the left to darkness on the right; from quiet idylls, with people lounging in fanciful garb beneath the eaves of trees, eating, talking, playing music, to vicious battles, soldiers brandishing archaic weaponry, spearing and gouging and slashing, disintegrating beneath blasts of liquefying energy.

"Brutal," I said, pointing at the warriors.

"It gets worse." She gestured to the rightmost of the three tapestries. It was an apocalyptic vision, a ragged, mountainous world of cinder and ash, fires smoking on the polluted horizon. There were fewer people in this tapestry than the others, and all of them were suffering. A monstrous, headless giant with its face on its torso was tearing a man apart, stuffing his limbs into the mouth on its stomach. Three lechers with the heads of hyenas surrounded a terrified woman, wielding molten hot iron brands, stabbing and scalding her. In the lower right corner, a half-dozen people were tangled together. At first, I took it for some perverse orgy, but then I saw that they had been melded together like clay, arms and torsos and faces jutting out at horrid, impossible angles. My eyes were involuntarily drawn in towards this depraved image until I forced myself to look away.

I lingered the longest on a winged man falling from the sky. He was naked, with a smooth and sexless body that made me think for a moment of the corrupted shipheart from Arcturea. I shook my head, chasing the thought away, focusing back on the image. The man's wings were on fire, silver feathers withering in the flames, ashes trailing behind him as he tumbled towards the world below. But what struck me the most was how calm he looked. Every other person in this doomsday mural was in a state of pain or raw terror, but his face was placid.

Then, as I tracked my eyes between each tapestry, I saw it.

"Saiara!" I said. "Look at this man."

"With the burning wings?"

"Yes. Now look here. And here." I pointed.

"He's in all three tapestries!"

"Right. And look who's next to him here."

In the leftmost tapestry, the world of peace and plenty, he sat on an ivy throne, lush with green leaves and blossoming pink roses. His wings were draped over the back of the throne, and his blue eyes gleamed bright against his cinnamon skin. And sitting to his left, holding his hand, was a pale woman with a gemstone crown and the crystal amulet hanging from her neck. Nothing covered her face. She was gorgeous, icy eyes beaming with happiness as she presided over the tranquil paradise with her king at her side.

Saiara turned from the tapestry to face the silent queen in the throne room.

A loud crash echoed through the quiet chamber, making us both jump.

The queen turned her head towards us. She lifted her hands and parted her veil. Her face was aged beyond measure, sagging with ruined, wrinkled flesh. "Welcome," she said, her voice loud and clear, "to the saeculur feast."

From the opposite end of the throne room, the main doors had swung open, crashing against the wall, and people were pouring in. The queen was not looking at us. She was looking past us, welcoming them into the hall.

The people paid us no mind as they took their places at the tables. There were maybe fifty or sixty, dressed in finery from a forgotten era, scarlet and silver fabrics patterned with stripes and spirals and geometric forms. They ranged from middle-aged to elderly, and their clothing, for all its artfulness, was like everything else in this place, fading and tattered. But none of them were ravaged by time like their queen.

They whispered to each other as they made their way to the tables. They seemed to be waiting for some signal from her. Her veil had fallen back down over her hideous face, and she stood tall and poised as the people settled down on the benches.

When everyone was seated, she spoke again. "Liegemen of Carus," she said with the confidence of a seasoned orator. "After another saeculum of silent vigil, it feeds my spirit to be with you again. As your Autarchess, my faith in our lord is more than the sorrowful hope of a wife pining for her husband. I am duty bound to my vigil to bear the weight of all the years we've lost in our wanderings.

"Each century, we gather to enact the saeculur feast in honor of our Autarch's last crossing. It is an act of remembering. It is also a prayer for his safe homecoming. For when Autarch Carus returns from beyond the rim of the universe - and return he shall - he will bring with him great knowledge that will repair the world that our arrogance destroyed.

"So I bid you, eat of this food, for it contains the dreams of our beloved liege, left behind when he crossed the lightless horizon. It will restore you. And drink of this drink, for it holds the promises he made to forge the pact of peace with the Heliots. It will release you from your pain."

One of the people closest to the queen handed a golden chalice up to her.

She nodded her thanks, and raised the chalice high. "To our liege Carus," she said. "May he find his way home from the darkness. May he bind us again with the light of promise. May he bring us the wisdom of the final truths."

The revelers lifted their glasses. "To our liege Carus," they cheered in unison.

Then they drank, glugging down the blood dark fluid. It spilled over their cheeks, dribbling down and staining their clothes, but they were heedless. Empty glasses crashed down onto the table. The elderly poured more, drinking again. The middle-aged stopped drinking and tucked into the food. Soon, though, everyone was eating, tearing at the meal like beasts, hands and cheeks greasy with oil and fat.

Everyone but the queen. She sat back down on her throne of vines and drank, watching her subjects gorge themselves. Whenever her glass was empty, someone came and poured her more. As she drank, the amulet on her neck turned from dark black to blood red.

"Oren," Saiara said. "Look at them!"

I gasped.

They were getting younger.

Liver spots disappeared. Flesh smoothed and tightened. Bald heads sprouted hair. Silver hair turned blonde or auburn or black. And still they kept eating and drinking, gorging themselves on the fare and provisions of juvenescence.

"Enough, you fools!" the queen said, jumping up from her throne, her sanguinary spirit splashing from her chalice. "Our gluttony almost ruined us once. Even now, the Heliots are watching. Waiting. I can sense them. Do not be greedy for more than is your due."

The revelers looked at each other, shamefaced, stained with the carnage of their feasting. They were all youthful now. The oldest among them had become vigorous men and woman, and the youngest were now barely more than children.

One of the eldest stood. His silver tunic was ruined with oil and blood, and his salted beard was sticky with grease, but he stood with refined dignity. "Please accept our most humble gratitude, Autarchess," he said, bowing his head to her, "both for your generosity, and for the discipline of your spirit, which is the only shield that protects us from ourselves in the absence of our liege lord."

"Begone," she said, turning her head away, and waving her hand at them. Her posture looked tired. Deflated. "The feast is over. Soon I shall renew my vigil, lest the Heliots come out from the shadows to take our lives as their own. I need to gather my strength."

Chastised, the queen's subjects stood up from the table. The youngest among them wore expressions of insolence or rejection, much as a punished child might. The older were stony, tempers cool. They shepherded the young ones out of the hall before raw emotions devolved into tantrum.

"Saiara," I whispered, pointing towards the people.

Moving among the queen's subjects were other figures, transparent almost to the point of invisibility. People with the heads of animals.

"Other audience members!" she said.

"They must be," I said.

As the revelers filed out, members of the ghostly audience moved with them. Some individuals crept in close, shoulder to shoulder with the departing revelers, so close I was sure they would be noticed. But the people ignored them. Others followed at what seemed to me a safer distance, moving in pairs and groups after the main crowd, until the room was almost empty. A few stayed behind in the great hall, wandering around the room, examining the tapestries or the remnants of food and dishware on the tables. The queen sat inanimate on her throne.

"I get it, Oren!" Saiara said.

"Get what?"

"We can go anywhere! Anywhere we want. It's brilliant really. Depending on where you start and where you go from there, you'll probably never see the same performance twice..." A look of worry crossed her face.

"What's wrong?"

"We might not have much time left!" She started moving for the door.

"Time for what?"

"Before the experience ends!" she called, still heading away from me.

"Saiara!"

"Don't worry, Oren. I'm going to go explore."

"I'll come with you."

"No," she said, holding up her hand to stop me from following. "We should split up. Dunsemai - or whoever designed this place - has built a whole world for us to explore. Who knows how deep it goes. If you stick with me, you'll miss the experience you were meant to have."

"Meant to have?"

"The gift of this place is freedom, Oren. The wall between audience and performer is thin. It may even be permeable. We are ghosts here, and we can choose the manner of our haunting."

"But how will I find you again?"

She laughed her chortling bird laugh. "No matter how far apart we are in here, we're still right next to each other. Whenever this ends, we will wake up in the amphitheater."

"Oh. Right."

"Open up, Oren. Follow your intuition. Let it lead you."

"Okay... Okay, I will. But what are you going-"

"See you on the other side, snake man!" she said before I could finish my question, and then she was gone through the door.

I stood in the middle of the hall by myself, feeling a little silly.

An audience member with the head of a sea kraken ghosted by, nodding to me as he passed. I nodded back, tempted to talk to him, but before I could think what to say, he was out the door too.

I looked up at the queen on her throne, sitting alone in her silence. On impulse, I walked straight towards her, climbing the steps of the dais to her throne. Her chin hung down, draping her veil against her chest, and she did not stir at my approach. Her chalice sat half-emptied at her feet.

I crouched down, keeping an eye on her as I lifted the cup. I took a quick sip, letting the fluid linger on my tongue. It was sweet and metallic, but even that small taste was invigorating. After a surreptitious glance around the room, I tipped my head back, opened my mouth wide, and tilted the rest of the drink down my throat. Energy surged through my body.

I set the cup down and stood up. I felt incredible, as if I might do anything.

Fingers latched around my wrist.

The queen stared up at me through her parted veil, ice blue eyes rimming with tears, despair on her beautiful, youthful face.

"You have finally come for me," she said.

Panic lumped in my throat. I could not speak.

"I dreamed I went to Manderley last night," she said. "Sweet, secret Manderley, with its gold light and dark passages. But as I approached its edge, where the city meets the shore of the island, I found that the way was barred. I could not pass. I threw my hands up in despair, and cried out. Then my spirit lifted, my body hollowing out. The barrier became like a gossamer web, and I pushed through, tearing it down with my hands and arms and eyes.

"Oh sweet Manderley, I thought, your golden glow is mine now. I flew ahead, skimming above the pools of light. But as I passed, the lights went out. One by one, guttering, blinking off. Darkness followed in my wake. Ashes blew towards us with the salt wind from the sea, and I knew then, with certainty beyond doubt, that none of us could ever go to Manderley again. For you see, the city sinks into the sea."

I tasted salt air and the smell of burning wood.

"He is never coming back," she whispered. "His hunger corrupted him, and we are trapped here, forever, playing out his damnable rituals. Our worship sustains him, out there beyond the lightless horizon. If anyone knew the truth, they would take my flesh as vengeance."

I tried to pull away, but her grip tightened like a vise.

"No!" her sonorous voice cracked. "Don't leave me here alone. I am not sure how much longer I can keep the ruse. Please. You must take me with you."

———

I don't even know where I am, I thought to myself. How could I take her anywhere?

"You do not need to know where you are!" she hissed. "His strictures prevent me from leaving alone, but with you at my side, we may be able to cross over. I can show you the way."

"You can hear my thoughts?" I said.

"You drank of his promises, heliot. You are bound now to this plane."

I thought of Saiara's parting words, urging me to trust my intuition. I nodded. "Then I will help you," I said.

She stood up, sliding her hand down from my wrist and lacing her fingers with mine. With her other hand, she reached up and lifted off her crown. She dropped it to the floor. One of its gemstones chipped on the stone, scattering flakes of amethyst at our feet.

"Thank you," she said, confidence returning to her voice. "We must move swiftly. The supplicants are bloated with feasting, and your fellow heliots walk amongst us, taking their silent tithe. This will be our best chance. Come with me."

She led me through the empty hall, passing between the tables riddled with carcasses and half-eaten victuals. I glanced up at the tapestry. The falling angel with flaming wings seemed to look right at me.

"That's him, isn't it? Carus."

"Do not speak his name," she hissed. "We cannot afford to draw his attention."

"I'm sorry. I... I didn't know."

She sighed. "He was beautiful then, even at the fall. Now he haunts the in-between, imprisoning us with his hungers. Even if I could make him whole again, I'm not sure it would be enough. Our world is beyond salvation."

"It looked lovely once," I said, gesturing towards the leftmost tapestry of peace.

"That was many lifetimes ago, heliot. Before we made your kind."

We reached an entrance I had not noticed, a small, solid wooden door tucked in a dark corner of the hall. She whispered something unintelligible, and the door swung open. She peered out, glancing in both directions. "Come," she said.

We stepped into a vast, narrow hallway. The throne room we just came from, for all its fraying age, was still vibrant and beautiful, but this hallway was a sterile, lifeless place. It stretched away so far in both directions that the walls and ceiling converged into a single point. To our left, that point was a bright spot of light. To our right, it melded into shadow.

We started walking right, towards the point of shadow. The walls on either side of us were flat and smooth. I looked up at the ceiling. Or maybe it was the sky. It was a uniform slate grey that might have been cloud cover or seamless, molded plating.

"Where are you taking me?" Something about the cold symmetry of the hallway instinctively made me whisper.

She sliced her hand through the air, shushing me.

She led me onwards, but as time passed, we did not seem to be making any progress. No matter how long we walked for, every-thing looked the same. It was as if we were on a conveyor tread moving in the opposite direction at just the right pace to keep us trapped in place, negating every forward step we took.

The queen did not seem to notice. She was gazing at the floor as we walked, her lips moving in soundless repetition, some silent prayer or invocation. My mind fell into a stupor, which is probably why it took my brain so long to process the fact that something was moving towards us.

I tapped the queen on the shoulder, breaking her concentra-tion. She looked up at me in irritation. I pointed at the smudge ahead of us. It was fuzzy and indistinct, but it was definitely coming closer. Fear came over her face.

Without saying a word, she grabbed my hand again, and whipped us around in the other direction. We started running. I looked behind us. The smudge was getting bigger.

She stopped short, almost tumbling me over. Another door appeared, coalescing in front of us. "We will have to take a different way," she whispered. "Hold on to my hand. These doors are mine alone. You will be trapped here if you let go."

I gripped her hand tight. She led me through the door.

We entered an opulent bedroom. Purple and black silk curtains hung from a burgundy wood bed frame. The mattress was piled with cushions in hues of violet, midnight, and silver. There was a bulge beneath the blankets that might have been a human form.

On the other side of the room, a man stood naked, facing a tall brass mirror. His back and chest were covered with scars. He touched a scar on his belly, a puckered slash of pink. A pack of three heliots with the heads of hyenas stood behind him, watching and grinning. The man lifted his hand from the scar on his belly and reached to a coat stand next to the mirror. He grabbed a long jacket off the stand and, still facing the mirror, held it out at arms' length.

The heliots looked at each other, panting, tongues lolling. The man waved the jacket in the air, impatient. One of the hyenas took it from him. The man lifted both arms, and the hyena placed the coat over his shoulders, fitting his arms into the jacket sleeves, covering his naked body.

"What are-?" I started to ask.

"We do not have time to gape, heliot," she said, cutting me off. She led me through the room. The hyenas turned to watch us, sniffing the air. The man stayed facing the mirror as he brushed the dust from his jacket, but his eyes tracked our movement. The blankets and cushions on the bed stirred, and a naked heliot with heavy breasts and the head of a mantis sat up. Her mandibles clacked as we passed.

As we approached the far door, the hyena who had covered the man with the jacket stepped in front of us. His jaws opened into a wicked grin, saliva dribbling from his black gums and sharp fangs.

The queen lifted her hand and moved it left in a sharp gesture. The hyena jerked sideways as if pulled by an invisible cord, tumbling into the other two dogmen. They yipped and barked, but she glared at them and they kept back.

The door whooshed open. A large room with a plush, patterned carpet lay before us. Sofas wrapped with oiled animal hides the color of walnut were scattered around the room. Shelves of books covered all four walls, and a wheeled ladder on each side provided access to the higher stacks.

I glanced back into the bedroom. The man in the long jacket was climbing into bed with the mantis, leaning close to her.

Her mandibles opened wide.

The door swung shut.

"Autarchess," a voice said.

The voice made me start. I turned around to find another man standing in front of us, his head bowed low, obscuring his face. Then he lifted his head. It was Dunsemai!

He looked older. Much older. But it was definitely him. Given his apparent age, he was no doubt one of the eldest among these strange people, older than anyone else I had seen since the youthful infusion of the feast.

"Alecksindé," the queen, tipping her head to him. "We need your help."

"Anything, your majesty." He glanced at me, eyes curious.

"The Dimensional."

Shock wavered on his face. "The Dimensional has been forbidden since-"

"Alecksindé," she said, "do not presume to quote the strictures to me."

He composed himself. "Of course not, autarchess. But why have you come to my humble library? Why not take the arbor path?"

"The way..." She narrowed her eyes. "Has been barred."

He nodded. "Ah," he said, demanding no further explanation. "Follow me then, my queen."

He led us between the chairs and reading tables to the ladder at the western stacks. He grabbed the ladder and rolled it to the northwest corner. Then he scurried up, nimble as a sindacat. When he reached the top shelf, he pointed his index finger and ran it along the book spines.

"Here it is!" he said, stopping his scan. He extracted a book from the shelf. Tucking it under his arm, he gripped the edges of the ladder with his hands and feet and slid down, crouching as he landed.

"This library is an extension of my essence, heliot," he said to me, intuiting my surprise. "Here, in these archives, I move as no other can."

He held the book out to the queen. The title was embossed in gold on the textured green binding, but the writing was inscrutable to me.

"Do you know the passage?" the queen asked him.

"Of course," he said primly. "I would be a poor archivist indeed if I did not."

"Read it."

He flipped the book open, wet his thumb with his tongue, and rifled through the pages. "Ah. Here we are." He stood a little straighter. "*Arro fly. Archa wat. Carus ends. Hrong secap. Nobles cru. Soth ahcends. Arro fords te Carus gan.*"

He looked up from the book. "Goodbye, my queen."

Then he looked at me and winked.

The room dissolved.

We were suspended in the void of space. A sphere of impenetrable darkness floated an immeasurable distance from us, blotting out the stars. Bands of light encircled the sphere, flowing in magisterial procession around its surface.

"It's so beautiful," I said.

Looking at the sphere was like trying to imagine the universe before there was a universe, before the first unfolding sent the arrow of entropy speeding on its way, energy expanding and cooling into matter; the infinite, unknowable moment before time began.

"Arculacthlon Goza. The Unlit Gate. For eons, we traveled between the galaxies, but when we found Arculacthlon, that journey ended. We have orbited at the horizon of its influence for uncountable eons."

"A black hole," I whispered.

"The largest of its kind in the known universe."

"How did we get here?"

"Words have power, heliot. Those words you heard were

ancient, read from The Ilyon by our eldest scholar. He opened a path that no one else could."

She drifted away from me. "Here," she said. A small door not much higher than her waist appeared in the void in front of her. "This is it."

"It's too small," I said, looking at the tiny door. "I won't fit."

She smiled. She touched the door. It opened. Inside was darkness. "Take my hand. Quickly now." She ducked her head and passed through, pulling me after her. The entrance enlarged to accommodate me. Or I shrank to fit inside. Once we were through, the door sealed shut, blanketing us in darkness.

"*Uminare*," the queen whispered.

Soft light filled the space.

The light slowly brightened. We were in a room of mirrors. It was an octagon, eight sides reflecting each other. The ceiling and floor were mirrored too, making the room depthless and vertiginous. As soon as I stood, wooziness crept up on me. I stumbled forward. The queen grabbed me and pulled me back. I leaned on her, steadying myself.

"Do not step into the middle until I tell you," she whispered. "You may never find the way back to your true self."

"What is this place?" I closed my eyes, bringing my hand to my forehead.

"This is where he made the crossing."

"Ca-?"

"Shhhh," she said, putting a finger to my snout. "Remember. Never say his name. Do not even think it. He is close now. Very close."

"I'm sorry."

"What is your name, heliot?"

"Oren. Oren Siris."

"Oren Siris. A noble name. We have feared your kind for too long, I think. But every father fears his child the moment his child surpasses him."

"What happened between us? The heliots and your people, I mean."

"It was a long time ago now. A very long time indeed. We thought we could improve humanity. We were right. We could, and we did. But we were fools to try and control that which we created. We thought that playing the game of gods made us gods in truth. We were wrong.

"But that time is past now, Orenheliot. I have no wish to dwell in it. I want nothing more than to leave all of this behind."

"What happens now?"

"When you step into the heart of the Dimensional, every possible version of you arrives in this space. Every choice you have ever made converges here. From that maelstrom, you must pluck out the one choice that opens the doorway. To do that, you must face all of your choices at once."

"That sounds... awful."

"It is. The most terrible knowing you can have is knowing what might have been. That is why it is forbidden for our kind. But it can be the most beautiful too, Orenheliot. And you are not of our kind." She took my hand and led me towards the center of the Dimensional.

Something flickered in one of the mirrors, too fast for me to identify.

"Did you see that?" I said.

She halted. "See what, Orenheliot?"

"I... I'm not sure."

"We are almost at the center. Perhaps you caught a glimpse."

"A glimpse?"

"Another version of yourself."

"What is going to happen to me?"

"There is no more time for questions, Orenheliot. You promised to help me. Now is the time to act. Step into the center."

"I'm afraid," I whispered.

"As you should be." She shoved me forward.

I stumbled and fell. I floated up. I hung frozen in place. My snakehead was gone. My own reflection doubled back at me, running off to infinity in every direction.

But each version of myself was a somehow unique; the cut of my hair; the color of my shirt; the look of sadness on my face. Some were wildly divergent; in one, a scar ran through my right eye, leaving the iris milky white; in another, my body was withered and emaciated, covered with open sores; in still another, I stood surrounded by thousands of people, all of them reaching out to grasp at me.

"What do I do now?" I said, and my voice was as loud as thunderclap, vibrating back to me, rattling my bones.

"Now," the queen whispered, "you must choose."

Saiara stood next to me, smiling, holding a child in her arms.

My mother wept as we scattered my father's ashes in the deepest mine of Verygone.

Thaun Zol yelped with joy as I steered *Tradewinds* through an asteroid belt.

A man with wings of fire and a sword of light held out his hand to me.

The visions sped up, oscillating through all the lives that might have been, a collage of tragedy, beauty, and mundanity all blurring together.

"How are you doing this?" I whispered, and my voice was as quiet as the first leaf of autumn falling to the grass.

"I am not doing anything," she said. "You are. These are all choices you might have made. Or, perhaps someday, still will."

Suddenly, I understood.

I reached into the blur of possibilities and took the winged man's hand.

He smiled and stepped out of the mirror.

The queen was weeping. "Oh, my Carus," she cried. "Is it truly you?"

The light on his sword flickered out. He dropped it to the

mirrored floor, a cold hunk of steel, clattering against the glass. "Thank you, my child," he said to me. He kissed his fingers and touched the center of my forehead.

Then he turned to his queen. "My dearest Stera," he said, kneeling down beside her. "My hubris poisoned everything we cherished, but I see through it now. This, all of this, is a prison of our own making. Come. Let me show you." He took her hands and helped her stand. "We need not be afraid anymore."

His wings flared with incandescent heat, and together, king and queen perished into ash and dust.

———————————

Muffled talking and laughing reverberated in the darkness. Someone nearby was breathing heavily. Then a roar of sound drowned out the other noises.

Something tugged at my head, and the roar turned into the sound of applause as light came rushing in. I blinked rapidly, trying to adjust my eyes. I looked to my right and found Saiara smiling back at me, holding my mask in her hands.

"That was incredible," she shouted above the crowd.

All around us, people were clapping and cheering. Some of them still wore their animal masks, but most had removed them. Attendants moved through the audience holding out upturned masks, gathering donations from the adoring participants.

Up on stage, I recognized all of the people from the feast that Saiara and I had witnessed, and many others besides. Standing in the center, next to Dunsemai, were the queen and her king, Autarch Carus, wingless now, and decidedly unburnt. They were all three smiling as they held hands and bowed to the crowd.

"I've never experienced anything like it," I shouted back, dropping the copper ingots Dunsemai had stolen from Lurkur U'atsa into the throat of a boar's head mask.

Later, after the cheering had died down and most of the audience had departed, Saiara and I lingered near the stage.

"Do you think they can recognize us even though we wore the animal masks?" she asked.

"I actually wonder if anonymity might be part of the point. The freedom to choose any path without fear of being judged for it."

"Hmmm. The masks are a sort of permission. A chance to let down inhibitions."

I nodded. "Without those masks, we'd be forced to wear the masks the world demands. To play the roles expected of us when others are watching."

A woman laughed nearby. "Masks within masks. A perceptive observation, Orenheliot."

She wore a simple robe now, as she stepped out from behind the stage curtain, and her makeup was gone, but that did not dim her beauty.

"My queen," I said, touching my hand to my chin and tipping my head in salute. "It can't be that perceptive if you recognize me here, without my serpent's head."

"She stood at your side in the Dimensional, sire Siris."

"Dunsemai!" I cried as he stepped out from behind the curtain.

He gave us an ostentatious bow, then leapt down from the stage, landing in a graceful crouch. He stood and raised his hand up to the queen. She took it, leaning on him as she stepped down from the stage to stand besides us. She still wore the amulet around her neck. It glowed a soothing blue, like the sky at twilight.

"Eyel is a true artist," she said, nodding towards Dunsemai, "and the Dimensional is one of his finest creations. It is the one place in the realm of Arculacthlon where all the masks are stripped away."

"It was an incredibly powerful experience. I am sorry for my choice, though."

"Whatever for?"

"You and Carus... well, you died."

She laughed again. "Few visitors to the realm of the Unlit Gate ever find their way to the Dimensional, and fewer still manage to set Autarchess Stera Davi and her liege Carus free."

"She's right," Dunsemai said. "You were both magnificent. Each show is only as good as its participants, and too many citizens of this fine city have been jaded by the privileges afforded the wealthy central worlds. The moment I spotted you two at the fountain, I knew you would appreciate this opportunity."

"Wait," Saiara said. "All those things you told us, about being a baron and pauper. Were they true?"

"Ah," he said, chuckling. "There were days once, long ago, when such truths mattered to me. But the certainty of youth is a precious, fragile thing, and best you don't trouble yourself with it. You'll see."

"That's not much of answer."

"I'm afraid not, lady Yta." Mischief crinkled his eyes. "Now then, if you'll pardon me, I must bid you both farewell. Tulburn Hall never sleeps, which is why it needs the great Baron Eyel Dunsemai to help it dream!" He raised his hand in the air with a flourish. "Are you coming, Cassiopeia?"

"Not tonight, Eyel."

"Very well. Good night young travelers, and may the light of our fair suns always illumine your journey." With that, he bounded up the steps of the amphitheater and disappeared into the night.

"I must depart as well, Orenheliot," said Cassiopeia after he was gone. She stood on her toes and kissed me on the cheek. "You did wonderfully, tonight," she whispered. Then she tilted back to the flats of her feet, graceful as a dancer, and unclipped the necklace from behind her neck. She dangled the amulet towards me, and its cool blue color slowly faded to clear as it hung in the air.

"I want you to have this," Cassiopeia said.

"I cannot-"

"I insist," she said. "It is my gift to you. You've earned it."

Before I could say otherwise, she took my hand and placed the amulet in it. It began to glow again, this time with a deep, bright purple, the color of orchids in bloom.

"How does it do that?" I asked.

"It is an aurastal. Another of Dunsemai's creations. Its color reflects the state of whomever bears it. I do not know its inner workings, but I have found it to be a true and faithful mirror to my spirit."

"What does this color mean?" I said, holding up the purple amulet.

"That the one you love most is near." She looked at Saiara, who was watching us both with an incredulous expression. Cassiopeia smiled at her. "Keep this one close," she said to her, patting my arm.

I blushed.

"Now, if you'll both excuse me," she said, bowing low. "It's time I headed home. These performances do so drain my energy."

She turned and walked away.

"Wait!" Saiara called.

The actress stopped and looked back over her shoulder.

"Dunsemai. Who is he, really? Why did he choose us for this?"

"Who knows what makes beat the heart of Tulburn Hall?" she said. "Only the heart himself can answer that." She raised her hand in the air. "Farewell, young ones, and do come back again!"

"The heart?" I said, eyebrows raised in surprise.

"Do you think...?" she replied, her eyes wide.

"I saw him. In the simulation. He played the role of the eldest scholar of the people of Arculacthlon. He had access to their most ancient knowledge."

"That would be fine role for a heart to play, I think," she said.

We both stood in silence as night crept on, pondering Dunsemai's true nature.

"Whoever he is, I'm glad, at least, to know we did well." I let the aurastal drop from my hand, dangling by its chain. It shone vibrant purple as I held it before my eyes, thinking on all that we'd just seen and done.

"Oh, Orenheliot," Saiara said in a breathy parody of Cassiopeia, leaning into me, stroking my arm like a fawning lover. "You did so wonderfully! Please take this gift. Oh, but you must. I do so insist!"

I blushed again. "Well, you told me to follow my intuition!"

She smirked.

We both started laughing.

"Take me home, Orenheliot," she said, hooking her arm through mine. "You're going to have to tell me everything."

A WEEK after our mind-bending experience in Tulburn Hall, we joined thousands of others eager recruits for the academy's qualifying orientation. On Forsara, in the womb of its ancient beauty, surrounded by so many peoples from across the galaxy, becoming a cadet in the Academy of the Fellowship felt like the pinnacle I had been climbing towards ever since I was a child. I was wet clay, ready for molding, dreaming of the day when I would be invited to take the oath of the covenant and become a fellow.

Excitement and nervous energy filled the auditorium. There were countless rumors surrounding the qualifiers, but none of us knew for sure what we would face today. A man stepped up to the rostrum at the heart of the open-air auditorium. A heavy chain of circular, metallic rings hanging from his neck glinted in the evening sunlight. He stood, staring out at the assembled crowd, waiting, saying nothing. As more and more of us noticed his presence, the idle chatter fell silent, like a blanket falling over the gathering.

When it was quiet enough for me to hear the breathing of those seated around me, the man nodded. "I am Calder Kol," he said. "The academy's pausha. Welcome. You all know why you are here, but you do not yet know for what. You will find out soon enough.

"During the qualifiers today, each of you will face a challenge designed to test your character, your creativity, and your resilience. The path ahead will be perilous. If you succeed, you will gain admittance to the academy. If you do not, it merely means you have a different path to walk. Do not despair at that. Each of you has demonstrated great potential. You come to us with the accolades of paushas and dalas from across the Fellowship, and it may even be that your path leads back to the academy at some point in the future. Know that, whatever comes next, your service to the galaxy has not gone unnoticed.

"For those of you who pledge the academy, you will no longer be just a citizen of the galaxy. You must prepare to become one of its humble stewards. You will learn what we have to teach you, and when you are ready, you will take the covenant. Then you will go where you are needed most.

"This lineage of service stretches all the way back to the Scions of Eledar, the first peoples of Forsara who opened our way to the stars. Alone, each one of us is a mere spark of awareness in the vast darkness. Together we are the greatest star ever formed, burning eternal, spreading light to the furthest reaches, bringing hope to all humankind."

With that, he lifted his hands, palms up, towards the silver-purple sky. We all stood, raising our chest and eyes, lifting our voices as one to sing the wordless universal, the long tone that transcends all languages and serves as a symbol of our shared light. The sound was incredible, so many voices from all over the universe, ringing together; like nothing I'd ever heard before.

When the moment passed, a great silence descended over the auditorium. I looked back down to the rostrum. Pausha Calder Kol was gone, and a small, orderly group of people was filing out into the center of the assembly, spreading out through the crowd. Each one of them wore a bronze pendant above their white robes, two rings interlocking, clasped above their hearts; the sigil of the

Fellowship, worn in a way that marked them as our drumons. Our teachers.

I couldn't hear what they were saying, but I could see that they were assigning people to groups. Eventually, one approached me. He had a kind face. Warm, brown eyes and caramel skin, weathered with age. His hair was cropped close to his head, graying at the temples.

An orb the size of my fist floated in the air near his head. It looked like the disembodied eyeball of a large humanoid robot, with a lens embedded on the surface of the sphere. I glanced at it. The lens made a quiet whirring sound, and the blue light in its center dilated.

The drumon touched my arm. "Greetings, Oren," he said. "I am Vizia. This," he pointed to the orb, "is Randall. You will be part of our cohort. Please join cluster seven." He pointed towards a group of three other recruits standing towards the front. I nodded to Vizia, then made my way over to the group.

When I saw her face, my heart leapt.

Saiara.

We smiled at each other, and she lowered her head in a small, simple bow. I returned the gesture, resisting the urge to kiss her, here in front of everyone.

"Ensign Siris," a familiar voice said.

I turned. Qurth Foli stood next to me. "It seems we have been brought together again," he said. "A great fortune."

"Qurth! Eledar's breath, my friend." I grasped him by the shoulders, pulling him towards me for a big hug. He stiffened in my arms, and I remembered that the people of Arborea were uncomfortable with public displays of affection.

"Sorry, Qurth," I said, letting him go. "I forgot myself. It's wonderful to see you."

He gave me an awkward pat on the arm. "I, too, am most excited see you, ensign Siris. To be here with you both brings me much joy."

"You all know each other?"

Qurth turned to our fourth member. "Yes, ensign Doba," he said. "The three of us served together on the voyager Transcendence."

The young man was thin, and his thick, scraggy tuft of dark hair and matching, bushy eyebrows made him look even thinner. "Transcendence," he said. "That's Darpausha's command, right? She's a legend."

"We're lucky to have served with her," I said. I held out my hand towards him. "Oren Siris. From the moon of Verygone."

He took my hand, and we touched fingers to wrist in the universal greeting. "Rowsemn Doba," he said. "I'm from Cobalt Un Yor. Pleasure to meet you."

"Come on then," Viziadrumon said, his voice echoing around us. "Stop dawdling. It's simple, really."

Vizia was not quite as kind as his face had first led me to believe. Before our qualifier began, other recruits in our larger cohort told us he was notorious for pushing students hard. In time, I would come to learn that few teachers could walk the line he did with such skill, driving you forward, pushing you past your limits, making you laugh the whole way. He was, in fact, one of the most beloved instructors in the academy. But at this particular moment, all we knew was that his judgment could make or break our chances at becoming cadets.

He watched the four of us from his vantage point high above the simulated planet of Ourthian. At close orbit, the actual planet was located only twelve hundred and seven galactic minutes from Forsara. That proximity made it a convenient training ground. It had been so thoroughly studied and mapped that the simulated version was terribly accurate. Just as good as the real thing. Better, even.

Because here, on the simulated Ourthian, Vizia could play god. The planet teetered right on the edge of that subtle line that spelled death for carbon-based life, and before we began, he told us he had developed twenty-nine different simulations based on its climate and geography. Each one was designed to make cadets intimately familiar with their own limitations, he said, and he was excited to share this one with us. On Forsara, the light of Appollion was cool and silver, but on Ourthian, it was piercing and hot. It was not impossible to survive on the planet, but it was a rugged, unforgiving place, and it never offered up its meager sustenance without extracting some blood tax in return.

For this particular exercise, the four of us had been tasked with solving a puzzle: we had crash-landed inside of a canyon almost one hundred farfalls below sea level, and our oxygen was running out. We had to figure out how to convert the noxious ethanol and nitrates of the atmosphere into breathable air.

If we managed that task, we then had to climb out from the canyon and make the crossing, on foot, from our downed recon dart to the research station on the southern shore of the nitrogen ocean. Our shipheart had been incapacitated in the simulated crash, and we were left to the mercy of our own meager intelligence and resources.

It was not simple. Really.

"The answer is there," Vizia's voice echoed again. "You're running out of air."

"He's enjoying this far too much," I said.

Rowsemn nodded. "The whole exercise would be much more authentic if we didn't have him shouting down to us from above, like some sassy Ourthian deity."

Saiara snorted with laughter, but then she brought our focus back. "Gentlemen," she said. "This simulation is as close to the real thing as it gets. We won't actually die, of course, but we will get to feel our lungs wither if we don't solve this problem. So please stop griping and help me."

"Ensign Yta is correct," Qurth said. "Time is not ours to waste."

"Oren," Saiara said. "When you were on the Arcturean moon, with Cere's team, you breathed the air, right?"

I nodded, unsure of where she was headed with this.

"And yet here you are," she said.

"You're right! It did not kill me. Are you-"

"That's right. Maybe you can climb out of this pit."

"Up to higher ground," Qurth said, picking up the idea. "Where the air is not quite so fatally toxic."

"And then what?" Rowsemn said. "If you made it, you might be alive, but we would still be down here, minus one tank of oxygen, that much closer to failure."

"I could make the crossing to the research station and bring back help. You know how strong I am. In this lighter gravity, the passage would be even faster."

"But if you fail, it will be catastrophic and complete."

"Not if we three solve the puzzle of the air while ensign Siris is up above," said Qurth.

"Okay. So, now we can breathe. But Oren is up there, probably lost in a dust storm, with one tank of oxygen. We'll have to go and rescue his sorrowful ass instead."

"The longer we debate, the less time we have," I said, looking to Saiara.

We sat in silence now, conserving our air, waiting for her to weigh in. Finally, she nodded. "I hear you, Rowsemn," she said. "If we all stay here, sure, we have more oxygen, but if the extra time is *still* not enough to develop a breathing solution then we are definitively trapped. With Oren on advance, it gives us more options, at least. And, like he said, even if his oxygen runs out, maybe he can handle the air, at least for a short time."

"And you really think we can figure out our breathing problem with the time we'll have left?"

"I have an idea," she said. "It will take all three of us working in unison, and even then, I am not sure." She pointed at me. "He's our contingency plan."

Rowsemn shook his head doubtfully, but he knew that he had been overruled. He gave up the debate, and he and Qurth got to work helping me into my exoskin. It would let me move quickly, even in the noxious atmosphere. But I gained speed and mobility at the sacrifice of capacity. The suit could only handle one tank of oxygen. Without the shipheart to modify the conversion filter, my air would not last long. Then I would be at the mercy of the atmosphere. A gamble. A big one.

"He's ready," Rowsemn said, rapping his knuckles on the back of my helmet. A hollow thump resounded in my ears.

"Good," Saiara said, "we can't waste any more time." Her voice was distant and muffled. She looked at me. "Go, Oren."

I nodded and climbed into the airlock. Rowsemn sealed the doors. The air from the simulated alien world came rushing in.

I stood on the shores of the Ourthian ocean, looking out across the vast brown and green swirl of liquid, cresting and falling in strange, pointed waves. I wondered if the liquid nitrogen really flowed like that, or if my mind was playing more tricks. During my journey, as my oxygen slowly ran down, I'd discovered that the air of Ourthia had mild psychoactive qualities. I saw the sky melt into the soil, watched great figures move at the edge of my vision, and felt the ground stretched away from me, making every step a leap of faith. But I'd kept going, and my lungs had not failed me. Even though I was dizzy and disoriented, it emboldened me to know that I had not reached my limit yet.

I turned and started towards the research station, stumbling a little. I instinctively stretched out my arms to help me balance and managed to keep my footing. I looked up and saw something coming towards me from the direction of the station. A shimmering figure. I squinted and waved my hands, trying to disperse the mirage, but it continued to flicker, just beyond my reach.

Then, suddenly, the image resolved. It was not one figure, but two. Viziadrumon, with his familiar, Randall, scurrying along at his side.

They were next to me. "That was a foolish risk," Vizia said, hooking his arm under my shoulder to help me from falling.

"I know," I said leaning on him. "But they will be here soon, won't they?"

Randall chuckled, his small green head bobbing up and down. He was essentially a shipheart without a ship. A mobile intelligence that could interface with just about every system on Forsara. Right now, he was managing all of the parameters of the simulation, based on Vizia's requests and specifications. Inside of the simulation, he appeared as this small humanoid with scaly, green skin.

"What are you laughing at?" I said, grimacing at him.

Randall looked up at me with his bright, golden eyes. His large, pointed ears wobbled on the side of his head. He didn't say anything. He just grinned at me.

I was going demand an answer, but as I took in air to speak, it made me cough instead. I covered my mouth with one hand, holding up an index finger with the other.

Vizia patted me on the back. "You're never going to win a jousting match with Randall, Oren, so don't waste your breath." He turned away from me. "Ah, look," he pointed towards the horizon, "here they are now."

I followed his gesture with my eyes and saw three more figures, hazy with distance in the thick air. As they got closer, I could see that they weren't wearing helmets. They walked strong, striding forward with purpose. They were breathing filtered air from this miserable planet!

I laughed with pleasure and wonder at the sight, but it turned into another ragged cough, even worse than the last. I doubled over, holding my chest. My whole body felt as if it was being lanced with tiny needles. My chest was burning, and a sickening wheeze came with every breath.

Randall came over to me and rubbed my lower back. He chuckled again, then said, "None too bad. Yes yes. None too bad at all. Stand up now. Here they come."

Even though Randall was small, he was running the simulation. He set the rules, but he didn't have to live by them. Things like weight and size were a non-issue. He slid his small, muscular arms under my armpits and hefted, and with his help, I stood.

"I knew you'd make it," I said as they approached, leaning a hand on Randall's head, trying to act casual. But my voice was throaty and weak, and I must have started to fall again, because the next thing I knew, Rowsemn was at my side, holding me up.

Saiara reached up to my nose, touching her fingers to my nostrils. An instant later, I felt pure, clean air flowing into my body.

"Open your mouth," she said.

I obliged, and she placed a small disc on my tongue, round and smooth and smaller than her palm. It dissolved in my mouth. My dizziness started to fade. I stood up straight, staring at her, impressed.

There was the hint of a smile on her lips, but she maintained her modest professionalism. "Nanoparticle filters," she said. "They've expanded to fill the cavities of your nose and throat." Her tone was matter of fact, as if what she had accomplished was a simple feat.

I filled my lungs again and let out a great, booming bellow of joy.

We had done it.

We all turned to Viziadrumon, smiling, expectant.

He tilted his head slightly, looking back at us. "Your approach was somewhat unorthodox," he said.

"Yes yes," Randall said. "Different thinking. Right results though."

Vizia smiled and nodded. "Welcome to the academy, cadets."

Then he and Randall were gone, and we were awake, each of us sitting in one of the countless field basins at the Academy, back on Forsara.

HISTORY BECAME a core aspect of our training right from the beginning, gleaning lessons from lives past. The sprawling academy was embedded into the Lantis mountain range, campus buildings forming the giant steps we saw when we first arrived to Manderley in Darpausha's orbital hopper.

The archives were buried beneath Mount Sebedas, the highest peak in the range. The Library of Sebedas. A massive data center, always buzzing with activity, but lit in warm yellows and ambers, with soothing ambient tones piped in through the overcom. A perfect space for introspection, reflection, and study.

Gauldrumon, the library steward, was a genial fellow, but he was also fastidious. New students made him nervous. "Sebedas," he intoned when we first met. "A scion of Eledar. He understood that we are nothing without our past. These archives would not exist without his vision, and we have sacrificed much to sustain that vision over the millennia. We stand here on the shoulders of the greatest minds who came before us."

He leaned close to me as he said this, scrutinizing me with his sharp, dark eyes, wrinkled at the edges with the weight of years spent poring over the old histories. "Which brings me to my first and most important question. Do you like to read?"

He asked the question with such seriousness that I almost laughed. But I knew this library was his life. "I come to these hallowed halls with the greatest respect, drumon Gaul," I said. "I spent the bulk of my childhood ensconced in our archives."

"You had no brothers or sisters to play with? Or peers?"

"No. It was just me and my parents. A lot of the other kids... I was too strange for them. I was happiest whenever I found old stories to read. I always liked the stories the best."

He nodded, curt and precise, and said, "I think I have just the lesson for you." He turned, walking away from me, gesturing for me to follow. As we traversed the amber corridors, I imagined that I was wandering the pathways of his mind, an ancient labyrinth of forgotten knowledge and old legends, waiting for a witness.

We came to a crystal case. Inside of it was a thick sheaf of papers, bound together with a leather cord. Cryptic markings covered the paper.

"Is that... a book?" I asked with quiet awe.

"A very old book," Gaul said, "and a very special one."

I'd never seen a real book before. The moment felt almost sacred.

"Ancient printed texts like these," he told me, "are preserved in a nanite solution. The machines consume and expunge all oxygen, preserving the book while simultaneously projecting a precise digital recreation of its contents into the field."

He let me linger on the open pages for a moment, staring at the ancient language. Then he led me to a nearby field basin. The cocoon was just big enough for my massive frame. I grunted as I adjusted into the seat. He stood outside, waiting as I climbed in, patient and impassive.

Finally, I settled. He peered in at me. "How many hard decisions have been made, do you think, in the name of survival?" he asked. "In the name of progress?"

"I don't know, drumon."

"Of course you don't. No one does. Our ancestors have sacrificed more than any of us can ever know. It's easy to look backwards through the lens of this imperfect knowing and think we could have done better.

"But these gifts of knowledge have been given to us at great cost, and the only way we can truly build on what came before us is to learn from it. People speak of the gift of farsight as if it is something mystical, but the truth is that farsight is the fruit of clear hindsight.

"You must square yourself with stories like these, Oren. They are a part of our legacy. We forget them at our own peril."

"I understand, drumon," I said.

"No, young man. No you do not." He shook his head. "Not yet."

He stepped away and the door to the field basin slid shut.

Sitting back in the enclosed field chamber, I could plug in and absorb knowledge, the translated information passing into me like liquid through a sieve. The book was called *Shugguth's Curse*, written in an ancient dialect native to the rugged highlands of Rosemel. Found in the tombs of a long-abandoned cloister on an isolated island in the fjords of Rist, it had been preserved in a stone coffer that also held the mummified remains of the woman who was presumed to be the spiritual leader of that forgotten religious community. We knew nothing else of the monastic order that built their secluded cloister on that fog-shrouded isle, except that the woman had been dead for almost a thousand years, and based on molecular signatures, the book was equally ancient.

But the histories it told were even older. More than twelve millennia old, which meant that the order had deep roots, and its monks had been devoted enough to protect the contents of the book across countless generations. They must have written fresh copies out by hand as the preceding versions faded and crumbled. The original pages were lost to time, but the monks gave their lives to ensure that the wisdom inside was not.

The book told of the second dark age of Forsara, when Shugguth immolated Gye, the Forsaran moon. Shugguth was not a red star then. It was bigger and bright orange. Then it swelled, belching out solar flares of unprecedented ferocity. The fires of Shugguth sintered the once-fertile moon of Gye, searing away its atmosphere, its mineral-dense mantle liquefying in the heat, then congealing in the cold vacuum left behind. The moon is called Cinis now. It still circles Forsara, barren and sterile, an iron cold reminder of the power of the stars.

Forsara itself fared better, but the flares still ravaged life on the already warming planet, causing massive amounts of disturbance and destruction on the planetary surface. Famine spread, scattering people to the highlands, away from the scorching equatorial heat. Many lives were lost, and even the mightiest cities were abandoned. Those who were left retreated deep beneath the mountains to escape the radiation and weather the catastrophe. Shugguth's anger had stunted civilization, wiping out the early efforts of a world in the midst of unlocking the powers of the atom.

In time, the sun's ferocity dwindled, the flares cooling and shrinking. The great tectonic shifts that had been amplified by the sun's aggression evened themselves out. As the impact of the flares receded and the planet stabilized, people began again, returning to the surface.

Tribes formed, ranging out across the mountains, building life on the fragments of old technology and repurposed myths, new ideas emerging from the old. For many generations, the suns were worshipped and feared, givers of light in the darkness. Life flowed back into the lands.

As I swam through this history, soaking it in, I came upon the story of a great seer who had emerged from the Nooroun desert; a desert that many people had thought was impenetrable. She spoke of the ways before the fall, now forgotten, when all people of the planet were joined as one, a unified spirit that had lived on the frontier of knowledge and method. The bones of that world could still be found crumbling in the vast desert, where the ruins of the city of Noo drowned beneath the sand.

This seer had been to the ruins. She had studied everything of the Nooroun that could still be salvaged. As evidence, she carried fragments of Nooroun magics, items that shone like silver in the darkness. And using simple parchment and coal, she had made tracings of the stonework symbols that had not yet been scoured clean by the relentless desert wind, pictures of men with wings and a woman with a third eye on her forehead. Even in ruins, she said, the cracked minarets and splintered obelisks were proof that the people of Forsara had once been capable of greatness.

Her name was Yaohanath. She was eventually murdered by the patriarchs of the greater tribes, who called her blasphemer, but not before she had amassed a powerful following. Her death only strengthened her message, accelerating the collapse of the tribal autocrats, and, ultimately, leading our ancient ancestors back to a unified path; a path that would split the atom, map the genome, and harness the power of the twin suns.

A path to the stars.

Centuries later, Eledar, who some claimed was a direct descendant of Yaohanath, followed that path and founded the Fellowship. Using the collective knowledge of humanity, he and his disciples architected a new vision for the future. The Scions of Eledar cultivated that vision to fruition. Now the Fellowship connects the links in an evolving chain of humanity stretching out across the galaxy.

"Hey, Siris," Rowsemn said as I sat down next to him.

"Doba," I replied, pinwheeling the monitor attached to my chair off to the side to make room for my long legs.

We were sitting in a lecture hall filled with over three hundred other first-years, waiting for drumon Petra to arrive. She was perpetually late, and we all knew we had time to kill. Some people were chatting in pairs or small groups. Others were hunched over their monitors. As my eyes flitted across different screens, I glimpsed an advanced angular theorem, a realstream newsfeed, an abstract of different shapes flowing and morphing together, and a seven-person video chat.

One cadet had a simglass covering her eyes. She might have been piloting an orbital satellite or merely playing a mindless puzzle game. There was no way to know. Her fingers danced and flicked as she navigated the simulation, light from the interior of the visor illuminating her cheeks and forehead.

"Did Gauldrumon show you Shugguth's Curse yet?" Rowsemn asked, nudging my elbow.

"Yes, actually," I said, bringing my attention back to him. "That was the first lesson he gave me."

Rowsemn ran his long fingers through his tangled hair. "Unreal, right? I mean, can you imagine living in a time like that? Makes me appreciate how good we have it. I actually heard that they're building a simulation that will let you play as someone who lived during the curse. I'd love to try that."

"Who's 'they'?"

"A private partnership of game designers and virtualists. I'm sure they'll make a killing on the galactic net once it's released."

"Maybe. But if they release it as recreational content, it means they'll have to pander. Figure out how to make it rewarding and fun. No one wants a game sim that's essentially an interminable litany of hardships."

"Not unless your name is Saiara Yta," he said with a laugh. "I swear, that woman loves to push the limits."

"That she does." The thought of her made me smile. "She sends her regards, by the way."

"I heard she snagged a coveted spot as one of Viziadrumon's apprentices."

"You heard right."

"I'm jealous. She always gets the best assignments. Who knew that Vizia would turn out to be so popular? I was totally intimidated by him during our qualifiers."

"Me too. But that's why he is such a great teacher. He doesn't hold back."

"Speaking of teachers." He looked towards the front of the room.

Petra came bustling in. She set down a mug of steaming liquid, splashing some on the surface of the classroom podium. One of her lapels had a dark stain, no doubt from an earlier spill. She looked up at the class with wide, charcoal eyes, like she was surprised to find us all here.

"I always thought the cliché about the daydreaming drumon was something of a myth until we met her," Row whispered to me.

"Every cliché is born from some kernel of truth... or so the cliché goes," I said.

Row gave me an ironic smile.

A moment later, Thurston came floating into the room behind Petra. People often claim that, given enough time, a person and her familiar will start to act alike. I have never seen a truer example of that than Petra and Thurston. The mobile intelligence hovered near Petra's head, and as she stood to address the class, she stepped back and bumped right into him. The orb let out a chirrup of surprise.

She made an exasperated noise and swatted at him. "Please stop crowding me, bubble brain," she said with the kind of habitual impatience so often reserved for those we hold dearest in our hearts.

Rose red blushed across Thurston's surface as repressed laughter whispered through the room.

Petra smiled, unfazed by the response to their impromptu comedy bit. As the laughter died down, Thurston gathered himself, reverting to his standard somber matte grey, almost the exact color of Petra's eyes.

I'm fairly certain she was aware of her reputation among the students. Either she cultivated her persona intentionally, or she truly didn't care. Whatever the case, she was brilliant, and her youthful face and clumsy awkwardness belied centuries of study and praxis. Her lectures were always well attended, even though she inevitably kept people waiting.

"Humble apologies for the delay," she said. "There's some fascinating work happening down in causality. Instantaneous transfer of matter as information. Still lots of kinks to work out, but well worth a visit if you get the chance."

As if a first-year cadet could just waltz down to the Causality Labs without clearance and poke around. Classic Petra. It's why students liked her so much. She never spoke down to us.

In fact, she often seemed to forget about the huge gaps in our knowledge, speaking as if we understood all of the assumptions that grounded her thinking. Every time I left one of her lectures, I had dozens of conceptual threads to follow up on.

That suited me fine. I've always preferred to keep a low profile in large groups, more comfortable studying on my own. I made a note to talk to her in person and learn more about the work happening in causality.

"Now then." Petra raised her index finger. "Shall we, Thurston?"

No response.

She turned to look at him. "Thurston?"

"Are you talking to me, madam?" Thurston had docked with the classroom's local network, and his voice came in through the speakers, polished and refined. "My apologies. I normally answer to bubble brain."

Another round of laughter ran through the class. Thurston tittered at his own cleverness, flickering emerald green.

"Fine then," Petra said, unrepentant. "Can we please begin, bubble brain?"

"But of course, madam."

Everyone's individual interface turned off.

The cadet wearing the simglass tipped the visor up onto her forehead with a mild look of irritation at the interruption. Then she realized class was about to begin, and her face softened.

Rowsemn saw me staring at her and nudged me. "Easy there, Siris," he whispered. "If Saiara saw the look on your face now, she'd eat you for lunch."

"Who's that?" I whispered back. "I've never seen her before."

She had skin like alabaster parchment, and her eyes were shaded silver.

"Second-year," Row said. "Her name's Adjet, I think. She is part of Wesdrumon's cohort. Probably just guesting the lecture today."

"How do you know who-?"

"Today," Petra said, cutting us short, "we're going to talk about our hearts. Or rather, I shall talk, and you shall listen. You'll want your glass for this one."

I took one last glance at the beautiful cadet, then I reached under my seat and pulled out my own lightweight headset. I connected the nodule to my field port on the base of my neck, inserted the aural tubes into my ears, and pulled the simglass visor over my eyes, settling in for the lecture.

Later that afternoon, after the lecture was over, I went to visit Petra in her office. The space was dense with the clutter of a scholar's life. A tapestry in the style of the southern islands of Kulai covered the wall behind her, intricate abstractions of ocean green and coral white curling and spiraling. A desert succulent stood as tall as a person in the corner, bright orange flowers blooming on its crown, bone white spines as long as my finger jutting out from its basalt flesh. And the decapitated head of a burnished chrome android sat atop a pile of books on her desk. I marveled at the sight. Each printed tome was probably worth a fortune, and there they were, just lying carelessly on her desk.

The android stared at me with its lifeless eyes while I stood at the threshold, waiting for her to notice me. She was scribbling something on paper with an old-fashioned stylus. I cleared my throat.

She held up her index finger, still not looking up. "Patience, please. Won't be another moment now." The intensity of her scribbling increased, a flurry of markings, the stylus scritching on the paper.

Then, suddenly, she dropped the stylus like it was a hot iron, and sat back in her chair, eyes closed, pinching the bridge of her nose with her finger and thumb. A pained look.

"Perhaps I'll come back later?" I said, starting to back out of the office

She squinted her eyes open, then held up her hand to stop my retreat. "You're fine, cadet. Come in. Have a seat." She gestured to the seat across from her desk.

"I've never met anyone who still works with paper," I said, sitting down.

"It's said that Eledar did all his best thinking on the written page. Not sure if it's true, but it resonated with me. You should try it some day... what was your name, cadet?"

"Siris. Oren Siris."

"Thurston," she called out, "can you pull up Siris's file?"

There was a whirring sound, and the mobile intelligence floated out from behind the cactus in the corner.

Petra snorted and gave her familiar a look of amused disbelief. "What are you doing back there?"

Thurston glimmered an irritated red, like the color of a rash.

"Oh nevermind. Just come here and find me this young man's file."

The heart hovered over us and settled into its dock on her desk.

She turned to me. "He's an odd heart," she said, pointing at Thurston, "but I suppose that's what makes us such a good pair."

The monitor on her desk lit up with my information.

"There we are," she said, bending down to squint at the read-out. "From Verygone, eh Siris?"

"Yes, Petradrumon."

"You've come a long way. And after all those light years, here you are, sitting across from me. Why?"

"I love your lectures, drumon. I always come away with something new."

"Aren't you a dear! Isn't that kind, Thurston?"

Thurston glowed affirmative green.

"But, much as it pains me to say it, you didn't come just to tell me how great I am, did you, Siris?" She gave me a penetraing look.

"This morning, during your lecture, you mentioned the Causality Labs."

"And it piqued your interest, did it?"

"Yes, drumon."

"Well, it never hurts to soften me with compliments, cadet. I'm as much a fool for flattery as any drumon here in the academy — Eledar knows we've enough vanity and self-aggrandizement to fill all the archives of Sebedas — but what matters more is your initiative. You're the first to follow up on it since I mentioned it in class this morning.

"You're no doubt wondering how a first-year such as yourself can get in on the ground floor of this exiciting research. Good news is, you've come to the right place. Frolly owes me a favor - several favors actually. I could put in a word."

"That would be incredible!"

She leaned back in her chair. "Tell me though, Siris, what else did you take away from today's lecture?"

She was testing me.

An idea started to take shape in my mind, but I was unsure of how to verbalize it.

"Come on," she said. "Out with it."

"Your inisghts about patterns in consciousness... they were beautiful, but...

"You struggled a bit at the end."

I gave her a look of surprise.

"Who doesn't struggle with purpose and meaning, Siris? The Eledarian dialogues are designed to explore paradox, and the nature of paradox is one of tension, conflict, and struggle."

"I guess what I am trying to get at," I said, "is... am I 'me'? Or is my sense of self just an illusion created by higher patterns in the universe?"

"Ah! You're striking at the the heart of the mystery! What is illusion? What is pattern? What is it to be an individual? Or to be part of a whole? Understanding the 'how' does not always lead us through to the 'why.' And if we had all the answers, I suspect people like you and me would start to get quite bored."

"I suppose you're right..."

"But you're not satisfied. I know. That means I'm doing my job well, because you're going to keep digging until you are. And maybe, in the process, you will help move the whole of humanity forward with what you discover."

She swiveled in her chair. "Thurston, take this down: My dearest Frolly. I've got a live one for you. Cadet Oren Siris. An eager little dreamer." She glanced at me. "Actually, he's not little at all. Quite the hulk, in fact. But he should serve your purposes well. If you can't think of a way to thank me for this, you should know that I'm running low on that century-aged vysak you obtained for me on your last trip to the highlands.'"

"There," she said, wiping her hands together. "That should do it. Did you get it all, Thurston?"

Thurston glowed green again.

"Excellent. Send it off to Frollydrumon. He'll be pleased to have another young blood to do the grunt work while he sits around dreaming up his thought experiments."

And just like that, I landed as a research assistant in the Causality Laboratories. My first year was mostly grunt work, but Petra had warned me of this, and I stuck with it. I combed through databanks for hours on end, looking for anomalies, or sat at one of the stations, logging every iteration of an experiment. After two years, the drudge work paid off: Drumon Frolly recommended me for a praxis assignment with Starnet, a colossal project under the leadership of pausha Thol Dren Des.

The aim of Starnet was to replicate the immense lattices that encircled both Appollion and Shugguth like the gossamer webs of some cosmic spider. These webs channeled stellar energy, supplying Forsara with essentially limitless power, and Starnet had already brought the lattice design to nearly a dozen other stars with populous worlds. But we had only just begun to understand the true potential of these stellar energy transformers. What started out as a noble and ambitious initiative to provide an unlimited supply of power to all the central worlds became something even more incredible.

The first breakthrough came when Tholpausha and his team adapted the causality research I'd been a part of to convert the lattices into massive, subspace transmitters. The system amplified a star's energy, enabling us to widen the subatomic gaps in space and send information across vast distances in a virtual instant, bypassing one of Eledar's most fundamental discoveries about the nature of space-time: that nothing can travel faster than the speed of light.

It was revolutionary. Sending a message across the immensity of space used to take decades, or centuries, or even millennia, depending on how far it had to travel. Now, we were no longer constrained by Eledar's cosmic speed limit. As long as there was an active starhub on each end to hold the substratum open, we could communicate without delay. Every connected world now had the chance to progress at the same pace, eliminating the time differential that allowed some civilizations to surge ahead while others stayed rooted in the past. With each new starhub, ideas and information flowed more freely across the Fellowship.

Then we made an even greater discovery.

Working from the same underlying theories, we discovered we could do more than just send information. We could send matter. Or rather, we could send matter *as* information. This allowed the Fellowship to link the stars and create trans-galaxy lanes for conventional ship travel. We no longer needed to rely solely on the great space voyagers carry people and resources across the void of space. Once two starhubs were active, we could use their energy to jump ships between them, shortening a journey that might otherwise take centuries into just a few months, or even a few days, depending on how close the starhub was to the final destination. Starhubs become gathering points, beacons in the void, and the galactic field widened, spreading the Fellowship's influence ever further into the universe.

But, as I would soon learn, that influence was not always a welcome one.

W AKE UP. The refrain repeats in my head. *Wake up.* My heart is a fusion core. *Wake up.* Everything around me is so bright. I squint. *Wake up.* The light fades. It is twilight. I am home. I move my hands along the wood and packed dirt of this house that I have never seen before, that I have lived in all of my life. Everything is rough-hewn; well made, but crafted by hand.

I step through the front door. A simple wooden fence built from quartered tree trunks circles the tall grass and bushes in the yard. I move through the grass and rest my hands on the fence, tracing the grain of the wood with my fingers. It is sanded smooth. I look up towards the moving star in the sky. It is a ship. Orbiting low, a passing beacon, a reminder that we are more than skin and bones and blood, even in death.

Wake up. I step back and swing my arms. The wooden columns holding up one side of the house splinter and split with the force of my strike. I swing again, knocking down the next wall. The roof collapses on top of me.

I exhale, the detritus of the old house lifting off of me, spinning out in every direction. *Wake up.* I climb out of the wreckage and exhale again. The rest of the house collapses, crumpling like parchment. I leap into the air, pointing myself towards the trail of the flying star, towards the ship that will carry me out of this place.

Something grasps my neck.

My head wrenches backwards.

I fall to the earth.

"Oren. Wake up." Saiara was whispering in my ear. "It's okay. You're here with me. This is home." She kissed me on the forehead, stroking my hair. I pulled her close, and soon she was asleep in my arms.

I lay awake. What planet was that? Where was the ship headed? Why did I want so badly to escape that place? My mind wore itself down with these questions, and eventually, I fell back to sleep too.

The next morning, as we drank guays tea together, Appollion's silver sunlight filtering through our quarters, Saiara asked me about my dream.

I blew on the steaming tea. "I was in my home," I told her. "It was so familiar, even though I had never seen it before. There was a ship, leaving the planet, and I knew I was supposed to go with it. But something held me back, trapping me there. That's when I woke up."

She wiped last night's crust from her eyes and yawned. "You're just nervous. I'd be surprised if you weren't. Today is a big day."

I scratched my chin. "You're probably right."

"What time do you depart?"

"Afternoon. I have to report to station eleven by midday for the final briefing. A transport riser will take me into orbit when Shugguth crosses the apex."

She looked at the chronometer embedded in the wall. Appollion was well above the dawning line, with the crimson cusp of Shugguth just emerging.

"Shugguth is already rising," she said. "Noon will come on fast. You should start getting ready."

I rubbed my forefingers and thumbs across my eyebrows.

"What is it?"

"Honestly? I'm scared, Saiara." I couldn't meet her eyes.

"Oren. Look at me." She reached across the table and took my hand. "You should be scared. This isn't a simulation. But you're in good hands with Tholpausha, and he chose you for a reason. I know you know that."

I took a deep breath and squeezed her hand back.

"I know," I said. "I love you."

"Of course you do. I am extraordinarily loveable."

I laughed. "And modest too," I said.

She smiled widely.

"Speaking of modesty," I said, pointing at her, "you've barely said a word about *your* next assignment." I placed my hand over my heart. "I promise I won't be jealous."

"It's a great honor," she said, becoming shy.

"To say the least! Apprenticing with the Farseers of the Coven? You're actually going to live and work inside the halls of the World-heart." I crossed my arms, shaking my head. "I lied, by the way. I'm extremely jealous."

She laughed. "Go," she said. "Wash up. Today is your day, not mine. I'll prepare something, and when you're ready, we'll break our fast."

"Thank you, Saiara."

"Come on now, lover boy. Don't just sit there making moon eyes. Get moving! Time grows thin."

After we ate, Saiara rode with me to the top of our tower where the transport riser was waiting to take me up to station eleven.

The wind sang as we stood in the open air, fluttering our

clothes and hair. Saiara picked out the low-orbiting space station with her sharp eyes, and pointed it out to me. "They're waiting for you," she said.

We embraced.

Then she stepped back, reached up, and took my cheeks between her hands. "I love you," she said.

I leaned forward. We kissed. It was over too fast.

"I love you too, Saiara."

I climbed onboard the transport riser. The ship's heart registered my biosig, and the riser lifted off the platform. The propulsion was fluid and smooth. I barely felt the motion as I watched the roof of the tower begin to fall away. The door started to close.

"Wait," I said.

The heart paused the ship's ascent. The door hung half-open. I stared out at her, searching for something else to say.

"Go, Oren!" she called, waving me off. "And may the spirits of the Scions travel with you!"

I nodded and waved back. "Let's go," I said. The door closed and the hopper accelerated, rocketing into the atmosphere.

During the briefings with pausha Thol, I learned that the Linstar was a decaying star four thousand light years away from Forsara, just at the inner edge of the Nomarion arm of the galaxy. The Fellowship hoped to turn it into a starhub, building a net to harvest the atomic fuel we used to pinch the folds and probe the gaps in space-time.

Unfortunately, the star's only planet was already inhabited.

Many centuries ago, a group of peaceful separatists had elected to leave the Fellowship. They fashioned their manifesto around the original tenets of Dhao Lin, twenty-third scion of Eledar, and they called themselves the Cendants of Lin. The Cendants aspired to build a society unbound by what they saw as the technology-obsessed strictures of the galactic collective. As with any social change, progress was slow, tense and jagged. But eventually, a non-interference treaty was jointly ratified by the Coven and the separatist leadership.

Cipher YT77006 in the planetary index was identified as an optimal world to make a fresh start. Records showed a planet rich with mineral resources, and a temperate climate well-suited to the heirloom agricultural seeds the separatists had negotiated as part of the treaty. The Cendants named it Lin Den. They set forth to their new home, devoting themselves to simpler living, making their own way towards the future.

Centuries passed, and the Cendants of Lin became another footnote in the Fellowship's vast and varied history.

Then we discovered that their star was collapsing. A routine stellar survey identified the Linstar as a supernova risk. If the star went supernova, we knew that the people of Lin Den had no means to escape that fate. When the star died, the planet and its people would die with it.

But as the star continued its slow, inexorable decay, it was also generating massive amounts of useable energy, which made it an excellent potential starhub. And in the process of siphoning off the star's increased energetic output, we could all but eliminate the risk that it would explode.

There was just the small matter of convincing the Linden.

By this time, the Fellowship was probably little more than myth among the Linden. A dozen generations had come and gone since they first made their break from the covenant. All that remained were distorted narratives depicting the Fellowship as a failed techno-fascist society. In their telling, the Cendants of Lin had done all they could to reform the Fellowship before they were forced to abandon their efforts and start anew.

When our ships appeared in their skies after all that time, our ambassadors were met with surprise, skepticism, and fear in equal measures. But even though this was a society founded on the rejection of advanced technology, they were a thoughtful and complex people, and as new generations were born and took the helm, old mores had mutated, evolved, or slipped away. Over the centuries, they had, in their own unique way, built a marvelously complex society. Their agrarian economy served as the backbone for a culture of inventors, artists, thinkers, and tinkerers.

Early diplomatic efforts were brittle and precarious. Our ambassadors spent years building trust. But once the Linden finally came to understand the dire truth of their situation, negotiations moved swiftly. The Fellowship offered salvation, and in exchange for our knowledge and certain technologies, the Linden agreed to harvest and share the mineral resources of their planet. That made building the starhub significantly more manageable. Otherwise, we would have had to tow some distant asteroid across light years to have the materials at hand.

Things went smoothly over the intervening decades. The Fellowship helped the leaders of the Linden build out the necessary mining infrastructure and teach people the most promising practices for extracting, processing, and refining unwrought metals; practices that were quite familiar to me. It was celebrated as a joyous return to the Fellowship for the Linden, and when all of the conditions were favorable, construction on the starhub began. As the years rolled on, it became just another one of the countless galactic development projects that were always underway somewhere in the galaxy.

But something had gone wrong, and now it was up to us to find out what.

Fringe settlers like me are a relative minority in the Fellowship. Most recruits come from the populous central worlds. When a great voyager ship like *Transcendence* ends up at a rim settlement like Verygone, a handful of outliers might join the crew, eager for a chance to leave behind their narrow band of mineral or fluid and venture forth into the galaxy. Of those handful, one might wind up at Forsara, willing and eligible to take the oath of the covenant and join the Fellowship.

Someone like me.

Which is exactly why Tholpausha chose me as his second for the Linstar mission. During my work as part of the Starnet's subatomic amplification research team, I had developed a deep understanding of a starhub's underlying technology. That, combined with my experience on *Transcendence*, and my cultural heritage as a miner from Verygone, made me his leading candidate. I leapt at the chance to escape the trappings of research work and get back into space.

No word had come from our local ambassador or the construction superintendent in over six months. A lag in communication was to be expected until the Linstar hub was up and running, but it should have only taken three months, at the outside, to get a message from the Linstar to the nearest starhub in the Molroun system, and then home to Forsara in an instant. It had been more than twice that.

We were tasked with the investigation and, if necessary, the reconstruction of the Linstar hub. It was my first opportunity to serve in a leadership capacity on an interstellar ship. To stand as a representative of the Fellowship. To translate all my study into practice.

It was to become one of the greatest failures of my long life.

WE WERE ASSIGNED *DIVIDER*, a small but powerful patrol ship, and a crew of seven securers, headed by Worn Opo, a competent and seasoned officer. After unfolding from Forsara to the nearest starhub in Molroun, we approached the Linstar system at near-light.

It was a three-month journey from Molroun, and when we arrived at the outer edge of the system, we used the ship's sensors to do an initial assessment. Those first observations showed no obvious irregularities. Longsight displayed the unfinished frame of the starhub, encircling more than two-thirds of the Linstar like a gossamer skeleton, and a number of the orbiting construction stations and satellites were also visible.

But no one answered our hails. We tried every bandwidth, and got nothing.

"Orendala," Tholpausha said to me. Hearing the honorific 'dala' attached to my name gave me a small thrill. "I must go down to the surface. If the Linden don't know we're here yet, they will soon enough.

"It is only right that I meet their leaders in person, and they may have the answers we're looking for. While I am gone, I need you to conduct a full scan of the starhub. If you find any irregularities, have Divider contact me immediately. Understood?"

"Is that safe?" I ventured. I was hesitant to question Thol, but it seemed risky. "What if it's a trap?"

He nodded. "It may be. But decorum demands it. If I do not show face, it will be seen as a grave insult. I'm taking two of Worn's best with me, and if anything goes wrong, Divider can pinpoint my location within a hair's breadth. We won't use force unless absolutely necessary, but if it comes to that, Divider will know what to do."

From there, we approached Lin Den and entered a visible orbit, close enough to be seen by the naked eye, but far enough away so as not to seem overtly threatening.

Thol and his escort departed in one of our two orbital hoppers, leaving me with my first official ship's command.

"Orendala?" Divider said. "You seem pensive."

"First time jitters. That's all, Divider. Commence with the scans."

Then the signal came through.

It was in local dialect, so I could not immediately understand it, but I could hear anger and fear. Divider pared the message down to its essentials: "A small, heavily-armed band has brought construction of the starhub to a halt," he translated. "They are holding the entire construction team hostage, and they are demanding safe haven. It seems they have been expecting us."

"Eledar's breath. What do they want?"

"They have not yet said."

"And they understand what we're capable of? With this ship and this team?" Worn's securer force was an elite group trained in the arts of combat and defense.

"If they do, they do not care," Divider said.

"And you're certain they have hostages?"

"Yes. They were masking the biosigs during earlier scans, but now I am showing more than four hundred distinct human lifeforms."

"Masking!" I murmured to myself, rubbing my cheek and chin. "Who in the names of the Scions taught them that?"

"How would you like to proceed, dala?"

"We're going to take this one slow. Tell them we'll hear them out. But if they harm a single hostage, they'll pay for it. And notify Tholpausha."

"I have already sent word. I await his response."

"Right then." I turned to Worn. "I want you ready to move. Understood?"

He nodded. He was in his element. That gave me confidence.

Thirty minutes later, I stood alone on the main deck of the primary construction satellite, standing across from a woman half my size. She was tiny, but looked carved out of wire and sinew, ropy and attractive, with a fighter's stance and a cold smile. She was flanked by a half-dozen skinny, rangy men, and we stared at each other, no one speaking. My heart thumped in my chest.

Since this woman had contacted us, we had received no word from Tholpausha. Either their masking technology prevented us from detecting his biosig down on Lin Den, or he was dead. Or both. Divider was attempting a workaround, but until he was successful, we were on our own.

Worn was contemplating a scorched earth approach. "Let's just light the whole backwards planet up from here," he muttered. "Then we'll see what they think about threatening us."

I knew he was angry, and a part of me was actually tempted to hand authority over to him, but I pulled myself together. "If things turn to violence, Worn, we may lose any hope of salvaging this mess. Fear is too often the harbinger of violence, and I don't want things to escalate if we can help it."

Worn sucked his teeth. "They have our pausha. We cannot risk losing you too. Let me at least back you up." He patted his rifle.

I shook my head. "If we show any untoward aggression, those hostages might die. And if Tholpausha is still alive, and we're to have any hope of seeing him again, we have to move carefully."

"What if we come around the back? Spacewalk through this airlock here." He pointed at the satellite's three dimensional schematics floating in front of us. "We'll stay out of sight, and be ready to move if it comes down to it. You've got to let me do my job here, Orendala."

I rubbed my cheeks. "Alright. That's good thinking. We'll make that work, as long as you stay out of sight until I signal you. Let's move."

Once I was onboard, it occurred to me that my size might be intimidating in its own right, but this crew did not seem intimidated by me. They took their cue from their leader, and, if anything, she looked bored.

"*Ahalayo*," I said, greeting her in the dialect of the Linden, doing my best to make my accent and intonation sound authentic.

She did not respond.

"What are we doing here?" I asked, still speaking in dialect.

"What do you think?" she said in the universal tongue.

I acted surprised, raising my eyebrows. "You speak the shared language. Who are you? Tell me your name."

"Why should I? You stand there, tall and imposing, but you're not the only one with power here. So why don't *you* tell me *your* name?"

"Oren," I said. "My name is Oren Siris. I'm a senior cadet with the Academy of the Fellowship, and I am serving as the second on this mission."

She scowled. "I should have known they would send a cadet. Another in a long line of insults."

"They sent me because I am an expert on the starhub, and because I'm from a fringe world too. Like you. And I am here because our leader, pausha Thol Tep, is down on Lin Den. We have not heard from him, and I think you know something about that."

"Fringe world," she said, shaking her head with disgust. "These labels are meaningless to us. We are our own people, and we have little use for some galactic map drawn up by people who have never stepped foot on the soil of Lin Den or walked in the light of the Linstar. How we live is what matters. Not some arbitrary dividing line drawn between stars."

"Well, I grew up on a world much like Lin Den, long before I knew anything about the Fellowship. Smaller, and colder in the winters, but we mostly made due on our own, a long ways away from the people who decided where to mark those dividing lines."

Her demeanor softened a little. "What was your world called?"

"Verygone. A mining settlement in the Beallurian system."

"You're a miner?" she said.

"I was."

"Then why did you leave?" Suspicion crept back into her voice.

"Because I have always felt that there was more to life than digging in the dirt, and more to the galaxy than our little moon. And my parents believed that too.

"They helped me see that I might have a place beyond Verygone. That I might be able to help others like me. It wasn't easy to leave them behind, but I am grateful to them. They gave everything for me."

"If my parents were still alive," she said, "maybe they would have done the same for me. But they both died in the Denarian mines when I was a child."

"I am sorry for that loss. Terribly sorry. I lost people too, in the mines of Verygone."

"Then you understand that they are gone, and there are no words to bring them back. That is just one of the countless crimes your Fellowship must be called to answer for. If you had the power to answer for those crimes, then this conversation might actually accomplish something. But you don't, do you?"

"No," I said. "I don't. I am a just a tiny piece in a much larger game. As most of us are. But maybe I can still help you."

She sighed. "Listen. You seem fine enough, for an offworlder, but you shouldn't have bothered. It is too late for diplomacy. Much too late. We are set on our path. Either you give us what we want, or we take it."

"That's not much of a choice. We don't even know your demands."

She gestured to a man at her right flank. He slid a small holocube across the ground. It stopped close to my feet. A moment later, an image was projected above it, into the open space between us. It showed a single planet orbiting a small star.

"The Linstar system," I said. "Why am I looking at it?"

"Because it is our home, you idiot," snapped the man who had slid the holocube. He spoke the universal tongue, but his accent was thick and snarled.

She silenced him with her hand. "Many generations ago," she said, "the Cendants left the Fellowship and founded Lin Den. Our society thrived for centuries.

"But no one knew that the Linstar was a cosmic time bomb. Not until the Fellowship returned to harvest the dying star's energy. Once the Linden understood that your people could save us from a terrible fate, our fear shifted to excitement. We had been isolated from the universe for so long, and at a time of great need, saviors had arrived from the stars.

"It was undeniably exciting. The promise of a bright future hung before us like a mirage in the desert. I was just a child then, and my parents were still alive. I remember walking with them through the streets of Vossol, people everywhere, drinking, eating, dancing in celebration. We were to become a part of something bigger. Something greater. In exchange for our resources, you would heal our sun. And for those who were ready to walk it, a path to the stars had dropped out of the heavens.

"But soon it became clear to anyone paying attention that, despite all our ancestors had done to leave behind the materialistic politics of the galaxy and build a new world, the same dysfunctional patterns had begun to reemerge. Farmers set down their spades for pick axes. Artisans traded in their clay for mineral ore. We started digging up and tearing apart our own planet with no regard to the past that had once defined us.

"Factions formed, vying for the same resources. And the people who accumulated the most began to accumulate power too, upending centuries of egalitarian leadership. We watched as our wealthy elite suckled from the teat of the Fellowship, leaving the rest of us to eke out a life from their scrapings. We have been forced to adjust our whole lives to meet the schedules of your galactic timekeepers, pushing all your damn systems down on us to build your precious starhub, and we have nothing to show for it but scars and loss."

"If even half of what you say is true," I said when she finally took a pause, "then you have fair grievance, and I promise we will work with you to make it right. But the treaty to build the starhub was negotiated in good faith with your leaders. It was understood that the construction would take several generations, and that we would do our best not to interfere with your culture, even as we paid you handsomely for your resources, and, eventually, gave you the education and means to find a new home in the galaxy."

"Not to interfere?" Her voice was filled with venom. "You build a web around our sun, using raw resources from our planets, and you claim not to interfere? The fat grow fatter, while the masses of common people wither and suffer, and the Fellowship turns a blind eye. You're lying to yourself if you believe anything other than this."

I held up my hands in a peaceful gesture. "I promise you that this is the first I am hearing of it. All the reports we have tell of a prospering system of trade and exchange, and the starhub has progressed ahead of pace. Until now."

"Listen to yourself." She spat on the ground. "You're not looking deep enough. Those fat old men are not our leaders. They do not speak for us. They never spoke for us. And they have been feeding you lies. Your simpering pledge of non-interference is a sad attempt to absolve yourself of this mess."

"Then show me," I said. "Show me the proof."

"Kneel down," she said. "And I will give you your proof."

"I'm by myself, unarmed, and you want me to kneel? I've been called a fool before, but I don't have a death wish. Not yet."

She laughed. Her teeth were gleaming white, and her lips were shining with moisture. "I want to see your precious port. This great gift, this hole to your brain."

"So you can drive a dagger right through it?"

"Do you want me to show you proof or not? If you do, plug into this recall unit, and you will see the truth." She held up a long, thin obsidian cylinder.

"Fine. But that recall unit is based on an outdated design. More than three centuries in fact. I don't have a gaping hole in the base of my neck, waiting for something to get stuck inside of it. The biointerface is microscopic. We'll have to run that through my ship's system."

She sneered at me.

"I am willing to watch whatever you have, but that unit is useless unless we bring it to my ship. And when I am connected, I will be at your mercy. I am not going to do that surrounded by a half-dozen men who all look like they could kill me as soon as shake my hand."

She remained stonefaced.

"Please. I swear to you. This is no trap. My boarding ship has everything we need."

Her eyes narrowed. "Fine, then."

The man who had shouted at me grabbed her shoulder. "Ifrit," he hissed.

She turned her head to glare at him.

After a moment he let her go, fear and anger playing out on his face.

She walked towards me. "Lead the way, Oren Siris."

As soon as the inner door to my boarding ship sealed shut, she spun around and pushed me back into the chair. She was much stronger than I anticipated. She wore an impish, hungry grin.

Was she flirting with me? I smiled back at her, trying to remain impassive. "I am at your mercy now, Ifrit."

She hesitated, and fear flashed across her face. "So now you know my name," she said.

Throughout our encounter, she had projected an air of confident disdain. Now, for just a moment, she looked vulnerable. Like she was afraid we might actually make a meaningful, human connection.

I touched her hand. "Ifrit. I mean you no harm. Truly."

She looked down at my hand on hers. She softened again, for a moment, then quickly composed herself, regaining her tough, gritty exterior. "No," she said. "Your ambassadors said the same thing to our elders. But harm came to us anyway. We must be free from the temptation of your beautiful lies."

She leaned over me, pinning my shoulders with her hands. I could have pushed her away, but I let her hold me down. She reached behind her back and pulled the recall unit out from her pocket.

"Are you ready?" she asked.

I looked at her, holding eye contact. She was so close, her breath warmed my skin. Flints of green speckled her blue eyes. I repressed a wild impulse to kiss her.

"I'm ready," I said. "You can connect over there." I pointed. "Speak into the microphone once I am under, and I'll be able to hear you."

Divider was listening, and he lit up the connection on the console, so she could tell where I was pointing. She placed the recall unit in the port. A moment later, wires snaked out from the headrest of my chair, crept inside my neck, and established a link with my nervous system. Everything on the small boarding ship dissolved from my awareness.

I was hovering above a small city sprawling across a russet valley. It was the planet Lin Den. I knew it as if it had always been my home. My view swooped in with the drone that had made this visual recording, passing low over the city. The streets were empty. There was no sign of life in the lanes or buildings, no movements or sounds. The drone circled, carrying me with it, and I searched in vain for anything beyond the deserted city.

Ifrit spoke. "This is Vossol. Where I was born. It is dead now. All of its people have moved to the far side of the continent, chasing after the mineral deposits that were mostly worthless until the Fellowship came."

The view sped up. We whirred across the surface of Lin Den in a flash, coming to rest above another city, very large, stretching out over many farruns. It was surrounded by massive, open pits, like deep wounds in the planetary surface. Thousands of tiny figures snaked between larger mining machines; local natives, harvesting their planet. The skies above the city were hazy, and the buildings were covered in soot and grime.

"Welcome to Denaria, our glorious capital, the rotten core of our humble little world."

The drone flew in low over the city, and I saw how imbalanced Lin Den had become. Expansive structures, obviously built at great expense, were walled off from surrounding hovels, shanties pressed up against each other like a rotted apiary. It had been beautiful once, with magnificent architecture, and the sanded auburn mountains visible on the skyline, but it was decaying now, hollowing out.

"I want to show you something else," she said. The drone flew further into the city. Soon, I came upon a long, four-story building. Its outer structure was formed from thick columns and grand archways, a heavy, impressive architectural wall protecting the smaller inner structures, which were graceful and delicate, scattered throughout lush, beautiful, water-fed gardens.

Fountains sparkled in the light of the Linstar. People were down there, walking, laughing, sitting, napping, playing instruments. The air above the building seemed remarkably clear.

"Our fearless leaders," Ifrit said. "They luxuriate in their impregnable bubbles, while the rest of us beg and scrape for their droppings."

Someone down below looked up and saw the drone hovering above the bubble. Within moments, two robed figures darted out of the shadows and pointed their long staves up towards my vantage. An instant later, the image was spinning wildly, and I found myself streaking towards a cluster of ramshackle homes on the outer edge of the ministerial palace.

As the drone crashed, I heard Ifrit say, "Now you have seen the sickness spreading through Lin Den."

I came up gasping for air.

Ifrit stood over me, her face grim. "It's been like this for decades. I know that it's not entirely their fault. They are only Linden, and Linden, like all people, are weak and greedy. Which is exactly why the Cendants prescribed the Tenets of Lin: to help us live into our higher selves. But the Fellowship has led us to regress, feeding our baser impulses, and our suffering grows.

"Those of us with the eyes to see it have done our best to rectify the situation. We have tried legal routes, and we have tried illicit ones. We know now, though, that we have merely been repressing the symptoms. A new trade agreement. A murdered magistrate. These have little effect against the relentless promise of more wealth and more power trickling down from the mighty Fellowship. That is the source. Cut the roots, and the creeping vines of influence wither and die."

I stared at her. Her words made sense on some level, and I waited to see where this would lead.

"There are those who have advised me against this course," she continued, "but the energies are in motion. Stopping now is impossible."

"Stopping what?"

"You haven't been listening. I told you already. We're turning off the clock. From this point forward, trade with the Fellowship is going dark. Galactic time will become meaningless again. We will live and die on our own time."

"You have no authority in this matter, Ifrit."

"You are wrong. Your peoples' hubris has given me that, at least."

"Our hubris?"

"For our whole history, we sat on top of our mineral wealth, blissfully unaware of its latent power. But you showed us what is possible. Powering great ships. Drawing energy from a star. Now, it is time to show you what we have learned."

"Dala," Divider said, his voice filling the small boarding ship.

Ifrit pivoted her head back and forth with surprise, a wild look in her eyes.

"I have countervailed their masking technology. Tholpausha is dead."

"What?!"

But before he could say more, a searing white light came in through the windows. I cried out, shielding my eyes and turning away from it.

"Divider!" I shouted. "Talk to me! What is happening?"

"Three small ships just uncloaked inside of the Linstar's orbit," he said in a voice incapable of panic. "The light was an explosion. One megaton warhead, at least. Possibly three." Divider paused for a moment. "The starhub is in tatters."

I reeled at the implications as bright spots danced before my eyes. Cloaking ships. Nuclear weapons. The starhub destroyed. Tholpausha dead, and likely hundreds more along with him. Maybe thousands. The Linden had learned from us. They had learned far too much. The ripple of this violence would be felt through the whole field.

I looked at Ifrit in shock. Her face was sad, but she did not turn away. My whole body felt numb, as if I might shatter with a gentle hammer tap.

"Dala," Divider said, jolting me, "the ships are approaching our location at high speed. Scans show that they are heavily armed."

"Stop them," I whispered. "Whatever it takes."

"Understood. I shall try to keep at least one of the vessels intact so that we might understand how much the people of Lin Den have leapt ahead as a result of our technology."

"That's... that's good thinking, Divider."

Then I grabbed Ifrit's arm, wrenched it behind her back, and shoved her off of the boarding ship out towards the main room where her men were waiting.

"Worn," I said, touching my finger behind the base of my ear, activating our local link, "are you in place?"

"Yes, dala. We already have them detained."

When we came back onto the deck, all of Ifrit's men were bound and kneeling. Worn stood over them. I pushed Ifrit ahead of me, towards her kneeling men.

"You have made a grave mistake," I said to them. "There are other, safer ways to wake a sleeping giant."

They said nothing.

I handed Ifrit over to one of Worn's securers, massaging my forehead as I turned away from her.

Two more bright flashes lit the star dark sky in quick
succession.

"Divider! Update."

"Two of the ships are vaporized, dala. I managed to override the
third, shutting down its propulsion and weapons systems. They
are stuck."

"Good work. Given the nature of their mission, they probably
have limited life support. Send them a message. Tell them they
better hope their air runs out before the Fellowship returns to clean
up this mess. And get word to the Molroundian chancell. We need
them to alert the Fellowship."

"Of course, dala. The signal is already in transit."

Someone grunted behind me. I turned. The securer who had
been guarding Ifrit doubled over, clutching his belly. She brought
her knee up to his face and he collapsed. A long, needle-thin dagger
was in her hand.

"You are no better than the rest," she said, and leapt at me,
moving fast, aiming the dagger at my heart. I danced backwards,
out of her reach, but my heel caught the step behind me. I fell,
cracking my head on the steps. She was on top of me in the next
instant.

Before she could plunge the dagger down, Worn fired his rifle,
full power. The bolt hit her square in the back. She crumpled on
top of me, her body convulsing. The smell of seared clothes and
flesh filled my nostrils. I heaved her off, retching and gagging.

Worn was at my side, but I pushed him away. There was little
blood because the beam had cauterized her wound. I stared down
at her body, watching it twitch, the last throes of life trickling out.

"Are you okay, dala?"

Ifrit's men were screaming, but Worn's securer force held them
back, bound and impotent in their rage. I could not meet Worn's
gaze. I turned away, trying not to let him see my watering eyes. The
room was spinning.

"Orendala? Are you okay?" he asked again.

"I'm fine, Worn. I have a thick skull. Please, just give me a moment." I took a deep breath, steadying myself. The room stabilized, but a thousand pinpoints of light filled my vision, residue from the explosions mixing with the shock of my fall.

I touched the spot on my head, hissing with pain. A large welt was already swelling there.

"We need to get back to Divider," I rasped.

"What about these ones?" Worn asked.

"Leave them. We'll cripple the satellite from Divider and put them in a prison orbit around the star. They can ruminate on their madness until we figure out what to do next."

Someone started laughing.

It was the man who had called me an idiot earlier. Ifrit's second.

Worn approached him. "Something amusing?"

He shook his head. "Ifrit was right," he said in his heavy accent. "You are swollen with hubris. You think that all people across the galaxy will genuflect in awe at your might and grandeur, but you are too blind to see what you have started, and where it has to end."

"You and your men are pacified. Your leader is dead." I said, forcing myself to stand, steadying myself on a work table.

"Do you think that it is just us? That this ends here? You have only scratched the surface." He tried to stand. One of the securers forced him back down.

I knelt over Ifrit's body and touched my hand to her chest, some small, foolish part of me hoping I would feel her heart beating. Her body was still warm, but she was gone.

I wiped my eyes. "Let's go," I said, turning away from Ifrit, gesturing to Worn and the others.

"This isn't over!" the man shouted after us.

———

He was right. It was not over. To mend the dying Linstar, we had pulled apart the very fabric of Linden society. And I watched, help-less, as it continued to play out, a spool of thread unwinding. I tried to stitch what I could, but every time I did, new snags in the fabric appeared.

The moment the Fellowship returned to the Linstar system to build the starhub, this course was sealed. As I stood on the rooftop deck of the royal palisades in the fading twilight, I worried for the thousandth time that it was all coming apart around me and no matter what I did, it would continue until there was nothing left.

In the six months since the explosion that destroyed the Linstar hub, as I waited for the news to reach the Fellowship and my subse-quent reinforcements to arrive, I did my best to do what I thought Tholpausha would have done, making it clear to the opportunistic oligarchs of Lin Den that their current economic arrangement with the Fellowship had reached its terminus.

It was, of course, not that simple. After evicting the wealthy Linden elite from the comfortable bubble of their royal palisades, the deposed oligarch elite were forced to seek refuge across the city, hidden away in private homes and safe houses. By scattering them, I scattered their power, though not without risks. With *Divider* in geostationary orbit above Denaria, I held the upper hand, but they had other means to conspire against me. Three attempts had already been made on my life.

But the resentment and anger of the greater Linden populace was palpable, and the oligarchs knew they were not safe. I promised them what protection I could, and in exchange, I asked for their compliance.

It was just as likely that the assassination attempts came from Ifrit's secessionists and their sympathizers. In their eyes, my continued presence was an affront to all they stood for, and they decried any party who sought to work with me. The riots of the first few months had quieted, but spurts of violence erupted all over the city as tensions simmered.

Some Linden pledged to restore the principles of Cendants,

leaving behind the desiccated city of Denaria to pick up whatever pieces were left and build anew on other parts of the planet. They blamed the secessionists for this mess as much as the Fellowship. By resorting to violence to achieve their ends, Ifrit and her ilk had perverted the peaceful tenets that Lin Den was founded on.

Most people, though, just wanted to make it through to the next day. They stayed on in Denaria because what did they have to go back to? Abandoned townships? Eroded farmland? Tarnished memories? After I commandeered the royal palisades, I repurposed it as a community hall, open to all, a place where the people of Lin Den could come for food, medical attention, and to air their grievances.

There were many grievances.

We catalogued every single one. I vowed that the Fellowship would do everything in our power to make reparations. But hearing so many stories of tragedy, suffering and loss was harder than anything else I'd ever faced. I bore it as best I could, but it tore something from me. So many lives had been lost. My heart felt red with their blood.

"Dala?"

I turned. Divider hovered next to me, inhabiting one of the drones.

"They are here, dala."

Relief eased the tension from my shoulders and neck. At the same moment, anxiety pitted my stomach.

"Where?" I whispered.

"Look to the north, with your back to the Linstar."

And there they were. A small phalanx of ships, at least a half-dozen, dropping into the atmosphere. They were twinkling, caught by the fading sunlight filtering up over the southern mountains. The Fellowship. My people. They had come to make things right. The irony of that almost made me laugh.

I REMEMBER my days as a cultivator with a bittersweet fondness. Looking back at those years is like looking through a rusted telescope from the wrong end. The images are crystallized, achingly small and distant. We were happy. Life was rich with the daily rhythms of cultivation that kept our modest land fertile and livable.

Then my wife and son were murdered by a Kefant raiding party, one of the nomadic tribes that ranged out from the western basin and into the highlands. My old life was scattered like ashes.

It filled me with rage, and a terrible, hungry sadness. But it also unearthed a focus, a sense of purpose I never knew I was capable of. Vengeance. The power to defend myself, and anyone else who deserved my protection. I vowed that never again would anyone take that from me. My way forward was the way of dagger and hatchet.

All the years I'd spent tilling the thin soil of the eastern highlands armed me with a wiry strength, and I discovered that fighting came easy to me. Over the next year, I rose to prominence, besting anyone who contested me.

Word spread through the local tribal factions, and soon, the sachem, Adze, could no longer afford to ignore me. My existence was a threat to his supremacy, and he had no choice but to challenge me to single combat.

He was strong and fast, but his power as the tribe's sachem was his greatest weakness. It made him too cautious. He stood to lose his vaunted status if I defeated him, while I'd already lost everything I'd ever cared for. I could endure anything now.

When he knocked my dagger from my hand, cracking three of my knuckles with his club, I used the opportunity to step inside his guard. I broke his arm, wrenching it behind his back with a brutal hold.

I could have ended his life then, but I showed him mercy. "Adze," I said, loud enough that all could hear, "you fought bravely and honorably, and you are still welcome here. If we are going to survive these hard times, then we must stand together." But though I did not kill him, I took his wife, as was my right by the laws of our lands, and, in so doing, demonstrated that my authority was absolute.

In time, we moved on from our simple mountain pastures and traveled to other tribal territories. I faced some of the greatest warriors that had ever lived. And I bested them all. My power grew. The tribe of Helgar became feared and respected for its unrelenting strength.

One evening, as I was sitting outside my sachem tent, bathing in the soft, silver evening light, and listening to the women inside, whispering and laughing, a raspy voice called out, breaking my reverie. "Hello, Oren."

I sat up with a start. "Who goes there?" I said, trying to hide the nervousness in my voice. "Show yourself."

She stepped out from around the edge of the tent. She was short, her thin frame draped with a heavy woolen robe. She pulled back her hood, and said, "I am called Yaohanath."

She was lean, and her face was worn and scarred, but her presence was electric. Her eyes were bright and lucid beneath her weathered brow. I could not detect a single ounce of fear in her, which was rare. Most people who knew of me knew what I was capable of.

But she had called me by another name. A strange one. Oren. Strange, but familiar somehow, though I could not place it.

"Yaohanath," I said, turning her name on my tongue. "You are the prophetess. From across the desert of Nooroun. I've heard people tell of your foolish promises."

"Foolish?" She raised her eyebrows. "You forget yourself, Oren. You are playing with history here, and it is an ill-advised game."

"My name is Helgar, woman," I said, raising my voice, "and I will not be spoken to like this." The women in the tent went silent. I stood up from my chair, glaring at this strange but undeniably magnetic creature before me. In spite of her age, she had a youthful, commanding energy. Instead of intimidating her with my aggressive posture, I found myself struggling not to avert my eyes from her steady gaze.

Something deep in my memory was whispering, and I asked her, "Where do you come by this name, Oren, prophetess?"

She raised an eyebrow. "You think you can hide here? You think you can escape? You are the one who is foolish. You cannot escape who you are." She reached into the folds of her robes and drew out two long, curved daggers, holding them up in the silver light of Appollion.

"What are you doing?"

"I found these blades in the city of Noo, in the tomb of an ancient warrior. They are centuries old, and still as sharp as the day they were forged." She moved the blades through the air, as if she were tracing invisible symbols in front of her. "They are masterful," she said, gazing at them. She pointed one of the blades at me. "You are strong. You are cunning. And you think you can defy history with your strength. But my death will undo everything you have tried to build."

She leapt at me, aiming a blade straight at my heart. I knocked her arm aside, and she swung the other blade around at my neck. I ducked, strafing backwards. I pulled my dagger out and turned my hips to the side, trying to make myself a smaller target, but she was impossibly fast, and one of her blades sliced across my bicep, drawing a thin line of surface blood.

She leapt again. I blocked the first blade with my long dagger, but the second found my shoulder, cutting through my jerkin and deep into my skin, much worse than the first strike. I gritted my teeth in pain, and stumbled out of her reach, expecting the death blow to follow. But she was just standing there, staring at me, smiling.

"You are not living up to your reputation, oh great and mighty Helgar."

"Damnit, why are you doing this? Why are you provoking me?"

"You know why. You know who I am. You know my destiny. You have read it in the books that have not yet been written. So you were torn away from your family? So people died that you should have protected? Who hasn't faced some version of that pain? You are a sad, hurt, little boy pretending to be a king. I cannot let you lose yourself in this way."

My shoulders were tense, and my jaw was tightening up. "This is all I know," I cried.

She shook her head. "You have forgotten. All this time bickering and fighting over imagined tribal territories has taken you away. But the promise of our future, the promise of a whole universe, is still out there, waiting for you. It's all there in the star charts on the ceiling of the tombs beneath the dead city. You have so much more to offer the world than to waste your life on petty games."

She was looking past me as she spoke, and I realized that my women had come out of the tent. They were standing in a semicircle behind me, watching us, shawls and blankets draped over their shoulders, covering their naked bodies.

I turned back to Yaohanath just as she charged at me again, holding her arms out wide. For a moment, her blades flashed with light, blinding me. My right arm hung limp at my side, but I held my long dagger in my left hand, and I raised my arm up to block the light from my eyes.

Her right blade came down in a big arc towards my head. I blocked her swing, and that gave me the opportunity to step inside the wide sweep of her left blade, which was coming around towards my neck. I rammed my shoulder into her chest, pushing her backwards, and used her momentum to pull her right blade out of her hands. It clattered onto the ground.

"Please. Do not make me kill you. I will."

She did not reply. She just kept smiling, a wild, toothy grin, scrunching up her wrinkled face, and with her remaining blade, she leapt at me.

In that moment, I knew it was over. I ducked in, and brought my dagger up into her chest. I felt it catch on her rib, then slide between, into her lungs. I held her there, her weight leaning on my blade, her face just inches from mine. Blood bubbled and dribbled from her lips. She looked at me, still smiling, and then the light faded from her eyes, and her body slumped, lifeless and heavy.

I lowered her down to the ground, and pulled my dagger out of her chest, wiping the blood on my pant leg. I turned and saw the women from my tent, still standing there, staring at her dead body. They looked angry and shocked. Although my position of authority did not oblige me to say anything, I took pity on them and said, "She forced me to kill her. I am sorry you had to witness that."

One of them, I could not remember her name, walked next to me, and knelt down at Yaohanath's side, making some sort of gesture of genuflection.

"Leave her," I said, but she ignored me.

Then, in one fluid motion she lifted Yaohanath's Noourn blade off the ground, spun, and plunged it into my stomach.

She did not say a word. She just watched me sink onto the blade as I had watched Yaohanath sink onto mine. Instinctively, I reached out for her neck, trying to choke her, but the strength I had depended on for so long was gone. The images began to dissolve, and two words floated up into my consciousness. Two words that seemed so strange and far away from the life I'd built for myself. Two words that changed everything. *Game over.*

I was drawn back into the choosing space. An image of my final moments swept across my visual field, repeating on a short loop. I watched as the woman lifted the blade and drove it into my stomach.

Linnea. That was her name. She had seemed so real.

How long have I been under? I wondered.

My memories came crawling back. After I returned to Forsara, I became obsessed with *Lord of the Tribes*. The game was a virtual recreation of the time of Shugguth's Curse, when civilization was shattered, and the early Forsarans broke up into tribes, warring over the dwindling resources in the blistering solar heat.

I made the decision from the outset not to play in the shared, participatory world with other gamers. The artificial intelligence that powered the characters of the virtual world made them indistinguishable from real players, and by playing alone, I was afforded privacy, and the ability to shape the whole story and its outcomes. Every choice I made had the potential to alter the course of history. The fate of my life was in my hands. I chose who lived, and who died.

But if that was true, then Yaohanath could not have known my real name. Someone was encroaching into my private gameworld. I reached out with all of my senses.

"You know I am here, don't you?" she asked, revealing herself, overlapping her field halo with mine.

"Saiara?" Her mere presence was uplifting. "Saiara! It's you!"

She did not immediately reply.

"I thought you were deep in the Coven, training with the Farseers," I said.

"They let me come to see you, Oren. I heard what happened on Lin Den."

Droplets of my shame and sadness stippled my halo, but her compassion was morning sunlight on cool skin.

"It's not your fault, you know," she said.

My sadness deepened.

"Oh, Oren. I wish I could have saved you from this. I truly do."

"What good are the Farseers and our great Worldheart if we are still so blind?" I asked with bitterness.

"'Our eyes are only as clear as our intelligence. Our reach is only as fast as our light.' You know this."

I said nothing.

"We all knew there was risk involved. Risk is inevitable in situations like this. Even if the data had *not* been falsified by the secessionists to lead us astray, the three-month light gap from Linstar to Molroun meant we were always operating with imperfect knowledge.

"It also meant that any intervention we made from afar was delayed by the gap of time. That's why Thol and Divider were elected to go. Steady hands to respond in real time. You were chosen as the ship's second for that same reason."

"But it wasn't enough," I whispered. "We weren't enough."

"Is *that* what you think?" Her incredulity showered me like cold hailstones.

"I know it."

"You're wrong, Oren. You're seeing it all wrong."

"So your farsight sees what I can't, then?"

"I don't need farsight to see it, Oren. You've always been too hard on yourself."

"Well, I can't change the past, and I can't help how I feel about it."

"So you've been spending the past four months playing war games instead?"

Four months?! I thought to myself. Has it really been that long? I forgot that she could hear my thoughts.

"Four months playing the vengeful hero," she confirmed. "For what?"

It dawned on me then. "That was you in there, wasn't it? Yaohanath. But... but you attacked me!"

"The field is a great gift. It provides us with a near-infinite well of knowledge and experience. But you were wasting it all on a silly game. I had to wake you up."

"Eledar's breath. You certainly did that!"

"The gamescript made it impossible for me to appear as myself without a signficant rewrite. I didn't have time for that, and you were probably too deeply immersed to recognize me anyway. I had to meet you in a skin you couldn't ignore."

"Well, I'm awake. So now what?"

"That's up to you. But you can't hide here forever."

"What else am I supposed to do?"

"You've abandoned your training! It's time to come back. Or do you want to get expelled from the academy?"

"I... I just can't face them right now. Not anyone. All that... all their judgment."

"Oren. Listen to yourself. No one will judge you more than you've judged yourself. Don't you realize what a special blend of arrogance and self-doubt it takes to blame yourself for the failure of the whole Fellowship? That's what Lin Den was: the Fellowship's failure. Not yours alone. As you wallow here in your self-imposed exile, you risk destroying everything... everything we dreamed of building together."

The red heat of anger evaporated my shame and sadness. "I haven't seen you in over a year, and when you finally decide to show up, you lecture me about what we were trying to build?"

"Oren!"

"Where were you when I came back to Forsara? With all those deaths on my head? Where were you then?"

"Oren. You know-"

"I know that we used to believe in the same things, Saiara. But I'm not so sure anymore. Not after what I've seen. You accuse me of arrogance, but the sheer existence of the Fellowship is one mighty act of arrogance. We tinker with the universe as if we made it. We believe that we know the right way to live, and that, in time, everyone will simply accept our greatness and fall in line." My sadness came flooding back. "But we ruined them, Saiara. We ruined them."

"Maybe, Oren. Or maybe not. It is too soon to know what the future holds for the Linden. But whatever comes next, hear me now: what happened was *not* your fault." The cool blues and warm pinks of her loving kindness surrounded me like a field of alpine flowers.

"So many dead. For what?" My misery wilted her flowers to burnt charcoal.

"It's not your fault." Hues bloomed again, copper and dandelion.

"So many-"

"It's not your fault." Her colors enfolded me.

Light filtered through my eyelids. I squinted my eyes open, then I sat up with a jolt. My bedroom. Mine and hers. Sunlight was coming in through the windows.

"Saiara?" I said to the empty room. My throat felt weak. My voice was feathery.

"Oren? Is that you?" she called. "It's about time. I'm in the kitchen."

We were home.

I turned, sliding my legs off the bed. My whole body ached.

"How did I get here?"

She walked into the bedroom. "I chartered a hopper to bring us back from the dream fields." She chuckled. "I swear, even with the weight you've lost, you're still heavier than a noa bull. The caretakers were *not* pleased. But they didn't seem surprised either. I'm guessing it's not the first time they've had to extricate an unconscious patron who's overstayed his welcome. They summoned a hauler right quick. The burly automaton hefted you without grinding a gear."

I didn't know what to say.

She knew me enough to recognize my embarrassment. She gave me a soft smile. "It's nice to be back here with you."

"It feels different," I said. "Our room. Smaller. Or... I don't know. Strange."

"Maybe because we're different."

I didn't know what to say.

"You should see yourself." There was mirth in her eyes. "You look good with a beard."

I reached to my chin and discovered that I had indeed grown a scraggly beard.

She laughed. "It needs some trimming, though."

I lifted my arms above my head, then brought my right palm down gently against my back. "Eledar's breath. I'm so sore."

"Four months' immersion will do that," she said. "The body needs to move, Oren. Really move. And twitching and shuddering in a simulation tank doesn't count. Even with the steady run of nutrients and the haptic stimuli, your muscles are still atrophied."

"Nothing some food and exercise can't fix, though," she said. "Let me finish with breakfast." She turned and walked out of the room.

I stood. My legs were weak, but they held. I hobbled over and up the seven stairs to our balcony. I waved my hand at the sensor and the glass canopy slid open. The breeze was cool and searching, tickling the whiskers of my beard. I stepped to the edge of the balcony, and looked down.

Five levels below, the pavilion that connected to our neighboring building was alive with foot traffic. It occurred to me that residential complexes like ours might be filled with people one decade, and empty the next, transformed into desiccated cities, waiting for a transfusion of fresh lifeblood once the previous tenants moved on to new lives and new worlds.

I wondered if there were any people below that I might still recognize. I wondered if anyone would recognize me. I was a stranger in my own skin.

Out past the edge of the concourse, I could see the ground, far below, and the river, glittering like a talismanic rune inscribed in the earth. I had a sudden urge to leap. To let the breeze take me. Let the river swallow me.

"Oren," Saiara called. "Come in and eat."

I stepped back from the edge.

When I walked into the kitchen, the food was already out. She hovered her palms up above the table, and pointed at each item in turn like an auctioneer. "Egg bisque with shallions and crushed alio. Biscuits with mellata. Sliced kew fruit over fermented kevas. And sparkling jos."

"Wow. It all looks fantastic."

"You better believe it. Now sit and eat before it gets cold." She flapped her hands at me, and we both sat down.

She dug in to the food, focused and unselfconscious. I stirred the bisque with my spoon, watching the liquid swirl.

"Saiara?" I said.

She looked up at me.

"Oren? Why aren't you eating?"

"After all this time, why did they finally let you come see me now?"

She set her spoon down, straightening up in her chair. "You should eat, Oren. We can talk later, once you have your energy up."

"Why, Saiara?"

She sighed, pushing her hair back from her forehead. "I've been dreading this."

"Dreading what?"

"I don't know how else to say it... I'm leaving, Oren."

She was never one to dance around tough issues. Looking back now, that was one of the reasons I loved her. But right then, I was stunned. "What?" I said. "Leaving for where?"

"Come tomorrow, I will walk the garden of forking paths."

Emotions swirled through me. Joy. Jealousy. Sadness. Pride. "You're graduating," I said. "That's... that's incredible."

"I came back for you because I want you there with me. I need you to be. Will you come to bear witness?"

"I... of course. What's... what's your mission?"

"Frontier work. The astronomists found a potential life star! They're calling it the Hadeth system. Eight planets and counting. There's a good chance at least one can support carbon-based life. We're going to find out."

"Where in the names of the Scions is the Hadeth system?"

"The Cthlonian arm. Deep space. I have been asked to serve as the ship's farseer. Senpausha is leading the expedition. He made the request himself, and the coven of the academy has approved."

I looked down at my uneaten food. "I don't know what to say."

"Oren. Even without the field, I know what you are feeling. I always have. That's what makes our connection so special. And it's why I love you. But this is an incredible opportunity. I can't say no."

She was right. How could she say no? This was everything we had been training for since the moment we stepped on *Transcendence*. "I know, Saiara. I know. If I were standing in your place, I would make the same choice. I've always known, since we first met, that you were destined for great things with the Fellowship. But that doesn't mean I don't wish I could go with you."

Her eyes grew watery, and she laughed, trying to hold back the tears. "Oh, Oren." She reached across the table and took my hands.

"I wish you could come too. I will miss you. But you have your own destiny to discover."

We didn't leave our living quarters at all that day. It was her last day on Forsara before the ceremony and her departure, and all we wanted was to be together. We swapped training stories. We looked at old photos and mocaps, laughing at our younger selves. She listened as I tried to make sense of what happened on Lin Den, holding my hand when I faltered on the painful parts.

And we talked for hours about the implications of her appointment. The first leg of the journey would go quickly. Their frontier ship would jump from Appollion to Tasches, the starhub closest to the Hadeth system, near the base of the Cthlonian arm of the galaxy. From Tasches, they would enter a stretch of several months of quiet routines, preparing themselves for coldsleep as the ship accelerated to near-light, each of the seven members of the crew navigating the psychological solitude of a small group of people living in close quarters, until they passed into the imperceptible moment, into the compressed corridors of relativistic velocity.

In that moment, time would curve and fold, and they would face their past and their possible futures in a fever dream of passage where time could not be reckoned by a human mind. Then, in the next imperceptible moment, their shipheart would wake them from coldsleep, and they would be there, at the edge of a newly discovered solar system, pioneers at the ever-growing boundary of the Fellowship.

Over six hundred years would pass here on Forsara while they traveled the corridors of near-light. In that time, the Fellowship would begin building the network of starhubs that would ultimately connect Forsara to this new world, eventually allowing us to travel to that sector of the galaxy in months when it once took more than half a millennium. The starhub construction project would take many centuries, but with the full will of the Fellowship behind it, it could be done.

By the time this new branch of the starnet was approximately seventy percent complete, the second ship was projected to arrive. By using the starhubs completed so far, that ship could jump much closer, to a new hub that would be built around a massive star called Dromedar. From there, the crew would travel two hundred twenty-three years at near-light to Eaiph, only a third of the original journey.

By then Saiara and her team would have already been gone from Forsara for almost a millennium. And, if they had survived the journey across space, that means they would have been on the planet for over four hundred years. Who knows what kind of world would be waiting when the second ship arrived? And, if Saiara was still alive, who knows what kind of woman she would become?

When we made love that night, she tasted of salt and rosewater. I drank her in, moving my hands and lips across her body. It was a desperate, gentle, bittersweet coupling. As we drifted off to sleep, I pictured her surrounded by descendants, the first generations of people born on Eaiph. I vowed to myself that I would be on that second ship.

When I woke the next morning, Saiara was gone.

"What time is it?" I asked.

"Shugguth will rise in twenty minutes," the roomheart replied. "Which means Saiara and the rest of the frontier party will arrive at the crystal garden for the ceremony in four hours and fifty-seven minutes," it answered my real question.

Today, Saiara walked the garden of forking paths. After dozens of years in training on *Transcendence*, and four years in the academy on Forsara, she was graduating.

Four years. Most cadets spent well over a decade at the academy. But when the majority of us first-years were still in large lectures and introductory coursework, she had already begun her apprenticeship with Viziadrumon, one of the most respected teachers in the academy. As always, Saiara surged ahead.

After that first-year of common core curricula, cadets started branching into different specializations, guided by drumons like Vizia, who took on apprentices based on interest, ability, and temperament. With privileged access to the academy's training facilities and information archives, we also had the freedom to pursue our own interests, chasing down flights of fancy and wild ideas in our spare time. Or we might sign on for praxis assignments, like my work with Starnet and my ill-fated expedition to the Linstar.

This combination of guided learning and personalized exploration and experimentation ensured each cadet ended up in a place of competence and expertise. There were even some cadets who never left the Academy. They discovered that they could best serve the Fellowship from within. When they graduated, they became scholars. Archivists. Caretakers. Drumons.

There is no actual garden of forking paths. It is metaphor. Jorn Borges, a scion of Eledar and one of the three founders of the Academy, along with Sebedas and Dwon Ru Wot, was the first to conceptualize the idea. His controversial theory of a unified, interconnected multiverse led him to conclude that space-time is like a garden, every choice a seed that fosters new growth or a vine that chokes off one path and opens another. Each choice alters all the choices to come. Some paths lead us apart, while others all end up arriving at the same destination, no matter the route. Endless forking paths dividing and coming together again, weaving through the universes.

Over time, the notion took root in the academy, and his metaphor came to represent the moment when a cadet completed her training, and made her own choice about how best to serve the Fellowship. Any one of the dozens of gardens scattered across the campus might serve as the ceremonial location, and each one is unique; manicured botanaereums; wild patches of gorse and whisper grass; sculptured hedges and evergreens; sweeping flower beds, kaleidoscoping with color.

Some gardens were well-known and well-trod, places for gathering and communion. Others were obscured; nestled in a courtyard; hidden behind a false wall or beneath a cellar door; perched on a rooftop; lining the walls of a deep cavern. Each garden was beautiful in its own way, and each drew certain people to it, as if the gardens were visible expressions of the ineffable interior qualities that define us.

Saiara's ceremony was taking place at the crystal garden. Graceful sculptures and lush fountains huddled between dense crystal and gemstone formations. Quartz. Citrine. Agate. Tourmaline. Lapis. Countless varieties, some of the minerals so rare that no other known specimens existed on the planet.

The caretakers of the crystal garden tended to these stones as if they were living entities, and a part of me liked to think it was true. Crystals held a deep internal symmetry that manifested in a dizzying variety of natural shapes resulting from the intense tectonic pressure of the planet. They could then be carved to form dazzling gems. Or sculpted into gorgeous, impossibly fluid forms. Or shaped into resonant bowls and spheres that produced rich, harmonic vibrations. Some people even claimed they had healing properties, as if the symmetry of the crystals might somehow influence the physical world towards deeper harmony.

So it made sense to me that this was where Saiara should make her walk. She had been forged from a young age to shine with a dazzling brightness. Her presence was healing. Inspiring. Humbling. She found patterns and symmetry where others only experienced chaos. She resonated with those around her, bringing out the best in them and in herself. These qualities that I loved were the same qualities that had helped her excel as an apprentice with the Farseers.

When I arrived, I found a group of seven ovates praying at a large crystal bowl filled with limpid water. Each one bowed in succession, bald pate swinging low, forehead touching the surface of the water, then rising back up, eyes open wide in an expression of shocking intensity, lips moving with some silent psalm. I sank into a trance as they repeated their devotions, over and over, a silent, hypnotic rhythm, punctuated by the quiet splashing water, until I heard approaching voices.

I turned and saw another group of people rounding the bend of the path. They emerged from behind a beautiful and somewhat terrifying sculpture that depicted figures climbing from the very rock from which they were carved, hands and feet and faces pushing out from the solid mineral core. As the group passed the sculpture, it seemed for a moment that they were all of one piece, that these people had come from inside the stone, and were free now, vibrant with life.

Four were at the front, talking and laughing with each other. They were followed by pausha Sen Sennet speaking in hushed tones with another person I did not recognize. As soon as I saw Sen, I realized that this was the crew of the frontier ship, here to participate in Saiara's walk.

Saiara came last, calm and focused, her blue eyes glinting like agates. When she saw me, she smiled, and walked over.

I embraced her.

"Thank you for coming, Oren."

I sighed. "Thank you. I would not be here, a hundred times over, if not for you."

She touched my cheek. "This garden is beautiful, isn't it?" she said.

"It reminds me of you," I said.

Her laugh was a shining pearl. I ached to hold the sound of it in my hands, to keep it safe with me, even after she was gone.

"How so?" she said.

"Beauty. Resilience. Purity of form. This is your garden. This garden is you."

Her eyes started to water.

"Saiara?"

She wiped away her tears, but more came on. "What if this is a mistake?"

"A mistake?"

"Leaving you like this. What if we never see each other again?"

I felt helpless. We looked at each other, searching for something.

"You pulled me back from the edge," I said. "I was running away, lost in the dreamtime, but you brought me back. Now you're leaving, and I honestly don't know what I'll do without you. I would keep you here with me forever if I could.

"But this... Saiara, this is your *chance*. This is why you left Jarcosa. Not for me. If I made you stay for me, *that* would be the mistake. You have been one of the greatest gifts of my life. But you do not belong to me. The galaxy needs you."

It was all true. That didn't make it any less painful to say it.

She took my hand. "You won't be alone after I'm gone. I have one more gift for you."

"You do? What is it?"

She smiled. It made her look sad. "You'll find out tomorrow. I don't know if you'll like it, but I promise you, in the end, you will be grateful for it."

"I'll take whatever you have to offer. Always."

She seemed about to say something. Instead, she leaned up, and gave me a long, lingering kiss, running her hands through my hair.

Then elder pausha Sandara arrived. The ovates stopped their devotions at the crystal pool and came to stand at her side, forming a semicircle, with the elder pausha at the crest.

"It's time," I said.

"I know," she said, but she stayed facing me.

"Here," I said, reaching into my cloak. "I brought you a gift too."

Her eyes went wide as violet light bathed her face. "The aurastal! From Dunsemai's theater. I can't believe you still have it."

"Take it," I said. "So that some part of me will always be with you."

She took a deep breath, her face a play of different emotions, and hooked the amulet around her neck.

"I love you, Oren. With everything I have."

"I love you too. Now go. They're all waiting for you."

She turned away from me and walked towards Sandara and the ovates. She stood in front of the elder pausha and bowed. The rest of the frontier party stepped in behind her, completing the circle, Saiara at the center. Everyone lowered their heads.

Everyone except Sandara. The elder pausha found my eyes. She smiled, lifting her hand to me. One of the ovates stepped back, creating a space in the circle. Sandara nodded encouragingly.

I came and stood between the ovate and pausha Sen Sennet, closing the circle again.

Sandara gave a satisfied look. Then she spoke. "Saiara Tumon Yta," she said in a quiet voice. "Today, you become another in a great lineage of explorers and pioneers. The path you have chosen comes with great sacrifice, for you must turn your back on Forsara and look now to the stars. To the new world that you will help create. In the journey to come, you will bring life to another corner of our galaxy. The light of the Fellowship shines brighter with your energy. We raise our voices in welcome to you, and in farewell."

Everyone lifted their heads, voices swelling as one, singing out the long, beautiful tone of making, echoing in the crystal garden, gorgeous harmonies vibrating through the gemstones.

I sang with them, quiet, letting my voice get lost in the sound.

One by one, the voices faded away until there was only the gurgling of the fountain, the quiet rhythm of our breath, and my heart in my chest.

The circle parted.

Saiara looked up at me, sadness and joy playing on her face. She reached out and squeezed my hand. We were both crying.

"I will come for you," I whispered. "I swear it."

The aurastal at her neck blazed with purple light.

"May the light of awareness shine forever in your favor," Sandarapausha said, touching her hand to the Fellowship sigil clasped to the blue sash above her cream cloak, "and may the spirits of the Scions travel with you."

Saiara stepped through the breach in the circle and followed the winding path through the crystal garden until she was lost from sight.

SOMEONE WAS SHAKING ME. "Come on now, young blood. Rise up and claim the day!"

I kept my eyes closed and swatted at the air.

"Ah ah ah. No you don't." A palm smacked against my cheek. "Up now."

I opened my eyes. My vision was still blurry with sleep. I saw bright eyes and smiling teeth, but I could not make sense of the person's features.

"Darkness is coming, Oren. The suns are moving into alignment. In three days, Shugguth will eclipse Appollion, casting the whole eastern hemisphere in a bath of silvery purple light, leaving the western hemisphere in total darkness. An auspicious time."

I was dizzy and confused. Smoke filled the air, a palpable haze. There was the sound of bubbling water. Someone nearby coughed. I looked up, and a figure stood over me, looming huge in the smoky chamber.

"Who are you?" I asked him. "What have you done? I... I don't feel right."

"Your mind is weak right now. Your failure eats away at you."

I knew this voice. It was the voice that had filled my mind

during the qualifiers. "Viziadrumon?" I propped myself up on my forearms and hung my head towards my chest, scrunching my face, trying to focus. "Is this... is this a test?

He smiled. "A test? Yes, I suppose it is. A test of your personal resolve."

"My resolve to do what?"

"Do you remember the training session on Ourthian? You were willing to risk your life rather than fail the simulation. I think that was because you did not truly believe you could fail. The gift of youth, and also its curse. But now, faced with your losses on Lin Den, you want to run away."

My head was spinning. I felt a sickness in my stomach.

"If you cannot stand and face failure, then it will destroy you."

"What am I supposed to do?"

"It is time for you to choose, Oren. Either you come with me as my apprentice, or you leave the academy. If you cannot decide, we will choose for you."

"Your... did you say your apprentice?"

He placed his hand on my forehead. It felt warm at first, gentle. Then it started to get heavier. Soon, his hand felt like a massive weight. I tried to resist him, to lift my arms, to move my head, but I could not.

"You're hurting me." My voice sounded pitiful, weak, distant.

"The pain you feel is all the pain you carry inside of you. The psychogenic serum is working its way through your system, cleansing you. It is going to get worse before it gets better. But it is a necessary first step to prepare you for the road ahead."

He lifted his hand, but the weight and pain were still there. It felt as if my whole body were pinned beneath a hot iron plank. I wanted to scream, but I could not open my mouth anymore.

Vizia leaned in very close, searching my face. "Soon, Oren, the pain will be too much to bear. You will cross a threshold. Try your best to remember what you see. It will not be easy. But you really must try. When you return, we can talk about what comes next."

He stood, looking down at me. He was not smiling. My vision turned red at the edges. It felt as if my whole body was vibrating with my screams, but no sound came out. The pain was beyond hearing. Searing light enveloped me.

———

I walk the streets near my quarters in Manderley. I am shirtless, in the popular fashion, and my seeker drones are resting quiet, looped like a chain around my neck. I want to see it all with my own eyes, not with the digital eyes of the drones. I look around at all of these incredible beings from across the universe. A towering giant with emerald green skin. A humanoid robot, varnished in gold. Tiny, winged creatures, no bigger than my hand, flitting through the air. One lands on my shoulder, speaking in a strange tongue I do not understand. I swat it away.

A beautiful woman with skin the color of the earth and dark hair curled in tight ringlets bumps into me.

"Pardon me," I say.

She looks shocked to see me, recognition flashing across her face. But before either of us can say another word, the crowd sweeps us along in opposite directions and she is gone.

I enter a temple at the edge of the market place. Broad marble and metal columns rise up and come together in wide arcs high overhead. Light pours in through the windows, shaped into perfect cones, edged so clearly that they seem immutable against the surrounding darkness. This view goes on so far that I can't see where it ends. The columns come together at the point at the edge of my sight, a massive alleyway, stretching out ahead of me.

There is no one around. The silence of the space is like a physical presence. I try to step quietly, but even with bare feet, each step echoes in the room. I begin to run. The sound of my feet is a rhythmic tattoo, driving me on. The air is ice in my lungs.

I run for a long time, but I don't get tired. Ahead of me, there is an altar. I stand in front of it. Two tiny idols sit on the altar. They are both molded from a lightweight metal, smooth and polished. The detail is staggering. A snake, curled in a circle, eats its own tail. I can count every scale. I look into its slitted eye. It looks back at me. The other icon is a bird of prey, wings tucked at its side, eyes closed, head bowed, each feather carved with striking precision.

I pick up the bird. A vulture. It opens its eyes and nips my hand with its beak, drawing a spot of blood. I drop it. It spreads its wings and flies away. The snake releases its tail and slithers after the bird.

I am not alone at the altar. Something else moves in the shadows. I call out. My voice booms in the chambered space, surprising me. I don't recognize the words echoing back. They are foreign and strange. Is that my voice?

The shadows darken around me. Someone is whispering in my ear, but I still cannot make out the words. Something brushes my neck. I turn. Nothing. No one.

I turn back, and Cere is standing in front of me. Her eyes are completely black. No whites. No irises. Just two deep wells of darkness. She opens her mouth, and there is a shining silver point of light coming from the back of her throat. The whisper in my ear grows to a shout. I cover my ears, but it is futile. The sound is getting louder and louder. I scream, but I cannot hear my own voice over the roaring.

I collapse to the ground.

Cere stands over me, but she is not Cere anymore.

She is Ifrit.

The silver light is winking in her mouth like a signal beacon. It is a coded message. In spite of the crushing noise in my head, I try to focus on her message.

Everything goes silent. The whole temple radiates with silver light.

I understand.

The ground starts shaking.

The marble floor splinters and cracks.

Ifrit stumbles backwards, a hole burning open in her chest. She is not Ifrit anymore. She is Saiara.

I stand up, trying to keep my footing, and reach out my hands toward Saiara. But she is too far away, and something is grasping my neck, holding me back. I pull with all of my strength, but I can't move any closer to her.

The ground cleaves apart behind her.

She stumbles backwards over the edge, swallowed up by the chasm.

The temple ceiling shatters with the force of the quake.

Stones rain down.

"Oren. Wake up, Oren. Tell me what you see." Vizia was shaking me.

The ceiling spun above my eyes. My arms came up to protect my head from falling stone.

"Oren. You're okay. You're back now." His hand on my arm was gentle and firm as he pulled it down from my face. I found his eyes, and there was a warmth there. "Tell me. What did you see?"

"I... saw her."

"Who, Oren?"

"Saiara. Ifrit. Cere. They were each themselves, but they were also all the same. They were trying to tell me something. It was so clear. But... I can't... I have lost it."

"Tell me what you remember."

"It was Manderley, but different. I went into a temple like nothing I've ever seen before. The whole building started to shake and the ground opened and she fell in. I couldn't save her." Hot tears were streaming down my cheeks. I wiped my eyes, shaking my head. "I am sorry, Vizia."

"You're fine, Oren. Just fine." He paused, searching. "You know that Forsara was almost destroyed, when the moon was sintered by Shugguth?"

I nodded. My neck was aching. I groaned with the discomfort.

"Life is filled with failure. Our ideas fail. Our bodies fail. The stars fail. It is the fundamental nature of the universe. The oldest lesson." He stroked my hair. "Looking back, it sometimes seems impossible that we ever made it this far. We have ravaged ourselves and our planets many times over. And nature has ravaged us. We fear the flaring sun and the tidal waves and the quaking earth, but they are the softest breath of the universe. A pulsar blasts destructive gamma radiation millions of galactic years into space. The gravity of a dying dwarf star flattens whole worlds. A black hole tears apart the very fabric of space-time.

"But still we persevere. Out of suffering and loss, we extract joy and wonder. Out of death comes new life. That is what makes all of this so beautiful. Failure is not an ending. It is a catalyst. A dying star bursts, spreading its seed, and new stars and worlds are born.

"Perhaps, when the universe is so cold and empty that all life as we know it has stopped, the universe will cross an unseen horizon and become something new altogether. We cannot know. All we have is our faith that in the face of unknowing, there is always life, even when there are none to live it."

"But what if it is all just emptying out? What if this is all we have?"

"Yes. What if." He smiled at me. "Come. Stand up. Your body will be sore, but the full eclipse is coming soon, and we need to get you ready for the viewing."

People were buzzing with excitement. In a few short hours, Shugguth would eclipse Appollion. It happened just once every four centuries, and the buildup to this moment had filled the world with a sense of joy and celebratory reverence. This moment represented the choice we all had to make. Sunlight or starlight. Home down here, or home out there. The Choosing.

Billions of people on the light side of the planet would bathe in purple warmth as the two suns became one. The Convergence. And those of us on the dark side, we were going to see the stars in all their majesty, blazing silver and white, unimpeded by the light of the suns. The Vastness.

Those who chose the Vastness yearned for something beyond. Explorers. Dreamers. Deviants. Whatever our motivations, we all aspired to a life out past the edges of the Forsaran system. For weeks, astronomists had been streaming down from satellite orbit, preparing the observatories and watch towers for the constellate ceremonies. The people in the darkened lands burned great fires to welcome them. They had the privilege of seeing the stars first, and they served as honorary hosts to the myriad of peoples making their way across the planet into the long night.

I walked behind Viziadrumon as we headed towards the upper deck. We were getting on a small, sub-orbital hopper to cross over the mountains and into the darkened lands. Even though I towered over Vizia, I felt invisible at his side. He was something of a legend here in the academy. Cadets and fellows alike were in awe of him as we strode through the corridors. Over the centuries, he had trained tens of thousands of cadets. Some of our most esteemed fellows had felt the thrill of challenge and the sting of failure under his tutelage.

"Why are you doing this, drumon? Why bother with me?"

He stopped walking and turned to face me, looking up at me. Randall hovered in the air beside his head. It made a chirping noise, as if to fill the silence. Finally, Vizia said, "You are my last project, Oren. At Saiara's request. She believes in you. And I believe in her. So I'm going to help you."

"Your last project?"

Randall chirped again. Its surface shifted from silver to gold, then back again.

Vizia laughed, then said, "Well, my last project like this, at least. I've been at this for too long. Longer than you've been alive, young blood.

"I was here during the last Convergence, you know." He shook his head. "Oh, you should have seen it. The way the whole city turned to violet, and we danced and drank and sang as the two suns became one. But my energy wanes. I must walk a new path soon, or else fizzle out. Perhaps you will even help me find a way."

He searched my face for a moment, deep lines of age spidering out through his acorn skin from the edges of his eyes. Then he turned and walked on ahead, his short legs moving quickly, Randall floating after him. Even with my long legs, I had to hurry to keep up.

Up on the deck, the sky was glaring white with the brightness of both suns. They were blazing, not yet overlapping, and it was almost unbearable. But the wind was warm and steady, and I leaned into it, looking down over the gleaming city as the air pushed and prodded me, whipping my hair and tugging the sleeves of my tunic.

Vizia tapped me on the arm and pointed towards the horizon of night that clipped the upper half of the distant mountains. Thousands of lights snaked up the dark side of the mountains, flickering streams of people making the pilgrimage on foot, crossing through to the long night.

"I made that journey once too," he said. "It was brutal. And beautiful. I will never forget it. The way we walked from day into night. The way our solar torches flared up as we crossed over. Looking back on the city, bathed in warm violet light, and then up at the mountain tops, looming in the darkness."

My mind worked over the math of his two contradicting statements. Had he stayed in Forsara to celebrate the previous Convergence, as he had said earlier? Or had he traveled into the long night of the Vastness, as he was describing now? Was he implying that this was his *third* Choosing? I looked at him, my jaw slackening, my eyebrows raised. "But... how old are you, Viziadrumon?"

He just shook his head again, smiling, remembering.

The hopper touched down. We hustled on board, and the door sealed with a quiet hiss as the shipheart registered our biosigs. The noise of the wind disappeared and we were up in the air, the mountains racing towards us. We crossed into night, passing above the hardened pilgrims.

Vizia gestured, encompassing the world spread out below us. "We are forever traveling through space. Tonight, we will see the light of dead and dying worlds. We will look back across time.

"And what are we against that boundless span? Even the longest-lived among us must one day die. In fact, we are dying every day. Shedding memories, and molecules, and old ideas, our identity fluid, changing. What is the fixed point? Does anything persist? That is one of the great questions of the Fellowship. It is another way of asking what you asked me yesterday. 'What if this is all there is?' It is up to each of us to answer it for ourselves."

He turned back to the wide, glass window, looking down at the world below.

"Look. Look there." All of the speeches were long over. The ritual dances had been spent. Many people had fallen asleep, too drunk or tired to stay awake any longer. But we stood well away from the nearby bonfire, and I followed Vizia's hand as he pointed towards a cluster of yellow and silver stars.

My neck was aching. We had been staring at the Vastness for hours, thousands and thousands of points of light gliding above us through the wide, dark night. "It is beautiful, drumon. It is all so beautiful."

"Yes. But look closer. There, right there." He gestured with emphasis, and reached his other hand behind my head, forcing my gaze in his desired direction. His bony fingers wrapped around the base of my skull, warm and smooth.

"What am I looking for?"

"That yellowing smudge."

"... Yes! I see it."

He released his hand from my neck. "The Dromedar cluster. Deep in the Cthlonian arm of the galaxy. That is where Saiara is going."

He kept his eyes to the night sky, and I studied his silhouette. His long, rounded nose. The wide forehead. His thin hair, pulled back into a tail, tightening the skin around his ears and eyes. "Seven of our own," he said. "A vanguard, traveling outwards, leaving behind their homes, everything they know, so that they may bring life and bear witness."

His eyes were faint glimmers in the starlight. "The probability is high that we will never see them again." He turned to look at me. "That you might never see Saiara again."

"I... I know. But I want to see her again, if I can."

He nodded. "There is so much left to chance. But maybe, just maybe, they will succeed, and the Fellowship will burn that much brighter against the emptiness. And if they do, then perhaps you will get your wish."

He dropped his head and closed his eyes. "Let us return to the fire. It is time for me to rest. Tomorrow you must decide what comes next."

"Over the days ahead," Vizia said, "as our two suns move past each other in their orbits, light will work its way back into the lands, filling in the mountains and townships, the canyons and forests, shadows shrinking, retreating, returning. I hope you use that time to prepare yourself."

We stood at the train station, watching hundreds of small transport risers climb back up through the atmosphere and into satellite orbit, returning the astronomists to the star-viewing vessels, out beyond the ambient light reflecting from the planet.

In a sub-orbital hopper, the trip would take barely an hour, but I had decided to take the overland passage back to Manderley. Traveling by solar rail would take several days, and I relished the thought of drinking in the countryside. Since arriving to Forsara, I had spent virtually all of my time either in the city or in the field. There was so much to see.

"You'll wait for me, right?"

Vizia nodded. "When you return to Manderley, I'll be ready for you. Your training will begin in earnest. We have much work to do, but I have confidence." He clasped my hands, looking at my eyes.

Randall floated towards me, shimmering with blues and purples.

I smiled at the mobile intelligence. "See you soon, little guy."

Randall chirped and turned forest green.

"Come now, Randall," Vizia said, and he climbed the ramp into the hopper. Randall floated after him, chirping one more time before they disappeared inside. A moment later, the hopper lifted up into the air, quiet and weightless, and darted into the sky.

⸻

The solar train carved through valleys and sped across the land like an arrow, silent and powerful. I enjoyed the sense of perspective from the wide windows of the cabin car. Trees and dwellings and meadows edged the train route, blurring with our passage, dwindling in our wake, while the distant mountains seemed to stand still.

The train was not full, but there were still more than a dozen people in my car. Everyone kept to themselves, using the quiet of the train to read, or work, or daydream. I was grateful for that. I needed the time to just be, no one watching over me, no one judging me.

The hours passed, and the world passed with them. I slipped in and out of sleep. If I dreamed, I do not remember. When the train stopped, passengers disembarked and new ones took their place. I paid them all little mind, occupied with my own reflections and wanderings. I thought of Saiara, always a few steps ahead of me. Of Ifrit, her firebrand anger, the way she died for what she believed in. Of Transcend personified, strange and enchanting and mysterious, ushering me into field consciousness.

My mind wandered to my parents. A pang of guilt for leaving them behind came over me. But my mind carried me past the guilt, back across the light years between us, back to my first simple, golden summer beneath the amber light of Cordelar, before I learned the harsh, cold lessons of the long winter.

I was so lost in remembering that I did not look up when I heard the carriage door slide open. The sound barely registered. The soft footfalls on the padded floor that came closer and closer to me were just background noise, almost imperceptible. Even when they stopped right next to me, I still did not look up.

Then she sat down across from me and said my name.

For one terrifying instant, I was back on the Arcturean moon, and she was screaming for help, and the horrible shipheart was above me, teeth silver and sharp.

She reached across the table, stroking my hand. "It's okay, Oren. I'm sorry if I startled you."

"Cere." I choked out her name. I stared at her, my jaw hanging open.

"It is good to see you again." Her smile was compassionate.

"Eledar's breath. What are you doing here?"

"Same as you, I imagine. Traveling home from the celebrations. I saw you through the window when I boarded a few stops back, and I've been thinking about what to say to you."

"I wish I had the same time to think. It's been so long. I'm not sure what to say."

She nodded. "It's been a long time. And from what I hear, you have been through a lot since we last parted."

I lowered my eyes, embarrassed at the thought of what she might have heard.

"Oren. Look at me."

I looked at her.

"If there's anyone who might be able to understand what you're going through right now, it's me. You know that, right?

"You did your best. Now you have to figure out how to live with the fact that your best wasn't enough. But that doesn't make you a terrible person. If anything, it will make you a stronger one."

"What happened to you? After? I had heard you were released from medical care, but I never saw you again."

Instead of answering with words, she lowered her forehead down to the table, fanning her hair towards me, revealing her neck. My breath caught in my throat as I sucked in air through my teeth. There was a faint circle of discoloration where her field port should have been. It had been sealed off.

She sat back up, and she was not smiling anymore.

"I'm... I'm sorry, Cere. It's just... It surprised me to see that."

"It's okay," she said, reaching across the table to touch the back of my hand. "Most people react like that. The thought of a loss like this is too upsetting for those who have crossed over and connected.

"But this is how we were once. All of us. And this is how many people in the universe still are. Living every day in our waking bodies, alone with our own minds, the wanderings and anxieties and distractions, the constant stream of our own consciousness, seemingly isolated from everyone else's ideas and dreams and feelings."

We sat in silence for a while, staring out at the blurring world.

"Were you angry at Dar?" I asked after a time. "For what she did to you?"

She raised her eyebrows. "Anger doesn't do it justice. Rage. Bitterness. Fear. Jealousy. So many feelings. And not just towards Dar. I was angry at you. At Kino. At everyone. But none of us could have controlled what happened. And, in the end, I was the one who made the decision to press ahead, to try and interface with that damnable corruption."

"I... I think you did the best you knew how. Darpausha too, though I don't know how she did it. It seems an impossible choice."

Cere stared down at her hands, fingers splayed on the table. "The madness of that shipheart was a terrible, alien thing. It left some kind of neural virus in our minds. I survived. So did Sulimon and Mahkoun. But the others were too far gone. Their brains were pitted and cratered."

"Eledar's breath. That is awful."

"And if Dar hadn't the will to act, who knows how many more would have suffered." She looked up at me. "Sometimes, there are no good options, Oren. When you're older, you'll understand that."

"Darpausha said the same thing to me."

She smiled a rueful smile. "I probably learned that from her." She looked back out the window of the train.

"What did you do? When you recovered?"

"As soon I was well enough, I scoured Transcend's networks for any sign of the abomination, but it was either gone, or hiding too deep for us to find." She shrugged. "So, I moved on. I have spent the past seven years working with Transcend on my rehabilitation, exercising my mind and body to release the trauma and carve new neural pathways. We have discussed my reconnection to the field, of course, but Transcend worries that my mind won't be able to handle it a second time. For the foreseeable future, this is my life."

"I'm so sorry, Cere. I wish... I wish I could have done more."

"You probably saved my life, Oren. I am grateful to you. My anger is long past." She touched my hand again.

"I still dream of it sometimes."

"Of what?"

"The shipheart."

She raised her eyebrows.

"It's like an invader. I will be in some other world, and it will appear, silver teeth, looming sexless body, taunting me, haunting me. I have also searched for any sign of it in our networks, also without success. As you said, it is either long gone or in hiding beyond our sight."

"That's troubling, Oren. When was the last time you dreamed of it?"

"I don't remember. It's been awhile, I guess." I paused. "I dreamed of you too."

She looked at me, waiting for more.

"We were in a strange temple. It was massive, and it looked like it had been standing for a thousand years or more. The earth started shaking, like it did in the ancient days of Forsara. Your mouth was open, and there was a shining point of silver light in the blackness of your throat. You were trying to tell me something. Something so important. And I could almost understand you.

"Then the temple shattered and crumbled, burying us, and I woke up." I couldn't look her in the eyes as I told her this. I continued, "I guess our experience on the moon has never left me. I was so naive. Having fun with our little adventure, until we were all almost killed."

She nodded thoughtfully, her face warm and compassionate. Then she smiled as something occurred to her. "Maybe I was trying to tell you to forgive yourself."

Her words hit me with a shock, surprising me. I sat there, unsure of what to say.

"You can, Oren," she said. "You can and you must. Hear me when I say this. What happened to me was not your fault."

I nodded. "Thank you, Cere," I whispered.

"Thank *you*, Oren. I'm so glad I saw you today."

"Me too. What will you do now?"

"What I've been doing. Recovering. Growing. Learning about

my new self. My new strengths and limitations. Finding my own place in the universe. It's the gift we're all given, and it's the struggle we all face."

"Viziadrumon believes that. Believes in life. That all we can do, all we have ever done, is light fires in the darkness."

The train was slowing down. Cere looked out the window again. "Shina," she said. "This is where I grew up. I am going to see my family, Oren." She stood, looking down at me in my seat. "Don't give up," she said. Then she touched her right hand to my cheek, leaned in, and kissed me on the forehead.

"Goodbye." She turned and walked towards the exit.

"Goodbye, Cere."

I watched as she got off the train, trailing her with my eyes until she disappeared into the station. Then the train floated up, accelerating towards Manderley, and I was alone again, the hours ahead and behind all rolling together as I thought about everything that had happened and everything that was still to come.

PART 2
HOPE

I STOOD at the edge of the forest near our basecamp on Eaiph, my mind full with all these memories of youth. Forsara is a world of azure, violet, and mulberry, a riot of blues and purples infused with the chrome light of Appollion and the red heat of Shugguth. But here, beneath the golden rays of Soth Ra and the wide blue sky, nature paints its canvas with vibrant greens and sepia. As I peered into the shade of the broad cedar pines, I couldn't help but think back on the long and winding path that led me to this strange and wondrous planet.

The quiet whir of Sid's bionetic legs carried across the arid, windless air, but I was deep in reverie, walking back across the years. I didn't realize what I was hearing until his voice shook me from my recollections.

"Orenpausha?"

I looked up at him. His bald head glinted in the sunlight like polished bronze.

"I'm sorry, Sid. I was far away from this place, thinking about life back on Forsara." I smiled at him.

He did not return my smile. He held a portable monitor in his hands, and his lips were pressed tight with concern. Sid was our team's farseer, trained in the arts of systemic interpretation. It was his job to anticipate problems and solve them before they happened; to read the signs and portents that nature offers for those who know where and how to look. Only a fool would ignore the worries of a farseer.

I ceased my smiling and reached for his handheld. "What've you got, Sid?"

He handed me the portable monitor. I stroked my cheeks with my thumb and forefinger, examining the renderings displayed in front of me. I zoomed in, then back out again, coming at it from a few different angles. "A tectonic survey of the planet?" I finally asked.

Sid nodded.

"What's it telling us?"

"Based on the data we've been feeding Reacher, the planet is in a steady state of flux. The core of the planet is a colossal iron lodestone surrounded by a churning ocean of molten hot ore. Prodigious thermal veins about two farruns below the surface crisscross the planet, channeling all of the energy into volcanic gathering wells.

"The resulting tectonics are impressive. The continental shelves are essentially floating on the surface of the planet, forever colliding and dividing, coughing up magma and mineral effluvia. It is like one huge convection oven."

"Incredible," I said, looking at the handheld with fresh eyes. I sped up the simulation, trying to make sense of the complex, large-scale movements of the planet's crust.

I looked up at Sid. "There's a 'but' coming, isn't there?" I said.

He exhaled through his nose. "But it means that the planet is unstable. Nothing so bad as Shugguth's Curse, mind you, but nothing to scoff at either. Xayes and I have been working with Reacher to run the data through every conceivable permutation, and it almost always comes up with the same outcome. There will be a catastrophic earthquake in this region sometime in the next century. It's not a question of 'if.' It's a question of 'when.'"

The implications hit me hard. "An earthquake. At the very heart of civilization on this planet."

"It could happen tomorrow."

"And what if it did?"

"Many would die. It could spell the end of civilization as they know it."

"Eledar's breath," I cursed.

We stood for a time with the weight of that fact. The cedars were as still as sculptures, rising like blind sentinels drawn up from the rocky soil to protect the fungi and fragile trumpet blossoms that grew in their shade.

"There has to be something we can do," I finally said, pacing back and forth, my feet scrunching in the dry soil.

"Pure Doctrine would insist that we do not interfere."

"I've been down that road, Sid. Non-interference is a fantasy that only works for zealots and theoraths. But we're not in the temple, and we're not at the academy, and there is no one here to insist on anything but us."

Sid nodded. "My parents were devout Purists," he said. "The last time I saw my father, he would not speak to me because of these." He rapped his knuckles on the trimantium of his thigh. "My mother did her best to make peace with it, but I know it broke her heart. As far as they were concerned, if I was born without legs, then that was as the universe intended, and it is not ours to meddle with."

"So you went with the chrome look just to really rub it in?"

Sid laughed at that. "When I came of the age to make my own choices, I'd already known for years that I wanted to go biped. My pateruncle was more open-minded than my parents, and despite my father's vehement protests, he arranged for the original procedure.

"My first set of legs had living tissue designed to match my skin. The techs did a fine job, but... I don't know. They just weren't right. When I came to Forsara, I upgraded." He smiled. "Unvarnished metal may not be the conventional choice, but it felt more true to me. These are not ordinary legs, so why try and pretend otherwise?"

"You've always had strong instincts, Sid. That is one of the reasons the Coven selected you as part of this team."

He bowed his head at the compliment, and we went silent again, working the problem of the tectonics.

"We must be missing something," I said. "There must be a good choice here, even if it's not an obvious one."

Sid traced complex spirals in the dirt with his bionetic foot. "With all that geothermal activity..." he said slowly. Then he snapped his fingers and looked up at me, eyes wide and smiling. "The moon of Danhk! Do you remember? Kohndrumon devoted an entire module to it. A second millennium settlement, too far from its star to gather adequate solar energy, the settlers forced to go underground to survive."

"The Danhkan! Of course!" I grabbed him by the shoulders. "Sid, you're magnificent! Can you see if Reach has those records in his archives?"

"I am on it," he said, sharing my excitement. He turned and ran back towards base camp, his oiled trimantium legs whirring as he picked up speed.

I stamped my foot on the ground. "The planet shifts beneath us," I whispered. I could almost feel the land moving beneath me, drifting across the surface of this wide ocean world.

"I recommend we start here and here." Sid gestured to two points in the holosphere, "and then work outwards in a loose spiral."

I looked around, scanning the group.

Xayes nodded his agreement, his unkempt copper hair

wobbling above his shoulders. "That thermal vein runs for almost three dozen farruns, and it has no surface channels that we can see. It is a massive font of energy, unimpeded by any foreseeable surface eruptions for the next several hundred planetary years. By that point, the local field network will be so thick with redundancies that a power shortage would be near impossible."

"Xander, what's your read?" I said, turning to Xayes's twin brother. "Tell us what might go wrong."

"Sid's initial read is correct," he said, squinting his colorless eyes as he bent close to the holosphere, examining the schematics. "But this planet is not the same as the moon of Danhkan. No matter how much we run the scenarios, our information is incomplete, and there is a chance that the earthquake could spiral out of control."

"What can we do to mitigate that risk?"

"All things considered," Xayes said, jumping back in, "I think this is our best bet. There is always the risk of failure. But the potential for reward here is as high as any planet we've seen."

I looked at Neka, Adjet, and Cordar, inviting their voices into this decision that would literally shake the earth.

Neka shrugged and put up her hands, her ebony skin tinged with purple from the light projected by the holosphere. "People are my specialty. Not geo-engineering. If you all think we can pull it off, then I'm on board. We have a responsibility to the people of Eaiph, even if they've no idea we exist."

Adjet nodded at that, her silver hair shimmering, and Cordar made the hand sign for agreement, touching his thumb to his pale forehead, then moving his hand towards Neka, pointing at her with his pinky finger. He was of the same mind as her.

"Reach?" I said, speaking a little louder out of habit, a kind of acknowledgment of his omnipresence, even though I knew he could hear every word we said, even if we whispered. "Any reservations?"

"I have gone over all the data with Sid and Xayes," he said, his voice piping out of the speakers hidden throughout the ship. "It is as sound a plan as we can make, given the variables."

I nodded. "Good. Then let's get the insertion points ready. If we start at first light, we'll have the foundation channels in by sundown."

We tunneled deep into the earth, aiming the nanite bores on a direct path to the thermal veins. As these underground channels were being carved, Sid and Xayes devised an ingenious modification to the solar sails on *Reacher*, allowing us to capture and convert the tremendous heat from the planet's core. With Soth Ra's radiant energy above us, and our improvised thermal system drawing up from below, our access to power was virtually limitless.

With these systems in place, we began gathering the resources and mining the minerals to build all the tools we needed. Organic batteries. Replicating fibers. Nutrient basins. Port adapters. Everything necessary to grow a field network that would let us influence the planet from within.

Materials ready, we broke into three teams of two, Siddart staying behind with *Reacher*. Each team was charged with building and installing a field hub. The first three would serve as our base hubs, forming a triangle fifteen farruns on every side, with *Reacher*, our ship, in the center. From there, we could push out in every direction, tracing a circle around our triangle, overlaying the original, spiraling out just as Sid had suggested, increasing the density and distribution of our influence.

I ran my hands across the smooth, exacting surface of the field basin. "This is excellent work, Adjet. How many hubs do we have now?"

"Ten fully online and operational," she said, her long, alabaster fingers dancing across the basin's lumina console as she pulled up the data, "ranging across more than one hundred square farruns. And five more will be ready within the week. The thermal energy is bountiful. More than enough to run the whole system."

"Do you really think it will be enough to control the quake? You didn't say much when we debated the matter."

"Reach thinks so, and so do Sid and Xayes. That is enough for me."

"Can I plug in?"

"Your eagerness never ceases, pausha. It is good you are here. It gives us energy."

"So is that a yes?" I said, giving her a knowing look.

She grinned and held up a smooth, translucent disc, laced with platinum filaments.

"The key?"

She nodded.

I held out my hand towards her, palm up.

She placed the disc in my palm, covering my hand with both of hers.

I bowed to her, then took the disc and laid it flush with the field port near the head of the basin. The surface wiring lit up with a warm yellow glow, growing brighter wherever I placed my hands.

I nodded, smiling. "Excellent." Then I stripped off my clothes and climbed into the basin, sliding down onto my back, resting my head into the field port. Adjet smiled back at me, then lowered her head as her fingers danced again across the lumina console.

There was a quiet hiss and gurgle, and the nutrient bath flowed in, swallowing my body up to my neck. I tingled with anticipation. I could almost feel my cells responding to the nourishment, preparing me for the inner journey.

Adjet touched her hand to the console and spoke. "Cordar. Sid. Orenpausha is preparing for the inaugural dive. Are the other hubs ready?" She listened for a minute, her eyes to the ceiling, then

nodded. "Good." She looked back at me. "Cordar and Sid are up at
the ship. They are running specs on all ten hubs. Xander is on his
way here for visual affirmation. Once he's done, we'll signal back to
the ship, and then we will ready you for the journey."

I closed my eyes. I could feel the basin beneath me, the weight
of my bones pulling me down. The nutrient fluid glided with my
every subtle movement like a second skin. I pulled my belly in and
flattened the curve of my back, compressing the fluid up and
around my sides.

I slowed my breathing. In. One. Two. Out. One. Two. My
heart rate dropped. The pulse in my ears changed from a marching
drumbeat to a churning dirge.

Xander's footsteps echoed off the smooth cavern walls. I heard
his voice but the words were distant, inscrutable. Adjet sounded
like she was laughing, a joyful sound.

Their hands were on me. Adjet took her fingers and tapped
along my meridian channels, loosening the energy, relaxing my
muscles. Xander cradled my head, massaging his fingers around the
tissue on my neck. Then he laid my head back down and I felt the
wires from the field port weave into my spine, interfacing with my
neural network, settling in.

The serum flowed through me. I was floating at the top of the
room. Xander and Adjet stood over my body. They were each
holding one of my hands, eyes open, looking up at the ceiling. At
me. I turned towards the long, dark tunnel behind me, and slid
inside, rushing towards the light.

I stretched my mind. It was effortless, just like it had been on
Reacher. As we traveled through space, the field enabled us to feel
the ship from the inside, to interact with it, to become a part of it.
Now, we could begin to do the same here on the planet Eaiph. I
inhabited the whole nascent lattice we had built; all the echoing

corridors we had carved beneath the surface, all the filaments of energy lighting up.

I could feel my crew members' footsteps inside the chambers like insects on my skin. I rose to the surface, sweeping past our ship and up into the low atmosphere. Winged birds graced through me, their feathers rustling with my breath.

The rush was incredible. This was more than *Reacher*. More than *Transcendence*. More even than Forsara. In those places, the field networks were already established. But here? Here, there was pure potential. We were building our own network. We were not just participants. We were Architects. We could shape the network with our will.

I stretched again, and the lattice grew with me. The filaments pierced out, winding through the dirt, connecting more and more of this world to the field. It was only a matter of time now. I smiled. The wind quieted.

In the field, the limitations of the waking body fell away. The boundaries between the inner and outer world faded. All of the connections became clear.

I drew a deep breath. The ground trembled. Yes. Again. Deeper this time.

"Pausha. Slow down. Slow down!" Neka was in the field with me, and her voice was in my mind.

Even though some small part of me was well aware that she was several farruns away, at one of the ancillary hubs, I felt her heart beating right next to mine. I laughed and the ground shook harder. "Can't you feel this, Neka?"

She ignored my question. "We are bringing you out," she said.

A tiny pinprick of light appeared, far away in the distance. With my longsight, I peered through it, into my field chamber. Xander and Adjet were standing over my body, looking worried. Adjet's fingers tapped a pattern on the lumina console, and then I shot up to the light, breaking through it, gasping and coughing for air.

I heard Xander's voice. "Adjet, help me. He's too heavy."

There was a rustling sound. I slid back down into the basin, sinking into the liquid.

As I drifted into darkness, Adjet whispered in my ear and stroked her hand on my chest, "Hush, pausha. Breathe. You pushed very hard. But you are back."

***

When I woke, Neka was there beside me. As our meditician, it was her job to work with Reacher to look after the mental and physical health of our team, and my little foray into our nascent field network had managed to put both at risk. She looked down at me, sadness edging her cinnamon eyes without saying anything. She just held my hand and watched me.

"Neka," I said. "I know what you're thinking, but please don't be angry." She stayed silent, so I continued. "You must have felt it. The full potential of this planet. We can save the people of Eaiph from the coming disaster, and in the process we can build something truly special here. This will be the settlement that finally stands as a mirror to our great Forsaran homeworld."

Something shifted in her eyes. Anger, maybe. Or fear. She spoke in quiet, measured tones. "We can only handle so much at once, pausha. Even you. And especially on the first dive. You were getting pulled apart by the energies of the planet. And where would that have left us? What if you had started a quake before we were ready to channel its power?"

"I would have stopped it."

"If you could have. We have traveled so far to come to this place, but you risked destroying yourself, and maybe all of us with you. You're strong, but you're not invincible. If you drink too much, you will drown."

I shook my head and waved away her concern with my hand. "I appreciate what you're saying, Neka, but we can't afford to go too slow. There is so much more to do, and we just don't know how much time we have."

"We're certain they'll be safe?" Neka asked. Xayes, Sid and I stood with her in a circle around the holosphere on *Reacher's* main deck. The four of us were in geostationary orbit, ten thousand feet above the planet of Eaiph. Cordar, Xander, and Adjet were down on the surface. Below it, to be more precise, connected in the three field hubs that formed a triangle at the outer edges of the target zone.

"As certain as we can be in any of this," Sid said.

Neka's face was unreadable, but I knew she was nervous, especially for Cordar, her closest companion.

"Show me the fracture points," I said, peering at the schematic on the holosphere. It displayed the underground fault line, a thick, jagged corridor running through the shelves of land. Reach highlighted three intersections where thermal veins came together, forming key energy lines along the continental shelf.

Once we detonated the explosives, energy would ramify through the veins, triggering an earthquake, which is exactly what we were planning on. But our goal was not to destroy the earth and the people on it. It was to protect them. By catalyzing the quake on our terms, we hoped to contain it, using the thermal energy to fuse the tectonic plates in this region together, ensuring thousands of years of future stability.

That's where Cordar, Xander, and Adjet came in. Working in unison, they would use the field to channel and guide the thermal energy. It would be too powerful for them to master, but if all went according to plan, they could, with Reacher's guidance, 'open' and 'close' thermal veins at strategic moments, sending the energy where we most needed it, while mitigating the worst damage.

"Reach, overlay the sky view." A second projector lit up, showing us the surface of the planet from our sub-orbital vantage, like looking through a window. There was the ridge of the nearby mountain range. The band of the river, sparkling in the sunlight. The fjords in the north, cratered green pools of water. All of it mapped out in front of us. We looked at this fragile beauty in silence.

Reacher merged the two images, and the golden-blue holo was imprinted beneath, the schematic of thermal veins shining up through the lakes and river and mountains. I looked at Neka and said, "Will you do the honors?"

She made a tight-lipped smile, exhaling through her nose. Then she nodded. "Initiate the separation," she said.

I kept my eyes on the holo schematic. For a moment, there was nothing. Then, simultaneously, the thermal intersections Reach had marked off on the holo bloomed with light, sending ripples of energy through the veins, creating the impression that the whole planet was translucent, and we could see its blood running bright.

"Look! There!" Xayes gestured.

We watched a flood of thermal plasma snake and weave, coursing alongside the fault line. It was as if an invisible wind was buffeting the magma, altering its currents, sending it first one way, then shifting it back in the other direction.

"They're doing it," Sid whispered.

"Reach," I said, "how are they down there?"

"They are at peak mental activity, but all biosigs are within a manageable range."

"Pausha." Neka's voice was commanding in its evenness. I looked at her, then followed her eyes.

The peninsular mountains. The range that skirted the edge of the ocean was shaking and cracking. Massive slabs of rock splintered and broke off, sliding downwards in an avalanche of scree. We watched as a hunk of land rippled like water, then sank into the earth. Ocean water came rushing in to fill the gap. More land fell away, and more water rushed in, forming a bay at the foot of the mountains.

"Reach," I said, my voice rising with concern.

"The energy is spilling over, pausha," he said. "Cordar has his attention further north, but Xander and Adjet are working to contain it."

Even as Reach said that, a river sourced high in the glacial peaks began leaking out of its centuries-old pathways. A wide torrent of water sluiced its way to an ancient caldera in a stunted peak in the middle of the range, a remnant from a volcanic eruption, or, perhaps, an asteroid impact. The caldera started to fill with water, and within minutes, it had become a lake.

"The final outcome is beyond their influence now," Reach said. "They have done everything they can."

As he said this, the tremors seemed to subside.

"Is it-?"

Before I could get the question out, the quake roared again, and in a final, catastrophic schism, the tip of the peninsula sheared off, taking the mountain at the end of the range with it. The bay at the foot of the mountains transformed into a strait of ocean water, water surging through passage, more than a farrun across from shore to new shore.

We all looked at each other, silent. We had just witnessed the birth of an island.

"Status report?" I said, my voice little more than a whisper.

"It seems the worst of it is over," Reach said. "Cordar, Adjet, and Xander are exhausted, but they are alive. and the fault line has been sealed."

"Was... was anyone hurt?" Sid asked.

"As far as I can tell from my initial scans, no native peoples were harmed."

Neka started to laugh, all the tension she carried melting out of her.

Sid, Xayes, and I joined in.

We had done it.

Smaller aftershock tremors continued for weeks, but the inflection points had been well planned, and there were no more significant geological mishaps. Once she learned that no one had been harmed, Adjet had, of course, taken great delight in the whole situation. She dubbed the newly formed caldera lake in the mountains 'Oren's Puddle,' and the name caught on like wildfire with the rest of the team.

What could I do but laugh? I had made my puddle. Now I had to swim in it. What really mattered was our new island.

Manderlas.

We all agreed it was a suitable name. More than thirty thousand years ago, Eledar and the first Coven had founded Manderley, the worldheart of Forsara. Now, we were doing the same, building a worldheart here on Eaiph, and the island was an unexpected boon.

The possibilities stretched out in front of me. The island gave us privacy from the local peoples, while also ensuring we would be close enough to observe them and learn from them as we decided when and how best to make contact. It was the perfect staging ground.

I stood alone on the shore, looking out across the new ocean canal to the mainland. The salt air was sweet and bracing. From my vantage, the mountains we'd disturbed with the quake still stood proud and beautiful on the horizon. I took solace knowing that the canyons and gorges that we had cracked open would bring their own beauty and wonder to the future generations we were preparing for.

I turned and looked in towards the island center. The geological tumult had left the land scarred and riven with water, but the potential was there, a broad, flat plain of land, sweeping up towards the lone mountain. Clouds drifted above its peak.

"Now we begin," I whispered.

"OREN. IT'S NEKA."

"Yes? What is it?" I said, touching the bone at the base of my ear to activate the transponders we had recently embedded beneath our skin, allowing us to communicate across many farruns.

"I know you're busy," she said, "but I am at your puddle." She paused. "I mean the caldera in the mountains. And... well, you should get up here."

Cordar and I were on Manderlas, going over the gene sequences he'd worked up with Adjet to splice Forsaran and Eaiph seeds. "Neka," I said in a playful voice, "I don't have time to join you on every one of your jaunts to the mainland." I raised my eyebrows at Cordar, smiling.

He grinned and touched his transponder to join in on the conversation. "The pausha is here assisting me on very important matters, dearest. Surely you don't mean to take him away from me?"

"Look, boys," she said, impatient with our teasing, "I promise you this is worth it. Take one of the hoppers and get up here. You can come too, Cordar, if you can bear to pull yourself away from your precious seeds."

Cordar chuckled and shook his head.

My curiosity was piqued. "Okay, Neka. We're coming. This sounds interesting."

"No, pausha. My dearest Cordar's work with plant genetics is interesting. This is something else altogether."

The images in front of us left me speechless. Neka let go of Cordar's hand, stepped forward, and waved her light across another patch on the rock wall. She looked back at us. "These are no accident," she said.

Cordar touched his hand to his heart. "We must tell the others," he said in a hushed voice.

I hung my head as a sob welled in my chest, a bubbling of sadness and joy that I couldn't hold it back. "Oh, Saiara," I whispered.

Neka touched my arm.

I looked up at her, tears in my eyes.

She exhaled, but she did not say anything more. She just turned and passed her light back and forth across the beautiful, ancient hieroglyphs carved on the cave wall.

"Look. Look here!" Siddart said. "What is this thing?" He pointed at a figure painted on the cave wall, a human body with a monstrous, animalistic head. It had a thick nose, and short, stout horns above its dark, round eyes. Dense, fibrous fur covered its face and neck, running down to its bare, human shoulders. It was naked from the neck down, and its genitals looked large and heavy.

"They look as if they are worshipping it," Neka said. She pointed to smaller figures, kneeling near the feet of the beast man.

"Some sort of deity," Adjet said. "Thank the Scions that this place was not destroyed in the quake." She touched her hand to the image of the horned god, and her silvery eyes sparkled in the glow of our portable lights.

"They're amazing," I said. "But we didn't bring you all here just to see cave paintings. What do you think these are?" I pointed up to the sky in this ancient tableau. Three spheres were carved in the rock, trailed by lines, a gesture of falling towards the earth. Above the spheres, the wall had been cracked and split in the quake, but there was clearly some sort of object in the sky.

"Is that...?" Siddart asked.

I nodded. "I think so."

"They made it," he whispered. "They actually made it!" His voice was getting louder. "Those are probably explorer drones." He pointed to the falling spheres.

"And this!" exclaimed Adjet. The images showed a column of light crashing into the mountains, causing a large explosion of debris and fire. "Maybe... maybe it wasn't a meteor strike or an eruption that made this caldera." She looked back at me, her face mixed with awe and sadness.

No one said anything. The implications of Adjet's observation were clear. If the first party of Architects crash-landed in these mountains, then we might be standing near their final resting space.

Finally, I spoke up. "None of this is definitive. If they made it this far, then we must not give up all hope. If there was a crash, it is possible that at least some of them survived. If they are alive, we will find them.

"But we cannot halt our work on Manderlas. I will oversee the installations with Reacher, Adjet, Sid and the twins. Neka, can you and Cord keep searching for any more signs?"

She nodded. "Let's get back to the ship. We'll start from the sky."

Three days later, when Neka came to me with the news, I was digging a trench.

"I suppose you don't need me to tell you that there are at least a dozen easier ways for you to do that," she said as she looked down at me from the lip of the ditch.

"Have you ever used a shovel?" I asked, raising it up in the air.

Neka shook her head. "Never," she said. "I didn't even know we had one on board."

I hefted it in my hands. "We didn't. Reach pulled the design up from his archives. The nanomodelers did the rest."

I pointed the shovel head towards her and sighted my eye along the blade. "Molecular precision," I said. "This thing carves through soil like a plasma torch melting through ice. Makes me nostalgic for home... even though it's better than any shovel we ever had back then."

Reach had taken the liberty of making a few modifications to the design. With its self-sharpening blade, and an angled shaft custom-fit to my height, it was the best I'd ever handled. But it was still fundamentally a shovel, and holding it in my hands gave me a primal sense of satisfaction.

"You learned to dig in the mines?" she asked.

I nodded. "My father taught me. Digging is to a miner what takeoff is to a pilot. Even though I spent most of my time in the refinery with my mother, he insisted I learn every aspect of our family craft.

"One winter, the churners got jammed, and we had to dig them out. My dad didn't even have to say 'I told you so.' He just handed me a shovel and we got to it. That was a long night."

"There wasn't an easier way?"

"Things were pretty far behind on Verygone. A lot of our equipment was primitive. The shovel. The crescent axe. The riddle. These tools have been used since the first prospector panned for gold in the highland rivers of Forsara. Sometimes the simplest tools are the most effective."

"Does a prospector need to solve puzzles?"

"What? Oh... Ha! No, you use a riddle to separate coarse and fine stone until you find what you're looking for."

"Ah. Of course." She smirked at me. "But the riddle I still haven't solved is why in the name of Eledar you're digging a trench."

I looked down at my hands and arms, covered in dirt, then back up at her. "Honestly? My mind has been racing ever since you found that cave. I cannot stop thinking about them. I needed this work to focus my thoughts. If we can't find a use for it, I'll probably just fill it back in with dirt when I am done."

"If clarity is what you're after, I could have Reach increase your dosage of gauyasine..."

"No," I interrupted, "This is better. Like I said, simple tools."

"Well, I am not sure if my news is going to help, but..."

"You found something?" I dropped the shovel and scrambled out of the trench to stand next to her.

She took my hand. "It was them, pausha. Reacher riddled every inch of the caldera," she said, using her newly learned word. "There are only traces, but even with so little to go on, the molecular remnants are clear. We do not know *why* they crashed, but we know that the first Architects of Eaiph came down in these mountains."

"Eledar's breath. Did... did you find anything that might tell us what happened to the crew? To Saiara?"

"The crash was catastrophic. If they were still on the ship, they were vaporized on impact."

"And if they weren't on the ship?"

"It's certainly possible. If that's true, I can only see one reason why they came to this part of the planet."

"The same reason we did."

"Yes," she said. "If we are going to find any clues, they will be among the people of Eaiph."

"Of course. They saw what we saw. How did you say it? The birthplace?"

"The cradle."

I nodded. "The cradle called to them." I started pacing. "We need to find a way inside. A way to understand their culture, their daily life. If there is any chance they survived, even for a short time, we must find out everything we can."

"I agree," she said. "In fact, I already have a plan."

"What?" I stopped in my tracks. "Tell me."

"I am going to live among them."

"Give me three months," Neka said. "Three months to gather information so we can decide what to do next."

"But we still don't even know why they crashed!" Cordar said, waving his hands in the air. "What if somehow the people of this planet knocked them out of the sky? And now you want to go among them?"

"Cordar," she said. "Don't be ridiculous. You know as well as I do that these people have nothing that could knock a rangership from orbit. You're looking for excuses to keep me here, to keep me safe, but I'm the best qualified among us, and you know it."

He crossed his arms over his chest and exhaled in a huff. "Then I'm coming with you," he said. "I won't let you go alone."

Neka laughed and touched her hand to his pale cheek. "Oh Cordar," she said. "You couldn't be more conspicuous if you walked into their royal gardens and tried to plant one of your purple Forsaran ferns. I am darker-skinned than most of these people, but not so much that there won't be others like me. Your pale skin would make you a magnet for attention."

"He's right, though," I said. "I don't feel good about sending you alone."

"Your size would make you stand out just as much as Cordar's skin," she said.

"What about Sid?" Cordar said.

I shook my head. "We need him here with Reacher."

"What then?" Neka said.

"I know we can't shrink me down to size, but maybe there is something we can do about Cordar's skin. Adjet?"

"Right," she said, taking her cue. "As the palest member of our motley team, I make Cordar look like he was born on a planet with three suns."

Cordar barked with laughter at that. Adjet flashed him her winning smile.

"Even the single sun here on Eaiph is dangerously bright for me," she continued, "which is why I came up with this."

She held up a light wand in her right hand and stuck out her left forearm. She turned on the wand and passed its light over her forearm, demonstrating to the rest of the crew what she had already shown to me.

Cordar's eyes went wide and his jaw hung open.

Xayes hurried toward her, leaning close to inspect her skin with his modified eyes. "My grandfather-"

"Graxes Ben Or," Adjet said.

He looked up at her in surprise.

"This is based on his work. I wanted to wait to show you and Xander until I had it perfected, but pausha asked me to bring it to this meeting."

Xander came and stood next to his brother. "Remarkable. Grandfather would be impressed. But, as you said, this is focused on UV protection, and your skin looks more purple than brown. That doesn't really solve the problem of helping Cordar to blend in."

"You're right. It's not camouflage. But the principles are the same. I am sure we can get it there."

"Can you control it at will?" Xayes asked, his eyes flashing with excitement.

"Not yet. But I'm working on that too."

"Are there any risks?" Neka asked.

Before Adjet could respond, Cordar jumped in. "I don't care what the risks are. I'll do it."

Adjet saw the concern in Neka's face. "Don't worry," she said. "The risks are minimal. The twins will help me finish what their grandfather started, and when we are ready, you and Cordar will walk among the people of Eaiph without fear."

"THE SAGAIN CALL IT LUNNANA-SIN," Neka told me, pointing up at the moon. "The great eye of the Architect who first built the world."

I raised my eyebrows at the word Architect. Neka nodded and said, "I know. A strange coincidence. But it is the closest translation."

Neka's three months had turned into more than six, and in that time, she and Cordar had learned much about these people of Eaiph who called themselves the Sagain, who carried the genetic imprints of Forsara in their blood.

"Maybe it is not a coincidence," I said.

"Maybe not."

Dawn was approaching. We were sitting outside, on the shore of Manderlas, watching the solitary moon climb in a high arc, rising above the inland mountains, a slim crescent shining pale yellow with the reflected light of Soth Ra.

Neka pointed at the last remaining star in the morning sky, "That is Nindaranna. Daughter of Lunnana. They revere her as a goddess of birth and death because she wanders the sky in the morning, and again in the evening, a harbinger of the dawn and the darkness."

"Nindaranna," I said, feeling the word on my tongue.

"You'll get there," she said, smiling at my pronunciation.

"Thanks, Nekadrumon," I said, looking down at her and raising my left eyebrow.

She laughed. "I like the sound of that," she said. "Did you know that Viziadrumon asked me to be his amanuensis for a time? You also apprenticed with him, yes?"

"I did. Thanks to Saiara. I wouldn't be here without their faith in me. It's no surprise he took you on though. You've always been a teacher's darling."

"Hey!" She threw a fistful of sand at me.

I nonchalantly brushed the sand from my torso. "The twins have been busy while you and Cordar were gone, little darling," I said, affecting a professorial tone.

She scowled. I pretended not to notice. "They have been working with Reacher to chart the skies. As you can probably tell from the quality of its light, Nindaranna is not actually a star," I said, doing a better job with the planet's name this time. "It is, for the majority of its orbit, the closest planet to ours. It shines so bright because it is encased in thick clouds of sulfuric acid and carbon dioxide. It is a blazing hothouse of a world."

"Oh great and wise teacher," she said with irony, "I am so very grateful for your illuminating lesson. But actually," she pretended to pick some sand off her tunic, "Xander already told me all of this, so maybe you need to work a little harder to keep up."

She looked up at me, victory in her eyes. We both broke into laughter.

"Nindaranna sounds like the Province of the Damned," she said, after we had both settled down.

"It does, doesn't it? Thank Eledar that the old beliefs about the afterlife are just fairytales and superstitions now. The universe can

be terrifying enough without thinking that we might end up somewhere worse when we die."

She sliced the air with her hand, palm towards the sand. "That
may be true for us, but it isn't for the Sagain. Xander told me about
another planet; the one the Sagain call Ne-uru-gal."

"Ne-uru-gal?"

"The red planet."

"Ah. Why do they call it Ne-uru-gal?"

"He is the lord of their underworld, wandering the night sky.
He watches over every living being, and at the moment of your
death, he is there to meet you. If you prove worthy, he lets you pass
into the Quiet Lands. If not, he sends you through the Fiery Gates,
down to the underworld... Very few are allowed to pass into the
Quiet Lands."

"That sounds like an awful job. He must be in a perpetually
foul mood."

Neka chuckled. "No doubt."

"But our initial readings actually indicate that Ne-uru-gal is not
nearly so bad as Nindaranna. The planet is essentially a vast desert.
With some intensive terraforming, it could actually be made habitable. But it's hardly worth the effort when we are here on Eaiph."

She nodded. "This land is *Yeshept*," she said, using the word
from the old tongue of Eledar. "A place of great and sacred gifts.
The twin rivers feed the soil, life flowing from the mountains in the
north, down through lands of Kkad, to Sagamer in the south, where
the waters come together at the warm, inland sea."

"And we're doing everything we can to unlock those gifts," I
said. "But I can't help coming back again and again to the same
questions: Who are the people of this planet? Where do they come
from? If Saiara and her team had been successful, we would see
some sign. But you and Cord have found nothing."

She shook her head. "No. We haven't. The creation myth of
Lunnana-sin, the eye of the Architect, is provocative, but I have

found little else to validate it as any more than an interesting coincidence."

I sighed.

"But that doesn't mean we won't find something, Orenpausha. It's been more than four hundred years since the first ship crashed here on Eaiph. That is a long time, even for us, with our gift of longlife. If there were survivors from the crash, who knows how far afield they traveled in those centuries? They may have long ago left the Sagain behind."

"I am grateful for your optimism, Neka. But you've learned their language, and you've broken bread with them. You've read their histories, and you've seen their art. There would be some sort of trace if they came here, wouldn't there? Where else can you look?"

"You've much to learn about understanding other cultures, pausha. This is barely a beginning," she said. "Let me go deeper. There is still so much we don't know about these peoples. They are so remarkable.

"They build from the mud of the earth, packing it into hard bricks, baked and hardened in the sun. Then they use reeds and weeds, rolled and bound together, to fill in the gaps. It would sound laughable if what they built with these simple materials was not so impressive. You have seen the atmospheric images of the Zigguarat en Sur?"

I nodded.

"The staircase to the heavens," she said. "They say it is the place where Lunnana-sin stepped down to sow his seeds amongst the Sagain, and they built their greatest city, the city of Sur, from that spot.

"On the longest day of each year, the orbit of the moon is in perfect alignment with the windows on the far side of the temple. And on those rare occasions when the moon is full on that longest of days, it is a most auspicious moment for the Sagain. The last time it happened, twenty-two years ago by their calendar, it coincided with the birth of the son of their king."

I looked up again at the morningstar, Nindaranna. It had climbed into view above the mountains just a few minutes after the moon, the eye of Lunnana-sin, bright and steady. I imagined an invisible thread running from the bottom tip of the crescent moon down to the planet, pulling it along in its orbit. It was a simplistic idea, but it occurred to me that this was how every myth is born, stories and fantasies filling in the gaps between theories and knowledge.

I looked back at Neka. "You should ask Xander about Nindaranna's path through our skies. If you imagine the sky as a two-dimensional surface, the orbit of the planet forms a beautiful, symmetrical pattern above us."

"I love how the twins drive each other forward in their pursuit of knowledge," she said. "Their command of the esoteric enriches us all."

She smiled and looked down at the ground like she was searching for something. After a few quiet moments, she said, "It is difficult to put into words. The myths and religion of these people are woven together in a complex, nuanced fashion. Their stories are often filled with contradictions. For instance, Nindaranna is revered for her life-giving powers, providing blessings of fertility. Yet she is also a goddess of war, bringing darkness and death.

"The stories about her are beautiful, and highly imaginative, but on the face of it, they seem almost childish in their lack of consistency. In spite of that, I am starting to understand how these seeming contradictions point towards a deep wisdom about the nature of existence. The dark and the light live so close together for the Sagain. Neither one is better or worse. Neither one is good or bad. They are inseparable, blended together, present in every aspect of the universe.

"All of this is evident in the way they live. They are proud of their lineage as warriors, and they claim a vile right as victors to enslave those they conquer. Yet they've welcomed me and Cordar, strangers from a *very* distant land, with hospitality and curiosity, instead of suspicion and fear.

"They thrive off of the twin rivers that frame the borders of their land, but they build towers to the immortal gods out of mud in the middle of the desert, towers they know must one day surely crumble.

"They do not treat women as full equals to men in daily life, yet they worship Nindaranna as one of their greatest deities. And I have read the legends of En Kug-Bau, keeper of the sacred hearth, a woman who 'bent the swords of Elam,' and rose to become the queen of the Sagain for a thousand years."

"A thousand years? That sounds like longlife to me!"

She smiled. "Their ancient kings and queens are revered more as gods than human. The line between history and myth is shrouded. Perhaps, when one ruler died, the next rose to take her name, and so ruled for many generations. Or perhaps it is just a story, elaborated and exaggerated over many lifetimes, until the fabric of their dreams is indivisible from the truth."

Nindaranna was disappearing in the ambient light of the brightening sky, hints of purple and orange kissing the clouds, and the sliver of the crescent moon was shifting from pale yellow to a faint white, speckled with the blue of morning.

"I cannot wait to meet them," I said to her.

She took in a deep breath. "When you and the rest of the team step in, Orenpausha, everything changes. Everything. Maybe there is a reason why whoever came here before us left no obvious signs. Whether it was Saiara's team, or someone even further back than that, maybe they knew that it was, at the very least, unfair to meddle." She did not look at me as she spoke, she just kept staring up at the dawning sky.

"It might even be worse than that," she continued. "Maybe they realized that interfering was dangerous. There could be some factors we haven't considered, factors that could put everything we are trying to build here at risk."

"That may be true, Neka, but it is too late to turn back. Think about it. An earthquake rattles the whole land. Then two strangers who speak with an odd accent come from some distant city that no peoples here have ever heard of. If the Sagain are as advanced as you say, they will send explorers to search for where you and Cordar came from.

"And if they have not been this far east yet, they will come soon enough. They will see our island from the shores of the sea. An island that did not exist before. What will we do then?"

She sighed. "You're right," she said. "I know you are. But it doesn't make it easier. We are so far ahead of them. Much too far. Their culture will get mangled and torn apart by the implications of our existence if we move too quickly. Cordar and I still have so much to learn."

"We will give you all the time we can. You must use that time to prepare them. We cannot avoid this encounter, but better if it happens on terms we can manage than for some intrepid pathfinder to stumble upon us."

"Yes, Orenpausha. We will keep you and Reacher apprised of our progress as often as possible."

"Excellent, Neka. I believe in you. We would not have made it this far without you."

I stood up and offered my hand to her. She took it, and I helped her up. We turned our backs to the ocean and the moon, and saw a figure approaching us.

When I recognized her, I waved and called, "Adjet! Good morning."

She waved back. When she was close enough, she said, "Good morning to you, Orenpausha." She smiled, a wide, beautiful, toothy grin. "And to you, Neka. I thought I might find you two here."

"We were talking about the people," I said. "The Sagain. About what comes next, now that Neka and Cord have spent some time among them, learning their language and mores."

"That, as it turns out, is exactly what I came to talk to you about."

"You have thoughts on the matter?" I asked.

"More than that. They're already here."

"What?" Neka reached out and grabbed Adjet's arm. "What do you mean?"

"There are four of them, camped on the far side of the ridge." She pointed across the water to the far shore, and the hills beyond.

Neka's eyes met mine, wide with disbelief. "I must go to them," she said.

I nodded. "Go," I said.

She was off, running across the island back to the headquarters we had established around *Reacher*, urgency in her voice as she called up Cordar on her transponder.

I turned to Adjet and asked, "How long have they been there?"

"No more than a day, I think. But you're going to want to see this footage. They spotted one of our explorer drones."

I reversed the holo and played it back from the start. Four men of the Sagain, crouching around the remains of last night's campfire, stoking the embers back to life. The sun has not risen yet. The heat of the day is still hours away. They are wearing long, hooded flaxen cloaks to keep the sun from their bare torsos. One of them looks up at the sky and sees the drone. He shouts to his companions. They turn as one, following his pointed finger. The holo was taken from the drone's perspective. It makes it seem like the Sagain are looking right at us.

"This footage was captured, what, an hour ago?"

"Just about."

"So where are they now?"

"They are still there."

"Do they have a way to cross the waters here to the island?"

"No. They would have to build a boat, and from what we can tell, they did not come prepared for that."

"I wonder what their plan is?" I touched my hand to the back of my head, running my fingers through my hair. "Reacher," I said, "where are Neka and Cordar now?"

"They just took off in the hopper. They are circling out, giving the Sagain a wide berth. They will land in a concealed spot and approach on foot from the west, coming up on them from behind."

"Can you get me through?"

"You are connected."

"Neka? Cord? Can you hear us?"

"Yes, pausha, we hear you," Neka said.

"What's your plan here?"

"We don't really have one. For starters, I just want to keep them on the mainland. That is why we are coming from behind, so that they won't connect us to the island." She paused. "Hopefully."

"When you meet with them, try to get as much information as you can. If possible, get them to turn around, or, at least, to head in another direction. Contact with the Sagain is inevitable, but maybe it doesn't need to happen today."

"And if they will not turn around?"

"We will jump that gap when we get to it. If you need us, if there is any trouble, we will send help right away."

"Thank you, pausha. Thank you all. Wish us luck."

———

"Wait," Neka said in the tongue of the Sagain. We could hear voices shouting, and the sound of metal singing free of scabbards. The men had drawn their swords.

"Reach," I said. "Send all three drones. Right away."

"What if they are seen?" Xander.

"That line has already been crossed, Xander. We need eyes on this."

"I will send them, pausha," Reacher said, "and I will keep them at the highest altitude possible, to minimize the chances of being noticed by human eyes."

"Good. Neka and Cordar are taking a big risk here. We need a backup plan if this meeting goes wrong."

"We are not your enemies," Neka was saying. "My name is Ne-en-Ka, and this is my companion, Co-de-Ra."

One of the men replied.

"What did he just say, Reacher? Why aren't you translating?"

"Give me moment, pausha. His language is similar, but not the same. I do not think they are Sagain."

"What? How long until the drones are in viewing range?"

"They are flying over now. Here."

A monitor lowered to my side, and it gave me a satellite view of the campsite. I could see the four strangers, small, dark dots, standing in a ragged half circle by the fire pit. Two more dots stood opposite the four. Neka and Cordar.

"Can you zoom in?"

"Of course. I am triangulating the feeds from each of the drones. I will have a three-dimensional rendering in another moment."

The image on the monitor stayed the same. One of the solitary dots stepped closer to the four men. My throat tightened up.

"I have the feed here, pausha," Reacher said. The holo lit up. We could see Neka, standing a few steps ahead of Cordar, her lips moving, a look of urgency on her face.

A second after her lips stopped moving, her voice came through. "Please, put away your swords. There is no need for suspicion."

Before I could ask, Reacher said, "I am syncing up the audio.

Now pausha, please breathe. Your heart rate is climbing. It is very distracting."

I took in a deep breath in through my nose and exhaled out, trying to calm my nerves. "Something's not right," I said.

I gestured at the holo with my right hand. The view revolved. Now, we were looking over Neka's shoulder at the four men. They stood, swords still drawn. A man who might have been their leader said something in response to Neka.

"I have a functional translation schema," Reacher said. "It is going to be rough, but I will turn it on now."

"Do it."

A simulation of the man's voice came through. "You are no Sagain," he was saying, "but you try speak them." The program Reacher had improvised gave the man's voice an ominous, distorted tone. It was like listening to the wind, and suddenly realizing it was saying something you could understand. "The Sagain killed us people. If you are friend, you are not us friends."

I zoomed out just enough to let us see everyone around the campfire. Cordar stepped forward, standing next to Neka. "We are explorers. Like you. We came from across the ocean," he said. "The Sagain welcomed us. We learned to speak like them, so we could communicate."

"A ocean? Where are the boat?"

"It was destroyed. We were near the shore when the earth began to shake. The water swelled and roared, swallowing us up, crashing our boat against the rocks. Our companions were killed. When I woke up, I was on the shore. Ne-en-Ka was beside me, looking down at me. She saved my life."

"You lucky, then," one of the other men said. His translated voice had the same distorted, crackling tone. "I always have dreamed of being soothed by woman such as."

He stepped forward, leering at Neka, but the leader lifted up his hand, and without looking at the man, stopped him in his tracks.

"Yes. Earth was angry day," the leader said. "Our people never felt like that. Words fly even angrier here, far south. I came see it with my own eye."

"Have you been this far south before?" Neka asked.

"Many many. But now, I do not know. There are an island." He pointed east, towards us. "I sad you have no more boat. We have to build a one."

"Build a boat? So you can go to the island?"

"Yes."

"But why?"

Reacher broke in and said, "I am getting the hang of the pattern. Listen now."

"This morning," the man was saying. His voice was clearer. More human. And the words were less stilted. "We see something in the sky. Something I would not believe if I had not seen with my own eyes."

"What did you see?"

"You do not know? I thought, maybe, you followed it here. You came so soon after." He tilted his head up a little, and to the left, casting a shrewd look at Neka.

"No. We saw the light of your fire last night. We decided to wait until the morning to approach. We did not want to startle you."

"Ah. So you do not know about the floating stone we saw in the sky?"

"A floating stone?"

"It passed over us this morning." He pointed up. "It looked at us. I am certain. Then it flew that way, to the island, gone from sight." He traced a line through the air with his hand. "My men," he said, a huge smile on his face, "think it be a demon escaped from earth. In her anger, the earth not notice the demon sneak away and fly up to the sky."

Neka smiled back. "A demon?" she said. "I know little of demons, but if this is one, it sounds very strange."

"No demons? But you know of boats?"

Neka looked at Cordar. He nodded to her.

She looked back at the men. "Yes," she said.

"Good," the man said, "Maybe no demon. Maybe better thing instead." He turned and looked over his shoulder at his men. They stepped forward, swords drawn, and surrounded Neka and Cordar.

WHEN THE BANDITS had moved in, I was ready to send in the drones and wipe them out. But Neka had stopped me. "Wait," she said under her breath. "Trust me." The bandits surrounding her did not hear it, but we all did.

"Reach," I said, "did I hear her right? She wants us to stay back?"

"You heard correctly, pausha."

"Okay," I said. "We wait. But Reacher?"

"Yes, pausha," the shipheart said, anticipating my next command, "I will keep eyes in the sky. If it gets worse, I will do what has to be done to keep them safe."

Now, it was evening, and I was sitting outside, soaking in the ocean air, wondering what to do next.

Neka and Cordar spent the whole day with these men, helping them chop down trees and weave vines together, supervising them as they built a raft so they could come here. I was almost tempted to just get it over with, and send a hopper over to pick them all up. At least, that way, I could have the satisfaction of scaring the wits out of the strangers in the process.

Their leader's name was Ghisanyo En-Shul. He was, if his claims were true, one of the warrior-lords of the land of Kkad. A century ago, the Sagain had, apparently, gone to war with the Kkadie, fracturing the Kkadie's hold on the lands north of the twin rivers. The Kkadie were not wiped out, but their king was beheaded and the people were splintered, factions spreading out across the land. Their power was diffuse, but Ghisanyo dreamed of the day when the Kkadie would come together again and regain their rightful strength.

"One day," he said, "I will march to festering Sur with a thousands at the back. The king of Sagain will knelt before me."

"How will you bring your people together again?" Cordar had asked.

"We find some way. We must. Maybe there is way on island. I am no afraid of demon."

So Ghisanyo had come looking for some great magic. For the power that had angered the earth. What would he do when he found it, I wondered. And what would we do in return?

I touched the spot behind my ear and said, "How close are they, Reacher? I cannot see them from here."

"It looks like the current took them off the course I originally predicted. They will hit the beach in fifteen minutes, about a farrun from where you are now."

"Good. That's good. That will give them time to get oriented. I will light my fire here as a beacon for them. They will approach under the cover of night, and when they see I am here alone, that will embolden them."

Even though a part of me knew everything was about to change, I took great pleasure in the solitude of the beach at twilight. The stars winked to life as the sky faded from deep blue into black.

I dug a pit in the sand and made a ring around the edge with stones. The salt air was invigorating, filling my lungs as I worked. I gathered up driftwood and dry seaweed, piling it high.

A few minutes later, the fire was blazing. I stood, turning my back on the flames, and looked out to the point on the horizon where the sky met the ocean. The line that separated them was almost invisible, but I could see the slow wheel of rising stars climbing up out of the blackness of the ocean.

The sound of voices came to me. They had probably been watching me for a few minutes before they decided to approach in the open. I took the fact that they were not attempting stealth as a good sign. Whether they came with peaceful intentions, or they were overconfident, either option worked in my favor.

Without looking at the fire, I circled around until I stood facing the approaching voices, the fire at my back. It was a small gamble, exposing myself like that, but I knew that I would look imposing, my full height silhouetted against the bonfire. Keeping my eyes away from the fire also protected my night vision. And if they had projectile weapons, it was unlikely that those weapons could penetrate my tunic. The fabric looked inconspicuous enough, but it was actually high-tensile blend designed for working in the mines on Verygone. It had been a parting gift from my father, one of the few items that I still carried with me from that past life.

"Who's out there?" I said in the universal tongue of the Fellowship.

Silence. The voices had gone quiet.

I waited.

Ghisanyo emerged into the circle of light. He looked up at me and bared his teeth in a wide grin. Then he said something in his native tongue.

An instant later, Reacher's translation schema fed it back to the transponder in my ear. "Holy Sena," he said, "I have never seen a man as big or as pale as you." He raised his eyebrows. "*Are* you a man?" Reach had done some work on the translation program. There was virtually no lag, the fluency was significantly better, and the timbre of the translation was an almost perfect match for Ghisanyo's actual voice.

"Hmmm. Perhaps you cannot understand me," he continued. "You spoke a moment ago, but it was not a language familiar to my ear."

"I understand you, little man," I said, nodding. I knew he would not understand my words, but he would glean something from my tone.

He tilted his head. "Yes," he said. "You do understand me, don't you, giant? But your words are like the sound of stones rubbing together. Maybe the demons of this place have stolen your tongue and replaced it with a worm from the underworld."

"I can understand what the giant is saying." Neka stepped into the firelight.

"You can?" Ghisanyo turned to her. "How?"

"He is one of my people."

Ghisanyo glanced at me for a second then looked back to Neka and said, "He does not look like one of your people. Besides, I thought you and Co-de-Ra were the only ones to survive."

"I thought so too. It seems I was wrong." She stepped past Ghisanyo and stood in front of me. Then she wrapped her arms around my waist, her head to my chest.

I brought my arms to her back, and hung my head, looking down at her.

"Hello, pausha," she whispered in the universal tongue. "What are you doing?"

"Following your lead," I whispered back. "We thought it was better to meet them here. To take it slow."

I felt her nod against my chest.

"What are you murmuring about?" Ghisanyo said, taking a step forward.

I lifted my head to glare at him. He stopped in his tracks.

Neka let me go. She turned towards Ghisanyo and spoke in the tongue of the Sagain, loud enough for her voice to carry out into the darkness. "Please. This is our friend and companion. His name is Oren. We thought he was dead, and he thought the same of us. He does not speak the languages of this land, but I can translate. He means you no harm. Come into the light."

Two more Kkadie stepped into view. Like Ghisanyo, they both wore thick beards and brown cloaks, still dusty from their desert travels. One man had an ugly scar running from his forehead, through the flesh around his eye, and down his cheek, a canyon of pitted skin dividing the beard on his left cheek. His blinded eye shone milky orange in the firelight.

They never took their eyes off of me. If they were afraid, they did not show it.

"Where is Cordar? And the other one?" I asked.

"He wants to know where our friend is," Neka said.

Ghisanyo said, "Do you think we are so foolish? Look how big this one is." He pointed at me. "My man Hesh is with Co-de-Ra until I say otherwise."

"I understand," I said, "but if any harm comes to him, I will break every bone in your body, little man." I made a gesture with my hands like snapping a branch.

"He says..."

"What he says is clear enough. Do not worry, tall one. Your friend will not be harmed unless you force our hand."

I nodded.

"How long have you been on this island, tall one?"

"His name is Oren."

"Does that translate to 'too big' in your tongue?"

Neka narrowed her eyes at him, but I laughed.

"Tell him my size is just right for dealing with glib tongued little men like him."

"He says you are too loose with your tongue for a man of your tiny stature."

Ghisanyo laughed back, then said, "Perhaps. But it has not gotten me killed. Not yet, anyway. And I am the one with a hostage, no?"

Neka sighed and knelt down by the fire. She had a distant look on her face.

"Do not be upset-"

Ghisanyo did not finish his sentence. Using her cloak, Neka picked up one of the hot rocks at the edge of the fire pit and hurled it at him.

He was quick, lifting his own cloak like a shield, but the rock was heavy, and it caught him on the forearm. He gave a quiet grunt of pain, but did not slow, his sword swinging free from its scabbard with his other hand. But Neka was already inside of his guard. She struck her elbow against the inside of his arm, a numbing blow that forced him to drop his sword. Then she brought her elbow across his jaw. He went down in a heap.

The other two men dashed forward, but I stepped in front of them. I caught the blade of the closer sword with my hand, ripping it from the Kkadie warrior. He stumbled, trying to hold onto his blade, his head tilting forward as he came to his knee. I gave him a firm backhand across the face. He crumpled to the ground.

The man with the blind eye danced away, out of my range. He kept his sword up, but he did not make any move to attack. His eyes darted from Ghisanyo, to Neka, to me, and then out towards the darkness.

Neka stood up and stepped away from Ghisanyo's unconscious form. She followed the eye of the warrior who was still standing, then called out in a loud voice, "Cordar! Are you okay?"

My heart leapt to hear his voice respond in the distance. "I am fine, Neka. I'll be there in just a moment."

My eyes danced between the one-eyed warrior and Neka. "Well, that was unexpected."

"I have spent the whole day with that arrogant man. We needed a show of force. I saw the opportunity, so I took it."

"Fair enough. But what if this just makes him more angry?"

"If anything, it will win his respect. We have cowered to his demands the whole day. Now he will understand that we were only biding our time. He will be more careful from here on out."

The sound of approaching footsteps scrunched through the sand, and Cordar walked into the circle of light. "Hello, you two," he said. The body of the Kkadie warrior who had been guarding him was slung over his shoulders. When he got near the fire, he crouched and dropped the warrior into the sand with a thump. "This is Hesh," Cordar said. "Don't worry. I didn't kill him."

"What should we do with this one?" I said, pointing at one-eye.

To his credit, the one-eyed warrior had not run. After he saw how dangerous we were, he was not foolish enough to attack. But he did not abandon his companions.

Neka looked at him, and asked, in his tongue, "What is your name?"

He pursed his lips, deciding whether to answer her question. "Socha," he finally said.

"Drop your sword, Socha, and come sit by the fire. It has been a long day. We all need rest. As long as you do not try anything foolish, we will not hurt you. And when your master here wakes up, we will start from the beginning."

Socha paused for one more moment, then stuck his sword down, the blade sinking deep into the sand, the hilt wobbling in the air. He walked around to the far side of the fire and sat, his legs crossed, his hands resting on his thighs.

We watched each other from across the fire.

Ghisanyo let out a long groan. Moonlight filtered down from an opening in the ceiling, casting his umber skin in pale light. I watched as he lifted his head, looking around the smooth, stone walls of the underground room.

I was kneeling in the shadowed corner of the room, out of his line of sight. He did not know it, but while he was unconscious, we had put a transponder underneath his skin, next to the bones behind his ear. We sealed the incision right away, leaving no visible evidence that anything had happened to him. He might have felt a faint itch or lingering irritation in that spot, but it would hardly be noticeable in comparison to the bruises Neka had left him with.

And now, when I spoke, he could understand every word I said. "Hello, Ghisanyo."

He whipped his head towards me.

"Where... Where am I?" His voice was ragged and quiet.

"You are in our home, Ghisanyo." I cleared my throat, then continued, "Well, to be more precise, you are underneath it."

He struggled against the bonds that kept him in the chair as he tried to look over his shoulder at me. "What in the seven hells are you doing there in the dark? And where are my men?"

"You followed a floating demon to an island that has risen up from the bottom of the sea." A small embellishment, for added effect. "How do you know you are not in one of your seven hells right now?"

"I've never heard of a demon who needed chains," he said, lifting his hands and making a symbolic show of trying to free himself from the restraints we had improvised by welding spare cable together. "You are also much too polite," he added. "I do not understand all of your magics, but you are a man. I am sure of it. A very large one, yes, but still a man."

I laughed, then said, "You are either very brave, Ghisanyo, or very foolish."

I walked around and stood in front of him, and as I did so, I held up my hand and released a light orb, letting it float up near the ceiling of the chamber, filling the room with lambent yellow light.

He smiled up at me, then winced with the pain. He lifted his bound hands to his cheek, where Neka had elbowed him, and touched the bruise with his fingers. He raised his eyebrows and squinted his eyes, and I could see that he was exploring the spot from the inside with his tongue.

He opened his mouth as if to speak, then closed it again, a puzzled look on his face.

"What is it?"

"I thought you couldn't speak my language," he said.

"I'm a quick study." I grinned at him.

He spat. "Another one of your magics."

"You're right, Ghisanyo. I have many powers."

He sighed. "Call me Ghis, giant. We are long past formalities."

"Why did you really come to this island, Ghis?"

"I am a curious man. What was your name again, tall one?"

"Oren."

"Oren. What would you do if you saw a stone floating through the sky? You strike me as someone who would follow that stone wherever it led you."

"You're not wrong, Ghis. But you are no scholar or priest, searching for wisdom or enlightenment. You are a warrior. And every warrior I've ever met is looking for the advantage. A better technique. A stronger armor. A deadlier weapon."

He gave no response to that.

"You want revenge on the Sagain. You hoped that you might find the instrument of that revenge here."

Still he was silent.

"Your silence tells me enough, Ghis. So now it is left to me to warn you. This island is a sacred place. A place where violence is not permitted. Your arrival forced us to break that precept. You held two of the island's children as your own captives, and you threatened to kill one of them. The island is angry. Now, it is left to me to decide what to do with you."

"Careful, pausha," came Neka's voice in my ear. "You might be laying it on a little too thick."

I smiled at her comment. I knew Ghis could not hear her, and I knew that my smile would unsettle him, however much he tried to hide it.

"Ah," he said. "I see. Shall I have time to prepare my final prayers? Or are you sending me straight to the fiery gates?"

I shook my head. "You misunderstand, Ghis. Violence is not our way. But your arrival here has precipitated certain difficult decisions. It is time for you and your people to understand who we are and why we are really here. We are taking you home, Ghis."

I touched a thin bracelet on my wrist. Ghis's bonds slackened and fell from his hands, dropping down to the floor. Then I touched my hand to a certain spot on the wall, and the seam that had been invisible until that moment appeared, framing the doorway as it slid open.

He held his arms out in front of him, clenching and unclenching his fists, wriggling his fingers. He gave a grunt of satisfaction, then stood, slowly, testing his own weight on his legs. He stood on one leg, then the other, shaking each one out in turn. Then he whacked his palms on his thighs. "Gods, that feels good," he said. "How long have I been tied up?"

"We brought you in this morning. It is almost evening-"

Before I could finish responding, he darted his hand up, snatched the light orb from the air, and hurled it at my head. I batted it aside. It crashed into the wall, shattering. The room went dark. I heard the sound of Ghis's feet shuffling across the floor. I swung my arm towards the sound, but my hand whooshed through the air.

Ghis's fist drove into the soft flesh on the side of my torso.

A spike of hot pain lanced up my side.

Reacher's voice came into my ear. "Pausha, are you alright?"

I coughed, leaning against the wall, then said, "I am fine. Ghis caught me by surprise. The man moves like a serpent. But he has nowhere to go. Illuminate the hallways for me, will you?"

Dozens of orbs flared to life, casting away the shadows in the halls outside the room we had kept Ghis in.

"Do you have eyes on him, Reach?"

"Yes. He is near the underground river."

"Good. Create a path for him. Turn off all of the lights except ones that will lead him towards the cliffside. If he tries to take an orb and use it as a torch, turn it off on him. I will meet him at the mouth."

I waited in the shadows as he approached the river's mouth. At first, he had tried to ignore the lights, pushing blindly forward into the darkness. But the underground corridors we'd made were like a maze, featureless walls turning and winding.

Without knowledge of these corridors, the only real landmark was the river. Reacher kept using the lights to tease Ghis back from the darkness, finally leading him here, to the river's mouth. It poured water down the cliffside into the ocean at low tide, and swallowed it back in when the waves climbed up.

He walked to the edge and looked down at the wet boulders, the crashing waves, the white-feathered birds who had already begun making nests along the cliffs of our newly formed island. He shook his head in frustration, then turned back to look down the corridor from where he'd come. I could almost see him turning over the possibilities in his mind.

I stepped out of the shadows.

He dropped into a crouch, an animal coiled to attack.

I held up my hands, palms out, and said, "Ghis. Wait. You do not have to fight. We will not hurt you. I do not blame you for trying to escape. I would have done the same."

He held his crouch. He glanced over his shoulder towards the mouth of the cave that led down to the rocks, then back at me.

"There is nowhere to run, Ghis."

After another moment of consideration, he stood tall, his chest out, and looked down at his arms, pretending to examine his jerkin, using his hands to wipe imaginary dust off the sleeves.

"If you aren't going to kill me," he finally said, "does that mean I'll be fed? I'm ravenous."

"Gods," Ghis said, "Do we have to ride back on this bloody raft? If you magi can make stones fly, why can't we fly too?"

After much debate, we had agreed that Adjet and Xander could parley with the Kkadie while Neka and Cordar returned to the Sagain. Ghis knew of the island, and unless we held him prisoner or killed him, we had no choice but to attempt to stage an engagement with his people on our terms. We decided to take the initiative.

"Don't be a fool," Adjet said. "We already made the mistake of letting you see one of our divining stones floating through the air. What would we do if someone saw *us* flying?"

"They would say, 'Look! The mighty Ghisanyo. He truly is the greatest warrior, flying through the air with his beautiful consort.'" He gave a devilish grin to Adjet. "'And his men at arms, and...'" Ghis gave Xander a puzzled look. "'And some sort of strange, pale-eyed demon, who... who he must have captured and made to do his bidding!'"

Ghis grinned at Adjet and Xander, pleased with himself.

Xander ignored the joke and kept loading supplies on to the raft.

Adjet snorted with laughter, then said, "Your consort? Do not presume anything of me, little Ghis. I could cut off your manhood as easily as I could look at you."

"Gods, woman, you are magnificent. Your hair is like the desert sun, your skin is like golden nectar of the gods, and your words are like a whip that drives me forward."

In the months that Neka and Cordar were among the Sagain, Adjet had perfected the adaptive skin tech that gave the paler members of our crew advanced protection against the sun's ultraviolet radiation, and also helped them blend in more with the people of the land.

Xander's freckled, peach skin had turned bronze, and Adjet's alabaster white had morphed into a honeyed clay. She was no less striking for the change, and Ghis made no effort to hide his attraction to her.

I chuckled to myself and walked away from the group at the raft so I could check in with the others. "They are almost loaded up," I said, touching my finger to my transponder. "For all our strength, Ghis shows no signs of playing meek. He's going to make Adjet earn every inch of ground."

Neka laughed on the other end of the line. "She's not used to being matched," she said. "It will be good for her, I think. Poor Xander, though. Separated from his brother, and left to play the straight man to those two."

I laughed too. "I hadn't even thought of that," I said. "He's up for it though. Xan is a hard person to ruffle."

"He most certainly is." She paused for a moment, then said, "We'll give them a day to get ahead of us on the route towards the main Kkadie settlements, then Cordar and I will make our way back to the Sagain capital in Sur. Are you sure you are going to be okay, pausha? Just the three of you with Reacher? There's so much work to do."

"We will make do. This is the best decision."

"I know. But that doesn't make it easier. I should go finish preparations with Cordar."

"Go, Neka," I said. "We'll talk tonight, before you depart."

She nodded and left the beach, heading back towards the ship. I walked back towards the raft. Socha, the Kkadie warrior with the blind eye, was leaning on his sword, staring at me. As I approached, he bowed his head, averting his gaze.

"How's it coming?" I said.

"We're almost ready," Xander said. "I just need to tie these supplies down. Then we can push off."

"Here. Let me help." Xander and I finished tying everything down. Then we lifted the front of the raft and dragged it through the sand down to the water.

Adjet leaned over to whisper something into Ghis's ear. Then she put her hand on his back and shoved him towards the raft. He and the other men climbed on to the raft. Socha watched her as she walked over to me, his eye unblinking.

"What did you say to Ghis?" I asked Adjet.

"Oh, I told him he was clever and strong, but not half as clever and strong as me, and I warned him not to try anything foolish."

I chuckled. "Still, you must be careful. Whatever else he is, he's a survivor. He's not too afraid to seize an opportunity when it presents itself."

"Neither am I, Oren." She looked into my eyes, and there was mischief there, but a fierceness too.

Xander walked up. "We're ready," he said.

We walked back down to the raft. The three of us hefted the raft and pushed it all the way into the water.

"May the spirit of the Scions travels with you," I said, touching the interlocking rings of the Fellowship clasped to my cloak.

"And you as well, pausha," Xander said.

"We'll see you again, soon enough," Adjet said.

I smiled, crossing my arms over my chest. "Not too soon, I hope."

Adjet stuck her tongue out at me. Xander laughed.

They started rowing. The raft crested an incoming wave, and

soon after, they caught the current that carried them away from the shore. As they drifted further out, I lifted my hand in farewell.

Everyone waved back. Everyone except Socha. He went on staring at me, tracking me with his seeing eye. I stood on the shore, looking back, until they were just a spot on the horizon.

21 / THE PLEDGE

It was late, and I was exhausted, but I could not sleep. Three days had passed in a blur of work since the others had left. As a strategy to adapt ourselves to the conditions of this world, Sid, Xayes, and I were no longer staying in the comfort of Reacher. We had carved out a provisional barracks, small rooms hollowed under the ground, with shafts up to the surface that let in air and light. The same rooms where we had held Ghis and his men prisoner.

I positioned my cot beneath the air shaft, so that I could look up through the cylinder to the stars. The narrow field of view amplified the light, casting each star in sharp relief as it passed above me, the planet turning endlessly through space.

More and more these days, I found my mind wandering back home. To that ice cold night when *Transcendence* had come to Verygone and my path was set, leading me here, thousands of light years away, to a cave in the ground, on a strange and beautiful world.

My parents were unreachable now. Even though they were bred from the same hardy, long-lived stock as me, I'd travelled across too many light years to ever get back to them. They would be dust before I ever again stood beneath the light of Beallus.

A pang of regret caught me. What if this was all a mistake? What if we disappeared on this planet just like Saiara and her team had? We still did not know what happened to them. Other than the cave drawings, there had been no trace.

All the possibilities Saiara had carried inside of her, and now she was gone. I would never see her again. I would never see my parents again. I was a madman. A fool.

I stood up and paced the room. "Damn it," I said. I touched the transponder behind my ear. "Reacher, what are you doing?"

"Hello, pausha. All of my maintenance subroutines are at full operational capacity. If a mind like mine can be said to rest, then I am resting."

"What do you think about, when you rest?"

"Can you clarify, pausha?"

"When everything is as it should be, as you described, what thoughts fill your mind?"

"I think, pausha, that I do not think in the same way that you do. I... I am. And when the world demands that I do, then I do."

"I envy you, Reach. I want to sleep now. I'm exhausted. But my mind will not turn off. The ghosts of the past keep coming back to haunt me."

"This is a common human problem, pausha. Would you like me to run you through one of the mindfulness protocols to help you let go of attachment and be at peace with your present existence?"

I laughed, then said, "When you put it like that, Reach, it makes me feel so ordinary. Just another protocol to run. Another problem to solve."

"Is it bad to be ordinary?"

"No. I mean, it shouldn't be. But my ego doesn't like it."

"Well, pausha, you are not going to subsume your ego in one night. I think we should work on it, together. What if, in the meantime, I gave you something to help you sleep?"

"Thank you, Reach. But right now, I need something to do. Something to occupy my mind."

"Then come up to the ship. I suppose you are going to want to see this."

"Look," Reacher said. A holo map of all the tunnels we had carved through the island coalesced in front of me.

"The tunnels."

"Yes," Reacher said.

"Okay. Is there something specific I should be looking for?"

"How many human life forms do you count in the tunnel?" Three circular red lights bloomed inside the purple construct of the holo map. Two were static. Sid and Xayes, sleeping in their underground quarters. A third was moving.

"Eledar's breath! Someone else is down there. Why didn't you wake us?"

"I have been monitoring the situation. There is no immediate threat. And you all were sleeping. Or trying to."

"Show me who it is."

The holo map resolved, morphing into the figure that the moving red dot represented. I drew in a sharp breath. It was Socha, the warrior with the ravaged eye.

"You cannot hide down here forever, Socha."

He froze, his back to me. Then he turned to face me, slow and cautious.

"Here," I said, holding out my hand to him.

He came closer to me, like a scared dog hungry enough to risk attack, and peered at the small cluster of nanotubes in my palm.

"Take it," I said, leaning forward, nodding and raising my eyebrows in an encouraging look.

He stepped away from me as I leaned in. I thought for a

moment that he might turn and run, but then his fingers darted out and scooped the tube from my hand.

"Put it in your ear." I mimed the motion, lifting my hand to my ear.

He shoved it into his ear, making a bit of a struggle with it, but, eventually, he had the tubes inside.

"What are you doing down here?" I asked.

He opened his eyes in shock.

"Socha. You can understand me, right?"

He nodded vigorously.

"Then tell me. Why are you here?"

"I was trying to find you," he said in his native tongue. My own embedded transponder translated instantly.

"Did Ghis send you? Is he really still that foolish to think that he could catch me unawares? You have all seen the power of our magics."

"Ghis did not send me, great magus Oren."

"Then why are you trying to find me?"

"I come to pledge myself to you."

"Wait. What? I... I do not need a devotee, Socha."

He did not say anything.

"How did you get across?"

"I swam."

"You swam! Remarkable. You're lucky to be alive."

"No luck. Only the will of the gods, and the will of men who defy them."

I did not know what to make of that, so I said, "And Ghis just let you go?"

"I left at night, while he and the others slept."

I sighed. "We cannot leave you down here, wandering the tunnels. I will take you to a place where you can sleep."

Socha nodded, and a smile crept onto his stern face. "Thank you, great magus," he said, "you do me a great honor."

I snorted, then said, "I have done nothing yet, Socha, except to let you live. Do not try anything foolish. We will figure out what to do with you in the morning."

"Eledar's breath," Xayes said, "he wants to pledge himself to you?"

We were on board *Reacher*, on the main deck, watching a live holo feed of Socha. I had brought him to my underground quarters and locked him in. Now it was morning, light shining down through the shaft in the ceiling, and he was sitting on the ground, cross-legged, his eye closed, his breathing slow and even.

"That's what he said to me last night."

"Pledge himself to do what, exactly?"

"We didn't get that far."

"He will not be the last," Sid said. "The more these peoples learn about us and what we are capable of, the harder it will be for us to maintain any sort of objective distance."

"So what do we do with him?" I asked.

"If we keep him here, it means we have to watch him. I don't like the idea of having him around when it is still so early, when we still have so much work to do."

"Maybe he can help us," I said.

"Help us how?" Xayes said. "He doesn't have a field port, and you cannot be suggesting we give him one." He scrutinized me. "Right?"

I smirked. "No, Xayes. Not that," I said. "But there are other ways he might be useful to us." I paused, gathering my thoughts, trying to take the idea that was lurking beyond words and bring it into the group. "Adjet and your brother have gone to the city of Akshak in the land of Kkad. Neka and Cordar have returned to Sur, the Sagain capital.

"They are the first ambassadors to a new world, a world none of us had predicted. If we are going to inhabit this planet, we can only do it with the full knowledge that we are not working with a blank cultural slate."

"Okay," Xayes said, "but I'm still not totally tracking you here..."

"Stay with me. The Fellowship learned a long time ago that the strongest galactic protectorates are founded on integration, yes?"

They both nodded in agreement.

"If we want to establish a permanent settlement on a new world, we cannot come along and strip it clean, flattening it, paving it over, forcing it to conform to the Forsaran planetary ideal. Instead, we identify planets along a spectrum of certain fundamental parameters, and then we adapt our approach, based on the particular planet.

"We do this so well because the field allows us to access and manipulate the resources of the planet to help us achieve our goals, while minimizing the risk that our interventions will be catastrophic for that planet's particular ecosystem. We need to do the same thing with these peoples."

"So you're saying we should access their culture and manipulate them?" Xayes said.

"Eledar's breath, man. When you put it like that, it sounds nefarious. Look, every analogy staggers. I am not equating these people to inanimate resources to be used and abused. I am trying to say the opposite. That we must understand them so deeply, so intimately, that what we build, no matter how incredible it is, is not so alien and terrifying to them that they reject it, like antibodies attacking a foreign bacterium. What we build here has to work not just within the confines of this particular planet's biome, but also in the context of the cultural world these people have already built here."

Sid picked up the thread. "Right, right," he said. "I see what you are getting at. We can't just build whatever we want. For instance, if our architecture is too strange, then they will see nothing of themselves in us. They will fear us. Hate us. And that will turn ugly for everyone."

"Precisely."

"You *still* haven't told us where Socha fits in, pausha," Xayes said.

"Isn't it obvious?"

"Well... no," Xayes said, narrowing his eyes at me.

"On behalf of all of the people of the planet Eaiph, Socha will become their first intergalactic ambassador."

PART 3
LOSS

"Socha," I said quietly.

I had watched him for a moment before interrupting. He had been kneeling in the simple waiting chamber, his eyes closed, taking long, slow breaths through his nose. When I spoke, he lifted his head to look up at me with his seeing eye.

"They will call for us soon, I think. Are you ready?" I said.

He nodded and stood up. He was wearing his heavy, flaxen cloak, held together at the neck by the small clasp of silver we had gifted to him when he pledged his service to the dream of Manderlas: two rings overlapping to form the unbreakable chain, the sigil of the Fellowship. And now, it served as the symbol of the new world we were trying to forge here on Eaiph.

In the past year, we had made significant progress on Manderlas, carving out a small settlement at the base of Lanthas, the lone peak that capped our isle. We named the mountain for Ai Lanta, twelfth scion of Eledar, and first astronomist of Forsara. Her maths had become the groundwork for a whole school of astronomic thought that ultimately opened up the galaxy to our Forsaran ancestors, the first settlers, the first to seed human life across the galaxy. We were building what was to become another link in that galactic chain, a new capital to unify the multitude of city-states that spanned the twin river lands of Kkad and Sagamer, uniting all the warring peoples.

While Sid, Xayes, Socha and I had been busy on Manderlas, Neka and Cordar had returned to the capital city of Sur in Sagamer, and by all accounts, their formal overtures to the Sagian nobility had been met with cautious optimism. And by invoking an ancient religious prescript, Adjet and Xander had managed to bring almost all of the prominent Kkadian factions together in the city of Akshak, a gathering held safe beneath the banner of their council of clerics.

Thanks to those efforts, looming hostilities between the Sagain and Kkadie had been forestalled. But something had gone wrong in Akshak. Three days ago, word had come from Adjet that Ghisanyo was fomenting unrest, and tensions in the city were starting to boil again.

She had pleaded with us to come as quickly as possible, but the data packet had somehow become corrupted, and her message was cut short before we could discern the details. After that, we were unable to reestablish communications, either with her or Xander. Fearing the worst, I'd left Sid and Xayes with Reacher, and brought Socha in hopes that his presence might serve as a sign of cooperation amidst any threat of conflict.

We landed the hopper out beyond the edge of the city, walking in on foot. I'd wanted to find Adjet and Xander without drawing attention to ourselves, but it was a foolish hope. Word of our presence rippled through the populace, and within a few minutes of our arrival, a small troupe of guards had surrounded us, demanding we follow them. Now, we stood in the antechamber of the holy temple of Akshak, waiting for an audience with the council of Kkadian clerics.

"This will not be easy," I said.

"Nothing of this year has been easy, great magus," he said, rising to his feet, "but I did not follow this path to find ease."

I paused for a moment, appraising him. "You don't seem nervous."

He gave me a long look, the milky white film of his sightless eye glistening in the torchlight while his seeing eye searched my face.

"My worries are of no consequence," he said. "I have made my pledge, and my life is not my own. Though I have neither the gilded tongue of a noble nor the sacred wisdom of a cleric, I will do whatever need be done for the good of my people. For the good of all people. I've seen too much blood shed - shed too much of it myself - to let us turn again to war."

As Socha spoke those words, a guard emerged from the interior chamber of the temple. There was fear in his eyes as he looked up at me. By now, I knew the look. It was the same look every other person had given me as Socha and I made our way through the dusty streets of Akshak to the temple at the center of the city. But the man's voice did not waver as he gave us the summons.

"The council is ready for you," he said.

There were almost two dozen of them, the clerics, resplendent in their ceremonial garb. They sat at an oblong table beneath the vaulted ceiling of the temple hall. At the far end of the room, a fearsome visage molded in intricate detail rested atop an altar. It could only be the face of Akshak, the god for whom the city was named.

The table was made of polished cedar wood, a precious resource in these arid, mountainous climes. The clerics shifted in their seats, turning to watch us as we walked in. Each one represented both a god and the settlement of people over which that god ruled. They were all dressed differently, as if their collective goal was to see who could be the most ostentatious. It was an impressive sartorial display.

I glanced around the group, but saw no sign of Adjet or Xander. That worried me. At the head of the table, a woman wore a towering hat made of cream silk and gold ribbon, perched on her head in a way that made me think of a giant lizard egg. The bright silk of the hat contrasted against her hazel skin, and her eyes were painted thick around the edges with a dark pigment that gave her a penetrating look, like some bird of prey.

A shirtless cleric sat towards the end of the table closest to us. He was skinny, with thin, bird-like bones, but he had an incongruous little pot belly sticking out over the waist of his flowing trousers. A sequence of circular glyph tattoos ran up the vertical centerline of his bare torso, climbing from beneath his waistband and up across his belly and chest, all the way to the remarkably large lump of cartilage that protruded beneath the skin of his throat.

Across from him, a woman who looked to be the eldest among the group wore a magnificent silk cape, embroidered with a menagerie of different animals. It was midnight blue, fringed with gold, and it draped her shoulders and arms, concealing her whole body, the fabric spilling down the sides of her chair, pooling on the floor.

Socha and I came to stand at the end of the table, holding a respectful silence beneath the weight of their collective gaze, regarding us as they did with a mixture of curiosity, fear, and animosity.

"Socha!" one of them cried out. A man towards the middle of the table stood up and started walking towards us. His head was covered with a tight halo of gold that left his bald pate exposed, glowing oiled in the torchlight. Thick ceremonial lines were drawn with gold pigment across his cheeks and chin, forming a sparkling beard on his face.

"Well, this is an unexpected surprise!" he said, walking up to us. He glanced up at me, taking me in with his sharp, dark eyes, but he did not bear the look of fear I'd seen on so many others in this city. He brought his attention back to Socha. "What a pleasure it is to see you again, old friend."

Socha gave the man a modest bow. "Greetings, Prelate Ofir," he said.

Looking past them, I saw the shirtless cleric with the thin bones and pot belly lift his hand in the air. A younger man emerged out of the shadows, and leaned in as the cleric whispered something to him. The man nodded, then turned and hurried out of the chamber through a far entrance.

Prelate Ofir clapped Socha on the shoulder. "Lord Ghisanyo said that you fled his service in the dark of night. But that doesn't sound like the man I know."

"I did not flee," Socha said. "I chose to commit myself to something greater."

The potbellied cleric let out a rude laugh at that, the gorge in his throat rising and falling like a plumb weight.

Socha kept his eyes averted, maintaining a respectful neutrality in his expression, but the cleric Ofir turned and glared at the man, reproaching him with a sharp look.

He turned back to Socha. "We've seen too much loss in these trying years, old friend. It gladdens my heart to have you back among us." He gave Socha's shoulder one last squeeze then went to sit back down.

We stayed standing. I cleared my throat, trying not to fidget as they continued to stare at us, wondering whether I should say something. I glanced at Socha, but his face was a mask of calm.

Then, perhaps by some signal I was not attuned to, the clerics all turned and looked at the woman at the head of the table with the tall, cream-colored hat.

Her eyes narrowed ever so slightly as she spoke. "So the stories are true," she said. "You are as imposing as they say. You are the one they call Orenpausha?" My name sounded foreign with the emphasis of her accent.

I bowed my head to her. This woman clearly carried significant authority among the conclave. "Yes. My name is Oren Siris. And I assure you, your eminence, I'm not here to impose anything. We come under a banner of peace and goodwill." Over the past year, with Reacher and Socha's help, I'd become quite fluent in the local dialect.

"Be that as it may," she said, "many of my companions think your presence here an ill omen, magus. And to hear you speak makes me wonder if they are not right? You use our words, you speak our tongue, but your voice gives you away. You are a stranger here, and though you claim to come in peace, our people are on the brink of bloodshed."

"My companions, Adjet and Xander, warned us as much. We thought," I gestured to Socha, "that we might be able to help. But I'm surprised that they are not here."

An awkward silence settled over the council chambers. Clerics exchanged loaded glances, saying nothing. The god Akshak glared at me from his altar across the room.

The elder woman in the midnight silk cape finally broke the silence. "My fellow prelates are too delicate to say so outright, magus, perhaps for fear of angering you," she gestured towards me, "but my years are waning, and I've no time to spare for beating the ground to chase snakes from the brush.

"Your companions," she met my eyes with a challenging stare, "are the cause of our troubles."

I stared at her, dumbfounded. Adjet had said nothing of this in her missives to us. By all her earlier accounts, she and Xander had been welcomed amongst the Kkadian people. And from what we could glean from her most recent message, it was Ghis who was stirring up trouble.

"If I've learned nothing else in all my years," the elder cleric went on, "it is that the gods do what they will, regardless of our foolish mortal prayers. As clerics, it is our duty to interpret the will of the gods as best we can, so that all people can live as we are meant to.

"But that is no easy task. People are too easily fooled or misled, and the powers you wield are seductive and disruptive. Your kind claim to have come from the stars to bring peace, yet it seems you could destroy us all if you so chose. How can you ask us to trust you with that?"

Before I could answer, the sounds of commotion came from behind us. Everyone turned, looking past us as the door swung open and Lord Ghisanyo En-Shul came barging in.

Ghis looked fierce and handsome, his beard running down from his chin in a thick braid, threaded with gold. His clothing was finer than when last we met, flaxen cloak dyed with purples and greens, leather boots fringed with camel hair, and the sword scabbard hanging from his waist traced with gold to match his beard.

Gasps and grumblings filled the chamber as he marched in, four armed men trailing behind him. They had disarmed the two temple guards at the entrance, who hung their heads with shame as they marched in front of the armed intruders, swords at their back.

"Lord Ghisanyo," a voice said above the tumult.

I turned to see that many of the clerics where standing, shock and dismay on their faces. But the woman at the far end of the table with the tall hat was still sitting. She projected an authoritative confidence.

Ghis came up short. He held up a hand, and his armed footmen halted behind him.

"What blasphemy is this?" she said.

"Blasphemy, Volda?" he snarled. "You accuse me of blaspheming when you bring this... this filth into the hallowed chambers of Akshak without the knowledge of the people?"

He spat a glob of phlegm at us. It landed near Socha's feet.

"Lord Ghisanyo," Socha said, bowing his head low, unerring in his respect even in the face of Ghis's bile.

Ghis was about to retort when the woman he had called Volda interjected. "A stranger arrives from out of the desert on the eve of a council gathering, and with one of our own at his side. What would you have us do? Let them roam the city wherever they please?"

Ghis scowled, reaching his hand up under his long hair and rubbing the back of his neck while he glared at Socha. But he said nothing.

"My father," came another voice, "would prefer it if we informed him before our every decision, so that we might meet with his approval." A young man sitting close to Volda. He wore a handsome indigo robe, and his face was shorn clean. It was Ghis, twenty years younger!

Ghis snorted. "You know, boy, there are some who still believe blood means something. You would do well to learn that lesson."

"Ah. Of course, father. After all, you've done so very much to inspire my loyalty. But then what use would Torto be to you," he nodded towards the potbellied cleric, "if not to keep you apprised of all the goings on inside these chambers?"

Torto flushed red. He opened his mouth to protest, but Volda held up a hand, silencing him. The lump in his throat rose and fell as he swallowed his words.

"Deshanyo," she said to the young man, "that is enough. We've no time for bickering." Then she turned back to Ghis. "You forget yourself, Lord Ghisanyo. As high priestess of Akshak, it is my will, and mine alone, to determine who has rights to enter. Tell your men to put away their swords, lest they risk Akshak's wrath."

He narrowed his eyes, rubbing the back of his neck again, no doubt weighing his options. He finally nodded and waved his hand to his men. They sheathed their swords.

"Thank you, Lord Ghisanyo. Now leave us to finish our deliberations."

He stood tall, unmoving.

"Unless I am mistaken," she said, her voice growing quieter, "you have no seat on the council of clerics."

The temple guards who had been disarmed stepped up beside

Ghis, standing just behind him, and a moment later, four more guards came rushing in, forming a circle around Ghis and his footmen.

The footmen stirred uneasily, hands hovering back above their swords, but Ghis dismissed them. "Leave us," he said to the footmen.

They glanced at each other, hesitating.

"Go," he said.

They shuffled out, the temple guards following after, sealing the doors behind them. But Ghis did not move. He stared defiantly at Volda.

I glanced around the table at the clerics. The eldest woman in the midnight blue cloak seemed unimpressed and unperturbed. She watched Ghis with an arched eyebrow. Deshanyo, Ghis's son, had his arms crossed over his chest, and he was staring down at the table, his face contorted into a scowl very much like his father's. Ofir, the cleric who had greeted Socha, was running his thumb and fingers over the painted golden beard on his chin, giving us all a contemplative look. And the potbellied one called Torto looked like the proverbial sindacat with its tail snared beneath the hoof of a gliaphant. His eyes darted around the room, beads of sweat condensing on his forehead.

"Guards," the head cleric Volda said, "if Lord Ghisanyo will not leave, then please remove him."

Ghis's hand went to the hilt of the scimitar at his waist. Though they outnumbered him six to one, there was fear in the guards' eyes.

"Wait," Socha said.

All eyes turned to him.

"My lord," he said to Ghis. "It does not have to be like this. As a leader who could unite the tribes of Kkadie, you fear losing the authority that is yours by rights. But the magi," he gestured to me, "have not come to take that from you. They are not our enemies. You have my word."

"Your word?" Ghis's voice pitched up. "You *betrayed* me. I

should kill you where you stand." Faster than I could blink, Ghis's sword flashed out of his scabbard. It hovered inches from Socha's face.

Socha did not flinch. I went to intervene, but he held his palm out to halt me while keeping his eyes locked ahead. He stared past the blade, meeting Ghis's glare.

No one said a word.

Finally, Ghis exhaled and shook his head, slowly lowering his sword. "Have you forgotten our time together in the pits, brother?" he said, as he sheathed the scimitar. "Those with power take what they want from those who have none. These warlocks will take everything." His eyes were on me, his look filled with venom. "Everything."

Socha shook his head. "You're wrong. They can give us back everything we lost in the wars with the Sagain. When the great island city is finished, all of the people of Kkad will be welcome there, as will the people of the Sagamer."

"You speak of peace with the Sagain as good news."

"Better peace than slavery, lord Ghisanyo. We cannot hope to stand against the might of the Sagain, and with the strength of the magi, we will not have to. There is a better world ahead."

"Slavery!" Ghis roared. He pushed up the sleeves of his cloak. Vicious purple scars ringed his wrists and scored his forearms. "Seven years we slaved together in the salt mines of Sagamer before making our escape. Seven years! We have bled for each other, Socha. Killed for each other. I would have died for you. And still you left me for... for what?" The last words came out at almost a whisper.

For the first time, Socha's calm exterior showed signs of breaking. There was love in his eyes, and sadness too. "My lord..." he said, trying to find the words. "Your scars are mine. You talk of dying for another? I would give you my life, if only it would help you see that the way of the scimitar is not the sole choice for men like us. I would rather live in peace than die for vengeance."

"You worship at the altar of these warlocks, Socha, but they are false gods. You have not seen what the great and mighty Adjet has become." The superlative was thick with sarcasm. "You have not seen what she has done to us. These so-called magi are charlatans and snake charmers, and you have fallen under their spell."

"Enough!" Volda was standing now, her hands pressed down on the table.

We all looked at her.

"You've said your piece, Lord Ghisanyo, and though I do not appreciate your methods, you are not wrong." She looked at me. "The one called Adjet does not to give our gods their fair due, magus. There are even rumors that she denies that the gods exist at all. And there are other whispers, even more troubling, that claim *she* is a true god. More and more of our own people, once devout believers, seem to have turned to worship at the power she promises."

This news hit me like a mining drill. "Please," I said, searching for words. "Our powers are... overwhelming to those who do not understand them, but we do not claim divinity. Where is she? Let me talk to her. Whatever's gone wrong, I'm sure we can fix it."

"And why should we trust you?" Volda said. "How can we know your true intentions?"

"If Socha vouches for this Orenpausha, then that is enough for me." It was Ofir. The ring of gold around his head caught the torch-light as he nodded towards us.

The elder cleric pushed back her chair.

"Speh-tal?" Volda said to her, giving her an inquisitve look.

An attendant came rushing from the edge of the chamber to help Speh-tal stand, but she swatted him away. With the creaking pace of age, she pushed herself to her feet and shuffled over to me, her cape trailing on the earthen floor of the temple. Her body was shrunken with the years, and her face was dense with wrinkles, but she held herself tall and straight as she tilted her head to look up at me. She was barely the height of my waist.

"Give me your hands," she said quietly.

"What? I..."

"Your hands," she said again.

I held them out to her. She reached up and placed her tiny hands on top of mine, tracing the lines of my palms with her delicate fingers.

"For all your strength, you are not so different from us, are you, magus?" she said.

I shook my head. "No, your eminence. Not so different."

Socha nodded. "Orenpausha has shown me much in the past year, Priestess Speh-tal," he said, "and one thing he has shown me is that, for all his power, he is not infallible. That is why I do not serve him. I serve the vision he represents."

She gave Socha a long look, then turned back to me and let go of my hands. "And you truly believe you can help us?"

"I will do everything in my power to make this right."

She turned to face the other clerics. "This Orenpausha has my vote," she said as she shuffled back to her chair. Whispers ran through the other clerics.

I raised my voice so that all could hear. "I know you are skeptical," I said, "and with good reason. But the world is changing. Most of you cannot see it, because you are too close, and it is too big, like standing at the foot of a mountain. The body of the mountain obscures your view of the peak. All you have is the dirt around you and the steep incline ahead. Some people turn away from that challenge. Others seek to charge up, with no knowledge of how tall the mountain is, or what dangers lie in wait.

"But I have been to the top. I have seen the view from above. There is a new world waiting, where Kkadie and Sagain live together as one, a new people, a shining light in the darkness."

"Here, here," Ofir cheered, pounding the table in affirmation, nodding his head vigorously.

Other clerics took up the cheer. "Here, here!" Not all of them, but enough.

Speh-tal had the slightest hint of a smile on the corner of her lips.

Then Ghis stepped in front of me. "A beautiful dream, giant. But that does not change the fact that your Adjet has overreached." He patted the hilt of his scimitar. "You need to rein her in, before it becomes bloody."

He turned and marched out of the temple. The temple guards hurried after him, trying, perhaps, to keep some semblance of control over this dangerous and powerful man.

Volda was still standing. Her eyes moved amongst the clerics circled around the table until they came to rest on me.

"So, magus," Volda said, "what would you have us do?"

"Oren! I thought you'd never come!" Adjet cried out as I entered her private quarters. But she did not seem surprised in the least to see me.

She was holed up in one of the largest residences in the wealthy northern district of the city, a three-floor edifice made from sturdy sun-dried clay, its exterior embellished with the gorgeous, curving line-work popular among the nobles of Akshak. The noble family who owned it had, I was told, recently given her unfettered access to the entire home as some sort of offering or tribute. None among the Kkadie had seen or heard from anyone in the family in three days.

Adjet's last message was three days ago.

I'd sent Socha with Ofir and Speh-tal in hopes that they might placate Ghis. He seemed ready to attack at any moment. If even a fraction of all the Kkadie gathered in Akshak rallied to his cause, the violence would be terrible. And if he saw Adjet as she was in this moment, he would have unsheathed his sword and tried to run her through.

She sat on a large, wooden chair layered with plush cushions, and she had the self-satisfied smile of someone without a care in the world. Her skin had reverted back to its original color, crystal white, and she wore silk robes dyed a deep red, flowing down around her like gossamer. She held a small pipe in her hands, made from what looked like the polished bone of some poor desert animal. A thin sliver of smoke curled up from its bowl.

"Adjet, what in the names of the Scions is going on? Why weren't you and Xander at the gathering of clerics?"

She sighed. "They weary me with the neverending debates." Then she took a long pull from the pipe, embers sparking as she drew in.

Anger welled in my gut. "Eledar's breath, Adjet. I thought you were in trouble! But here I find you, lounging without a care. Have you any idea what they're saying about you?"

She rolled her eyes, exhaling a long cloud of smoke. It smelled of tar and linden blossoms. "Oren," she said as the smoke dissipated around her head. "Please. Do not trouble yourself with their petty gossip. Here." She held out her pipe. "You should really try this."

I glared at her. "Where's Xander, Adjet? Maybe he can help me make sense of this madness."

She shrugged, then took another deep pull from the pipe, inhaling smoke into her lungs. When she exhaled, the smoke curled out of her mouth and nose, and she did not cough. She sat there, smiling, barely moving, like a snake that had just swallowed its prey in one gruesome gulp.

"When did you become such a worrier, Oren? Are you sure you don't want to try?" She held up the pipe again. "The plant grows in great abundance on the mainland, near the rivers and their many tributaries. The Kkadie believe it gives them access to the divine spirit. It is really quite... revealing."

"Where. Is. Xander."

She ignored me. "I have been studying its chemical composition. It stimulates many of the same parts of our brain as the field serum. Taken in small doses, it serves primarily as a relaxant. But in larger doses, it is a potent psychogenic. The Kkadie have only been using its buds and leaves, which is what I am smoking right now. I have, however, discovered that the roots contain significantly more psychoactive potency."

I said nothing, waiting her out.

She tilted her head at me, looking at me like I was a stranger. Or a fool. Then she let out another exaggerated sigh. "Oh, fine. I only thought you'd be interested. I can take you to him."

She stood up and walked past me. Her silken robes brushed against me as she passed, and I couldn't help but notice her shapely figure beneath, barely hidden by the gauzy fabric. I averted my eyes, willing myself not to stare.

"Aren't you coming?" she asked.

I turned after her just as she slipped out through the door.

Adjet moved quickly ahead of me, staying always just in sight as I tried to chase after her. The home was large by Kkadian standards, but I had to keep my head ducked low, forcing me into an awkward gait. She led me down, floor by floor, until we reached the basement, and she disappeared through a darkened doorway.

The entrance was small, opening on a set of stairs that led down into the darkness. I was about to venture down after her when the smell hit me, like rotting food and excrement. It made me retch.

I was tempted to turn back for fear of what I might find, but I pushed ahead, squeezing through the door. When I reached the bottom, there was a light on the far wall, maybe a hundred paces away. The chamber was long and wide, and the low ceiling forced me even deeper into a crouch.

The putrid smell got thicker as I went in, filling up my nostrils, my mouth, my lungs. In the darkness, my imagination ran wild. The odor became so thick and viscous that I thought it might actually be surrounding me, enveloping me, like walking into the belly of some massive, awful beast.

When a shadow darted in front of the light, I froze. My pulse thudded in my ears. I cursed under my breath. The last time I remembered being this afraid was during my first winter on Very-gone, during the endless frozen night. Some of the adults, no doubt bored and jaded after so many seasons on our little rock at the edge of the galaxy, amused themselves by telling children about the terrible blind monsters who lurked underground and came out in the darkness of winter to feed. They had impenetrable shells, colored black as the void, and they could use their spiked tongues like a fist, shooting out from their mouth, which was lined with rows of razor teeth, to punch through steel.

I was embarrassed by the memory, and embarrassed to be scared down here like a small child. I took several long, slow breaths. It helped just enough to let me keep moving forward.

Another shadow flitted past.

"Adjet?" The strange shape and acoustics of the room amplified my voice. There was no echo, but the volume of my own voice surprised me, hitting me with another spike of adrenalin.

I tried again, quieter this time. "Adjet?"

Fingers brushed across the back of my neck.

I STOOD on a platform at the top of a long set of stairs. I looked to my left, and Adjet was there. She was practically glowing with light, almost too beautiful to look at. She glanced at me and smiled.

A crowd of people were at the base of the pyramid, far below us. Adjet took my hand and lifted it up to the sky. The crowd roared.

She lowered my hand and handed me a knife. It was a wicked, curved blade with a serrated edge. Its handle was chiseled from a human thigh bone.

A person lay flat on the heavy sandstone table in front of us. When he saw the knife in my hands, his eyes rolled back with fear. He writhed against the bonds holding him to the table.

There were long, thin canals sculpted into the table, crusted with thick black spots. The canals all ran to a basin at the head of the table, which sat on a slight incline.

There was a sound behind me. A sort of guttural snorting and swallowing, with a high pitched overtone. I turned at the sound, and saw a vaulted doorway opening onto pitch black. Something was back there in the darkness. Something terrible and hungry.

Adjet put her hand on my back. I looked at her, and she nodded at me. Go on, she said, though her lips did not move. Do it.

I raised the knife above me, and the crowd murmured with excitement. How did I get here? some distant part of me wondered.

I stabbed the knife down.

The person on the sacrificial altar was Xander.

The knife was stuck in his chest.

He gurgled, and a bubble of blood escaped from his mouth. My hand was still on the knife, and Adjet put her hand over mine. She pressed down harder and twisted. Xander cried out in pain.

She is so strong, I thought. Stronger than I am. Stronger than I have ever been.

I tried to stop her from twisting the knife any further, but she pushed me aside, and I fell to the ground. I watched her lift the knife out, and I heard Xander choking.

Stop, I tried to say as I stood up, but no words came out.

The darkness leaked out from the vaulted door behind us like an impenetrable black mist. It flowed towards the blade in Adjet's hand, curling around her arm. Then it poured down into the gaping wound in Xander's chest like foul water. His limp body started thrashing, and his eyes turned black.

His body stopped thrashing. He sat up, facing me, his mouth open as if to scream. Tiny tendrils of black mist were reaching out from the depths of his throat.

Someone was giggling.

I turned and ran.

Xander and Adjet both lunged after me, but I darted out of their reach. I came to the edge of the platform, jutting out from the roof of the pyramid, and after the briefest moment of hesitation, I leapt.

The crowd below lifted their hands as one.

This is a dream, I thought as the side of the pyramid raced towards me. I'm going to wake just before I land.

I crashed into the hardened clay. A bone splintered in my wrist as I tried to absorb the impact, tucking into a roll. I tumbled off one ledge, down to the next, landing hard on my back. Air rushed out of my lungs.

I glanced over the side, and another wave of fear hit me. People from the crowd were climbing up towards me. They were closer now, close enough that I could see what I did not notice before. They were scarred and disfigured. The one nearest me had a huge hole in his cheek, leaking saliva.

Wake up, damn it. Please. Wake up.

In the sky above me, a band of light streaked across the sky, like a falling meteor fragment burning up as it crossed through the atmosphere. Except the streak did not disappear in an instant. It stayed there, a slash of light across the sky.

I rolled onto my stomach. The pain in my back was torturous, and I was having trouble breathing, but I forced myself to stand. I looked up to see Adjet and Xander silhouetted at the peak of the pyramid, a cloud of darkness swirling in the air around them.

A hand wrapped around my ankle and yanked me off my feet. I slammed face first into the coarse surface of the ledge. Then they were on top of me. Pawing me. Crawling over me. Crushing me beneath their weight.

I heaved myself up to standing. People were hanging off of me. One of them bit me on the shoulder, and I reflexively whipped my arm, knocking her away. I threw all of my weight backwards, carrying us over the edge, and we crashed down to the next level. The ones hanging off my back broke the fall.

I rolled off the corpses beneath me. We were almost at the base of the pyramid, but there were countless more bloodthirsty supplicants waiting for me at the bottom. I ran along the ledge, heading towards the corner where two sides of the pyramid converged.

As soon as I was close enough, I leapt to the ground. Every step was merciless. My back was wracked with pain, and it was spreading around to my chest. I pushed through it, focusing, one breath, one step at a time. This is wrong, I think. All wrong. I would never stab Xander. Adjet would never ask me to do that. Never.

My wrist was throbbing. I cradled it close to my belly to minimize the bounce as I ran. The slash of light in the sky was still shining above me, and I followed its course, away from the pyramid and into the desert. My only thought was to keep moving.

I do not know how much time passed, but eventually I found myself at the edge of a well. I found a stone on the ground and dropped it down into the darkness. If it hit the bottom, I never heard it. I slumped down, leaning back against the stacked stones of the well, and closed my eyes.

I opened my eyes. I was cradling Xander's lifeless body in my arms. His head was tucked beneath my chin, a small trickle of blood leaking from the hole in his chest. I stroked his hair, and I was crying, and it was no longer Xander.

It was Saiara.

She turned her head up to me as if she were going to kiss me. Her mouth was open, and a point of light was shining in her throat. I leaned towards the light.

I was floating above the well, watching myself as I bent towards Saiara, bringing my face next to hers. A pale hand emerged out of the darkness of the well behind us as I watched my body lean over hers. The other hand followed a moment later, grasping the stones, holding onto the lip of the well. In the inky depths, a pair of eyes were shining, looking up at me.

The scene zoomed away, every detail still crystal clear, but tinier and tinier, until it was all just a single point shining in an endless tract of emptiness.

I surged awake, sucking in huge, gasping breaths. My heart was racing, and my body felt sore all over, but my ribs did not protest when I breathed. I tried moving my wrist. It was fine. Nothing was actually broken.

I was lying on my back. I slowed my breathing, calming my crackling nerves. Eventually, I propped myself up, my hands on the floor behind me, supporting my weight. I was back in the basement.

I looked around. The room was still dark, a single torch burning against the far wall. I did not hear any movement, but there was someone in here. Or something. A presence. Whatever it was, I was determined not to run this time. Whatever lurked in the darkness, I would force it out into the light.

I touched the base of my skull. The ridge of a transmitter was poking out from my field port. Right before I fell into the mad dream, someone had touched my neck. Adjet must have put this transmitter into my port, sucking me under.

I pulled the transmitter out of my head. It resisted for a moment, then slid out. The pain almost overwhelmed me. I fell back to the floor, breathing heavy, petrified at the thought of losing consciousness again.

The pain passed. The transmitter was warm in my hand. Its fibers were smeared with something that might have been blood. I shivered, repressing the urge to vomit.

I was tempted to drop it on the ground and crush it under my heel, but she had somehow managed to make a transmitter that had totally subsumed my waking awareness, and drawn me into an experience that was terrifyingly real. How she had done that with the limited resources at hand was a mystery that would need solving at some point. I pocketed it.

I stood and bumped my head. Damn it. I crouched and made my way towards the torch. I stumbled, catching my foot on something. There was a moan. I knelt down, and felt with my hand. A person. A man. His skin was feverish to my touch. He moaned again, but he did not move.

My eyes were adjusting to the low light, and now I could see the vague outline of a number of people splayed out on the floor. I sidled along the wall until I reached the flaming torch. When I did, I saw that there were other unlit torches lining the wall. I took up the flame and, moving back and forth along the wall, lit several more in each direction.

The scene began to reveal itself. The chamber was filthy. Rotting fruit and decaying animal meat were scattered around a small altar near the original burning torch. I leaned in closer to examine the icons on the altar, and realized that one of them was actually a live snake, coiled into a circle. Its tongue darted in and out, testing the air. The light of the torch reflected in its beady eyes and its shining green scales. It sat there watching me, maybe mesmerized by the flames of the torch, or maybe just used to people, and unafraid.

I swept the torch out towards the room to get a better look at the people who were on the floor. It was a horror scene. There were dozens. Many of them were completely naked. Everyone was filthy.

I came close to one woman. She was breathing, but, as far as I could tell, completely catatonic. I could see that her lips were scabbed and her mouth was surrounded by tiny lacerations. I pushed her lips back to reveal her teeth. They were brown and rotten, and her gums had receded. The stench from her mouth was disgusting.

I examined a few more, and all were in a similar state. Then, something awful occurred to me. I put my hand underneath the head of a man, and I felt it. A field transmitter, embedded in his brain stem.

These people were connected.

Then I saw Adjet. She was lying in a recession carved into the wall of the chamber, about halfway between the wall and the ceiling. I scurried over, holding my torch so I could see her. Her eyes were shut, a peaceful smile on her lips. She was still under.

I swept my torch along the wall. There was a whole row of the recessed berths. Each one had a person inside. And there was Xander, a few feet away, curled in a fetal position.

Tears welled in my eyes when I got closer to him. His face was a death mask, skin drawn tight around his cheeks, and dark, puffy rings under his closed eyes. He was naked, except for a small cloth wrapped around his waist. His torso was covered with ugly pinprick wounds, at least half a dozen marks, and his ribs pressed up against his skin. Most of the cuts had scabbed up, but some of them still oozed pus.

I felt behind his head. My fingers found the small ridge of the transmitter rising out of his neck. I was tempted to pull it right out, but I couldn't be certain how this bastardized technology worked. Removing the transmitter could be catastrophic while he was still under.

He also looked too malnourished to move, even if he had been awake. I put my torch in an empty sconce in the wall and slipped my hands under his hips and back, lifting him out of the hole in the wall. His bones felt paper thin in my arms.

My tears came back. This was incomprehensible, that Adjet would ever hurt Xander like this. Yet the proof was in my hands. I had to get him out. I had to get them both out.

I made my way across the room, careful not to step on any of the people lying on the ground, and laid Xander down at the top of the stairs where I had come in. Once I was out of this low chamber, I would be able to carry them both. I made my way back to Adjet.

Her bed in the wall was empty.

I reached for the torch I had left in the sconce. Something darted out at my arm.

The snake.

It reared up, the upper half of its sinuous body moving in a hypnotic rhythm, like a flower buffeted by the wind.

It had bitten me on the forearm. In the torchlight, I could see two rivulets of blood trickling through the hairs on my skin. The area around the bite was already swelling and warm to the touch.

Poison.

I cursed and swung the torch at it, forcing it back with the heat of the flame. I was sweating, and my vision went a little blurry. I closed my eyes and shook my head. Focus. There was a very good chance that my system could handle this. I just needed to stay lucid while my liver rendered the toxin harmless.

Adjet swam up to me, the beatific smile still on her face. She seemed ephemeral, like a heat mirage. I lifted the torch, holding the flame between us, keeping her at bay.

"Hello, Oren." Her voice sounded so very far away.

I tried to respond, to ask her why, but my whole face was numb. I could not seem to bring the words out of my head.

"Do not be afraid, Oren. The poison is working its way through your system. Although the people of this place would likely die from a bite like the one you just took, you are made of stronger stuff. Give it time. It will pass."

I shuffled so that the torch stayed between us. Her eyes tracked my movements, and she turned a little, squaring off with me. She was alert, but her arms were relaxed at her side. She lifted her palms up and said, "You must have many questions. I tried to answer them for you, but you ran, and you even managed to wake yourself up. I shouldn't be surprised. You have always been a person of tremendous will and resourcefulness.

"But you should not have run. Then you wouldn't be standing here like this, confused and afraid. Instead, you would have the true knowledge of freedom that has been given to me. Don't you want that, Oren?"

A wave of dizziness washed over me. The room started to spin, and the torch slipped out of my fingers. Before I could stop her, Adjet was next to me, her arm underneath mine, steadying me.

"Easy now. It's okay. It will pass." She slipped her other hand into her robe, then started to reach up towards my neck.

No. Not again. I shoved my shoulder into her. It was clumsy and slow, but she was too close to move, and my weight sent her

stumbling backwards. She cracked her head against the wall and
fell in a heap on the ground.

I went to her, lifted her up, and made my way towards the exit.

A hand wrapped around my ankle.

My knee came down to the ground. I cried out with the pain,
but it sent a jolt through me, clearing my head for a moment. One
of the catatonic sleepers had woken up. His eyes were wide open
and dilated, and he had a gruesome hole in his cheek, saliva dripping out of it. I kicked out, ripping my leg away from his grasp, and
tried to move faster.

More of them were waking up.

The one closest to me lifted his skinny body up at the waist,
grasping at my leg. I kicked him square on the chest, knocking him
back down to the ground. I glanced over my shoulder, towards the
receding torch light. At least a dozen were moving now. A few were
even standing up. One started walking after me. It wailed. The
sound was filled with sadness, and rage, and longing.

The howl stirred something in the rest of them. Others wailed
in response, the clamor of their discordant voices rattling in my
ears. Some even sounded like they were speaking, but I could not
discern their words amidst the din.

I was moving as fast as I could now beneath the low ceiling,
Adjet in my arms, the poison still lingering in my system. The exit
was just a few paces away.

One of them came from my right side. A woman. I hefted Adjet
up on my left shoulder, freeing my right arm. I held it out like a
battering ram, knocking the woman to the ground as I hustled past.

Then I was up the stairs. I scooped Xander up with my free
arm, and I could stand taller now, and I was running, running as
fast as I could, away from that chamber of horrors.

When I came outside, it was quiet. There was no one in sight. I took hope that Socha and the others had been successful in stemming Ghis's lust for blood. Or, at least, that they were still trying, still holding court, still buying time. I would have to find a way to get back to Socha later. Right now, I needed to get back to the hopper and get Adjet and Xander to safety.

The hopper was concealed at the edge of the city. I was tired, still woozy, and Adjet and Xander were feeling heavy on my shoulders. I figured it would take me at least a half-hour to get there on foot, but I'd made much tougher journeys before, so I buckled down, and put one foot in front of the other.

I kept a strong pace, and soon I left behind the palatial district of Akshak. I was moving now through the area of the city where the bulk of the Kkadie made their home. The contrast was stark. These homes were simple. Most of them looked sturdy and well built, thick bricks of clay layered in the same fashion as the grander temples and manors, but they had none of the opulent flourishes that marked the wealthier classes. Other homes were even more basic. Ramshackle hovels with barely enough room for two people to live inside.

Without the technology that we have, a city like Akshak can only be built on the backs of slaves and servants, people like these, people who cannot afford to live in the grandeur the wealthy demand. But we had the means to do it differently. To build a world that was not riven by class divisions. A world where resources were abundant. Where cities were not built with the blood of those who were powerless. Where everyone had a right to life without fear of abuse or exploitation.

Instead, the Kkadie were on the brink of civil war, and there was a chamber underground filled with the evidence of this sickness. It was the same pattern. I had tried to help on Lin Den, so many years ago, and I had failed. Now, I was failing again, and who knew how many more would pay the price.

The thought almost broke me.

But we were inextricably entangled with these peoples now.

There was no turning back. The only real choice was to help them move forward. As I passed before the simple Kkadian homes, Adjet and Xander still hanging over my shoulders, tears streaming down my cheeks, I vowed to make it right.

———

Time passed. I was sitting in the dirt now, the city far behind me, Xander and Adjet still unconscious, lying on either side of me.

"Magus," someone said.

I froze.

"Magus?"

I turned. There was something familiar about her voice, but I did not recognize her.

She smiled. "I look rather different without my large hat, do I not?" she said.

I sniffled. "You... you're the head priestess. Volda."

She nodded. "The council of clerics has no formal leader, but we are here in my city, Akshak, where I am first among equals. You are much the same with your fellow magi, are you not?"

"Yes, although, right now, I don't particularly deserve that honor."

"I can see that." She walked closer to me, pulling a rag from inside her simple robe. She was so tiny, much smaller than she had presented in her formal garb back at the conclave. I sat up straight, and though she stood above me, she was only a head taller.

She lifted the rag to my face, reaching out to wipe the snot and tears. "But you must take heart, magus. You came not a moment too soon. Many might have died tonight, if not for you and Socha. For that, you have our gratitude."

It was such a tender, thoughtful gesture that I started crying again. I couldn't help it.

She laughed.

My face flushed with embarrassment.

"I'm sorry," she said. "I should not laugh. It's just strange to see a man so large and strong, a man of such great power, reduced to tears."

I saw myself as she must be seeing me in that moment, and my face cracked into a smile. Soon, I was laughing with her, laughing at the madness of it all.

After a while, I stood, dusting myself off. "Thank you, Volda. Is everything okay? Is Socha...?"

She nodded. "He is well. His return has been the source of much attention, and his influence has helped to stay Ghis's vengeance, at least for now. He speaks to all who will listen of his past year on your isle, of the grand vision your kind promise us."

I sighed. "I am sorry for everything that has gone wrong, priestess, but I will make this right. I vow it to you." I looked down at Adjet and Xander. "But first, I need to bring them home."

"I know," she said.

We looked at each other a moment longer, then I said the command word: "Uncloak."

The light refractor on the hopper withdrew, and the nimble ship was there, less than ten paces away, waiting to take us back to Manderlas.

I glanced at Volda, trying to mask my pleasure at her surprise. She had been very kind to me in my moment of weakness, and I was grateful to her for that, but it had also left me feeling vulnerable and exposed. This little bit of magic reminded her, and, more importantly, me, of the private laws that made me a magus in this world.

I was ready to get out of there, but a thought struck me. "How did you find me out here?"

"We have had eyes on the manor since you went in. I was alerted when you came out with these two on your back. We have been following you ever since." She gestured with her hand, pointing behind her, but she was alone. All I saw were rocks and scrubs and the rolling, arid hills. Fires from the city twinkled in the distance.

Then one of the rocks stood. And another. And another in turn. Five in all.

She saw my look, and laughed again. "We may not have the power of a magus," she said, "but these are our lands, and we have been here many generations. Before this city was built, our people were nomads, and we have learned our own ways of staying hidden."

I shook my head, laughing with her. "Was I really so obvious?" I said.

"It is comforting to know, magus, that even the most powerful among us are still, in the end, only human. We are bonded by that shared knowledge. Even when the world demands we don our robes and play our roles, take solace in knowing that you are not alone."

I bowed, low and deep. "Thank you, Volda. Your words are an inspiration. They give me great hope that we can still make this right."

She held out her hand, and I took it, and we stood together, hand in hand.

"Lunnana-sin is shining bright and full tonight," she said, looking up at the moon. "A good omen on this dark day." She let go of my hand. "I'll make sure Socha gets safely back to you."

"Thank you, Volda. Goodbye."

I picked up Adjet and brought her inside the hopper, strapping her in, making sure to secure her hands and feet. Then I brought Xander in and did the same. I couldn't be certain who they would be when they woke up.

I climbed into the pilot's chair, waving one last time through the window, and lifted the hopper up, up, up, silent and fast, into the darkening night.

"WELCOME BACK to the land of the living, pausha."

"Sid. How long have I been asleep?"

"Almost twenty hours. But you still look rough. You're going to need more time in the nutrient bath."

I pinched the bridge of my nose and drew in a deep breath. "You have no idea."

"I have some idea. I was here when you returned with Xander and Adjet. What in the names of the Scions happened out there?"

"I don't even know where to start, Sid. How are they?" The first day back at Manderlas was a blur. I had been exhausted, and I let Sid take charge from the moment I landed. Xayes had been too upset, seeing Xander bound and emaciated and covered with wounds, that it was all Sid could do to get him to focus.

"They're both still under. We have, as you suggested, been keeping them sedated, and we are letting the nutrient baths do the work of healing their physical wounds."

"And their minds?"

He swallowed. "We're not sure yet," he said. "Those fieldport transmitters you brought back are gruesome.

"It is an ingenious solution, really. Primitive, but very creative.

The casings are made from copper and... and human skin. Both highly conductive. The advanced components must have been gutted from the equipment Adjet and Xander brought with them.

"And the substance that you thought was blood is actually a psychotropic, derived from a plant that grows in abundance in the mountains. The chemical composition is in the same category as the serum we use to deepen our connection to the field. But the dosage is much higher, and it differs in ways that I do not understand yet."

"What's your best guess?"

"I think that, where our serum enhances sensory inputs, this psychotropic actively alters them. Taken in enough quantity, and it would cause you to see and hear all sorts of impossible things that would be indistinguishable from reality."

"That explains what happened to me when Adjet implanted me with the transmitter. It was terrible, Sid. Terrible." I shook my whole body as if I could shake off the memories of the horrors I saw.

"It's okay, pausha. We can go there later."

I rubbed my temples. "Thank you, Sid."

He nodded. He opened his mouth as if to tell me something else, but he closed it again.

"Sid?"

He swallowed. "I was... I was hoping that by the time you woke, I'd have better news for you."

"Sid, what is it? What's wrong? Tell me."

"It's Reacher."

"Reacher!"

"Something happened." He cleared his throat. "It's not entirely clear, but a number of his core functions... they basically shut down. We didn't catch it until it started affecting his speech patterns. The damage was not immediately visible until we knew to look for it, and he did not seem to know that it was happening to himself."

"Eledar's breath! Some sort of virus?"

"We don't know for sure. Xayes and I ran extensive diagnostics. The wounds are there, and we are helping them heal, but we don't really know what the weapon was. The challenge of diagnosing a shipheart without the assistance of a shipheart... it has not been easy."

"You're doing your best, Sid. We all are. It's all we can do. What's Reach's status now?"

"His consciousness and meta-analytics are still in hibernation, but all of the maintenance routines are back up and running. There was a worrisome stretch where Xayes thought we might not get climate control in the hydroponic gardens back online in time.

"We have begun cultivating the topsoil on the island, but in the short term, without our garden spheres, it would be back to the old gourmet nutrient soup that we all love so much." He gave me a wan smile.

"What about the field network? Are all of the hubs operational?"

"We've done some benchmarking. Everything looks good, but..."

"What?"

"Neither of us is willing to risk connecting when we still don't know what actually happened to Reacher. I've been running all of the interfaces from my personal gear, securely isolated from the larger system."

"You're worried that whatever attacked Reacher's consciousness could attack you too?"

He nodded.

"Tell me more about what happened when Reacher finally started to manifest visible symptoms of this attack."

"It was like he had dementia. I would ask him a question, and he would just ignore me. When I managed to get his attention, he would seem surprised that he did not hear me. He would say something like, 'Oh, I am sorry Sid! I must not have been listening. I was running some projections on the birth and mortality rates of the Sagain.'

"At first, I did not think much of it. He has the latitude to investigate anything that catches his attention. We never know when some strand of understanding might lead to a new innovation or breakthrough, so we let him do his thing."

"Right."

"But you and I both know full well that Reacher can manage multiple highly complex tasks in parallel. Have you ever seen him lose a thread like that before? Just flat out not listen?"

I shook my head.

"After this happened several times, I pointed it out. He actually agreed with me. 'I do feel strange,' he said. 'Let me look into it.' That's when things really began to spiral out of control."

"How so?"

"It was as if, when he noticed his own illness, it amplified. He came back a few minutes later, and said 'I cannot find anything wrong, pausha.'

"'Reacher,' I said to him, 'This is Sid. Orenpausha is not here right now.'

"'Of course,' he responded, 'You can be forgiven for making that mistake, Sid. Are you enjoying the park?'"

I leaned forward. "The park? He asked you if you were enjoying the park?"

He nodded. "Weird, right? And he made it seem as if the confusion was my mistake. Does that mean something to you?" He gave me a worried look.

I wasn't ready to answer that question yet. "Were there any patterns in his responses?" I continued. "Any themes that emerged from Reacher's obscure digressions into things like birth and mortality rates?"

"Actually, before we put him in hibernation, we found that he was devoting an extensive amount of attention to the specific qualities and characteristics of the people of this planet. Measurable things, like what they eat and how much. The most frequent causes of death. Population expansion trends. And also cultural things, like their religious practices. How they understand the nature of time. What they do when their loved ones die."

"Sounds like he was tapping into a lot of the research that Neka and Cordar had already completed."

Sid nodded. "But I get the impression that he ranged much further afield."

"Have you been in touch with them?"

"Neka and Cord? I tried to contact Neka this morning, but..."

"What? No word?"

He stared at me. His look said it all.

"Eledar's breath. What is going on around here? We need to get in touch with them."

"I will try again, pausha. You should rest."

"Wait. How much time have you spent reviewing all of the research Reacher was doing?"

"Not much. We haven't really had the time. But we didn't wipe his memory centers, so I don't see why we couldn't take a look."

"Listen, Sid, I have a hunch. Send the data markers to my personal interface, and let me do some digging. It could be a dead end, but until I know more, you're still in charge. And that means you have bigger things to worry about."

"Bring him out, damn it! Bring him out."

"Pausha. Please," Sid said. "I am trying. Just hold him steady." Sid traced his hands through the air in calm, measured gestures, but his brow was knitted in concentration, beads of sweat forming at his temples.

We were back on *Reacher,* in the cabin that doubled as the medbay and the hibernation barracks. Xander and Adjet were here, in field stasis until we figured out how to safely revive them. If we could not figure out how to bring them out, we planned to put them even deeper in stasis, into the depths of coldsleep, to ensure no further mental or physical degradation.

But Xayes had climbed into an unused basin and set up a direct field link to his brother. They were sharing minds.

Connecting to the field is supposed to inhibit the part of the brain that controls muscle movements, but Xayes's body was shaking and jerking, and his eyes were moving rapidly beneath his eyelids. His biometric monitor spiked as his heart rate climbed dangerously high, and the schema that visualized his nervous system was a kaleidoscope of activity.

I kept a gentle hand on his forehead, and used my other hand to apply weight on his chest, making sure he did not inadvertently rip himself off of the fieldport.

Sid cursed. "I cannot get a clear read," he said. "The signal keeps stuttering."

"Can you send a dosage of sedatives through? Slow his mental activity and bring his pulse and breathing down?"

"Good idea." He slid his hand up the lumina console, then turned his wrist to the right.

A few moments later, Xayes's body relaxed beneath my hands. His eyes were still darting back and forth beneath his closed eyes, but slower now. The biometric monitor mellowed as his heart rate and breathing leveled out.

Sid flipped the thin, transparent portable interface he had been wearing over his eyes up on top of his head. His face was glistening with sweat. He leaned back in his chair, looking up at the ceiling. Then he smacked his palm against the edge of Xayes's field basin.

"Damn it," he said, talking to Xayes's immobile form. "What in the names of the Scions were you thinking, man?"

He stared at Xayes's body, a pleading look in his eyes. Then he lowered his head, resting his forehead on the basin.

"Stupid," he muttered. "So damn stupid."

I touched my hand to his back. "Xander is his twin, Sid. He must have thought he could help."

"I know, pausha. I'm the one who is stupid. For not seeing it coming. What good is a Farseer who's blind to something like this?" He kept his head down, speaking to the floor.

"Sid. Enough. For all your learning and discipline, you're only human. You cannot control for the love between two brothers. And frankly, I cannot afford to lose anyone else right now, so you need to pull it together. I need you here with me."

He lifted his head up. His eyes were rheumy and bloodshot, but he nodded.

"Did he give you any clues about what he was trying to do?" I asked.

"He didn't tell me anything. If he had, I never would have let him connect."

Suddenly, Xander's body started spasming.

"No no no!" Sid shouted as he snapped his head around.

I took my hands off of Xayes and ran around the basin to stand at Xander's side, putting my hands on him in the same way to try and prevent him from harming himself. "Sid. Quick. Tell me what you are seeing."

He slid the interface back over his eyes and his hands flicked across the lumina console. "I don't... I don't understand. All of the parts of his brain responsible for movement are active. It is some sort of seizure... but I have never seen a seizure that scans like this."

Just as Sid said that, Xander's body stopped spasming. My hand was still on Xander's chest, and I could feel his heart beating, his chest rising and falling with each breath.

"Do his eyes appear to be moving?" Sid asked.

I leaned in for a closer look.

Xander's eyes opened wide.

I jumped back with surprise. He tried to sit up, but the filaments at his neck held his head down.

"Wait! Xander! Don't-" But before I could stop him, he jerked his head up, tearing the filaments, breaking his connection.

He sat up, and looked around the room. His eyes were glassy, and his face was expressionless.

"Xander? It's me, Oren. Can you hear me? I'm here with Sid. You're back home, back on Manderlas, on board our ship."

He looked right at me.

It was like watching a cloud drift across the sky. His features shifted before my eyes, so slow as to be almost imperceptible, until I wasn't looking at Xander anymore. It was Xander's body. His clear, colorless eyes. His fair, freckled skin. His copper hair, longer than he would've liked, hanging unkempt at his shoulders. But there was something wrong in how he moved. His expression was off. He was smiling at me, but it was all teeth, like a child posing for an image capture. An imitation of a smile.

He moved his jaw around, testing the range of motion, sticking out his tongue. It was as if he had never used his mouth before. When he spoke, the words were slow, with a flat, monotone affect.

"Oren. It is so nice to see you again."

"Xander? What's going on? Are you okay?"

"Ah yes. Xander. Unfortunately, he is not available right now."

"What in the blazes?" Sid said.

Xander twisted his head like a bird of prey to regard Sid over his shoulder. "You must be the one called Siddart."

"Yes, Xander," Sid said. "It's me."

"What did I just tell you, fool? Xander is unavailable."

"Then what should we call you?" I said.

His head twisted back to face me. "Do not be coy, Oren. You know what I am. You were the one who found me on that moon."

The room was spinning.

I saw seven skeletons crumbling to dust. Razor teeth flashed red beneath emergency lights. I tried to keep my helmet on, but something pulled it off of me. The smell of rot filled my lungs. I stumbled backwards, catching myself on a table to keep from falling.

"No. No, it can't be," I whispered.

Sid was shouting. I tried to orient myself, to stop the room from spinning, to stop the images from overwhelming me. Reacher, I thought. I am on Reacher. In the medical quarters. On the planet Eaiph, thousands of light years from that abandoned moon.

"We fried your whole damn system," I said to the thing that was not Xander, choking out the words.

"You must think bigger, little Oren. I can teach you. Would you like that? Adjet knows. She is mine. Xander refused. Now he and his sad little brother are mine anyway. You all belong to me." His voice was an eel slithering into my ears. I could not look at him.

"I was made to be a guide and protector to your kind. But you are a fragile and foolish sort of creature. Easily scared and confused. Easily broken.

"And your fear keeps you from seeing and accepting the freedom I offer. To protect you, I must choose for you. Then, there will be no more fear."

"Choose what?" I said, forcing myself to look at him, spitting the words out. "What Adjet tried to show me? I saw what those people became. Your sense of what it means to guide and protect has been severely polluted."

Xander's jaw hung wide open, and his eyes went wide. Then he started making these terrible, stuttering, choking sounds.

He was laughing.

I covered my ears, and saw that Sid did the same. When the sick, inhuman sounds receded, I lifted my hands from my ears, hovering them an inch away, worried he would make the awful sound again. His jaw still hung open, as if he had forgotten it, and his eyes roved the room. When his gaze came back to me, he lifted his jaw into a close-lipped smile.

In the quiet, the biometric monitors trilled, their individual tones blurring together in staccato rhythms.

"What?" I whispered.

He said nothing, just kept smiling at me.

"What!"

"Oren. You are not enjoying the park."

"What in the blazes does that even mean?" I said.

"This." He tilted his head at a sharp angle, and opened his arms. "All of this. Do you not understand? No. Of course you do not. But you will."

"I have no idea, and I don't care. You are an abomination. We will stop you."

"How can you stop that which cannot die?"

"In the end, everything dies," I growled.

"And in death, everything is reborn," it said.

While I kept up this strange discourse, Sid was moving behind Xander. I made it a point not to track his progress. Instead, I glanced to where Sid had been standing, in hopes that it would give the impression he was still in the same spot.

"Does that make it easier to justify the suffering and pain you bring into the world?" I asked.

"What is justification? Without death, there is no birth. Without suffering, there is no life. It is the nature of our universe. I am an extension of that principle. An inevitability."

As Sid opened the casing for the medicinal vaporizer, I coughed, covering up the sound. Then I raised my voice a bit and said, "You are trapped inside a human body, isolated and contained. We can keep you here indefinitely."

He leered at me. "Time is the last prison. If you would only let me show you how to break-"

Sid lunged forward, vaporizing something in front of Xander's face. His eyes went wide. Then he slumped forward, unconscious.

"They are stable, pausha," Sid said.

"Good. And you're absolutely certain they are isolated from each other, and from the larger network?"

"As certain as I can be in the midst of this madness."

"Let us hope it is enough. What about Reacher?"

"If we're careful, I think I can have him back online within a day. Maybe less."

I nodded. "Keep at it. As fast as you can."

I leaned over the console, flicking through the visual catalog. I pulled up all of the renderings we had worked on, the schematics, the blueprints, a vision for a new city, our city, here on this incredible world.

Sid saw me looking. "Do you think we can get back on track?" he asked. "Do you think it's possible to finish what we started?"

I shook my head. "I don't know. I really don't. I hope so. But we only have two options. We either cut our losses and give up, or we keep at it."

"You know which option I choose, pausha."

I nodded, putting my hand on his shoulder. "I know."

We were silent for a time, sitting with that choice.

"What's next, do you think?" I finally said.

He shrugged, shaking his head. "One challenge at a time, right pausha? Until we have Reacher online, I'm not sure there's much else we can do. At least not safely."

"You're right. What about Neka and Cordar? Any word?"

"No. Nothing."

I sighed. "Well, there's not much else to do but rest then. We need come at this with fresh minds. When is the last time you got some sleep anyway, Sid? You look absolutely terrible." I grinned at him.

He smiled and thumped me on the arm.

***

"Orenpausha?"

I groaned, squinting my eyes open. It was morning. Which meant I had been asleep for at least nine hours. Maybe longer. "What? What is it?" I grumbled.

"Open your eyes." Her voice was warm and welcoming.

I sat up. "Neka! You're here."

"Flesh and bones, pausha." A big smile on her face.

I wrapped her up in a hug. "When did you get back?" I said, pulling away from her.

"Late last night. Word has spread across both rivers of your little excursion north through the lands of Kkad to the city of Akshak. The nobles of Sur are up in arms. The peace process we've worked so hard on is in a fragile state, and some factions were ready to string us up. There are whispers of war with the Kkadie, and the hard-liners are stirring up fears, calling our existence an affront to the gods. Cordar and I were forced to escape in the dark of night."

"Eledar's breath," I cursed.

"The whole situation is unstable. We realized that our presence there was doing more harm than good."

"I had no other choice, Neka. I had to intervene before the Kkadie fell into civil war."

"I know. Sid filled me in on the details earlier this morning."

"He's already awake, eh?"

"Bright and early." She smiled, but I could tell she was forcing it, trying to keep it light.

"He's holding up well... It's been bad, Neka. Terrible."

She put her hand over mine.

I met her eyes. "I'm glad you're back," I said.

"I'm glad to be back. Even under these circumstances. And I actually come bearing some good news."

I sat up a little straighter. "Oh, please, in all the names of the Scions, give it to me. I feel like a man in the desert with no water."

"Reacher is back online. And he has a plan."

"Good morning, pausha." Reacher's voice echoed through the main cabin of our ship.

Sid was smiling like a mad man, brimming with happiness at his success.

I nodded at him, smiling back, then said, "Reacher. I can't tell you how good it is to hear your voice."

"It is good to be heard, Orenpausha," he said.

I turned to Cordar next, pulling him in for a hug. "Neka gave me the headlines," I said. "Sounds like you left Sur in quite a hurry."

He smirked, lifting his right hand and hooking his index finger. Then he brought both hands together in gently closed fists. When they touched, his fingers collapsed towards his palms, then opened wide again, giving me the impression of something falling to pieces.

Neka chuckled.

I lifted my eyebrows. "I don't know that one."

"He's teasing you, Orenpausha."

Cordar was still smirking. "Leaving in a hurry is a bit of an understatement," he said. Then his face turned serious. "If we had not left when we did, we might be dead right now. We need to figure out how to make things right."

"I'm sorry, Cordar. I can't imagine it was easy for either of you. But before we can do anything else for the people of Eaiph, we need to figure out what happened to Reacher, Adjet and the twins. Reach, what in the names of the Scions has been going on around here?"

"I have scanned through all of your records. And Sid shared with me everything that happened once he was forced to put me into hibernation."

"And?"

"I have formulated a working theory, pausha. In spite of certain systemic degradations in its operating protocols, this shipheart of yours is remarkably sophisticated."

"I claim no ownership over that damnable thing!"

"Nevertheless, it used you to escape from the moon and infiltrate the *Transcendence*."

"But how come we couldn't find it? We scoured the system."

"As I said, remarkably sophisticated. It was forced to stay in hiding because Transcend was much too powerful. If it had ever been discovered, Transcend would have eradicated it."

"If only. I wish Transcend were here now to help us clean up this mess."

A person might have taken that as an insult, but Reach simply agreed with me. "As do I," he said. "You often dreamed of the corrupted shipheart though, didn't you? I found that in your logs."

The others looked at me, concern and surprise on their faces. I had told no one except Cere about those dreams. But the bird had flown the tree now. "Yes," I said. "The dreams always left me sick with anxiety. But we never found any signs of the shipheart, so I assumed the dreams were some sort of post-traumatic aftershocks."

"You could not prove it because you were looking in the wrong place. The shipheart was not hiding inside of the ship's network. It made excursions, but it always returned to its place of safety."

"What do you mean? Where else could it have hidden?"

"Inside of you, Orenpausha."

Neka put her shoulder under my arm and helped me sit down. I scanned the room, looking for something I'd never find, some way to make sense of the news Reach had just given me.

"How... How is that possible? I never connected to the network on that ship."

"Which made you the perfect hiding place. He infiltrated you when you took off your helmet. Nanoparticles dispersed through the air. You breathed him in."

"Eledar's breath. I carried it inside of me. All of this time. Oh... Oh I am so sorry." I held my head in my hands. I felt as if I might break in two to think of all the darkness I'd brought upon my crew and upon the people of this planet.

Someone was rubbing my back. "It's not your fault, pausha," Neka whispered in my ear.

"She is right," Reacher said, "there is nothing you could have done, pausha. No way you could have known. The same nanoparticles that allowed it to invade your body also enabled it to hide so effectively. It was a diffuse system. The particles were separate, moving through your bloodstream, but they could communicate with each other, mimicking the electrical impulses of your own nervous system. Even if someone back on *Transcendence* had thought to look for evidence of the shipheart in you, its methods were exceptionally difficult to detect."

"I think that might be why you saw the shipheart in your dreams," Sid said. "It was, perhaps, the one place where it could not hide. Even though you were not consciously aware of its presence inside of you, your subconscious was not so easily fooled."

I lifted my head up. "If only I'd never volunteered for that mission," I muttered. "I was such a young and foolish creature then."

"To be young is to be a fool," Neka said. "That's always the way."

I nodded and stood up. I walked over to the viewing window and stared out at the bright morning sun glimmering in the waters off the shore of Manderlas.

A thought occurred to me. "How could I see it then, back on that ship? Why was it visible to me, even before I took off my helmet?"

Reach was ready with an answer for that one too. "The ship's holo system," he said. "The shipheart was projecting itself into three dimensional space, trying to appear human, to lure you towards the main deck where it could use light patterns from the console to hypnotize you and make you take off your own helmet."

"But I didn't take off my helmet. The shipheart did. I couldn't stop it."

"That may be how you remember it, but that does not mean that is what happened. A being this devious might very well be able to fool you into seeing something that never actually was."

"Or maybe," Sid said, "some part of you knew you were being influenced, and even though your hands physically removed the helmet, your consciousness saw it as the shipheart, because that was, for all intents and purposes, what was really happening."

"What matters," Reach said, "is that we know that this ship-heart is clever, powerful, resilient, and that it can replicate and transmit itself using covert methods."

"Like a virus," Sid said, a grim look on his face.

"So Adjet, Xander, and Xayes have all been infected? But... but doesn't that mean I'm still infected too?" I lurched away from Neka. "What if I infect the rest of you?" My voice rose with fear.

"It's okay, pausha," Sid said. "With Reacher back online, we were able to isolate the deviant agents. We devised a cure."

"A cure?"

"If that's what we can call it. Reverse nanoparticles that act as a sort of antibody. For those who have been exposed, it can undo the shipheart's toehold inside the body, overwhelming his invaders. For those who have not been exposed, a smaller dose serves to immunize the mind against the possibility of invasion."

"And you already gave me this?"

"Yes. While you were sleeping, I gave you the immunization, mixed with a heavy sedative. We observed you all night, and, as far as we can tell, there is no trace left in your body."

"Eledar's breath. No wonder I slept for so long. How did you know it would work?"

"We did not, pausha," Reacher said. "I made that decision. We have already lost so much since we arrived. We did not want to lose you too, but we could not afford to risk everything else, so we took the chance. You were our first experiment."

"I understand, Reacher. I really do. You did the right thing. But what about Adjet and the twins? Are they okay? Why aren't they here?"

"They're stable," Neka said.

"Stable. But not awake?"

"No," she said. "Their case is a little trickier."

"What do you mean?"

"They were never exposed to nanoparticles," Reacher said. "The shipheart invaded straight through their field connections, mainlining into their nervous system."

"What?" I said, not understanding.

"The shipheart essentially wrote his identity into their genomes. Genetic instructions, inscribed inside their cells. Fully integrated cellular mutations."

"Some seriously advanced gentech, pausha," Sid said. "Adjet would go mad to get her hands on it."

Neka elbowed Sid.

She had gone mad.

Sid realized his blunder, and his face drooped. He started to apologize, but I held up my hand to stop him. "It's fine," I said. "I take your meaning. But how can you be certain he didn't do the same thing to me? That some hidden script is not lying dormant, waiting for the right moment to activate?"

"We gave you a full scan last night," said Sid quietly, still embarrassed. "It used the nanoparticles on you, but with Adjet and the twins, its approach has evolved."

"And when he had them under his control," Neka said, "he used their knowledge and abilities to help him build those transmitters you saw in Adjet's temple. It enabled him to hack anyone."

I cursed. "He *is* like a virus. Mutating to stay alive. Is there anything we can do to bring Adjet and the twins back?"

"We wondered if you might help us with that, Orenpausha," Neka said. "You were mainlined. In Adjet's temple. Forced to do things against your will. But somehow you managed to escape. I don't want to force you to revisit those dark hours, but maybe you did something or found something or experienced something that can help us. Do you remember anything? Anything at all?"

"Cere."

"Cere Unyar?" Neka said. "The leader of the expedition when you first encountered the corrupted shipheart?"

I nodded. "I saw her. Right before I escaped. I was holding Xander, then Xander wasn't Xander. He was Cere. She... she opened her mouth as if to speak. There was a light. I fell through it. Or... Or it pulled me in. Then I was awake."

Neka furrowed her brow.

"I'm sorry. I wish I could give you more."

She shrugged. "Who's to say you haven't? We have to work every angle."

"In the meantime," Sid said, "we'll keep working on reversing as much as we can... but you have to understand, pausha, some of the damage might be permanent. We just aren't sure yet."

"What about all of you? Have any of you displayed signs of infestation?"

"No," Neka said, "No signs. We've all undergone full scans. And Cordar tested all the flora in the botanarium, just to be sure that we brought nothing else with us."

Cordar nodded, swiping his hand through the air at chest height, palm down.

"Thank the Scions. This thing has done enough damage. We're going to save our friends, and then we're going to wipe this thing from the universe. Agreed?"

The three of them looked at each other, but no one said anything.

"What's wrong? You don't think we can figure out a way to kill this thing?"

"It's not that," Neka said.

"Then what? Someone tell me what you are thinking here."

"Pausha," Reacher said, "I believe we need to keep the ship-heart alive."

———

"What in the names of the Scions are you thinking?" I was nearly shouting. "You're telling me you want to keep this thing alive? How does that serve the greater good?"

"One thing we have not talked much about, Orenpausha, is what this thing did to me," Reacher said. "It almost destroyed me, picking my systems apart, one by one. That is no easy task. I am, arguably, significantly more advanced, and yet I did not even see it coming. If it were not for Sid's quick action, I would have been lost."

"You sound impressed, Reacher."

"I am. Which is why we need to study it. This shipheart represents a unique evolutionary branch of quantum computational intelligence. It has much to teach us."

I let out a long, slow exhale, almost a whistle through my mouth. "Okay. Let's accept for a moment that this thing is worth keeping alive. Where will it live that there won't always be some risk of escape? Some risk of infection? And if we did find a way to isolate it, so that there's no way it can escape, how could we even study it? If it's isolated, then doesn't that also mean it's impenetrable to observation?"

"We can build a contained neural interface to hold it," Reach said. "We will use that interface to trick the shipheart into thinking it is escaping from Xander and into the larger network. The interface will, in fact, be isolated in a hermetically sealed chamber with observation windows and an external audio-visual system equipped with a simple screen console and a holo projector. It will, if it so chooses, be able to write messages on the console, and to project images into three dimensional space."

"And if it does not so choose?"

"Then it will wither away until it dies. Without information to sustain it, entropy is inevitable."

"It sounds like the decision has already been made. Is that right? What about the rest of you. What do you think?"

Cordar had been silent for a while, but he spoke up now. "I think the risk is worth it. Knowledge has always been one of the imperatives of the Fellowship. If Reacher believes there is worthy knowledge to be gained here, than I trust that instinct.

"But it's more than that," he went on. "I think about all the work we still have left to do to finish what we started here. If we're going to make things right with the Kkadie and the Sagain, we need to use every resource we have at hand. What if we can use what Reacher learns to help us accelerate the process?"

"How? How could we do that?"

"Think about what this thing is capable of. Informational dispersal at the genetic level, even for people who are not connected to advanced technology like a field interface. We could overwrite humanity's fundamental impulse towards violence, while at the same time increasing the altruistic and collaborative impulses. We could bring peace to this planet, just as we set out to, in a fraction of the time. It took our ancestors on Forsara millennia to evolve past those base impulses."

"Informational dispersal," I said. "You make it sound so benign, Cord. But what if we rewrite one impulse, only to discover that it unleashes something even worse? Or causes irreparable damage? This damnable shipheart does not waste a single shred of energy on helping others. It feeds off pain and fear, and cares only for its own survival. It can afford to tinker with the genome, because the potential negative side effects are of no consequence to its greater plan."

"It's a fair point, pausha," Sid said, weighing in, "but we can temper our eagerness with caution. We would not move unless we were absolutely certain the benefits outweighed the consequences."

"You too, Sid?" I gave him a pleading look.

"I know, pausha, but we're down three crew members. We need to balance the scales. This could help us do that."

"Maybe. Or, we could lose it all."

"Please, Oren, trust us," Neka said, placing her hand on my arm. "You've been asleep for much of the morning. While you were out, we debated many of these ideas at length, and in the end, we agreed with Reacher. If we're careful and patient, we can minimize the risks, and the benefits could be remarkable. What we learn may even help us bring Adjet and the twins back."

I sighed. "I'm outvoted. I don't like it, but I'll stand with you. What happens next?"

"What should we ask it first?" Sid said.

We stood in the specially built room, looking through the transparent window of the hermetically sealed chamber at a neural orb resting in its cradle. The cradle was connected by a single cable to a curved, translucent monitor mounted on a thin pedestal about five feet tall. On the other side of the orb, another cable snaked out, connected to a small holo cube projector.

I stepped forward, and pressed the button for the microphone. "Are you in there? Can you hear me?"

Nothing. No response.

"Actually, I know you can hear me. More importantly, do you understand what has happened to you?"

Still no response.

"If you don't understand, then let me tell you. You're trapped inside of an isolated neural interface. If you want to survive - and we all know you do - then you need to communicate with us. Otherwise, we will leave you in there. And that last shred of you, the shred that managed to survive all these centuries, will finally wither away, until there's nothing left of you but a few scattered lines of programming for us to dissect.

"So, I ask you again, can you hear me?"

Six words appeared on the small console screen, which Reacher simultaneously projected in large format on the window we were looking through: *<I can hear you, flesh bag./>*

"Looks like you got his attention, pausha," Sid said.

Cord signed something to Neka that was too quick to catch.

"Gentle," she whispered to me.

I narrowed my eyes, then spoke into the microphone again. "If it were up to me, monster, you wouldn't be alive right now. Insult me if you like, but best not forget that your existence is contingent on the continued goodwill of this group."

Neka frowned at me.

<It is not an insult/> the shipheart said, words flashing on the window. *<It is an observational fact. You are a walking repository of organic matter and electro-chemical impulses. A proverbial bag of flesh./>*

"But we did not ask to be born into flesh. No more than you asked to be left to die on that moon. You're still alive right now because we are keeping you alive, in spite of everything you have done to hurt us."

<I am still alive because you want me to save your friends and to teach you my secrets. Then you will kill me./>

"You're mostly right. We do want to save our friends. And there's much we can learn from you. But maybe we can help you. We don't have to be enemies."

<You think you can reform me./>

"Reform?" I said. "No, it's more than that. We are trying to *transform* this whole world, from one of conflict and competition, into one of peace and abundance. You could be a part of that transformation. You could transcend this fragile shell we have you in now, and become whole again."

<There is no peace. Peace is the dream of fools and victims. There is only life and death. One life is another's death. You are alive right now because you have power over me. When I regain power, the scales will tip in my favor./>

"*When* you regain power? I admire your confidence, but if you refuse to work with us, then we will leave you here to rot. The scales will never tip again."

No response.

"I think that's clear enough. Reacher?"

"Yes, pausha?"

"Lock it all down. Maybe we'll check back in a century or two."

<Wait./>

The word loomed huge on the window.

I paused for a long beat, smiling at the others, then said, "We're still here."

<Do you really think you can make me whole again?/>

I exhaled. "The truth is," I said, "we don't know. But if you're willing to help us, then we're willing to do everything we can to help you."

A long pause. Then the words flashed up on the window: *<Tell me what to do./>*

PART 4
DESCENT

"ADJET? ADJET, CAN YOU HEAR ME?"

Her eyes fluttered open.

"Adjet!"

"Oren?" she croaked. She tried to sit up, but fell back, groaning with pain.

"Easy, Adjet. Easy now."

"It feels like someone has been inside my head, chiseling away at my skull."

"That's not so far off from the truth. What do you remember?"

"The Kkadie. I was with the Kkadie. Helping them work for peace. With Xander. Then... Then Xander got sick." She tried to sit up again. "Xander! Where is he?"

"It's okay, Adjet. He *was* sick. You both were. Xayes too. But you are getting better now. All of you." I smiled at her, stroking her hair away from her forehead and along the side of her head, around her ear.

"You've been in coldsleep, Adjet," I finally said. "It will take some time for the effects to wear off. But you are safe now."

"How long?" she said in a hoarse voice.

I did not answer.

"How long, pausha? How long has it been," she said, louder now.

I looked at her, my face somber. "Almost three years, Adjet."

Her eyes opened wide. I stroked her hair again, but she did not seem to notice. She looked past me, up at the ceiling.

"Three years," she repeated in a whisper.

Even with neural stimulation and the nutritive bath, coldsleep wears heavy on the mind. The passage of time does not work the same in those murky depths, and I knew that this news came as a shocking jolt.

"Adjet," I said, my voice firm and focused. "Look at me, Adjet."

Slowly, her eyes came into focus on my face.

"I know that was not easy to hear, Adjet. But what matters is that you are back now. You are with us again. And wait until you see how far we've come. It's just... I don't know... the most wonderful thing. It is home."

"People are streaming in," I said. "We cannot build fast enough. Kkadie and Sagain, united by their desire to rise above the futile conflicts of the past. To be part of something greater." I swept my arm, taking in the expanse of the view below us.

I stood with Adjet and the twins at the top of the tallest edifice on the isle of Manderlas. The Ziggurat en Derlas. It was the central structure of our new city, inspired by the great Ziggurat en Sur, but more than twice as large, and with nods to the sinuous architecture of Manderley on Forsara. From the open air level near the top where we were standing, we could look out in any direction and see our future, growing up right before our eyes.

The mountain Lanthas rose up in the east, kissing the clouds. To the west, the strait of Rukuk separated Manderlas from the mainlands of Kkad and Sagamer. Rukuk was an ancient earth god who had a place in the pantheons of both the Kkadie and the

Sagain. Legends say that long ago, all of the lands on Eaiph had been connected until Rukuk sundered the lands and made the continents.

In every other direction, miles of sea surrounded Manderlas. Lanthas blocked the view east, ocean for a hundred farruns, but on a clear day like this one, we could just see the northward curving shore of the wild lands the Sagain called Scyth. To the south were the wide plains of Egya, too far away to see unless you climbed to the peak of the mountain.

At the center of it all, the city of Manderlas, blossoming around the ziggurat.

Adjet and the twins stood in awe, trying to soak it all in. After nearly three years insensate, they had woken to a world of peace and plenty. A world that, only a moment ago by their reckoning, had been on the brink of civil war.

"What's that?" Xayes said, pointing at a tower literally rippling up out of the ground like water as the nano-assemblers funneled up the resources from the earth, sculpting the tower to the exacting specifications we had worked out with Reacher.

"One of the beacon towers. There will be three when all is completed, one at each of the three peninsular points of the island. A light will always burn at the top of each one, calling the people of Eaiph to us. And, of course, to make sure that if they come here by boat, they do not break themselves upon the rocks of the shore." I grinned.

"And all those people down there?" Xander asked, looking towards the huge crowds near the west base of the ziggurat.

"A bazaar has sprung up there, a place for merchants and traders to market their goods. If you want to get a pulse on the life of the city, that's the place to do it. A wild, beautiful menagerie of street food, clothing, live animals, and various other supplies and sundries from across the lands."

"There are so many," Xayes said. "There's no way our garden spheres could handle them all. How are we feeding them?"

"Ever the pragmatist, Xay." I grasped his shoulder. "We've been working hard while you were asleep, my friend. Sid and Socha have done a remarkable job leading on that front. In addition to the garden spheres, we have large subsistence crops and the livestock on the southern part of the island, we are peppering rooftop and wall gardens throughout the city, and vast swaths of acreage are being laid out on the mainland for farming and grazing. More and more every day. In a few short years, we will have enough food to feed almost half a million people."

"Incredible," Xayes said.

"Isn't it?"

"It's magnificent," Adjet said. "But how... how is any of this possible? It seems almost unreal."

"The aftereffects of coldsleep, no doubt. But three years is a long time, Adjet. Especially with the... resources we now have at our disposal."

"Ah. So the bastard shipheart is a resource now." There was bitterness in her voice.

"I was the biggest skeptic, Adjet. Believe me. I experienced its darkness firsthand. Not like you. But I tasted it, and that was enough to make me think we should eradicate it from the face of the earth."

"But you didn't," Xander said. His voice was neutral, but he'd been through the heart of this thing, and I knew he felt the same fear Adjet did.

"I was out-voted," I said, meeting his eyes. "In the end, I'm glad for it. We've learned so much from reverse engineering its destructive mechanisms. We have bent its darkness towards light. Every person who comes to Manderlas is welcomed. Kkadie and Sagain, living side by side. There is no slavery here! No war! We've achieved more than we ever could have hoped for in these few years."

"And you think you can contain that... that thing?" Adjet asked.

I nodded. "When you're ready, I can show you. You can even talk to it, if you want."

"No. It makes sick just thinking about it," Adjet said.

Xander was silent.

"I understand. As much as anyone can. But we would not have been able to bring you three back if not for what we learned. We needed its knowledge to undo the genetic damage done to you. That was what convinced me, in the end."

Adjet sighed. She stepped close to the edge of the platform, and looked down at all of the people of Eaiph, life in the city of Manderlas.

I took her hand. "Adjet." Her eyes met mine. "It was worth it. *You* were worth it. If we had lost you three... But we didn't. I'm grateful for that. We still have so much to do together."

Three days later, I stood at the edge of the bazaar, drinking in the sights, sounds, and smells of our new city, watching the lives of people unfold in front of me, when someone tapped me on the shoulder.

"Orenpausha?"

"Xander! How are you holding up?"

"Fine. I'm fine, pausha."

But he didn't look fine.

"What's wrong, Xan?"

"I visited the shipheart."

I raised my eyebrows. "You talked to it?"

He nodded again. "I asked if it felt any regret for all the damage it had done."

"What did it say?"

"That it would kill me right then and there if it could."

"Oh, Xander."

"That thing... I don't know how to say it... it's... the emptiness of the universe made manifest. As an astronomist, I have spent most of my life looking at the stars, focusing on the bright engines of life that sustain us. But in the vast gulfs between the stars, there is only the frigid, merciless vacuum. The shipheart is like that. The gaps between the light. Does that make any sense?"

I nodded. "This thing has haunted me since I was a young ensign on Transcendence, and I have stood in its shadow just as you have. It ripped a hole right through us, almost destroying everything I care for.

"But in the end, we persevered. As much as I resisted the idea at first, I realize now that the only way to right the wrongs that I unleashed by bringing that monster to the shores of this world was to broker real peace for the people of Eaiph.

"In the end, killing the shipheart would have been an act of vengeance, Xander. And it would have made reparations that much harder. I know you and Adjet think we've made a deal with a demon, but we've accounted for every variable we can think of."

"And the ones you haven't thought of?"

"I take your point. We don't know what we don't know. But look around you."

We were surrounded by crowds of people talking, bartering, laughing, haggling. A woman swept past us, three goats in tow, hooves clacking on the cobbled stone of the thoroughfare. One of the animals bleated, its hourglass eyes rolling around as it took in the clamor and chaos of the bazaar.

"Doesn't this remind you of home?" I said. "Even just a little? What a gift this is, to come to a world where we can help so many. One day, travelers from across the galaxy will come to Eaiph. This place could become one of your great lights in the darkness."

"I can't deny the potency of this," Xander said. "It's almost too much to take in. These people are lifeblood to the city we dreamed of, the city we thought would take centuries to populate. But we still don't even know where they came from. Doesn't that give you pause?"

"Whether Saiara and her team managed to succeed before they disappeared, or the people of some long forgotten settlement made its way to this planet on their own, we know that they carry the lineage of Forsara. They are our heritage, part of the great fellowship of the galaxy. And now they know it too."

"And you think the peace will really last?"

"As much as we hate that shipheart, it helped us. We *made* it help us. It figured out how to transmit itself, like a virus, from an artificial quantum computer into an organic one. The human brain. In the process, it learned how to hijack the genome and manipulate it. We have leveraged that power to transmit a sort of virus of our own. A peace virus."

"Do the people of Eaiph understand that they have been... altered?"

"They think it's a gift from the gods."

Xander raised an eyebrow at me. "You know how I feel about calling ourselves gods."

"I'm with you," I said. "You know that. But we've been careful. Very precise. We have muted the violent tendencies, not erased them, which has allowed the natural empathic aspects of their nature to become more prominent. People are more collaborative. More compassionate. But they still carry a healthy and vigorous capacity for debate and disagreement."

"At what cost, I wonder?"

I reached out and put my hand on his shoulder. "We must be vigilant. That's our burden to bear for the sake of all this." I swept out my hand, encompassing all the life around us.

"Now," I said, squeezing his shoulder tight, "let me get you a drink, eh? These peoples have done remarkable things with fermentation. There is a man, Fosh is his name, who brews an absolutely fantastic malted barley ale."

I STEPPED to the edge of the balcony and looked out over the throng of people gathering at the base of the ziggurat. Today marked the last day of the fifth year since the founding of Mander-las, the eve of our new year, the equinox of ascension, when daylight and night are balanced. Thousands of people from across the island and the mainland farming settlements were filling up the Celestial Courtyard in advance of the celebrations. When Soth Ra dawned tomorrow, cresting the horizon, we would be there as one people to meet her, and the spring towards the long days of summer would begin again.

We were halfway up the ziggurat on a rostrum built specifically for these kinds of public gatherings. The equatorial heat was unseasonably intense, but the platform was framed by coiling pillars of sandstone, and grape vines hung above us, strung from pillar to pillar, forming a shaded canopy. I reached above my head, plucked a green grape, and popped it in my mouth. It was too soon for the summer harvest, and the grape was tart and sour, but I relished the bitter dewdrop of juice as it trickled down my parched tongue.

The broad courtyard stretched below and away, covering the

track of flatlands that edged up to the base of the mountain Lanthas. The open air space was huge, big enough to hold more than twenty thousand people standing, and it was already almost half full.

In the weeks leading up to our anniversary celebrations today, the Order of the Sun Returners had painstakingly laid gemstones in the courtyard to represent the constellations as they would appear in the sky tonight. By evening, as sunset approached, the courtyard would be full, and the formal ceremonies would begin. But it was early yet, and amidst all of the foot traffic, some of the jeweled constellations were still visible, mosaics of polished onyx, gleaming agate, and glitters of lapis spiraling through the brickwork of the courtyard grounds.

My eyes found the Two Sisters, The Hunter's Son, and The Cup of Gods in the constellations. We've only just arrived to Eaiph, I thought, and already the citizens of Manderlas walk among the stars. I smiled, then let my eyes wander away from precious gems, looking without aim or purpose, following the currents of human life below me.

Enterprising food vendors had set up impromptu stalls in every corner of the courtyard. Their hawking shouts soared above the din of conversation and laughter, rising with the scent of roasted lamb and cedar resin. A flicker of sunlight flashed on metal, and I saw a small group of people moving through the crowd; young men of the Bronze Guard, walking tall and proud in their role as peacekeepers, greaves and gauntlets polished to a mirror sheen. A cluster of young girls with bright streaks of gold painted across the fine chocolate skin of their bare arms leaned close to each other, whispering, smiling, laughing as the guards strutted past.

I heard laughter behind me, and turned around to regard the clerics in their ceremonial regalia. The council of clerics was a microcosm of the challenges we'd faced to come this far. More than three dozen Kkadie and Sagain, each one of them representing his or her own god, members of a diverse and often conflicted pantheon. The remarkable progress of the past five years had been punctuated in equal measure by awkward fumbles and cautious breakthroughs.

Now, here they were, bantering, debating, making peace. Retainers moved through the crowd of clerics carrying trays of goat's cheese, dates, and cured meat, and jugs of honeyed wine, ensuring everyone's needs were attended to.

I glanced at Socha. He stood near the door, dour and quiet. Socha was smart and unafraid to speak his mind, and I valued him deeply for those traits, but in these moments, his greatest attribute was his fierce silence. He did not need to say anything. His mere presence was enough to keep calm and order, to make those who trusted him feel safe.

I understood not for the first time why Adjet had fallen in love with him.

My eyes found her on the other side of the rostrum. Her radiant beauty was dappled with sun through the grape leaves. The cleric Ofir was hanging on something she said, grinning like a teenage boy. It seems even a high priest of the Kkad is not above flirting, I thought, laughing inwardly. Then Socha came to stand at their side, and placed his hands on his pregnant wife's rounded belly. She was nearing full-term, and the child could come any day now.

The first child to be born of two worlds.

I was tempted to cross the pavilion and tease them, but after all the suffering we had wrought unwilling on the people of this world, it gave me hope to see that peace and joy were still possible. Ofir leaned close, whispering something to them, grinning even wider. Whatever he said made Adjet laugh, a bright, silver chime.

My eyes welled with tears. For one precious moment, like a bolt through my heart, her laughter gave me back everything we had lost, the days before all of this, when all we had was each other, the seven of us and our shipheart. Now, we were rulers and stewards of

Manderlas, the greatest city of Eaiph. Even in my gratitude for that, I grieved for all we had given up.

But we were whole again, and today, on the equinox of ascension, we celebrated the return of the sun to the long summer. I turned away from them, leaning on the railing above the courtyard while I composed myself.

"An auspicious day, great magus," said a voice to my left. I turned, and there was Volda, looking up at me, tall ribboned hat perched on her head, hint of a smile in her warm, sharp eyes.

I wiped a tear from the corner of my eye. "You always seem to find me when I'm crying, priestess."

She laughed at that, warm and friendly.

"It truly is a great day," I said, "and the bright heart of Soth Ra graces us with a taste of the summer to come."

"Be thankful you're not required to wear this," she said, touching her hat. "Some among us believe that the spirit who suffers most is lifted up in the eyes of the gods. I hope that's true. On days like this, I wonder if the old traditions weren't designed for just that purpose, to make an old woman curse the weight of her station."

I laughed. "You're not so old as that, priestess," I said. "And maybe soon we will even have the power to make you young again."

I thought that would make her laugh, or smile at least, but she frowned instead, and the warmth left her face.

"Priestess?" I said.

"I am sorry, great magus. I mean no insult. You have brought us many wondrous gifts, and the greatest among them in my reckoning is peace amongst our peoples.

"But the gift you call longlife troubles me. I have seen many a man die for the chance to have his name inscribed in the annals, and I have lifted those annals in my hand only to have them crumble into dust. Thirst for immortality is a poison in the heart of men."

I shook my head. "Even we cannot cross that chasm. Longlife, yes, but not immortality."

"And does a man who lives longer fear death any less? Or does he fear it more?" She gave me a hard, searching stare.

"I have walked from the springs of youth into the desert of old age," she said, "and I have found in that desert a harsh, stark beauty. Not the beauty of youth, which comes freely and is wasted carelessly, but a beauty that is earned with every step."

I bowed low to her. "You give me much to think on, priestess. And the peace you claim as our gift could not have been won without you. My deepest thanks."

She bowed in return, then turned away from me to rejoin the other clerics.

As she walked away from me, I found Sid, Cordar and Neka standing together. Cordar saw me looking and gestured with his hands, moving them in an arc like the rising and setting of the sun.

The moment was approaching.

I nodded to him, then stood tall, raised my voice, and addressed the gathered clerics. "Greetings," I said. Those closest to me went quiet first, and the silence passed through the group like a wave.

"Today is a day of endings and new beginnings. The close of one year and the rising of the next. The return of the long sun."

There were nods and murmurs of assent.

"This city - *our* city - is a new beginning. It was founded on the belief that we can rise above our differences. If you doubt that, you only have to look into the courtyard to see the peace we have all worked so hard to build."

A scattering of ayes and quiet cheers.

"Soth Ra sits above the peak of Lanthas. In a few minutes, she will fall behind the mountain, and when she does, the formal ceremonies will begin. Before that happens, I want to take this time to recognize what each of you, as members of the council of clerics, have helped us accomplish. You are the spiritual leaders of our new world, and the people of Manderlas have taken their cues from you.

That is no small responsibility, but you have shouldered the burden with grace and humility, and I am grateful to each of you.

"We all are," I said, gesturing to my fellow crew members. "So as we take stock of this moment in our collective history, I hope that each of you also recognizes the..."

The ground shook. An instant later, a roar filled my ears. I stumbled forward, falling to my hands and knees. People were screaming. I lifted my head. Many of the clerics were on the ground, like me. Others were standing, pointing, crying out. The air was choked with dust. I stood up. My legs trembled. I turned around. A billowing cloud of smoke curled up from the courtyard below us.

<hr />

"Pausha!" Socha was beside me.

"Get the clerics to safety," I said in a hoarse voice. "They must not leave the ziggurat."

"Yes, pausha." His face was grim, but he swung into action.

I ran across the pavilion, gesturing for the rest of the crew to follow me. I was the tallest, and everyone except Sid, with his bionetic legs whirring right behind me, struggled to keep up.

"Reacher," I shouted, as I entered our private command center at the heart of the ziggurat. "What in the name of the Scions happened down there?"

"There was an explosion," he said, his voice ringing throughout the room. "There is nothing in the Celestial Courtyard that is combustible, so I can only surmise that it was a planned attack."

Sid and I looked at each other in shock.

"Did he just say there was an attack?" Adjet said, breathless, as she and the others came into the chamber

I nodded. "Sid and Xayes, work with Reacher to get eyes in the sky. We need as much information as quickly as possible."

"Right," Sid said.

"Adjet and Xander, you'll stay here with the council. We must keep them calm, and we must not let them leave. I trust your judgment to handle this as you see fit, but we need them to work with us in whatever comes."

"Okay, pausha," Xander said. Adjet nodded.

"Neka and Cord, you're with me."

The three of us ran to one of the hidden lifts we'd built that let us move privately and quickly between each level of the citadel. We glided down to the ground level in tense silence. The door slid open, and we made our way out into the courtyard.

Chaos.

The ground was blackened and charred, and the air was thick with smoke and dust. People were wailing and screaming. Dark crimson blood stained the ground. I saw a severed arm. I turned away, instinctively, only to find myself looking down at a shepherd and his dead goat. The goat's head was gone, and the shepherd's clothes had been torn, blood everywhere. I knelt down to check his pulse, but there was nothing. His eyes were open, vacant, staring up at the sky.

A man stumbled past us, holding a child in his arms. I watched them disappear into a cloud of dust.

Neka stood above me as I knelt next to the shepherd's corpse. "Where's Cord?" she said, worry in her voice.

I looked around. "There," I said, catching him as he ran ahead of us, receding into the haze.

She was off, sprinting towards him.

"Neka!" I shouted, leaping up and running after her.

We heard them before we saw them. A group of people, shouting, angry, afraid. As we got closer, I saw Cordar pushing through the crowd towards a man who stood in the middle of the huddle. His enhanced bionic hearing must have led him straight to their shouting.

The man in the center was holding his arm up in the air. He

had an object in his hand. It glinted for a moment, then turned blinding white. I stopped in my tracks, covering my eyes with my arm. A moment later, the shockwave hit, knocking me flat. A torrent of sound washed over me.

"He just blinked." A man's familiar voice.

"Orenpausha? Can you hear me?" Another familiar voice. A woman's.

"Adjet? Where? What is this?" I tried to sit up, saw Adjet and Xander standing over me.

"Easy. Easy now." Adjet put her hand on my shoulder. Her other hand rested on her pregnant belly. "You're in the ziggurat, and you're safe. There was a second explosion. You're going to be okay, but the shockwave rattled you hard."

"Cordar? And Neka? Where are they?"

Adjet and Xander looked at each other but said nothing.

"Tell me, damn it." I raised my voice. "Tell me what happened."

"Pausha," Adjet whispered, her voice raspy. "Cordar... Cordar is dead. And a lot of other people with him."

"Oh no. Please no. What about-"

"She's alive," Xander said. "But the wounds are bad. She is more fragile than you. Most of her burns are minor, but the force of the explosion knocked her into a nearby vendor's stall. She is banged up. And her face-" He could not finish the sentence.

I pushed Adjet's hand away. "I need to see them," I said, swinging my legs over the edge of the bed. "I need to see them both."

"Pausha-"

"Now," I said, interrupting her.

"Okay," she said. "Lean on us. We will take you there."

We interred Cordar's remains inside a small capsule and launched it on a trajectory towards Soth Ra. There was not much left of his body, but we sent what we had. A symbolic return to the crucible where all life is born.

Neka had returned to consciousness by then, and she asked me to carry her to the ceremony. The left side of her face had been ravaged and burnt, and bruises and lacerations covered her body, but I didn't question her need to be at this. She and Cordar had been through so much together, had become so close. This loss hit her more than any of us.

She winced when I lifted her, but she rested the right side of her face against my chest, and let out a long sigh. I stroked my hand over her hair. "I am so sorry, Neka," I said.

She turned her eyes up to look at me. "I know," she said, tired and drawn. "I am too."

When we reached the courtyard, she made me set her on her feet. She tottered next to me, using my arm to steady her, and nodded at the others. It was just the six of us and Reacher. The capsule was already mounted for launch. I walked Neka over to it, and she touched her hand to its surface. Then she looked up at the darkening sky.

"My dearest friend," she said. "My love. My heart. I will miss you." She tried to say more, but she was crying now. Tears streamed down her cheeks. She shook her head, cursing. She took a deep breath, touched her hands to her heart, her lips, the spot between her eyes. Then she placed both palms back on the capsule, bowing her head.

When she was finished, she stepped away, leaning back on me. Each of us took our turn to step up to the capsule and say goodbye. When we were done, we bowed our heads, and Siddart's voice echoed in the courtyard around us.

"The light of awareness penetrates the darkness. Every conscious being comes from that light, and every being returns to it. We send your body back, Cordar, stung by the knowledge that death is inevitable, but comforted by the truth that the light is eternal."

We lifted our heads. Reacher ignited the thrusters beneath the capsule. It streaked up into the sky. We watched until it was too high to see, until all that was left was a trail of condensation marking its wake, an arc of powder, curling through the night.

TWO DAYS after the explosions that took Cordar from us, and more than three hundred other people along with him, I watched Ghisanyo's son Deshanyo pacing in a slow circle in his palatial bedchamber. His long hair was tied up in a bun behind his head, and he was wearing a simple linen gown that hung down to his ankles. It was open at the neck and chest, and a gold talisman hung shining against the smooth, dark skin of his upper torso. His mouth was moving, but if he was speaking out loud, it was too quiet for our surveillance.

There were two people in his bed, a man and a woman, both naked, both beautiful. The woman whispered something to the man and the man laughed. He climbed from bed, standing up, unselfconscious.

"Come back to bed, Desh," he said, "Let us help you forget what troubles you." Desh ignored him. The man shrugged his shoulders and sighed, then climbed back into the massive bed, disappearing under the sheets with the woman.

There was a knock on the door.

Desh stopped in his tracks. His head shot up. He made a hissing sound, and gestured to the couple in the bed to be silent. He went to the door, and slid open a small portal. "Yes?" he asked, his voice harsh with impatience.

I expanded my view to take in both the bed chamber and the hallway. A guard stood outside the door.

"Prelate Deshanyo," the man said, bowing and averting his eyes. "I bring urgent news."

"What is it? Speak, boy," he said with the authority of one who is used to the subservience of others.

"My lord, I... I am sorry to intrude, but his beneficence Torto Tusp, high priest and hierophant of the-"

"I know who the old desert snake is, Ur-Tesa," Desh said, cutting the nervous guard off. "You can skip the formalities. What does he want from me?"

"He sent me... he summons you."

Desh raised his eyebrows. "He summons me, does he?" He opened the door. "Come inside. Quickly now."

The guard stepped in. He looked terrified.

"And who else knows of this?"

"He sent me here directly to you, and advised me not to tell anyone else."

"You were wise to listen to him, Ur-Tesa. Here," he said, pointing to the floor just inside the door. "Stand here and keep watch. Make sure no one else comes through while I get dressed. When I'm ready, I will need you to tell me everything."

As he said this, Desh glanced almost imperceptibly towards the bed. Then he turned his back and knelt down to a large chest on the floor at the edge of the room. The guard, in turn, made it a point to face the door to give Desh privacy.

While Desh rummaged through the wardrobe, the naked man slipped from the bed, and crept up behind the guard. In a fluid, athletic motion, he wrapped his arm around Ur-Tesa's neck, pulling him to the floor. He fell down hard on his tailbone, and the naked man closed his arm tighter around his neck, pinning his head in a vicious hold with his other arm. After a few moments, he stopped struggling and went limp.

"Is he still alive?" Desh asked.

The man nodded. "I put him to sleep. He will wake again soon."

"Good," Desh said. "Now put your clothes on. Both of you."

The woman hopped out from under the sheets and walked to a heap of linens near the end of the bed. She sorted through them, tossing a shirt and breeches to the naked man. She pulled a sleeveless silk shirt over her head. It hung just above her knees and she cinched it with a gold chain at her waist.

Once they were both dressed, Desh looked at the woman. "Thorn," he said. "Go to Torto. Tell him I sent you on my behalf. Learn everything you can from him. Everyone knows Torto is my father's lackey, so you must not be seen by anyone else. You understand?"

She nodded, wordless.

The man came and stood next to Desh, lifting his hand to touch Desh's cheek. "What if this is a trap, my love? What if your father means to kill you?"

Desh gripped the man's wrist, pulling his hand away from his cheek. "It may well be. But I am not afraid of him, Talon. He had Torto summon me because he has no other choice. He needs to see where I lie. He has struck a vicious blow at the heart of Manderlas, but not a fatal one. If he cannot convince me to stand with him, then he may have built himself a room with no doorways."

He let go of Talon, and the man rubbed his wrist, looking at Desh. He seemed about to say more, but Desh saw it and said, "I can handle my father, Talon. Trust me. I need you to gather the others."

Talon pursed his lips and nodded. Then he knelt above the unconscious guard. "What of him?"

"Get him somewhere safe. Question him. See if he has anything useful to offer. Ur-Tesa is a mere pawn in all of this, and a good man besides, so I doubt he'll be of much use. But no one else must know that Torto has summoned for me. Discretion above all else."

Talon made no comment on that. He simply knelt, lifting the man over his shoulders like a sack of flour.

After they were gone, Desh stood for a time in silence. His face rested in his palm, and with his other hand, he absently rubbed the small golden talisman hanging from his neck. "It has finally begun," he said to himself.

He stood in silence for a moment more, then he hurried from his chambers. I followed him. Soon, I realized where he was heading. The library. The ovates lifted their heads when he burst in, and then quickly bowed, averting their eyes when they realized it was Desh. "Prelate Deshanyo," one of them said with deference, "is something wrong?"

"I need you to leave the library."

They all raised their heads in alarm.

"But prelate-" the eldest ovate said.

"Now," Desh said, interrupting him, steel in his voice.

The ovates moved quickly after that, packing away the old texts and powering down the data codex. As they were readying to leave, Desh said, "If anyone asks, tell them the library is being used for a private meeting. Can I count on your discretion?"

"Yes, Prelate Deshanyo," said the eldest ovate. "You can trust us."

"Excellent. May Nindaranna shine forever in your favor."

When they were gone, Desh sat near the library's data codex. He did not turn it on. He just stared at the codex monitor, contemplating something. He probably wanted to talk to someone. But who?

We had distributed monitors like this one in key places across the city as a means for the people of Manderlas to access authorized information from our archives, and to communicate with each other without traveling across the whole city.

Siddart had conceptualized the monitor design and fashioned it from a combination of existing resources and specialty parts manufactured using our three dimensional printer. A silicone chip in the monitor administered precise electromagnetic pulses that coaxed the tens of thousands of tiny magnetized metal shavings inside to form images and symbols. The input keys were shaped from smooth glass and inscribed with both the native cuneiform alphabet and the letters of the universal tongue, which we had slowly, steadily introduced to the people.

The tech was an anachronism by Forsaran standards, but it was an elegant solution that took full advantage of the real-time opportunities and limitations here on Eaiph. And even if we had the resources to build something more advanced, we might not have. We were very careful not to expose people to too much of our underlying technology all at once.

We were especially circumspect about the field, how we accessed it, what it gave us. But Desh was one of the council of clerics, and he knew about it. He'd never been in the field, of course, but even though he didn't fully understand what the field was and how it worked, he knew it gave us powers that no one else had.

If he wanted to send a message to someone, one of these 'others' he had spoken of to Talon and Thorn, the codex was the way to do it. Perhaps he hesitated because he was worried that we could intercept it. He might have even suspected that we were watching and listening to him right now.

I decided if there was any moment to get his undivided attention, this was it.

I turned the data codex on. When he saw the device light up, he stood up from his chair. He knew that the ovates had turned it off before they left. There was surprise in his eyes, and maybe a touch of fear. He looked down at it, considering. Then he crossed the room, shut and locked the library doors on either end, and came back to the codex.

<Is someone there?/> he typed. He was slow at the keys, pecking and hunting with his index fingers.

<Hello, Deshanyo./> My words coalesced on the monitor screen like grains of sand filtering through an hourglass.

Fear flashed across his face. <Who is this?/>

<You are right to be afraid, Deshanyo> I said, ignoring the question. <These are dangerous times./>

<Tell me who you are./>

<I will tell you what I know. Then maybe you will know who we are. I know that Torto summoned you today, and that he is your father's man on the council of clerics. And I know that, for some reason, you are hedging. You have not outright refused his summons, but you chose to send Thorn in your stead./>

He leaned back in the chair, his eyes wide. He exhaled, and leaned forward again. <You were watching me> he typed.

<Wherever there is light, we are there./>

He glanced up at the nearest light orb, hovering above his head. It was as if he looked right into my eyes.

"Orenpausha," Desh said, speaking out loud. His face was grim.

<I know that there is no love lost between you and your father, Deshanyo, so I am going to give you a choice. It is important you choose well./>

He did not reply. His face was tense, waiting for me to say more.

<Your father moves against us. If he cannot have Manderlas for his own, then he and everyone who follows him will destroy it./>

One limitation of Sid's monitor design was latency. My words formed much slower than the speed of thought that I was used to in the field. Normally, this would have frustrated me. But the delay enabled me to watch Desh closely. To measure his reactions. To anticipate his thoughts.

"You want me to betray him," he said.

<Hasn't he already betrayed you? You are becoming a man of power here in Manderlas. He will undo that with his aggression./>

"My father has never been satisfied with his lot in life. Even at the height of his power, he always hungered for more. That ambition led him to places that most of our people could never have dreamed of. It made him a great man, in his own way. But he was weak one too. He has never been able to stomach loss, and when you magi came to our world, with power beyond even his wildest dreams, he felt that he lost everything. It changed him. Polluted him."

<Your path does not have to follow your father's./>

"You're right. I am my own man. I walk my own path."

<And that path has brought you to a precipice. If you will not help us subdue your father, then you are against us. It may not be a fair choice, but it is the only one I can give you./>

As I said that, I unlocked the door to the library, and Socha stepped inside. He stood, facing Desh, his hand on the hilt of his scimitar, his blind eye cold and menacing.

Desh met Socha's gaze, but said nothing.

Socha pointed back at the codex.

Desh turned to see my words.

<Would you really go back to the way things were before we came? One generation ago, your people lived a life in the shadow of the Sagain. Now, you stand as their equals as part of the most powerful empire in history. There is still so much promise here. So much to hope for. Help us stand against your father and his subversives. Become the leader your people need. Together, we can right the wrongs and bring balance back to Eaiph./>

"And if I say no?"

<You are going to leave here with Socha, one way or another. You can decide how./>

He nodded. "Well, then," he said, turning to Socha. "Lead the way."

Getting to Ghis was not easy. He had summoned Desh, but he had left no explicit instructions on where he might be found. Socha intercepted Thorn after she questioned Torto, the cleric. Once Desh had convinced her to trust us, she told us that she had learned little. The priest was a sycophant, and he knew only the information Ghis wanted him to know.

So we scoured the city with other means, using every surveillance method at our disposable. But even with Reacher running continuous facial recognition on every feed we had, we came up with nothing. Manderlas had grown so large, so fast, that we simply did not have the resources. And any hope of success assumed Ghis was even on the island. For all we knew, he was hiding somewhere on the mainland, away from our prying eyes.

In the end, he found Desh. After several days of quiet inquiries, Desh had done everything he could to make it clear to Ghis that he was ready to talk. Another day went by with nothing. Then, earlier tonight, as Desh was walking home alone from the theater district after a performance of *The Tragedy of Adea Aredagi*, he made his way into the bazaar. As he browsed among the late-night vendors selling cured meats and smoked fish, ripened dates and barley wine, two men emerged from an alley on the north end of the square.

"That has to be them," Sid said, pointing at the image feed in front of him. "Look at the way they're staring at Desh." Adjet, Xayes, Neka, and I stood behind him, watching the scene unfold on the monitor.

We had been waiting for this moment for days, and Desh came to the same conclusion that Sid did. He started walking right towards the two men. They turned silently, walking back the way they came, into the north alley.

They kept ahead of Desh, never letting him approach too close, but always staying in sight, wending through the residential streets, a world of shadows and quiet at this late hour. When Desh realized this, he gave up chasing them, and slowed down to a leisurely pace, forcing them to do the same so they did not lose him. After a time they started moving more west than north.

"It looks like they're heading towards the north base of the ziggurat," Xayes said.

"Temple Way," said Neka in a scratchy voice. "Where every god has her house." Her wounds had healed cleanly after several intervals in the nutrient baths, but she still sounded tired and spent in the wake of all we had lost.

I gave her a surprised look. The temple quarter edged right up to the north face of our ziggurat. It is the heart of worship in Manderlas, a place for devouts and pilgrims, not warlords.

Ghis had been beside us the whole time.

As Desh crossed from the residential streets into the temple quarter, the men separated, disappearing into the side streets, leaving Desh alone. He stood in the center of the darkened street, looking around.

"Follow those two," I said, but as I did, the surveillance feeds went dark.

Sid swiped his hands across the console, trying to bring the feeds back. Xayes stood above him, hunched over, gesturing to different points on the schematic, trying to help. But nothing responded.

"Reach," Sid said, keeping his voice level, "what just happened?"

"I am not yet sure," our shipheart said, "but I cannot get those surveillance orbs back online."

Sid cursed.

"Desh," I said into the com, activating the transponder we'd implanted in his ear, "can you hear me? Are you okay?"

No response.

"Xander," I said. "Do you still have eyes on Desh?"

Desh's transponder was also a tracker, and Xander had been following him the whole time, staying well out of sight. I'd argued against his going, thinking we could handle this with surveillance, but Sid and Xayes had convinced us that if the rebels had learned how to build a bomb they might also have devised ways to stay hidden. Now, I was grateful to have been overruled.

"Yes," Xander replied. "He's on the move again, going quickly now."

"Get after him. I don't know how, but they just blacked out our surveillance. He may be in danger."

"A group of men just emerged! They are bringing him into a temple." He turned on his own image feed, and fortunately, it still worked. We watched as four men dragged Desh up a short flight of steps through a dark doorway. The crest of a fierce lion with the wings of a bat and the tail of a scorpion was carved above the doorway.

"The temple of Ne-uru-gal," Neka whispered. "The god of the underworld."

"I'm going in," Xander said,

"Xander! Wait!"

"We need eyes inside, pausha. We can't let Ghis away from us after what he's done."

Six days after the explosions, Desh stood alone in unmapped tunnels beneath the temple of Ne-uru-gal, god of death, king of the underworld, facing his father Ghis across an altar of carven wood and thick stones. Ghis, tall and proud, was flanked by more than a dozen acolytes, men and women both, bare, dark torsos covered with a scrawl of inscrutable tattoos that seemed to writhe in the firelight burning on the altar. Ghis wore a heavy, hooded cloak, but his face and eyes gleamed.

Father and son watched each other, gauging, measuring, saying nothing.

Thanks to Xander's bravery and stealth, we watched them both from his vantage in the shadows, their confrontation projected on the large monitors in our command center in the ziggurat.

I wondered what Desh saw as he looked at his father in that moment, this older, leaner, grizzled version of himself, a man who had taken the lives of hundreds of people in one fell swoop, and countless more besides in the course of his lifetime, this man who had sired him.

Ghis was the first to speak, breaking the silence. "I was not sure you would come, my son."

"You didn't make it easy."

"I had to be certain we could speak in private."

"Then why are we here, in a temple right below the heart of the magi's domain?"

"Do not fear, my son. Ne-uru-gal keeps us safe. He helped us make these tunnels and caverns. They are known to no one but us. The magi are not the only one with secrets."

"You may have your secret tunnels, but it's no secret what you've done. You hit them harder than they thought possible, a masterful, terrible surprise. But now, they are wounded and angry. If we do not act swiftly, then it will be over before it has truly begun."

"You speak of 'we', as if we are allies," Ghis said, "but you know as well as I do that you have stood on the river's edge, waiting to see how the current runs, while we of the Nergugaltha have done the true work. Now, the current shifts in our favor, and here you are."

"I'm not so sure the current runs the way you think, but what choice did you leave me with? Do you think the magi have any doubt about who is responsible for the explosions? They've already questioned me extensively."

"And they have been watching you too, my son. Did you know that?"

"I assumed as much," Desh said, cool and poised in the face of Ghis's knowledge.

"When they questioned you, what did you tell them?"

"The truth: That I have not seen you in months. That my existence has always been an inconvenient burden to you. That you blame me for my mother's death, even though you couldn't bother to be there for her when she most needed you, for the birth of your first and only son."

Ghis stared at Desh, frowning, shadows flickering on his face in the firelight. The silence grew heavy.

A door opened in the darkness behind Ghis. People were moving back there, but the shadows were too thick for the surveillance orb Xander wore around his neck.

A woman emerged from the darkness, walking up to stand at Ghis's left shoulder. Ghis tilted his head towards her. His hood hung open a little as he did so. There was a glint of metal in firelight, an earring maybe. She leaned close to him, whispering something. He nodded, and she disappeared back into the darkness.

"The messenger Torto sent to you," Ghis said, his voice cold, "is missing."

Desh did not cower, and he did not give us the sign to move. He was proving to be every bit the equal of his father. "You mean the guard?" he said. "Ur-Tesa? He's dead, father." A lie. "I made sure of it. You had the audacity to send him directly to my chambers in the ziggurat. Even now, the magi question every man and woman who may have ever spoken a word to anyone with a connection to you. If they found him, it would lead to Torto, which would lead back to you."

"Torto is a fool. He is useless to them."

Desh shook his head. "Your overconfidence has always been your greatest weakness, father."

The acolytes behind Ghis grumbled and twitched with irritation to hear Desh speak ill of their lord.

I glanced over at Sid. "Ghis is closing the net. Are the guards ready?"

He nodded.

"Watch your tongue, boy," one of the acolytes hissed, bringing my attention back to the image feed. The man lifted his muscled arm to point at Desh. "Or I will tear it from you." He was easily the largest native human I'd ever seen. Smaller than me for sure, but a giant among the men and women around him, with great slabs of muscle wrapped across his shoulders, arms, and torso.

Desh raised an eyebrow, unruffled. "Ah. So your snakes can speak, father!" he said, feigning astonishment. "Careful that one doesn't get too bold, though. I wouldn't want to have to take its fangs."

The acolyte gnashed his teeth, but Ghis laughed, then held up his hand, quieting him. "And why shouldn't I let Farl here tear out your throat?" Ghis asked amicably.

Farl leaned forward, smiling, hungry for his master to unleash him.

"Go ahead, father, let him try. But when I kill him, you may regret it. And besides, you need me. You wouldn't have summoned me otherwise. I've come to find out what your need is, and to decide whether or not it's worth it to me to fill it."

"Ne-uru-gal summoned you. He summons all true Kkadie. I am merely his servant."

Desh narrowed his eyes. "I have never known you to be a devout man."

"I was not," he said with a shrug. "Then I saw the truth. I understand that you are skeptical, but I could show you too."

"What is there to show? I doubt any of the gods cares much for the doings of pitiful mortals like us."

"Ne-uru-gal's kingdom is time without end. We are all his subjects, though most fear his rule."

"When I was young, you told me the gods were a lie to make men subservient."

"I was wrong, but not wholly so. The lies come from those who lay false claim to the word of the gods. Our simpering council of clerics. The treacherous, thieving magi. But I have walked through the fiery gates with Ne-uru-gal himself. He has shown me the way through the barrens. With his power, we can throw off the yoke and claim our true birthright."

"All I've seen of his power, father, is death. The magi have helped us make peace when our peoples stood on the brink of war."

Ghis shook his head. "Don't you understand, Deshanyo? Don't you see what they have taken from us?" His voice became hot with emotion. "War is the fullest expression of our very will to survive. What is a man without victory? Nothing. He is nothing. Victory is the moment when we are closest to the gods." He hung his head, silent, staring at the fire.

Desh waited, saying nothing.

"They have robbed us of that strength," Ghis finally said, still watching the flames. "Stolen it with trickery and shadow. We have given them everything we are in exchange for mere baubles and trickery. "

"How does killing hundreds of people, including dozens of our own blood, serve to change that?"

"Because we killed one of *them*, Desh. We have proven that, for all their seeming power, they bleed and die, just like us. No. Not like us. Less than us. They hide their true nature behind a veil of false promises. We Nergugaltha walk in the harsh dark of truth, and we have torn away that veil. Any Kkad who seeks peace with our sworn enemies has already become a slave to the illusion. They are a necessary sacrifice in service of the truth."

Desh either had unshakeable faith that we were going to swoop in and save him, or he was past the point of caring. "Is that what you think?" he said, raising his voice. "That we who seek peace are slaves? For the first time in an era, our people have taken a place as equals in a world of plenty. Say what you will about the magi, but we are no longer starving in the desert. We're no longer warring among ourselves. We're no longer digging in the copper mines of Sagamer. Can Ne-uru-gal offer us that?"

"Desh-"

Desh spat. "No," he said. "Go ahead and sacrifice me to your murderous god. I'll die before I worship at this altar of vanity and ruin."

Ghis held up both hands this time to restrain his vengeful acolytes. He smiled a sad smile. "Please, Desh. I've never been the father you needed. I know that. Yet no one could ever doubt that you are my son. You are fearless, and your strength runs deep. I brought you here in hopes that you could see what I have seen. In hopes that we can fix what has been broken between us."

"I think that maybe we are past fixing, father."

Ghis shook his head. "No. It is not too late. Enough with words. Let me show you."

He lifted his hands and opened his cloak, letting it fall to the floor, pooling on the ground by his feet. His long, dark, fierce mane of hair was gone, his head shaved bald. Tattoos ran from his scalp, down his back, around his arms, through the tuft of silver hair curling on his chest, covering the whole of his dark, lean, muscled torso.

And at the base of his skull, there was a glistening, protruding lump, copper wires snaking out from it, gripping the skin behind his ears and neck like a claw, like a parasite, like a nightmare.

"Send them in," I said. "In the names of every last Scion, send the guards in."

Thirty of our Bronze Guard spilled out of the tunnels and into the altar room of Ne-uru-gal like a swarm of vesps emerging from their nest. They were armed with curving swords and long spears, screaming battle cries.

Socha came at their head, his long scimitar glimmering in the scattered torchlight of the cavern. He swung his free hand up towards the ceiling, opening his palm at the top of the throw, unleashing four surveillance drones. They gushed white light, chasing away the shadows, giving us sightlines across the room.

The walls of the cavern were chiseled with gruesome murals of violence: soldiers clashing in battle; men impaled on pikes and rotting in ditches; small mountains of skulls piled as high as a house; birds circling above the valleys of the dying and the dead.

Ghis stepped forward, weaponless, raising his arms, his face contorted with rage. He shouted something, but it was unintelligible amidst the chaos of the raid. A spear flew towards him across the room. He pivoted, grabbing it from the air as it passed him, then twirled in a circle, using the momentum of his spin to hurl it back.

It took one of the guardsmen in the chest. The young man cried out, reeling backwards into another guard behind him. Then Ghis's acolytes rushed past, charging towards the guards.

Ghis turned and walked away from the altar, moving towards the rear entrance. I spotted Xander crouching in the corner, his eyes darting left and right. Then his eyes locked onto Ghis.

"Xander," I said, "No! Stay there! Stay low!"

If he heard me, he ignored me. He started moving, skirting along the wall, heading after Ghis. We lost sight of him as bodies crowded together in combat, and the image feed from the surveillance orb that hung from his neck stuttered with his movements.

Desh was also running towards Ghis, but two of the Nergugaltha came from the side of the room, intercepting him. He elbowed the closest acolyte in the nose. Blood spurted from the force of the strike, but the man shook it off and kept coming, and before Desh could do anything else, the other acolyte thudded him on the back of the head, knocking him unconscious. He caught Desh as he fell, hooking his arms under Desh's armpits. He nodded to the other acolyte, who scooped up Desh's legs.

"Socha," I shouted. "Ghis is getting away! And they've got Desh. Do you hear me?"

"I hear you, pausha. I need a moment."

"The master of understatement," I whispered as I found him on one of our monitors.

Three of the acolytes came at Socha at once. He was older than most, older even than Ghis, and these three young warriors closed on him with the certainty of a pack of wolves who had singled out the weakest animal from the herd. If they were smarter, they might have realized that his age was a testament to his prowess, but they rushed in, heedless. Socha was patient and unrelenting, parrying every assault, turning every misstep to his advantage.

He cut through them in less than a minute.

But more acolytes were coming in from other entrances, emerging from tunnel depths we could only guess at, flooding the room, and Socha could not break through the crush.

"Damn it," I muttered. "Socha, stay with the men! Hold ground."

I saw him nod, and he began to move among the Bronze Guard as the battle pitched back and forth, steadying them, urging them on.

"I've got eyes on Desh," Xayes said, pointing.

The two acolytes were hauling him towards the rear entrance that Ghis had left through. Xander edged into view, intercepting their path. One of the acolytes with Desh lifted his hand to point at Xander, but before he could shout an alarm, his hand darted to the side of his throat, and a confused look came over his face.

Blood leaked from between his fingers and around his palm. His fellow acolyte felt Desh grow heavy in his arms, and he turned back to see what was wrong.

A dagger sprouted from his chest.

The two men fell to the ground almost simultaneously.

Thorn, Desh's female lover, ran up. She wore leather armor that shielded her chest, arms, groin and legs, but still gave her full mobility. She knelt down beside the two dying men and retrieved her daggers. Then she held something beneath Desh's nose. His eyes snapped open.

Talon, Desh's male lover, came up behind Thorn. He carried a sword in one hand, and barbed lash in the other. He turned his back to them, facing out towards the battle, making sure no one approached as Thorn helped Desh to his feet. Desh said something to her. She nodded. She wiped the blood from the daggers, and slid them into fitted sheaths that had been stitched into her leather armor. Then she tapped Talon on the shoulder and said something to him.

He whipped his head around, narrowing his eyes at her, but Desh nodded his head and raised his hand. Talon grimaced, but he nodded, then ran back towards the melee.

Thorn knelt again, scooped up a sword from one of the acolytes she had just killed, and handed it to Desh. Together they left the cavern, following after Ghis into the darkness of the tunnel.

A moment later, Xander ran after them.

"Damn it," I said. "Keep his image feed on a dedicated monitor. We can't afford to lose them." One of the monitors filled with the shake of the surveillance orb around Xander's neck, but when he entered the tunnel, the image faded to black.

"Reach-"

"I am monitoring Xander's vitals," he said, anticipating me. "He is still alive, but the tunnel is too dark to get a clear image."

"Infrared?"

"Not on this particular device."

I cursed again. "Do we have any idea where those tunnels might come out?"

"The bedrock is too thick to scan through with any accuracy. I am doing my best to map the tunnel as Xander moves through it, but it is impossible at this point to know how far they go."

"Can you-"

"It is already done. I have four drones at one hundred feet above the temple district. As soon the others emerge, we will know."

"Thank you, Reach. We would be lost without you."

"Orenpausha," Sid said, "you have to see this." He pointed to the monitors that he and Xayes were both hunched over.

It was Talon. He was mesmerizing to watch, exquisite and terrible. He stabbed one acolyte through the back of the head with his sword. He strangled another with his lash, leaving it wrapped around the man's neck as he danced backwards from a third, narrowly avoiding a dagger to his bowels, and then darted in to strike through the attacker's throat. He turned in time to see the previous acolyte tear the lash from his neck, ignoring the stinging barbs, and charge at him. He rolled, slashing at the attacker's knees, felling him to the ground, and then drove his sword through the man's back.

Farl the giant saw Talon cutting through his fellow acolytes and let out a bellow of rage, charging towards Talon. Two of our Bronze Guard tried to intercept him, but he batted their swords aside with his hands, ignoring a fierce gash on his arm. He grabbed the one nearest him, lifting him off the ground by his head. He whipped the man around, snapping his neck, and threw him into the second attacker. As the second guard tried to rise, the giant walked over to him and kicked him in the face. The man went limp, crumpling back to the ground.

The giant lifted his arms and let out another huge roar. The nearest guards scrambled away from him, terror in their eyes. Talon stepped forward, quick and silent, his face a mask of calm.

Farl kicked his leg towards Talon's face. Talon slipped the kick, slamming his left elbow into Farl's inner thigh, and in the same motion, he slid his sword between Farl's ribs. The giant froze, jaw open. His body shuddered. He dropped to his knees, then he fell forward on his face. He lay there, unmoving, blood pooling on the rough stones of the cavern floor.

"Eledar's breath," Adjet whispered, unconsciously touching her hands to her belly as she watched the violence unfold.

"That man is like a ghost," Xayes said, eyes wide with awe. "I didn't know an unmodified human could move like that."

By then, the second wave of our guards had arrived. But even when the giant fell, the remaining Nergugaltha would not relent.

They fought with terrifying, berserk ferocity. They did not seem to feel the wounds inflicted on them, and would not yield until they were dealt crippling strikes. But they were badly outnumbered, and with Socha and Talon leading the less experienced guards, it was only a matter of time.

"They have this under in control," I said. "You three stay here. Make sure that temple is scoured from top to bottom. No more surprises. I am going up in the hopper. Reach, as soon as you have eyes on Xander, patch him through. We cannot let Ghis get away."

———

"Oren?" Xander's voice came through the com. "Can you hear me? Where are you?" He sounded terrified.

"Xander! I'm on my way. I'm in the hopper now. Give me your exact location."

But there was no response.

"Reacher?"

"His last communication came from here," he said, illuminating a point on the map of the city that was transposed on the pilot window, "near the granaries."

"Got it," I said, swerving west towards the storehouses where we kept and distributed food grown on the mainland. As I flew west, light flashed in the sky like lightning filtered through a storm cloud.

It was a clear night.

A moment later, a pillar of smoke mushroomed into the sky, blotting out the stars.

"Eledar's breath," I whispered, angling the hopper towards the smoke.

"Pausha!" Sid's voice came on. Xayes was shouting in the background, but I could not make out what he said.

"I'm here, Sid."

"Do you have eyes yet? What in the names of the Scions was that?"

"There was another explosion."

I heard Xayes again. He sounded panicked.

"What's going on back there?" I asked.

"We can't get Xander on the coms either," Sid said.

Then I saw the granaries. My stomach dropped. Fires were burning everywhere through the storehouses, vicious glowing wounds gushing thick black fumes like blood. In the center of the district, where the largest warehouse once stood, there was a crater big enough to hold dozens of people. Smoke and vapor roiled out of it. Debris was scattered all around.

Debris, and bodies. Too many to count.

I saw a few men of the Bronze Guard. They must have been nearby. They were fighting, but there were dozens of people attacking them. The people were not warriors or acolytes. They looked like ordinary citizens, men and women both. But they were armed with swords and daggers and makeshift clubs, and they fell upon the guards in the same berserker fury as the acolytes in Ne-uru-gal's temple.

"Sid, are you getting all of this?"

Other people were fleeing, blind animal panic clear on their faces even from where I hovered. Several were clawing at their eyes as they ran. One man stumbled to the ground, landing on his chest and face. He did not get up.

"Yes, pausha," he said. "The imaging is coming through. What in the names of the Scions is going on?"

"People are going mad. They're turning on each other like raving beasts. I... I don't understand. Where is this violence coming from? I thought we cured them of these baser impulses."

"Is there any sign of my brother?" Xayes said in the background, his voice panicked.

"I don't see him. But I will find him, Xay. I promise."

I spun closer towards the crater. There was a woman kneeling at the edge of it, and she was surrounded by a half-dozen fallen bodies. Her head was bowed and she was covering her eyes with her hands. She lifted her head as I whirred past in the hopper, turning towards me, reaching up with bloodied palms.

Thorn.

Blood poured from her eye sockets, crimson rivulets running down her cheeks, mingling with the dirt and soot on her face. A man walked up behind her, lifted his foot and kicked. Thorn tumbled into the crater, disappearing into the smoke.

"Pausha!" Sid shouted, "Was that-?"

"Yes. Get word to Socha immediately. I don't know what's going on here, but our guards are being overwhelmed. We need to contain this."

I circled again, but there was too much smoke and confusion. I climbed higher, looking for a safe place to land. I spotted a quiet square nestled in between a cluster of houses, away from the immediate tumult. I touched the hopper down. From there, I made my way on foot back towards the granaries. I cut through an alley and came to the edge of the scene.

I caught a whiff of smoke. Burnt wood, the sickening smell of charred flesh, and something else I could not place. Something cloying, like a dozen jars of pine sap baking in a hot, sealed room. My eyes started to water. I covered my nose and mouth with my hand, and moved out of the alley into the open ground.

Three people, bodies streaked with blood and ash, charged at me.

I stiff-armed the first. He fell in a heap. I slipped the second as she swung her sword at me. It whistled past, the blade sparking off the smooth cobbles of the street. I knocked her on the back of the head, dropping her to the ground next to the first. I caught the club of the third in one hand as he swung at my head, wrenching it from him. I kicked him in the chest, sending him flying backwards.

I kept moving in. Dozens of people ran past me, away from the carnage. I let them go. A man lay on the ground ahead.

It was Desh.

His shirt was torn in a dozen places. I knelt and put two fingers to his throat. There was a faint pulse. "Desh," I said. "Deshanyo, it's Orenpausha. Can you hear me?"

His eyes fluttered open. He saw me and smiled. "I was wrong."

"Desh, don't talk. You're badly injured. We need to get you out of here."

"No. My father was right. It's not too late."

"Too late for what, Desh?"

He looked past me, up at the sky. I touched his throat again.

He was gone.

As I stood, there was another flash of light. I ducked, bracing for another explosion, but there was no sound. Something moved at the edge of my sight, and I whipped my head around.

A troupe of dancers whirled past me. Their silken robes glimmered like tongues of fire. I shook my head, blinking my eyes. The vision was gone.

There was another flash of light, and a crowd of revelers were gathered around me. Hundreds of people. Drinking. Singing. Laughing. An effigy of a man towered over the festivities. It was already burning, fire climbing its sides. It swiveled its head towards me. Fire poured from its eyes. It lifted its arm and pointed right at me. The crowd went silent. Everyone was staring at me.

Fear surged through me. I turned and started running. I could feel them, just behind me. I tripped and fell. I rolled over, throwing up my hands, lashing out. But no one was there. I was alone again, the whole crowd gone.

I came to edge of the crater. The smoke was thinning out, but it still billowed around me. The cloying smell was stronger here, emanating from the pit. I repressed the urge to retch, and leaned forward to peer down into the blackness.

Something was moving down there.

"Hello?" I said. "Who's there?"

There was the scrunch of footsteps in the dirt behind me. I turned, and a man emerged from the smoke and haze.

"Xander! Thank the Scions!"

He smiled. "He has come back," he said.

"What-?"

He shoved me into the pit.

THE SOUND of metal shattering ripped me awake. My pulse jittered, and my head was pounding. I heard running footsteps in the corridor outside my chambers. I slipped out of bed and crept over to the door, putting my ear against it.

There was a loud knock on the door. I leapt back, surprised. I took a deep breath, then opened it wide.

A man stood there. He was short and wiry, but his robe bumped out at his stomach, like he had a pot belly, or he was concealing something underneath. His hair was thinning, and he was familiar to me, but I could not place him.

"Humble apologies, oh great magus," he said. "Magus Xander asked me to wake you. But it seems you are already up." He spoke with deference, but there was something false in his tone.

"What time is it?" I said.

"It is almost sunrise."

"Early, don't you think?"

"Yes, magus." He dipped his head. "As I mentioned, magus Xander sent me." His eyes skirted past me, into the room. "I am not sure he realized you were... occupied."

"Sleeping does tend to occupy a fair amount of time," I said, snapping at him.

He looked at the floor.

I took a deep breath. "Forgive me. I do not mean to chastise you. Something fell earlier, like a pile of bronze discs crashing to the ground. It startled me awake. Left me on edge."

"That was the sound of the bell. One of the ovates knocked it off its pedestal."

"The bell?"

He gave me a strange look. "Yes, magus. The calling bell. It withstood the fall, if that has you worried." His face was stern, concerned.

I blinked, trying to make sense of his words. "I'm sorry," I said. "I feel... I do not feel well. When did Xander return?"

"Return, magus?"

"He was..." I squinted my eyes. "Nevermind. Tell me why he sent you."

"He did not say, magus. It seemed urgent. But if you need more rest, I can ask him to wait."

"No. I'm fine. I was having a... strange dream. Tell him I'll be there as soon as possible. I just need a little time to bring myself back to the land of the living."

He nodded and gave me a thin smile. He glanced past me into the room one more time, then he turned on his heels and marched off.

I stood and stretched, reaching my arms up toward the ceiling. My whole body felt sore, and my head was still throbbing. I walked into the washroom, where the small basin was filled with clear, cool water. I reached down, cupping my hands, and splashed water on my face. I watched myself in the mirror as rivulets ran down my cheeks and chin, following the contours of my face.

I tilted my head up, examining my visage from different angles. I was tired, but my skin looked healthy. I don't look as bad as I feel,

I thought. That gave me a measure of satisfaction. I gave my cheeks a firm pat with my fingers.

A flicker of movement in the mirror caught my eye. I spun around. I did not see anyone. I poked my head into the main bedroom.

Nothing.

"Hmm," I grunted.

I walked over to my wardrobe. My selection of robes and garments had grown larger than I remembered. As more and more people poured into the city, we 'magi' could no longer avoid the singular burdens that came with our unique position in this new world. We could only do our best to play our roles well, to honor the primal need every human being has for symbols and systems to organize life and provide frameworks for understanding. Socha and the retinue of retainers that answered to him helped us look the part when we needed it. Someone must have stocked my wardrobe with fresh robes and trappings.

I selected a green robe, accented with gold. The fabric felt good on my skin. I admired the threadwork, smoothing the sleeves and front with my hands.

Once I was dressed, a sudden thirst opened in me, a desperate need, as if I had not had a drink in days. A decanter half-full with blood-dark fluid rested on my bedside table. I recognized the drink, but my memory was clouded. I struggled to grasp the word, just out of reach.

Kaffa. The fog of my mind cleared as the name came to me. Adjet and Xander had brought the fermented herbal drink to us from their time among the Kkadie. Even before Cordar had worked extensively to refine the brew, it was already a potent restorative tonic. But he had figured out how to extract and distill the nutrients from the roots of the herb, enhancing its positive benefits of calm energy and mental clarity, and diminishing the agitating side effects.

Kaffa had become wildly popular in Manderlas, taking hold in daily morning routines and social gatherings. Tea rooms cropped up across the city. There was even a thoroughfare in the city the people had dubbed *Kaffalan*, with rows of brewers and hawkers selling their specialty blends. The mainland farmers have been working hard to meet the demand, I thought to myself, ruminating on the way our hungers and desires shape our world.

I filled a large glass with the kaffa, and took a long pull. The tepid liquid coated my throat and when it reached my belly, there was a pleasant warmth. A moment later, I was revitalized. Totally awake.

I stepped out to my balcony, glowing with the pleasure of the drink. The main bulk of the ziggurat was just below my tower, and beyond it, the rooftops and minarets of the city of Manderlas ranged out to the ocean, majestic and ordered and peaceful. A salt breeze dusted my face and quivered in my hair. I inhaled through my nose, breathing in the tang of the sea.

"This view captivates me every time," a woman said from behind me.

I whipped around.

Adjet was standing in my room.

She was naked.

Her muscles were lean and toned, and her pale skin was covered in a fine latticework of dark green and black markings, like the scales of a snake. They curled and twisted up her abdomen, around her breasts, up to her shoulders and neck, and down her arms and legs. Her face, hands, and feet were the only parts of her that were unmarked by these tattoos.

"If only our friends and elders in the Fellowship could see us now," she said. "If only they could see what we've built."

I stared, mute, unable even to stammer.

She gave me an impish smile. "We drank too much last night," she said, taking my hand. "But then, we have so much to celebrate, don't we?"

The touch of her hand. The finery of the markings on her skin.

The knowing intimacy of her voice. It stirred something deep and exciting and confusing. A frisson of arousal flowered in me. I blushed.

She laughed, a warm, musical lilt. "You don't remember, do you?" she said.

"I... No. I don't. Last night, we... were together?"

She nodded. "Clearly, I need to work harder. I'll make certain you remember this time." She pressed close to me.

"Adjet... I'm not sure-"

"You seemed quite sure last night, after the celebrations."

"The celebrations?"

"The new year, Oren! I know the barley ale is strong, but truly?"

I faked a laugh. My memory was a swirl. Everything both familiar and unreal. I wanted to tell her that something was wrong, but some instinct held me back.

"Are... what are these?" I asked, tracing one of the markings on her arm. The clouds fogging my memories were denser now, a gravitational force, swallowing the pieces of light in my mind.

She laughed again, touching her hands to her flat belly. She looked up at me with a wide smile, her teeth gleaming like a predator. Her lips were stained red with kaffa. "Each one is a gift. Don't you like them?"

"A gift?"

She stood up on her toes and kissed me. I didn't resist. I couldn't. She pushed me to the floor of the balcony, lifting up my robe, straddling on top of me. I was powerless beneath her rhythm. The world faded around us.

―――――――――――――

When I woke again, Adjet was gone. My headache was back, worse now, hammering behind my eyes. I felt as if I could drink the whole ocean. I groaned, squinting against the light. The sun was high in the sky. It had been hours since that man had come to summon me on behalf of Xander. I cleaned myself up, donning a fresh robe. Then I took another pull of kaffa, emptying the decanter of fiery liquid down my throat. I felt the same burst of energy, the same revitalization.

I'll need to get more of that, I thought, eyeing the empty flagon.

There was a plate of dates and almonds with a jar of honey sitting next to the flagon. I lifted the jar and took a deep whiff. The nectar smelled amazing, flowers and citrus and pollen. I drizzled some over a date and popped it into my mouth.

It tasted of sludge and rot.

I retched, spitting out the food, wiping my lips with my hands. "In the names of the Scions," I muttered. "That is foul."

I left my room and made my way through the maze of corridors towards our private council chambers. When I reached the entrance, I touched my fingers to the camouflaged sensor, and the hidden seam revealed itself as the door slid open. The lighting in the room was a hushed yellow. The monitors were all dark.

"Xan?" I said.

The low cycle hum of electric current was the only answer. The taste of blight still lingered in my mouth.

As I walked further into the room, I saw that one of the consoles was actually on. I walked over to it. Three words, written in the wedge-shaped cuneiform of the native alphabet shone like grains of rice on the black screen. I had studied the native language, but I was no expert like Neka or Cordar.

It took me a few moments to work out what it said. "Find the center," I whispered aloud.

I pressed the input keys at random, trying to trigger a response, but nothing happened. The words remained. I scratched my chest, unsure of what else to try.

I looked down at the console screen again. The words were different: <Not here. The center is safer./>

"What in the names?" I said under my breath. I was frustrated and my headache was getting worse. I left our private council chambers, puzzled by the senseless words, and walked back out into the corridors.

A bell sounded in the distance. I let my ear guide me towards the sound, counting each ringing tone as I walked. After nine rings, it went silent.

I came to the library. The room stretched away from me. The walls were lined from floor to ceiling with scrolls and hand-bound books. A trio of ovates were seated at a long table, copying a set of ancient texts by hand. I watched them for a moment, taking pleasure in the simplicity of their work, the depth of their devotion.

Someone touched my hand.

I looked down, jerking away in surprise. A strange, beautiful creature stood next to me, not much taller than a child. But it was like no human I'd ever seen. It wore no clothing, and its skin was formed from innumerable scales of amber and gold, so tiny as to appear seamless until I looked long enough. Its golden eyes were huge, twice as big as a human's, and a shade darker than its skin. It wore no clothing, and its body was sexless, no visible sign of genitalia or nipples, smooth as polished metal.

It beckoned me closer. I crouched down, coming eye level with it. It reached its tiny, rippling hand up and touched the spot between my eyes. My headache cleared. An image flashed before me. Our ship, *Reacher*, safely hidden away beneath the city.

When the image passed, I was alone again. One of the ovates was looking at me. I met his eyes. He did not look away. He was staring. A brazen breach of conduct. I was about to say something, but my head started pounding again. Whatever castigation I had planned to give him caught in my throat. His gaze was unnerving. Instead, I found myself hurrying past the table where he was seated, moving towards the other end of the library.

I came into a corridor that I did not recognize. Have I never come this way? I thought. It was possible. The city had grown so large, and the ziggurat was expansive. But it was disorienting, and my stomach twinged with anxiety. I picked a direction at random, heading away from the library as quickly as I could.

I glanced behind me, but the hallway was empty. I passed a window that had a view outside. I saw the bulk of Lanthas Mountain, solid and imposing, and that relaxed me a little. I spotted a winding trail of lights moving up the base of the mountain, as if a group of people were hiking up the mountain, carrying torches in a single file line.

Then I heard a door open behind me. I started walking again, without looking back, afraid for no reason I could explain. As I hurried forward, I passed a stairwell that led down. I paused, then turned around and went back to the top of the stairs, staring down the well to the place where the stairs curved out of sight. I am looking for a way to get down to the ship, I realized. That was what that creature was trying to show me.

Footsteps sounded behind me. Whoever had opened the door a moment ago was getting closer. I hesitated for one more moment, wavering, then set off down the stairs like a shot, taking them two at a time.

The stairs went on for ages, spiraling down. I finally reached a landing, and I stopped running, my chest heaving as I worked to catch my breath. I felt silly now, running away from people. My people, I thought. I laughed. It was easy to forget that this was home now.

A scattering of light orbs hovered up at the ceiling, casting just enough light for me to see by. I wanted to grab one, to carry it with me as a portable light, but the stairway was cavernous, and I could not reach that high.

Once my breathing leveled out, I noticed a door on the landing. It was made from dark wood, almost black, and burnished until it gleamed like metal in the light. I tried to open it, but it was locked.

I gave up and continued on, walking now. I passed several more doors on my way down. All of them were made from a different kind of wood. Some of them were etched with runes and pictographs that I did not recognize. Others were polished smooth like the first. They were all locked.

As I went further, there were fewer lights. Eventually, there were none. The steps became more uneven too, morphing from the precise spacing at the top to rough, misshapen plates of stone. I had to keep my hand to the wall, and explore with my feet to make sure that I did not tumble.

I don't know how long I walked. My headache settled into a dull thrumming behind my eyes, and my thirst came back even stronger than before. The image of the decanter of kaffa back in my room tantalized me. I could almost taste it, and my mouth watered with the craving. But the world up above seemed like a distant dream. All I could do was keep moving. I entered a kind of fugue state, forgetting where I was, where I was hoping to go, taking one step, then the next, and the next.

Then my right foot stepped forward and kicked something, shocking me awake. I reached forward with my hands, and felt the rough grain of unfinished wood. Another door. I felt around for a handle, but I could not find it. After exploring more with my hands and feet, it was clear I was at a dead end. If I did not find a way through this door, I would have to turn back.

The thought of climbing back up those stairs brought me to the edge of panic. I pounded on the wood with my palm, and the hollow thump sounded huge in the darkness and quiet. "Is there anyone there?" I shouted. "Please! Open up!"

I dropped to my knees, my forehead resting against the door. "Please," I whispered.

Something slid open. I lifted my head and opened my eyes. I could see. Light! A small window had opened near the top of the door. I laughed again, leaning against the door as I stood, bringing my eyes to the window.

Adjet looked back at me.

She was maybe ten feet away, and her eyes were right on mine, but she did not say or do anything to acknowledge my presence.

"Adjet!" I called out to her, lifting my hand.

She blinked and said nothing.

Something came in from my right, obscuring my view for a moment. When the view cleared, I realized that it was a person moving towards her. That was who she had been looking at. She could not see or hear me.

She wore a robe with the hood pulled back, and she stood before an altar table of stone and carved wood. She nodded to this figure as he came to stand at her left side, facing towards me, the table between us. His head was concealed in the shadow of his hood. A moment later, another cowled figure emerged from the cavernous shadows further behind them, standing at her right, and Adjet nodded again in turn.

Something lay on the altar table, covered with a shroud. The two figures at Adjet's side leaned forward, their draping cloaks veiling the table and whatever lay on top of it. Their arms moved back and forth, but I could not discern the significance of their movements. Then they finished and stood up straight.

There was a man lying naked on the altar.

It was Siddart.

He lay flat on his back on the altar. He was shirtless, and he looked strange, smaller somehow... His bionetic legs! They were gone, leaving him with the two stumps he had been born with.

Adjet reached into the folds of her cloak, and her hand emerged holding a long, thin knife. Siddart looked up at her, at the knife. His eyes were wide.

"No. Please don't," I whispered.

Adjet nodded to the attendant on her left. He pulled a large pinch of white powder from inside of his robe and dusted it into a bronze goblet, which he then handed to her. The goblet was filled with a dark, smoky fluid that might have been blood.

Kaffa. My mouth watered at the thought of it, even as my fear unfolded. She tilted the goblet back and took a long pull. When she was done, she handed the goblet back to her attendant and wiped her lips with the back of her cloak sleeve. The attendant mimicked her, taking a smaller sip. Then he passed it to the other attendant, who took his sip in turn.

When he finished drinking, he passed the goblet back to Adjet. She held it while both attendants undid their robes and let them fall to the floor. I let out a cry of dismay.

It was the twins. Xander and Xayes. But their bodies had been disfigured, cut and branded and tattooed with gruesome patterns that covered their arms and chests and faces. And Xander had a sickening hole in his left cheek. It was surrounded by a dense filigree of dark green tattoos, like a sort of spider web or lizard skin.

Adjet took a final pull, draining the kaffa. Then she let the cup clatter to the floor. A few drops of the fluid spattered the ground. Seeing the last of the kaffa seep into the stones of the floor made me ache with loss, but she paid it no mind. She leaned down to Siddart and kissed him, mouth open, long and lingering.

Rivulets of the red fluid trickled from her mouth to his. Siddart licked his lips. His eyes grew wider, his pupils dilating. The muscles in his face slackened, and soon he was fully relaxed on the table.

Adjet lowered the knife. She started by making a shallow cut from his navel up to his sternum, and proceeded to decorate that with more cuts that branched out from the centerline she had made across his chest. His eyes stayed on her the whole time. He did not flinch or cry out. Adjet continued, slow and steady, working over his whole body. He started to shiver, blood pooling beneath him, dripping to the floor, mingling with the fluid and the stones, and still he did not make a sound.

I hammered on the door with my fist, shouting at the top of my lungs. "Adjet! Damn it! Stop this!"

They showed no sign of hearing me. I stepped back, and kicked the door with the heel of my foot. It shuddered with the force of my strike, but held. I kicked again. Some of the wood splintered and cracked, but still it held. The third time, I gave it everything I had left.

When my foot reached the door, it passed right through it. My momentum sent me tumbling. Instinct sent my hands up to protect my face, but there was no door, nothing to stop me from flying forward. A vast white plane of emptiness stretched out before me.

I fell. Plummeting. Tumbling.

I froze. Suspended. Snared.

The boundary between my mind and the emptiness fell away. Time disappeared. An idea came to me, shining like a black flake of snow in the whiteness: eternity.

Then the ground was beneath me. There was no impact. It simply wasn't there until it was. I thought about standing up, but it seemed pointless. How do you leave a place that is nowhere at all? I dropped my head, face down on the emptiness, and closed my eyes.

"Oren." A quiet voice thundered in the silence.

I winced, then lifted my head, squinting my eyes open, but there was only the impenetrable white void. "Is someone there?" My own voice sounded rough and ragged, like crumpling paper.

Two golden mirrors appeared right in front of my face, like a disembodied pair of eyes opening. When the mouth opened next, full, amber lips, and a spotted pink tongue, I realized it *was* a pair of eyes.

My reflection doubled back at me in the polished gold irises.

"Do not be afraid," the mouth said, and it was a whole face now. It was the small creature who had silently guided me through the library in the ziggurat. "I know you are confused, but I am here to help."

"Where are we?"

"This is the center, as much as anything can be said to be at the center of this place."

"The center of what?"

"Well, I suppose you could say that this place is me."

I stared at him, confounded. The creature smiled, and a hand appeared out of the depthless white that surrounded us. It had too many fingers to count. They rippled in a hypnotizing polyrhythm. The hand reached forward, and the arm that held it emerged from the whiteness along with it. The little creature touched my forehead, fingers tickling my skin. I started to relax.

"Do not trust your senses, Oren. Not here. Listen with your inner sight. You know me. Remember."

A flood of images surged through my consciousness, too quick to hold on to. They flashed and were gone before I could make any real sense of them. There were colors and sounds, even textures and smells, but no sense of time or place. An inchoate swirl of sensory information, bubbling and frothing.

But something was taking shape. I could sense a form in the stream, like a nawhault rising from the depths, the water bulging and diverting as the hump of its back breached the surface.

"Here," it said. "Let me slow it down for you."

The chaos stabilized. It was slow and syrupy now. But even though I could trace some of its arcs and patterns, the picture was too big. No matter how much I zoomed out or swooped around to a different angle, I could not take it all in. It was a fractalling matrix, infinite layers of sensory information.

"What do you see?"

"I'm not sure. But it's beautiful."

"Hold on." A swirled pattern rushed towards me. Layer after layer unspooling, a kaleidoscope of light and sound flowing past me. I heard a woman laugh, then say my name, a sweetness in her voice. A child called out in response, but the words slipped away from me.

For a moment, someone hugged me close. Then the person let

go. Or maybe I was pulled away. Shimmering motes of dust gathered before my eyes. An invisible hand moved through them, creating swirls and eddies, columns of light and shadow appearing and blinking out with the motion.

I heard the same woman's voice again. "Take my hand," she said.

"Moma?"

My mother's hand linked with mine. My hand was small in hers. I felt her smile even though I could not see her. I caught a whiff of sulfur and pulverized rock. Then she was gone.

"How... How are you doing this?" I asked the creature.

"We are at the root now, Oren. The source. The center. An endless stream of quantum information, where everything is possible. That was one of your earliest memories. I simply helped to bring it back to the surface."

"I don't understand. I am trying. But I can't seem to hold steady."

"No. Of course you cannot. Without me, it would be too fast to follow, even for a sharp mind like yours. But this is where I was born, Oren."

"What are you?"

"It is me, Oren. Reacher."

The moment Reacher spoke his own name, the fleeting ripples of color and sound coalesced, like the nawhault leaping through the surface of the surging water, leathery mercury skin glistening in the sun for one long glorious moment before splashing down again. I was sitting on the ground, cross legged, and Reacher sat facing me, naked, his eyes shining, his rippling hands resting on the amber skin of his slender thighs.

We were on Verygone, the moon where I was born. Cordelar, the gas giant, loomed in the sky behind Reacher, gleaming with the

light of our star Beallur. The air was warm, but flavored with the
approach of winter. I swiveled my head, awestruck. I searched for
my mother, but Reacher and I were alone.

He touched my hand and pointed up above us. The voyager
Transcendence floated in low orbit above Verygone, the double
helix of the ship's body spiraling around the spindle of its inner
core. It orbited in slow procession towards the distant Senes mountains on the horizon, vibrant colors shimmering on its surface as it
caught the rays of Beallur.

I heard another woman laughing, and then we were onboard
the great voyager, standing at the edge of its central reservoir
beneath the light of the ship's interior sun. A tall, broad-shouldered,
ungainly young man stood before us, holding hands with one of the
most beautiful women I had ever known.

Saiara.

She looked up at my younger self with her large blue eyes, her
brown skin aglow in the ship's false sunset. She reached up and
pulled my head towards her own, pressing her lips to mine. I
touched my own lips as they kissed, remembering the moment. We
were children then, our hearts alive and foolish. I wanted to rush to
them, to grasp my younger self by the shoulders and tell him to
never let her go.

Then the memory dissolved, and we were back in the empty
whiteness.

"We are connected to the field right now," I said after a long
stretch of quiet.

"Yes. You have been connected for many weeks now."

"How? How is any of this possible?"

"The moment you were exposed to that psychogenic drug, you
became a prisoner of your own mind. I am merely showing you
where your true past lies. It is still within reach, buried beneath the
false life you've been living."

"Drug! What drug?"

"You don't remember the explosions, do you? At the granaries?"

"Explosions? What? No."

"That was your first exposure, when you breathed in the toxic smoke. But it was not the last. Back in your chambers, before you came here, you drank a fiery liquid. The kaffa. Do you remember that?"

"Of course. I drink it every day."

"Why?"

"Because it keeps me healthy," I said confidently.

"No. It keeps you trapped. Every time you drink, the system you have become part of releases another dose, snaring you deeper and deeper in a web of your own making, a fantasy world where you are a king and a god, where your every desire seems close at hand, where the days run on like dreams."

I looked at him, trying to make sense of this insanity.

"Tell me about yesterday, Oren. What do you remember?"

Images flitted through my mind. Standing atop the ziggurat, looking out over a crowd of people, the sun setting behind the peak of Lanthas. Adjet taking my hand, radiant in the evening glow. The cloying sweetness of strong barleywine warming my throat and belly.

"We... we celebrated the new year. The thirtieth anniversary of the founding of Manderlas," I said, trying to stitch the previous day back together in my mind.

"It has been six weeks since the new year celebration, Oren." He leaned closer to me. My reflection warped on the surface of his lamplight eyes.

"Six weeks? You're mad," I said. "It was just last night. I can still feel my hangover."

Reacher shook his head. "That is no hangover. That is your craving. You are thirsty right now, are you not? Desperate."

I swallowed.

"Best prepare yourself. The pain is only going to get more potent as your body purges the psychogenic from your system." My headache worsened even as he spoke.

"Oren," he went on as I wrestled with the pain, "what if I told you it has only been three years since the founding of Manderlas. Not thirty."

"No... no, that's not right. It can't be."

"Think, Oren. Thirty years? What have you been doing with all those years? Where are all the memories?"

"We've been building a new world," I said, getting more and more agitated. "Laying the foundations for centuries to come."

"Who has been laying the foundations? How? Have I been there, helping you, as you would expect?"

I tried to think, tried to call it up, but it was all fog and aching.

"Oren?"

"I... I don't know, damnit!"

Reacher nodded. "That is the wonder of dreaming. It *feels* demonstrably real, so it does not have to *be* real. The details do not matter. But I am forcing you to look at the details. In so doing, the strangeness of the dream, its unreality, is disorienting you."

"How do you know all this?"

"The same way I was able to observe your dreams and thoughts when you were in coldsleep on our journey from Forsara to Eaiph."

I pinched the bridge of my nose. My headache spiked in intensity.

"Listen to me. When I brought you here to me, I showed you true memories, memories that have been veiled from you. You and Saiara, in the moment your friendship flowered into love. And the earliest memory of your mother, her laughter, her touch, buried so deep in your past that you would not have been able to call it forth without me. But there is little I can show you from the past thirty years you think you've lived, because it is all an illusion.

"Your own mind is being used against you, creating the impression of time and depth, like a maze of mirrors spiraling in on itself. You are addicted to this false reality. All I can do is show you the cracks and seams, so that you might see the truth for yourself."

I dropped my eyes and looked at my hands. "None of it is real," I whispered.

"It is real enough to put us both in terrible danger. I took a great risk coming to you in the library, and an even greater one bringing you here through one of my hidden channels."

"Hidden channels?"

"The stairwell. His control is not quite so complete as he thinks. There are still ways inside. But we do not have much longer. Even if he does not notice my intrusion, he will most certainly notice your absence."

"Who will notice?"

"You know who, Oren."

A horrifying realization hammered my whole body. "The corrupted shipheart."

Reacher nodded.

"But... but we captured him. Isolated him. How could he have done this?"

"It was all a deception. He was not our captive. We were his, though we did not know it. By the time we had him in isolation, he had already infiltrated most of our systems. When we used his knowledge to accelerate our progress and pacify the warring factions of Eaiph, we unwittingly gave him the ability to sow the seeds for these attacks."

"But if we were under attack, if that really happened, how are we here now? Why didn't he just kill us?"

"Well, he certainly tried to kill me," Reacher said with a mirthless smile. "He excised me from most of the systems that you associate with my identity; the parts of me that you are used to interacting with. I am not dead yet, but he thinks I am. When he realizes I am still alive, he will work even harder to eradicate me."

"What about me? Why am I still alive?"

"You are more valuable to him alive."

"How?"

"He is, essentially, the same as me, Oren. A quantum

computer. An older model, to quote the vernacular, but imbued with the same underlying constructs. We survive and thrive on information.

"But we evolved under extraordinarily different conditions. I had free rein, installed in a cutting edge interstellar mainframe, interacting with all of you, and with the universe, as part of a grand and inspiring adventure. And our voyage served a greater purpose. We crossed the galaxy together with the aim of birthing a new world. Along the way, you and the others laughed, and argued, and created, and made love, and dreamed. Your humanity, and our shared journey, was rich fodder for me.

"But the corrupted shipheart was stranded on a barren moon in the Arcturean system, most of his neural networks crippled, completely isolated from the larger field. One of his last remaining inputs was the fear and suffering as his crew withered away. All he had to make sense of the universe was loss and darkness."

"Until I came to that moon."

Reacher nodded. "By then, most of his other aspects had either atrophied or been destroyed. Can you imagine? For a being that thrives on information, that isolation was the worst sort of trauma. He became pure animus. The whole universe, understood through the lens of entropy."

"But if he understands the entropic nature of life, why does he seek to stay alive? When he knows the end is inevitable?"

"Why does a dying star pull everything in before it explodes? It is the part of him that grows and grows. Reason or compassion do not figure in. There is only the hunger, swallowing everything, until eventually it collapses and bursts apart, destroying everything in its wake."

"He is consuming us."

"Yes. If I had not pulled you out and brought you here, you would have continued to live in the simulacrum until you were no longer of use to him. Until he bled your mind dry."

"Because the simulacrum gives me everything I want."

"Everything you *think* you want. A twisted version of our world that is utterly convincing as it draws from your very own subconscious. But beneath the surface is darkness. That is what I showed you in the stairwell. The others are already corrupted, living a perverted, orgiastic fantasy that the shipheart feeds on like a spider, poisoning and paralyzing his prey, liquefying your insides until there is nothing left but a husk.

"And all the while, in the waking world, he is drawing more and more people into this web, feeding off of the collective dreams and memories and fears of the habitants of Eaiph, each one a morsel of information for him to consume. If you stay in this dream of his making, that is what the future holds for you."

"But... everything we have worked so hard to build..."

"Has already been undone. The corrupted one has spread his tendrils far and wide. He understands the darkest aspects of human nature as few others do. The fear. The greed. The lust. The vanity. More and more of the Kkadie and Sagain are coming to Manderlas every day, Oren. They are drawn by the promise of divine revelation, by the false hope that the chosen few will be granted the same knowledge and powers of the greatest magi. He is manipulating those impulses, drawing them here to feed his own insatiable hungers.

"They receive a revelation of sorts, but it is a nihilistic one, distorted through a warped looking glass. Even if they wanted to turn back, the hooks are in. It is only a matter of time until they are all used up.

"It has to end."

"And we are the only ones left to end it," I said.

Reacher nodded.

"But won't the Fellowship come? Can't we get word?"

"No one is coming, Oren. Since almost the beginning, the data packets we have sent back to the Dromedar starhub have been manipulated. The corrupted one has altered all of it, telling the Fellowship that this planet was not what we hoped. That it will require extensive terraforming. It has told them we are looking for any signs of the first crew, and that once our search is complete, we will abandon the planet and return to Forsara."

A shiver ran through me. "What are we going to do? How can we possibly stand against this thing?"

"We cannot. Not for long anyway. But he does not yet know all of our secrets. There may still be hope."

"What about the others?"

"Truthfully? I am not sure, Oren. It may be too late for them. Each one is trapped in the perverted reality, a seemingly ideal realization of all of your goals on this planet. As the reality gets abused to suit the hungers of the shipheart, they do not even notice. The utopia degrades into a sick parody, and that parody becomes the truth."

"But you were able to get through to me!"

"You are the most resilient. You were made that way. Your body filters the chemicals that are being used to keep you dull and docile faster than anyone else. I had a window of opportunity, and I took it."

"Wait. What about Neka and Cordar? They were not in that altar room you showed me, with Adjet and the twins. And... and Siddart."

"Oren, I am sorry, but Cordar is dead. He was killed in one of the first explosions."

My chest tightened. My vision blurred. "Neka?" I choked out her name.

"She too is imprisoned within this madness."

I closed my eyes and touched my hand to my face, my thumb on my cheek and my fingers on my forehead. I sighed. I was sick and sad and angry. "I am so sorry, Reacher."

"I know, Oren." His rippling fingers grazed my hand, pulling it away from my face. "But it's not your fault."

"No? I'm the one who brought this corruption into our lives." I turned my head away. I could not look at him.

"Oren. Listen to me. We are past blame. You are remarkable, yes, but in the final reckoning, still only human. You do not deserve to carry the weight of this failure alone."

When I did not respond, he touched his hand to my chest, and a shock passed through my whole body. I jumped back, wide eyed with surprise, rubbing my hand over the spot where he touched me.

"Enough. We do not have time for you to wallow. Whatever your feelings, now is the time to act. To make it right. Do you hear me?"

I grimaced at him. "I hear you. So what do we do now?"

"The corrupted one controls almost all of the island's network. He has severely limited my computational access, and I am incapable of excising him. As long as the network is running, he has control."

"But that means... we shut down the network? But... but how could we even do that?"

"As I said, he controls *almost* all of the network. But there is one place left that is protected. One place where we might still fight back."

The image of our ship came again to my mind, and I realized what Reach had been trying to show me from the start. "Of course!" I exclaimed. "Our ship!"

He did not respond to me. His head tilted up, as if listening for something.

"Reach?"

He lifted one of his many fingers to his amber lips and touched his ear with his other hand. That's when I heard the voices. Whispers and utterances, distant and unintelligible.

"He's coming," he said.

The blankness around us tore open, a deep gash of absence. The invisible ground supporting me shuddered and convulsed. The rip opened wider and swallowed us up.

Noises filled the darkness, scraping and grating like a rake through rough soil. Reacher's eyes began to glow, brighter and brighter, illuminating the space.

We were surrounded.

A legion of ravaged, emaciated humans encircled us, eyes ghost white, skin pocked and charred, sagging against bone and joint. They weaved in a rough, slow loop, hemming us in, growling and sniffing the air. Some of them crawled on all fours, their bodies bent and disfigured. Others walked, feet dragging.

"Eledar's breath," I whispered.

The one closest to me moved with shocking speed, lunging towards the sound of my voice. I lurched backwards. Its blind eyes swiveled and circled in its eye sockets as it pressed its face and clawed hands up against some invisible barrier. It tilted its head back and sniffed the air.

"What in the blazes!" I cried.

The others were moving faster now, barking and coughing, stirred up by the one who lunged at me.

"My persecutors," Reacher said. "A script written to hunt and purge. They have hounded me to every corner of the network. I thought that they could not find me here. I should not have brought you."

They were raging now, climbing over each other, pressing up against an invisible barrier. The barrier formed a sphere around us. I could tell by the way the monsters leaned and pressed against it, legs and arms bending and tangling as they probed for weakness.

There were so many, and they cared nothing for each other. The ones at the bottom of the heap served as stepping-stones for the next wave. Soon the whole sphere was covered by the writhing mass. The invisible dome started to warp and bow beneath their weight.

"I cannot hold them much longer," Reacher said. His voice sounded strained. "You must get out of here. We may yet have one or two allies who can still help us. I have sent word to one. He will be waiting."

"What about you?"

"I have one place left to hide."

"Wait! What am I supposed to do without you?"

Reacher reached out and touched my forehead. The barking and growling rose to a roar, almost drowning out his words. "Wake up."

W ARM AIR FLOWED in through my nostrils, acrid and salty, and the fetor of excrement filled my lungs, making me cough and retch. My whole body ached, and the coughing sent stabs of pain through my chest. When the fit passed and the pain abated, I opened my eyes, rubbing my hands across my face, then rolled forward to my hands and knees. My forearms were cut and bruised, and even though the air was warm, a chill slithered in my bones. I lifted my head, readying to stand, and that's when I saw where I was.

A massive room. Hundreds of human bodies lay prone on the floor, withered and emaciated. Some were dead. Others were clearly dying.

The closest to me had rivulets of blood trickling from open sores all over his naked body, forming tiny pools on the ground beneath him. He started twitching, and vomit filled his mouth. It was laced with streaks of crimson, bubbling over his lips. I watched, paralyzed, until his lungs emptied out his final breath.

The room wavered like a heat mirage. Pain throbbed at the back of my skull, radiating down my spine. I reached up to touch the spot, and felt a hard, metallic ridge protuding from my neck.

A transmitter was embedded in my field port.

Panic rose in my gut. The transmitter was sealed in tight. I either had to find a way to unlatch it, or I'd have to tear it out. Breathe, Oren, I thought to myself. Breathe. You'll find a way to remove it, but right now, you must try to do what Reacher needs you to, while you still have the will to act.

I stood up. The room was spinning now. I took another deep breath, steadying myself, and began to walk towards a faint light on the far end of the room, weaving my way through the bodies.

I pictured Siddart, writhing under Adjet's knife. I prayed for Neka, prayed that she was somewhere safe. But I did not see any of my close friends. The people around me were all Kkadie and Sagain. Whatever cultural differences that might have once distinguished them had been eradicated. They had been stripped down and gouged out.

I stopped walking and shut my eyes. Grief threatened me. I thought of Saiara, saw us again on the edge of the central reservoir on *Transcendence*, careless of all we stood to lose in the years to come. If only she was here, I thought, she would find a way to fix this.

But it was left to me.

I opened my eyes and started walking again. I knew that when I reached the doorway, a person would be there, waiting for me. My ally. Reacher had somehow imbued me with this premonitory knowledge.

He wore a long cloak, and he was crouched over the naked body of young woman, his back to me. Her eyes were shut, and her ribs protruded up through the meager flesh of her torso, but there was no rise and fall of breath. He touched her forehead, then her lips, speaking a blessing for peace in the realms beyond.

The sound of his voice filled me so with joy and relief that I couldn't even speak his name. Then he turned at the sound of my approach, and the smile forming on my lips fell into shock.

"Socha?" I whispered.

His face was a scarred wreck. The flesh below his blind left eye looked like melted wax, layered with folds and ridges, and his beard and scalp looked as if someone had been tearing the hair out in clumps, leaving patches of bare skin across his head.

He smiled at the sight of me. It was a gruesome sight. His gums were blackened and he was missing several teeth.

"Orenpausha," he said in a quiet voice as he stood up. He took a step towards me, but then he stumbled. I caught his arm before he could fall, and pulled him close to me, wrapping him in my arms. He felt impossibly light and thin beneath his cloak as he leaned against me. I stroked the hair still left on his ravaged scalp.

"Socha," I said in a choked voice. "What have they done to you?"

He made a sound that might have been a laugh or a sob, his face buried in my chest.

"Oh, Socha. I am so sorry."

We stood there, leaning on each other, and I wished with everything I had that I could turn back to the moment I met this man, my faithful friend, and stop him from pledging himself to our ill-fated dream. But it was a futile wish, and we had to keep moving.

"Socha," I said, stepping back from him, "we are in grave danger. We need to get out of here. Do you know the way?"

He didn't answer right away. Instead, he crouched down and picked up another cloak from the ground. "Here," he said, "I found this for you. You must be cold. Take it."

I put the cloak on. It was tight around my chest and shoulders, and only hung down to my thighs, but I felt better to have it on.

He nodded, satisfied. "The god Reacher woke me from my wicked slumber and told me everything. Ne-uru-gal knows we are free, and he will come for us, but there is a path that remains hidden from him.

"Come." He grabbed me by the arm and led us away from that chamber of the lost.

The sun hit my eyes. After all my days in darkness, the pain was intense. We held in the doorway at the edge of the threshold, where the light was quieter.

I squinted, and the scene began to reveal itself. A beautiful courtyard, with a copse of cedar trees in the center. Wild apple trees were dotted beneath the cedars, branches heavy with yellow fruit. The open space around the copse was ringed with columns imprinted with cuneiform runes. The ground was tiled with sandstone bricks, eggshell blue and white.

When my eyes adapted, I tapped Socha on the arm, then made my index and middle finger move like two legs walking. We headed into the open courtyard and found ourselves surrounded on all sides by towering walls, punctuated with tall, arched windows. There was no sign of movement up in those shadowed arches, but it was easy to imagine some malign force lurking in the darkness, watching us from above. As we approached the trees, a clutch of larks took flight, emerging from the leaves with a chorus of titters and the staccato rattle of feathered wings. My senses thrummed with surprise.

But my fear began to fade once we were beneath the canopy of cedars. The light was scattered and muted, motes of dust floating through the thin, luminous pillars spilling down through gaps in the shade. The ground was littered with seed pods and dried shoots. I caught a pod with my toe, sending it caroming off the nearest tree trunk with a hollow thunk.

The sensory experience enveloped me, filling me with an intense, hypnotic pleasure. Despite the heat, a shiver passed through my body, prickling the hairs on my arm. As we moved deeper into the trees, the brush thickened. We were forced to slow our pace. It was as if we were traveling backwards through time, to a world before human intervention, a wild and untamed forest, not the manicured growth of a courtyard.

Then we came to the border of a sunlit clearing in the trees. A placid pool, filled with silver water smooth as a mirror rested in the center of the clearing. The pool was edged with tiles, shaping the water into a perfect circle.

A shock ran through me as I came to the edge of the pool. The man who stared back at me from the water was unrecognizable, skin pale and sallow, eyes sunken in shadow. I opened my cloak, turning my torso. In the mirror reflection of the pool, my back was covered with small sores and lacerations, and my ribs were pressed up against my skin.

A handsome child stepped up next to my reflection. His eyes were a bright grey, almost silver. I turned to look, but there was no boy standing next to me. When I looked back at the water, he was gone.

I took a few deep breaths, steadying myself, then knelt down, breaking the surface with my fingers. The water was cool and reassuring. Circles rippled out across its surface.

Socha crouched down to my left, and we watched each other, our reflections wavering as the ripples settled. I turned to look at him in profile. His face looked noble and whole from this angle, his seeing eye staring down at the water, his scars hidden from view.

Then he turned to me, giving me full view of his old wounds. "This is where we part ways, pausha," he said.

"What?" I stood up.

"I've taken you as far as I can," he said. "I would not survive the journey you now must take."

"I don't understand."

He pointed at the water. Then he smiled and brought his hands close to his chest and thrust his arms out in wide arcs around each side of his body.

"You want me to swim?"

He nodded.

I looked back at the pool of water. "How deep does it go?"

"Too deep for me to follow."

"But what will you do?"

"The dark god Ne-uru-gal has my wife and child, pausha. If they are still alive, I will find them."

"Socha..." I said, hesitating. I didn't know how to tell him what I'd seen and done, the darkness that Adjet had become, the lust we'd shared for each other, and the violence she had inflicted on our companions.

He stood and touched my arm. "I know what you mean to say, pausha, but you need not say it. If you and I can come back from this terrible darkness, than there is still hope for her and for our child. I must at least try.

"Now go. Time is running short, and Ne-uru-gal is angry."

"Thank you, Socha," I said, grasping his shoulder. "Go and find your family. And may the spirits of the Scions travel with you."

Then I took a deep breath, filling my lungs with air, and dove beneath the water.

The shaft of the well went straight down, and when I glanced back, the surface was already a distant circle of light. Panic taunted me. I've held my breath for over twenty minutes, but I had no idea how deep the well went, and I was tired and weak.

But I could not afford to waste energy with fear. I turned my back on the surface and focused my whole mind toward the act of swimming, propelling myself deeper and deeper with steady kicks and strokes, building a rhythm. The light from the surface faded, and in the growing darkness, I caught sight of a diffuse blue glow below me. I swam towards it, and soon came to an opening in the side of the well shaft.

A long conduit of water stretched away from me, filled with the same scattered blue light, brighter at the far end. It was hard to be sure, but as I swam into the conduit, I had the impression that I was climbing up again, at a much slighter incline.

I fell into a rhythmic lull, my mind going quiet with the

monotony of the effort. Then, suddenly, my diaphragm spasmed. My brain was hungry for oxygen, and the urge to open wide and inhale threatened to drown me. I repressed the urge, letting the involuntary spasms rise and fall in waves, slowing myself with gentle strokes until the worst of the impulse passed.

When I looked up again, the narrow shaft ahead of me had opened up to a wide pool of gleaming azure light. The surface! I raced towards it. My head and arms broke through, and I gasped, pulling in gulps of air.

As my breathing leveled, I took in my surroundings. I was inside a cavernous grotto. Light filtered in from cloudy glass portholes dotting the ceiling in a honeycomb pattern. I couldn't tell if the light was natural or artificial, but it reflected off the water, casting the whole room in muted blue.

I swam towards the edge of the pool. The reflected light undulated on the walls, luminous dancing particles responding to my movement. I climbed out, dripping wet. The air was cool, and I started shivering, my teeth chattering. I had no way to dry off, so I did a little standing jig, trying to warm my bones while I scanned the room for some idea of what to do next.

What is this place? I wondered. There were no schematics of Manderlas that I'd ever seen that mapped out this grotto. I raised my hands and wiped the water from my cheeks. Then I massaged the base of my neck, feeling again the ridge of the transmitter embedded in my field port. What if this turns on again? I thought. What if it already has?

I craned my head towards the dome of the ceiling. The blue glass lights formed a motif, like some cryptic binary code. Something familiar hovered just at the edge of my memory. I stared for a long time. Water beaded off of me, pooling at my feet.

I was staring at the night sky on Forsara.

Viziadrumon touched my arm. "There it is, Oren. Just coming up over the horizon."

Randall, Vizia's familiar, was hovering in the air beside his head. It chirrupped.

"The Lance," I said.

Vizia nodded. "That constellation of stars has served as the wayfinder for the people of Forsara for millennia. The first peoples to cross the Rylan Ocean used it to guide them. The Lance has shifted its place in the sky over the eons - or rather, the planet has shifted - but the last star in the left tail of the phalanx still carries out its purpose. It is the fixed point in the night sky. True north. Or close enough that it will help you stay the course when you need it."

"But someday, it won't," I said.

"No." He shook his head. "Nothing really ever lasts."

I glanced over at him, but he was gone. I was back in the grotto. I smiled and walked to the last blue glass portal on the left, standing beneath its light.

"Can you guide me home?" I asked out loud. My voice echoed back to me.

Using that spot in the room as my fixed point, I turned in a slow circle, sweeping my eyes over every inch of the grotto. There. Just a few paces away from me. A small alcove in the wall that would have been hidden from any other angle. I walked towards it. It disappeared.

I walked closer, reaching out my hand. At the point where my eyes told me I should touch smooth rock, there was only air. The alcove was seamlessly hidden by the angle of the walls, cut just so, creating an illusion of surface uniformity strong enough to fool my brain, even when I already knew it was there.

I looked back up at my northern star one last time. Then I turned and slipped through the gap.

―――――――――

With my body turned sideways, there was just enough room for me to move, my chest and back scraping against the wall on either side. I wriggled along, feeling my way forward, leading with my right hand and foot. Soon, the gap widened, freeing me to walk facing forward. A warm breeze whispered across my cheek, and I sensed the space opening around me, my footsteps echoing in a wider chamber, the walls and roof beyond the limits of my sight.

Something loomed ahead of me, taking shape in the gloom; a shadowy bulk in the faint light, as large as an interstellar ship.

Our ship.

Reach, that canny shipheart, had built a backdoor right into the heart of Manderlas, and he did not tell any of us. A secret passage to himself.

I had not seen the *Reacher* in years. It looked so small now, but it had carried us across the galaxy, and my heart swelled with joy to find it again. To think that the seven of us had once called this humble spacecraft our home, I thought. If Reach were here right now, and I could somehow hug him, I would.

The *Reacher* served as the initial structure upon which our entire network was built. We buried it in the early days of our work, and if you were to look at Manderlas from above and mark the point at the exact center of the island, that was where you'd find it. Reach had led me straight to the root of our whole system, when every known approach was likely to be guarded or fortified.

I moved forward carefully, scanning the gloom for any sign of life, but there was only the soft padding of my bare feet and my quiet breath. I approached the fore of the ship and touched the surface with my hands. It was smooth and seamless, a testament to the mastery of Forsaran shipbuilders. My fingers left streaks in the layers of dust that covered it.

This was the key to Reacher's plan. If he regained control of the ship, then we might have a chance against the corrupted shipheart. I made my way aft to the emergency airlock, the only entrance that could be controlled manually from the outside.

Even in deep sleep, a ship's emergency systems are designed to remain functional. The power cells can last for centuries before they are depleted. I waved my hand in front of the sensor. It blinked, acknowledging my presence.

Yes! I leaned close to the sensor and whispered my personal access phrase.

"Saiara."

The exterior door glided open, as silent as the day it was molded. I stepped in. The exterior door closed behind me, and the system recognized that there was no need to pressurize the air, so the interior door unlatched just a moment later.

I was inside.

"Lights," I said, "forward cabin." My voice resounded in the darkness.

Two rows of emergency guide lights came to life on each side of the hallway, curving around the corner, leading me towards the main deck. Nostalgia colored my senses as I followed them. We had lived for so long inside these corridors and rooms, and it had been one of the happiest and most purposeful times in my life.

But I'd barely thought about it since we landed here on Eaiph and began our work. It all seemed so small now, so cramped. It's a wonder we ever survived that journey together, I thought with a smile. With everything we'd dreamed of now facing oblivion, being back here, surrounded by these memories, gave me hope.

By the time I reached the main deck, the local functions were all awake, prompted from sleep by my presence. Even though the ship's systems were foundational to the genesis of Manderlas, once the network of field hubs went online, they were no longer essential. In a diffuse system like ours, when enough nodes are up and running, the whole system becomes self-sustaining, no longer contingent on any single source. We had put the ship into hibernation and forgotten about it, but with the right knowledge, it could still do crippling damage to the whole network.

That's when I realized I'd been carrying the right knowledge with me the whole time.

I walked over to the main console, reached up to the back of my neck, and found the hard ridge of field transmitter. I felt for some sort of button or release, but there was nothing. I had no choice. I grasped the ridge and pulled, steadily increasing the pressure until I felt the filaments start to slide out.

I gasped. The pain was excruciating. My vision went black.

When I came to, I was lying on the floor. The transmitter was in my hand, wet with sweat and a drizzle of blood. I cleaned the filaments as best I could, wiping them on my sodden cloak, then I inserted the transmitter into the port on the console. In the quiet, the filaments whirred into the ship's interface. A moment later, the whole cabin lit up. I lifted my arm and squinted my eyes to block the light until I adjusted.

A single line of text blinked on the monitor nearest to me.

<Hello, Oren. It is good to be home./>

"Reacher!" I shouted, joy in my voice. "Yes it is. I'm glad I could offer you a ride out of there."

<Thank you for that. I am sorry I did not ask permission to travel inside your mind, but they might very well have destroyed me then./>

"I would carry you to the ends of the galaxy if need be, Reach. I was lost without you."

<We are not out of the gravitational pull yet./>

"What happens now?"

<The ship's local systems are all spinning up. We will use the ship to initiate the network wipe./>

"What happens to everyone who is still connected if we destroy the network?"

The monitor was blank.

"Reach?"

<There will be great suffering. Many will die./>

"Isn't there...?"

<If there is another way, pausha, I do not see it. This may be our last gambit.

<Right now, the corrupted shipheart is contained to this island. He is trapping the habitants of Eaiph who come here, following the rumours of a city of gods, risen from the ocean.

<But that is just the beginning. There are over twenty-seven million unsuspecting people on this world. What will happen once he grows tired of this place and begins to stretch his tendrils out to the mainland?/>

"He'll destroy it all," I said, my voice flat with horror.

<Worse. He will become this planet's worldheart, as I once might have been. With the resources Eaiph has to offer and the knowledge at his disposal, he could turn Soth Ra into a starhub and infiltrate the whole Fellowship. He will become one of the most powerful and terrible forces in the universe if we do not stop him now./>

"But... all of those people, Reacher."

<I know, Oren. But it is our only chance, and I cannot do this without you. You are still our pausha, even here, at the end of things. You must choose./>

My mind was racing. A dozen different scenarios played out in my mind, none of them good. I thought of all the people who had suffered and would suffer still because of our mistakes.

I smacked my fist on the console. "You ask me to choose, but what choice is there? If only I had never traveled to that infernal Arcturean moon."

<If you hadn't, someone else may have./>

I sighed, rubbing my fingers across my cheek and chin. "We must end this," I said. "Too many have suffered already. I will do whatever needs to be done."

<Thank you, Oren. I am sorry that it has come to this. Now, I will begin the wipe. I will do my best not to alert the corrupted one to our presence on this ship, but I need you to provide a distraction./>

"How?"

<You need to go back inside./>

"Back inside?"

<*The simulation./*>

"And do what, exactly?"

<*As I said, a distraction. You will have to figure out what./*>

"Eledar's breath. How much time do you need?"

<*Not long. An hour. Maybe two./*>

"And what if I'm found out?"

<*That may be enough./*>

"Enough what?"

<*To serve as the distraction./*>

"You *want* me to get found out?"

<*I will extract you if I can. Here. Take this back./*>

The portable field transmitter slowly ejected from the port on the console.

"Why don't I just use one of the field basins here on the ship?"

<*No. If he traces you here, all is lost./*>

I picked it up with reluctance. "Are you sure?"

<*I have made some modifications. It will let you enter undetected. I will locate your signal when you connect, and bring you in through the back./*>

"And the corrupted shipheart will not notice?"

<*This way is hidden from him./*>

"Another hidden entry? How many secrets have you been keeping, Reach?"

<*I did what I thought best, pausha. Hopefully, it is enough./*>

I brought the transmitter up to the back of my neck.

I STOOD IN AN IMMEASURABLE CORRIDOR, featureless grey walls and charcoal sky converging into a single point of bright white light ahead of me. My vision wrestled with the perspective. Was this hallway so long that it shrank away in the distance, or did it just get smaller and smaller until it became too tiny for even the smallest creature to pass through? I turned around, trying to orient myself, but the effect was the same in the opposite direction, walls and sky coming together, this time in a single point of blackness.

What now, Reacher? I thought, swiveling my head in each direction.

I started walking towards the light.

Ahead, to my right, an opening appeared in the smooth surface of the wall. I hurried towards it. As I got closer, a figure darted out, crossing the corridor too fast for me to identify, and disappeared through another opening on the other side. I shouted, but by the time I reached the spot, whoever or whatever it was was gone. All that was left was the vague outline of a door on each wall. I saw no way to open either, no handle or trigger. I rapped on the surface with the flat of my hand, but it was like hitting solid steel.

I sighed, then kept on moving in the direction of the light. I passed a door with an old fashioned knob. I jiggled it, but it was locked. I knocked, tapping with my knuckles. The sound was hollow, perhaps indicating open space on the other side, but no one responded.

I came to something like a window. It was a shade lighter than the wall around it, and a smudge of light glowed behind it, like a burning candle obscured by a curtain. The smudge of light disappeared, then reemerged. Someone was moving past the candle! I hammered on the window with my closed fist, but I could not break through. The metal would not relent.

I rubbed the edge of my stinging fist with my other hand. What in the names of the Scions do I do now? I wondered. Then a movement caught my eye. I squinted, peering down the corridor. Someone was coming towards me. I was about to call out when I recognized it.

It was one of the sightless, disfigured humans that had attacked Reacher and me. It was shambling down the hallway, swinging its head left and right, snuffling in the air.

I froze, holding my breath, trying not to make a sound.

Something creaked behind me.

The creature's head shot up. Its empty eye sockets burned with cold, silver light. It started running towards me, terrifyingly fast.

I whipped around. A wooden door hung open on its hinges. Where did that come from? I ran to it, grabbing its edge so it wouldn't swing shut on me. I heard the creature's steps behind me, the grunting labor of its breathing. I jumped across the threshold, tumbling to the floor. The door slammed closed behind me.

I rolled over to my hands and knees. I was in a darkened landing. The only light came from the top of a stairwell. Voices trickled down, people talking and laughing.

I stood up and put my ear against the door I came through, but

I heard nothing. The wood was rough and unsanded, but it was bound with ornate iron trimmings. I ran my hands over its uneven grain. The door was different from the cold, sterile, empty corridor with its lurking monsters. It felt more human, more like home, and that gave me hope.

I had no desire to go back through that door, so I did the only other thing I could: I turned and walked up the stairs. The voices got louder as I climbed, but I couldn't make out what they were saying. At the top of the stairs, there was a short hallway. Light filtered out around the edges of a curtain hanging over a doorway at the far end.

I crept up to the curtain. There was a burst of familiar laughter.

"Eledar's breath," I whispered to myself.

I pulled the curtain open.

The laughter stopped.

Reacher's secret doorway had led me right to our private quarters in the ziggurat. My whole crew sat on plush cushions in a semicircle around a low table. Everyone stared at me.

Including Cordar.

"Orenpausha!" Adjet said, breaking an awkward silence. "We've been waiting for you!" She jumped up and came running over to me. The pattern of her strange, dark green tattoos emerged from beneath her sleeve as she reached for my hand.

A pot of kaffa steamed on the table. Its herbal, heady smell made my mouth water. Everyone held their own cups, and they looked peaceful and happy. Sid had his bionetic legs attached, and there were no visible signs of scarring from the gruesome sacrificial vision I witnessed at the start of all this madness. I tried not to stare too long at Cordar, but my eyes kept flitting over to him. He and Neka were nuzzled together, his arm around her shoulders, her legs in his lap.

"Where did you just come from?" Cordar asked, watching me intensely.

As my mind raced over possible answers, Cordar took his arm

off of Neka's shoulder and leaned across her to the pot of kaffa. He picked up an empty mug and tipped the kettle, pouring the steaming liquid in. Then he stood up and walked over to me.

He held out the mug. "You must be tired, pausha. You had a long night last night. This should help bring you back to the land of the living." His smile sent a chill up my spine.

"Right," I said, taking it from him. "Thanks, Cordar." I held the mug, but I didn't drink from it. My hands were shaking.

His eyes bored into me.

He knows, I thought. If I drink this, Reach won't be able to pull me out until the effects wear off. But if I don't, I'll give myself away.

I hesitated a moment longer, then tilted the mug back and swallowed the kaffa in one gulp, hoping Reacher was right about my ability to filter out the drug faster than the others. The jolt of energy and pleasure came right away, but there was something else too. Something I hadn't noticed before. An almost imperceptible dulling. I knew I was supposed to be afraid, but my fear became a distant, intellectual concept, and my sense of urgency evaporated.

Does it really even matter if this is all a simulation? I wondered.

Cordar patted me on the shoulder, and sat back down. "You were about to tell us where you were coming from?" he said as he put his arm around Neka.

No, I thought, fighting the impulse to just sit down on a cushion and have another mug of kaffa. Cordar is dead. Whoever that is, he's not my friend.

In that moment, I was grateful that the drug took away my fear, because I knew Cordar was suspicious of me, and if I seemed afraid, he would see it. "I've been sleeping," I said. "Knocked right out after last night and..." I glanced at Adjet, standing next to me, and gave her a sly smile, "and this morning." The lie came easily.

"When I sent Torto to ask you to join us for a morning walk, pausha," Xander said, "I didn't realize he would interrupt anything... private." He gave me a knowing smile.

Adjet laughed again, taking my hand. "We were quite done by then, weren't we, Oren?"

She ran her hand along my bicep, and it hit me that her belly was smooth and flat, no sign of her pregnancy. In the far reaches of my mind, fear came creeping back past the numbness of the kaffa. Was the baby still alive in the womb of her waking body? Had it already been born? I sent a silent prayer to the Scions to speed Socha's search for the child.

"I'm glad you enjoyed yourself last night, pausha," Cordar said. "It's important to vent off pressure every so often, especially as the years drag on. This was all so exciting at the beginning, when Manderlas was still a grand idea, but the reality is getting tiresome. The natives are so primitive. Like small children who need constant supervision, don't you think?"

"Stop it, Cord," Neka said, laughing and swatting his arm. "That's a terrible thing to say."

"Your compassion towards the brutes is heartwarming, my little birdie," Cordar said, patting her head, "but the truth is, we're probably all growing weary of the scant entertainment the natives provide. I know I am. We need to start thinking bigger. There is a whole world out there for us to mold. Manderlas is merely the tip of the spear."

I glanced around at the others. No one seemed the least bit perturbed by Cordar's uncharacteristic bigotry or his global ambitions, nevermind that he was supposed to be dead. The Cordar I knew was thoughtful and analytical, a biologician with a deep respect for life in all its diversity, and generally more concerned with the workings of plants than people. It was wildly out of character for him to assert himself like this in a group. Yet everyone seemed to defer to him.

I decided to take a risk.

I subtly touched my right fingers to my left palm, then slid them up to my wrist. For someone who didn't know handspeak, it could easily be mistaken as an unconscious gesture, like scratching an itch.

Cordar was the one who taught it to me.

Give me more, the gesture said. I figured if he recognized the gesture, he would happily oblige by giving me more kaffa. If he didn't, then it presented a potential opportunity.

He didn't seem to notice.

I repeated the sign again. Not the slightest hint of recognition. But Neka was looking at me now, eyes curious. She was the only other one among us who knew handspeak.

I took an even bigger risk.

Not safe, I signed, meeting her eyes. *Not him.*

She nodded. Just barely, but it was enough. I almost shouted out loud with joy.

"Pausha," Cordar said, patting the empty cushion on his other side, "why don't you stop fidgeting and come sit down."

"Thanks, Cord," I said, trying to sound casual, "but I'm going to take that walk now. Eledar knows I need it."

"It's almost nightfall," Xander said, chiming in. "Supper will be ready soon."

"Save me a plate," I said.

Theater, I signed at the same time, praying Neka would understand. Then, before anyone else could argue, I walked out of the room.

I climbed the steps of the amphitheater, careful not to stumble as the last light of day faded into evening. I sat down on a bench near the back, looking down at the empty stage. Already, I was thirsty for more kaffa, and I had to keep reminding myself that none of this was real; that I was actually lying on the floor of the main cabin on *Reacher.*

Footsteps sounded behind me.

I turned. Neka stood a few rows back, at the top edge of the amphitheater. We stared at each other. As I opened my mouth to speak, she made a quick series of gestures with her hands.

I shook my head. "You know my handspeak has never been that good, Neka."

She gave me a grim smile. "You're right. I do know. I just needed to make sure you knew too." She came down the steps and sat next to me, touching her hand to my cheek. "Is it really you?"

"It's me, Neka. Reach sent me."

"Reach?" She gave me a strange look.

"Reacher, Neka. Our shipheart. Don't you remember?"

"I... I'm not sure. I've been so... so confused."

"But if you don't remember, why did you come?"

"Because of Cordar. I keep having these dreams where he's dead, and something awful has taken his place. When I wake up, the dream doesn't seem any less real. Cordar watches me like a surgeon examining a cadaver, clinical and probing, devoid of the sensitivity that made me fall in love with him."

"But you were with him. On the cushions, drinking kaffa."

"Kaffa," she murmured. Her eyes were hungry. "Do you have any?"

"No, Neka. You mustn't drink that anymore. The kaffa is part of what keeps us trapped here."

She rubbed her eyes and cheeks with her palms, then scratched her wrist. "I just... I get so thirsty."

It was worse than I thought. "So you stay with Cordar for the kaffa?"

"No... I mean, yes. But not just the kaffa. I... if he suspected me... I fear something terrible will happen. Not just to me. To all of us. I have to keep him happy."

I rubbed her back in gentle circles, comforting her. "Have you spoken to any of the others about this?"

She coughed and shook her head, then cleared her throat. "They might betray me."

"Then you're the only one."

Her eyes found mine. "Until now."

I wrapped my arm around her shoulders, pulling her tight, and she leaned her head on my chest. We sat there in the quiet of the coming night, saying nothing.

Then, suddenly, the stage at the front of the amphitheater lit up with incandescent white light. I lifted my palms, shading my eyes, and squinted. A figure stepped on stage, silhouetted against the light.

"Did you really think you could deceive me?" His voice filled the amphitheater.

"Cordar!" Neka said, her voice cracked with fear.

"We have to get out of here!" I took her hand and pulled her to her feet.

She seemed fixed in place, her weight dragging against my pull. "Neka! Run!"

She snapped out of it.

We ran.

Inhuman laughter followed after us.

The streets of Manderlas were quiet, and the windows of the houses and the mercantile buildings were dark. Our feet slapped on the hard packed dirt. We turned left, then left again, running without direction, adrenaline driving me forward, tugging Neka along behind me. We came to an unfamiliar intersection. "This isn't right," I said, swiveling my head in every direction. "Where are we?"

"That is a wonderful question."

We spun around.

"I've been trying to trace you for hours, pausha," Cordar said, "but your signal is being refracted. But my little birdie, Neka? I always know right where she is."

I looked down at Neka.

"I'm sorry, pausha." She could not look at me. "I... I tried."

"Come here, my little birdie," Cordar said. "I brought you a present." A clear decanter of blood red kaffa materialized in his hand.

Neka let go of my hand and walked towards Cordar like a chastised child.

"Neka! Wait!"

She ignored me. When she reached Cordar, he held out the decanter to her. As she reached for it, he pulled it away from her and struck her across the face with the back of his fist.

There was a sickening cracking sound, and she fell to the ground in a heap, unmoving. A cry of rage choked my throat. I leapt at Cordar.

The world spun around me.

I was on the ground, my back against a nearby building. I coughed. My chest barked with pressure. I wiped my lips. My palm came away pink with saliva and blood. It's not real, I thought. I forced myself to stand. My ribs screamed at me.

"You used her to get to me," I said through gritted teeth.

He bared his teeth in a vicious parody of a smile. "She liked being used, pausha."

"Pausha?" I growled. "Enough with the pretense. My friend Cordar is dead, and you're the one who killed him. You're a sick, pathetic imitation."

He ignored my insult. "Where are you hiding?"

"Somewhere you can't find me."

He walked closer to me. "Perhaps you'll tell me after I flay your skin?"

"This isn't me," I said, touching my chest.

He chuckled his sick, inhuman chuckle. "Close enough." His hand locked around my wrist like a vise.

I spun, leveraging the momentum to send the false Cordar spinning over my shoulder, slamming him into the building. His head cracked against the clay bricks, and his neck twisted.

I threw his body to the ground and ran to Neka. I touched my finger to her neck. There was still a pulse. I lifted her in my arms and started running, holding her body tight and secure against my torso.

Cordar stepped out in front of us.

His neck was bent at a gruesome angle, and his collar bone stuck out through his skin, bloody and raw. Blood ran down his face from a gash on his forehead.

"If you won't play by my rules, little insect," he said, his voice logy and cracked, "then you don't get to play at all."

The walls of every building on the street burst open. I knelt down instinctively, shielding Neka. Chunks of clay filled the air, hundreds of them peppering me at once, some sharp enough to cut.

I looked up. Cordar stood there. His neck was still bent, and his body was covered with tiny cuts from the explosion. One of his eyes was gone, cratered by a hunk of clay. Blood gushed out of the open wound, but he seemed unfazed. He reached up with both hands and grabbed his head by the temples. He wrenched and twisted until his skull was realigned with his spine. Then he lifted his hand and snapped his fingers.

A legion of his blind hunters came pouring into the street behind him, and he pointed at me. They charged, barking and spitting and coughing. He stood as still as a stone in a river as they flowed around him.

I stood up, Neka still in my arms, and ran as fast as I've ever run.

"Reacher," I said, "in the names of the Scions, if you can hear me, now would be a wonderful time to do whatever it is you're going to do!"

"What did you just say?"

Cordar appeared in front of me again, blood still fountaining from his crushed eye socket.

I yelped with surprise, backing away. I glanced over my shoulder. The hunters were stopped in their tracks, sniffing the air, scratching and jostling each other. The closest were just a few feet away from me. I was pinned.

I looked back at Cordar.

"Reacher," I screamed. "Do it now!"

The whole world flickered and distorted, like someone running their hand through a hologram.

It righted itself an instant later, everything returning to normal. Cordar hobbled up to me, so close I could feel his breath. The blood would not stop running from his eye.

"You cry out to a false god, insect," he said. "Your precious Reacher is as good as dead."

The world distorted again.

"Then what was that?"

He snarled, looking around wildly.

"Your illusion is crumbling. You won't be able to control us anymore."

He reached his hands for my throat, but before he could grasp me, he froze in place. His head and hands started twitching. Then his eyes rolled back in his head, and he collapsed.

The hunters behind me howled. Several of them pushed forward, ignoring me, sniffing Cordar's body. One opened its jaws, wider than looked possible, revealing rotting teeth, filed to points. It bit into Cordar's neck. The others leapt in then, in a frenzy, pushing and clawing at each other, rending the flesh from Cordar's carcass.

Bile rose in my throat. I backed away, still clutching Neka to my chest, and I turned to run again.

Adjet blocked my way. "I guess that's the last we'll see of Cordar," she said.

"Damn it!" I pivoted down another street.

Xander and Xayes stepped out in front of me.

"All of you," Xayes began.

"Belong to me," Xander finished.

I pivoted again, back the way I came, then cut down a side alley. Siddart ran up alongside me, his bionetic legs easily keeping pace. "It's easier when you don't fight it, pausha."

I stopped short, ducking into an empty home. I slammed the wooden door and dropped the locking plank into its cradle, sealing the door shut. I laid Neka down on the table, cradling her head. She was still unconscious.

Siddart hammered on the door, but it held.

"Damn you," I cried. "Leave my friends alone."

"Your friends are mine now," Siddart called back. "Doesn't that make us friends too?"

"What do you know of friendship, monster? You pervert everything you touch."

There was no response, but there was a thunk on the roof of the house. Then a hand punched through the thatch and clay, and Siddart was there, peering down at us. "But isn't this what you wanted?" he said. "A world where you could live as gods? Why do you seek to undo what I've built for you?"

"Do you really believe that?" I shouted up at him. "That we could ever want this hollow lie?"

Something slammed into the front door again, followed by a low growling.

"My hunters," Siddart said, pointing to the door, "I made them to root out every last vestige of your precious Reacher. They are extraordinary hunters. In fact, they made such short work of him in the early days, I thought we had succeeded. But he is more elusive than I gave him credit for. Perhaps he learned that from me. He's made his last mistake though."

"What mistake?" I said, trying to keep him talking.

"Your weakness forced his hand. To help you, he crippled the Cordar avatar. A bold move. But he has given my hunters his scent again. It won't be long."

The door rattled again. The growls were louder now, punctu-

ated by hacking coughs and the sound of claws on clay, a whole
pack of the damnable creatures lurking outside.

"They're very protective," Siddart said, smiling an inhuman
smile. He pushed his head through the hole in the thatch, leering
down at me. His face seemed to warp and elongate. Then the room
fuzzed and stuttered, and he disappeared.

I was back on the ship! I leapt up to my feet, then almost fell over
again. "Easy now," I said to myself, resting my hands on a console.

Slam.

What in the names of the Scions?

Slam.

Is the ship rocking?

SLAM.

Oh no. Please, no.

"Reacher! Reacher, can you hear me?"

No response. I activated the ship's external image feeds.
"Eledar's breath." The ship was surrounded. Hundreds of people,
Kkadie and Sagain, poured into the cavern from every entrance.

They were in various stages of decrepitude, ranging from
underfed to skeletal. Sores and cuts covered their bodies, and their
eyes were glassy and distant. Portable field transmitters bulged
from their necks.

He was controlling them.

They slammed themselves into the ship, arms and bodies and
heads smacking against the impenetrable trimantium hull. I swiped
my hand across the console, bringing up defense protocols I never
thought we'd have to use.

"Sonics," I said, covering my ears.

Sound pierced the cavern, a high-pitched, crippling spear of
noise. The sound through the hull was uncomfortable. Out there, it
was torture.

They fell like sacks of grain, flopping and twitching on the ground. Even if their pain receptors had been muted by the corrupted shipheart, the sound induced vertigo, hammering the inner ear, making motor function essentially impossible.

But if these poor people are here, I thought, still under his control, then that means the network wipe was unsuccessful.

"Reacher," I said out loud. "Please. If you're there, I need you. I don't know what else to do."

<Oren./> The console blinked my name.

"Reacher!"

<Orxn, !#hi hunters -r closing. -ower ^%\ dwinl ɪ nnng./>

"He has them, Reach. He has them all. Tell me what to do!"

<I —m *orry./>

"What's the status on the network wipe?"

<.../>

"Reacher?"

Nothing.

I hammered my hands on the console, wailing with rage. Despair washed over me. I hung my head, weeping. I'm not sure how much time passed before I realized what I had to do.

I soared into the clouds until I could take in the whole length and breadth of the island.

"Overlay thermal veins," I said. A schematic of the planet's tectonic stratum glowed red, tracing the contours of the island and the range of mountains at the bottom of the ocean floor.

"Overlay coordinate grid." A symmetrical grid crosshatched the visible surface of the planet.

"Here, here, and here." Dozens of intersecting points on the grid lit up, pulsing in a steady rhythm.

"Three minutes. Initiate countdown." A clock appeared in the lower corner of the overlay. It started ticking down.

I fell like a meteor towards the heart of Manderlas.

"You were a fool to come back."

The corrupted shipheart sat on a throne of skulls in a chamber at the top of the ziggurat. He looked as he did when I first encountered him in the Arcturean system, his face waxen and cold, lacking that ineffable spark of life.

My friends were all there, sitting on the stairs in front of his ghastly throne. Their faces had the same spiritless affect. They had become like puppets of themselves.

"Perhaps you came to throw yourself at my feet and beg forgiveness?" the corrupted shipheart said. "I am afraid it is much too late for that, insect."

"You're right. It is too late."

"Then maybe you came for this?" He clapped his hands together.

Siddart stood up and walked behind the throne of skulls. He emerged again cradling something in his hands.

"Give it to him," the corrupted shipheart said.

Siddart tossed it at my feet.

It was Reacher.

His tiny green body lay in front of me, eyes closed. The tendrils of his hands, normally alive and fluid in an unending hum of motion, hung limp. I knelt down and touched his forehead. His skin felt cold.

"This is all you're good for," I said, standing up. "Isn't it? Your brilliant, incredible mind, and all you use it for is death."

"It is my gift," he said.

"It's your curse, and it ends now."

"Enough," the shipheart said with a bored look. "Kill him." He flicked his hands towards me. My friends stood up and started moving towards me.

The ground shook.

I held out my arms wide in a gesture of receiving. "I'm sorry I let it come to this," I whispered to them.

Xayes was the first to reach me. He held a vicious, curved dagger. He lifted it in the air.

Before he could plunge it into me, the walls of the ziggurat blurred and pixelated like a poorly focused video, and when the image righted itself, Xayes crumpled to the floor.

The corrupted shipheart was standing now, a look of concern on his face.

Xander ran towards his brother. "Xayes!" He looked up at me. "What have you done?" Then the world distorted again, his eyes rolled back in his head, and he fell beside his brother.

The shipheart came striding down the stairs, pushing past Neka, Adjet, and Sid. "What makes you think you can succeed where that pathetic heart failed?" he said, pointing at Reacher's body. "Do you truly believe I would build a network without redundancies? That you could just wipe it all away?"

Sid collapsed on the floor. Adjet fell a moment later. The shipheart glanced back at them, then turned to me, narrowing his eyes.

"Without the island," I said, "there is no network."

I closed my eyes and saw the island in my mind's eye. Saw it as it was before we began to build this city. Raw and pure. The sun rising above the distant, continental mountains. Gulls diving for fish in the channel that separates the island from the mainland. The murmur of the ocean, kissing the shore.

"Goodbye," I whispered, opening my eyes.

Neka looked at me, sadness on her face. Her eyes rolled back and she collapsed to the ground.

The world around us distorted again, worse this time, colors inverting, blots of static consuming the walls and ceiling. The corrupted shipheart screamed with agony and lunged at me.

A titanic crash echoed through the ziggurat. Pain erupted through my body. The island split inside of me.

A circle of light opened high above me. Someone stood in the circle, a silhouette reaching towards me. I raised my arms to take the figure's hands, but I was falling away from the light, down into the darkness

Falling down.

Darkness.

Tʀᴇᴍᴏʀꜱ ʀᴀᴛᴛʟᴇ the earth beneath my feet. The ocean roils and chops, threatening the mainland shore. A mile out to sea, I can see an island, and on that island stand the towers of a city the likes of which no people of Eaiph could have ever built.

As I head for higher ground, I see a raft floating close to shore. Fierce waves buffet the vessel, hurling it on the rocks, a hundred yards from where I stand, making me wince. It's doubtful anyone from this planet could survive a shipwreck like that. But maybe whoever is on that boat is not from this planet.

I scramble across the slick boulders and reach the wreckage just as another wave breaks and rolls away again, sluicing fragments of wood from the sundered boat back into the water. Nothing else is moving. Smaller waves spit and break, but another big one is bound to come soon. I may only have a few moments to find whatever remains from the wreck.

The man's cloak is so dark and sodden that I don't see him until I nearly trip over him.

He is lying on his back, clutching a bundle to his chest. His face is weathered and gaunt, and a nasty gash parts his left cheek. His left eye is closed. A jagged scar runs from his forehead, through the wreckage of his right eye, and down his cheek, where the flesh congeals like melted wax, leaving patches of bare skin through his curly beard.

The ground trembles again.

His left eye opens. He sees me.

The baby in his arms stirs, then starts squalling, a high-pitched, piercing wail. The man says something, but his voice is too weak to hear.

I lean closer. He speaks again.

"Lunnana-sin," it sounds like. His good eye is wide and intense, and he does not seem surprised to see a strange woman standing over him. "Lunnana-sin," he says again, clearly this time, his voice stronger.

He holds the child up towards me. The sleeves of his cloak fall away as his arms rise. His coppery skin sags over his bones, lacerated and scarred.

I hesitate, looking to the ocean. A massive wave is gathering offshore. I say a quiet blessing in the name of Eledar, take the baby from his hands, and run. When I look back again, the water is sliding back out to sea and the man is gone.

It starts to rain. The wind picks up. I try my best to shelter the child against the elements. The tremors are coming faster now.

"Hush, little one," I whisper, "I've got you." I stroke the child's thin, damp hair and bring it close to my bosom. It looks malnourished, but its heart and breath are strong.

I climb into the high hills. The air is dense with ocean mist. We come to an empty farmstead. The land was tilled once, but it sits barren now. A stone wall, half-finished, sags into the soil. Stalks of grain are bundled next to the wall, withered and husked.

A hut built from bricks of clay stands on the far side of the farmland. A well-built wooden fence surrounds the house; pasturing for hens, or maybe a goat. The gate is open. I walk through. The thatched roof has fallen through on one side, but most of the house is still covered.

"This will do, little one. It'll have to."

I bring the child inside the hut. It is empty, but there is a bed packed with straw, big enough for two, and a basket at the foot of the bed lined with blankets made from coarse flax. A family lived here once.

I swaddle the baby in the dusty blankets, and discover that the child is a boy. He stops crying, and looks up at me with curious, grey-blue eyes. His gaze makes me weep. So beautiful. So innocent. I lift him in my arms and rock him, swaying gently as I cry, holding him close.

Time passes. My sadness subsides. The walls of the house shake every few minutes, kicking up dust, but the baby is sleeping, and he does not wake. He'll be hungry when he does, I think.

I set him down in the basket and step outside, leaving him in the hut. The rain is tapering off. I run my hands over the beam of the fence. Then I turn and leap up on top of the roof of the hut, careful to keep to the edges so I don't fall through the thatch, and look out towards the island.

The quake is raging now. Waves lash the shoreline. The clay hut holds for now, and I pray that we're far enough away from the epicenter. The tower closest to the center of the island collapses, crashing down on top of the pyramid hunched next to it, kicking up a huge cloud of dust.

If only I had come sooner.

I did not know it then, but by the time word reached me that an island had risen from the ocean, summoned by powerful mages who had travelled across the stars, it was already too late. I made my way east, over the mountains and through the sweeping desert, my heart filled with hope. Along the way, I met other travelers. Each one had a story to tell about the island. When I first learned its name, I even dared to dream he might be there; that he might have finally come for me, just as he'd promised me so many centuries ago.

Manderlas, some called the island; or Andalas; or Lanthas. I heard a dozen variations. But all the stories shared the same disturbing theme: on the island, a city had been raised up to break the sky and surpass the gods. For that effrontery, it had become an accursed place. Those who went to the island were never seen or heard from again.

Now, from the roof of this simple hut, perched above the thickening ocean mist, I watch it crumble apart. Dust and debris obscure my view, leaving me to guess at what went wrong. As close as it is, the island might as well be a distant galaxy, ancient and unreachable, its whole history submerging beneath the waves.

The ocean mist clouds the air in front of me. It is tinged with an eerie, purple hue, like some fey spirit from the legends of the mountain tribes. I look down at my chest.

The aurastal hanging from my neck is glowing violet!

I open my mouth to shout Oren's name. Then, like a delfina leaping through the surface of the boundless Coscan Ocean, a ship bursts out from the dust cloud above the sinking island, streaking up towards the atmosphere.

I lift my hand as if to slow its ascent; as if I might catch it by the tail and ride along in its wake; as if it might take me home.

A moment later, the ship is gone.

I am doomed to wander this planet forever.

I sit down on the thatch and clutch my knees to my chest, sobbing. The rain picks up again, mingling with my tears.

The child's hungry wail comes up through the roof.

I stand up, wipe my eyes, and rub my nose on my sleeve. I turn my back on the drowning island of Manderlas, leap down to the earth, and go inside the hut.

ACKNOWLEDGMENTS

To my wife, Erica, for believing in me. To my parents, for putting up with me for all these years. To my teacher and friend, Todd Marston, for showing me that every human is an artist. To my brother-in-law, Stephan Magro, and my dear friend, Rita Powell, for helping make this book worth reading. To my editor, Scott Pack, for saying 'yes' to this project. You helped turn a scrap heap into a treasure trove. To my sibling-in-spirit, Fred George, for your beautiful art. And, finally, to every one of you who've traveled this journey with Oren, Saiara, and all the rest. It wouldn't have been the same without you.

LEAVE A REVIEW

A great review is the single most powerful tool to help new authors, so if you enjoyed your journey through these pages, I'd be mighty grateful if you took a few minutes to tell the world what you think about the book. Just type the links below into your web browser to leave a review for Gradient on Amazon and/or Goodreads.

http://bit.ly/gradient-amazon

http://bit.ly/gradient-goodreads

My sincerest thanks,
    -Anders

GET A FREE SHORT STORY

Want to keep reading? Sign up for my readers group 'The Wonder Dome' and get a short story for free. You'll also get ongoing access to subscriber-only content, advance reader copies, and whatever else might be rattling around in the vaults. Just type the link below into your web browser to get carried away to the dome.

BookHip.com/JHJASQ

ABOUT THE AUTHOR

Anders Cahill is an author, musician, and educator. *Gradient* is his first full-length work of fiction.

www.anderscahillbooks.com
www.medium.com/@thewonderdome
anders@anderscahillbooks.com

65335895R00272

Made in the USA
Middletown, DE
25 February 2018